# SEASON OF IRON

# SEASON OF IRON

## A Rebecca Temple Mystery

# Sylvia Maultash Warsh

A Castle Street Mystery

THE DUNDURN GROUP

TORONTO

Editor: Barry Jowett
Copy-editor: Andrea Waters
Design: Andrew Roberts
Printer: Webcom

National Library of Canada Cataloguing in Publication

Warsh, Sylvia Maultash

   Season of iron / Sylvia Maultash Warsh.

(A Rebecca Temple mystery)

ISBN-10: 1-55002-616-X
ISBN-13: 978-1-55002-616-0

   I. Title.  II. Series: Warsh, Sylvia Maultash.  Rebecca Temple mystery.

PS8595.A7855S42 2006      C813'.6      C2006-901333-0

1   2   3   4   5      10   09   08   07   06

Conseil des Arts du Canada      Canada Council for the Arts      Canadä      ONTARIO ARTS COUNCIL
CONSEIL DES ARTS DE L'ONTARIO

We acknowledge the support of the Canada Council for the Arts and the Ontario Arts Council for our publishing program. We also acknowledge the financial support of the Government of Canada through the Book Publishing Industry Development Program and The Association for the Export of Canadian Books, and the Government of Ontario through the Ontario Book Publishers Tax Credit program and the Ontario Media Development Corporation.

Care has been taken to trace the ownership of copyright material used in this book. The author and the publisher welcome any information enabling them to rectify any references or credits in subsequent editions.

                                                      *J. Kirk Howard, President*

Printed and bound in Canada      www.dundurn.com

Dundurn Press
8 Market Street, Suite 200
Toronto, Ontario, Canada
M5E 1M6

Gazelle Book Services Limited
White Cross Mills
High Town, Lancaster, England
LA1 4XS

Dundurn Press
2250 Military Road
Tonawanda, NY
U.S.A. 14150

# SEASON OF IRON

# *chapter one*

## Rebecca

**Toronto, November 1979**

People look different in hospitals. Quite apart from the illness. Even the self-confident ones become cowed in a hospital bed, frightened by their IVs, by the unequivocal nurses coming around to prod them in intimate places, by the specialists and students who discuss the ailment as if it were a gnome sitting on the patient's chest, a third party, utterly separate and deaf.

Rebecca understood their distress at their loss of control and did her best to reassure them when they went into hospital. Always felt duplicitous because she so keenly loved Mount Sinai. She had to suppress a frisson of excitement whenever she walked through the doors. Magically, the tragic part of her life fell away. The black moods, the sleeplessness. She had trained here, an eager sponge absorbing knowledge, and now she was doing her part to make life better for people.

She stood near Mrs. Fiori's bed. More than a year had passed since Rebecca had seen her patient. She recalled the robust energy of the stout but handsome woman, her thick dark hair sprayed into place. That person was hiding inside this pale rendition, the usual bloom of her skin now faded. Gently, she turned Mrs. Fiori's hand palm up and, holding her wrist between thumb and fingers, took her pulse. No matter how she felt about a patient — not all were as pleasant as Mrs. Fiori — this somehow intimate gesture never failed to rouse in her a protective affection. Maybe it was the measure of their vulnerability, a reminder of her own, that struck her so tenderly. Mrs. Fiori smiled at Rebecca, her eyes still sparkling. This was not the time to tell her again to stop smoking. That could wait. She was fifty-three and had just suffered a stroke.

"How are you feeling?" Rebecca asked.

"Not so bad. Just tired. Can't even do my hair."

"It'll take time." Recovery depended on so many factors that she knew better than to promise anything. "I'll come by tonight to check on you on my way home."

Mrs. Fiori smiled feebly and nodded.

Rebecca picked up her Jaguar coupe from the staff lot behind the hospital and drove back to her office on Beverley Street. The rest of the day she spent dealing with the usual ear infections, stomach upsets, and women who were terrified they might be pregnant.

After office hours she wasn't in the same hurry and usually walked the four blocks back to Mount Sinai. She could air her brain and get some exercise at the same time.

She realized later that she had barely given Mrs. Fiori a thought all day. Was that why it hit her so hard when she walked to the nurses' station that evening? She felt it as soon as the nurse looked up at her. The eyes gave people away. Some unintentional message written on the underside. The way the muscles of the face realigned themselves.

She wanted to be anywhere but here because she sensed the nightmare playing out in the room down the hall. No, she *heard* the keening of the nightmare, a barely human voice. The wailing that rose up from that part of you that lay quiet most of your life if you were lucky. That part of you that understood the real world viscerally, the careless cruelty and unfairness of it, and only surfaced when summoned by your own tragedy. Not others', only your own. Otherwise how could you live?

Rebecca stopped in front of the nurse, trying to wrap herself in a layer of professionalism. A doctor didn't fall apart. A doctor helped others cope. A doctor …

"What happened?" Rebecca asked.

The nurse, a tall middle-aged woman, handed her Mrs. Fiori's chart. "I tried to phone your office. She just had another stroke." Her cheeks sagged from effort.

Rebecca stared at the file, but the writing wavered before her eyes. When the words stopped moving, she read that the internist had seen Mrs. Fiori within the last hour. Right in the hospital. Still nothing they could do for her. Blood clot in the brain. Such a small thing to stop a life.

Still in her wool coat, she walked down the hall toward the frantic weeping. She hovered in the doorway, hating her own cowardice. Mrs. Fiori lay facing the ceiling, her once lovely face white, dark hair splayed on the pillow, mouth open.

*David.* A flashbulb went off and everything stood still in an instant. David lying in the hospital, the same hospital. The same white. The same gone. *Gone.*

The moment passed. Rebecca saw a nurse in the room, speaking in a low voice to the husband and teenage son. Rebecca had met the family when Mrs. Fiori had been admitted four days ago. It was the daughter, maybe twenty, who keened shrilly, slumped over her mother's body. The daughter, who resembled her mother so much, with her dark hair and wide cheekbones, she might have been mourning for herself.

Rebecca watched the nurse approach her, gently but firmly lift her from the bed, murmuring words of comfort that slid right past the face swollen with tears.

"Nobody said she would die!" cried the young woman. "She can't die!"

The nurse looked up and saw Rebecca in the doorway. Now she had to go in. Try to console a family who would be inconsolable. As was their right. She had been through it all herself. She understood only too well. People try to comfort, but there's really nothing anyone can say. Nobody found the magic words when *she* was inconsolable.

She stepped into the room. It was airless. She could barely breathe, but she placed her hand on Mr. Fiori's arm. "I'm so sorry. I didn't expect it."

He shifted damp brown eyes to her and nodded. The boy had his arm around his father's shoulder and seemed to be protecting him from her.

The daughter noticed her entrance. "I don't understand! She wasn't supposed to die! I don't understand!"

"I'm so sorry," Rebecca said. "There's always a risk, but she seemed to be doing so well ..."

"You didn't say she might die!" cried the daughter. "Why didn't you tell us?"

The words hit Rebecca in the stomach. She blinked from the pain.

"She threw off a clot that blocked the artery to her brain. That's the danger with stroke."

The daughter stopped wailing and stared at Rebecca as if she had said something offensive. It wasn't the physical cause of death she didn't understand. That wasn't the answer she wanted. Rebecca didn't have that answer. Would never have it.

"I'm so sorry," she mumbled and flew from the room toward the elevators.

Don't think. Just go! Don't let it break your heart. She stared at the floor numbers descending. Darted out onto the main floor, past the life-sized portraits of the Mount Sinai benefactors hanging on the travertine marble. How many years had she been hurrying down this hall? Past some elderly lady volunteer posted next to a table of used books outside the hospital gift shop. The never-ending lineup of visitors and staff at the coffee stand, impatient for that jolt of caffeine that would hold them to dinner. How many years had she sprinted by it daily?

She didn't know what was happening to her. It was just over a year since David had died. She'd thought the despondency would subside. That her body would adjust to his absence at the table, in her bed. That she would be able to wake up in the morning without remembering, before anything else, that he was dead. But she became weepy at unexpected moments and sometimes had to excuse herself from company.

She had been a happy person before fate turned her into a widow at thirty-three. Fate? She didn't believe in fate. Just blind rotten luck. Bad genes and circumstance. If only he hadn't developed diabetes. If only he hadn't been so goddamed funny. If only his red hair hadn't glowed like that above the milky complexion.

His death had robbed her of her optimism. Had she really been an optimistic doctor? Didn't that just make her stupid — ignoring everything they taught her in medical school about the vulnerability of the human body? Stupid and ready for a fall. After that first big fall, she just seemed to keep falling. She couldn't have helped Mrs. Fiori. Nobody could. Her daughter probably understood that now. Maybe she had been an optimist too, but the ground had opened up beneath her and swallowed her mother. Maybe the weeping *had* been for herself.

No point hurrying today. Other Friday evenings she would head out to her parents' house for dinner. But they were in Santa Barbara for the month. No one was waiting for her to come home. Her mother-in-law had invited her for dinner, but Rebecca had declined. She couldn't enter that house without finding David everywhere, and all the sadness she was barely keeping at bay threatened to break the delicate barriers she had built around herself, ready to engulf her.

She walked along Elm Street, buttoning her coat against the November chill. Barely glanced up at the grey brick residence for married interns where she had spent the happiest year of her life. David had been healthy then, busy with his painting. They had both been immortal, the way the unthinking young are. She saw death and disease often during that year in the hospital, yet never dreamt it would seize her own life so soon. They had been buoyant with hope then, innocently looking forward to a life together. But the universe hadn't unfolded as it should. David had lived for only seven more years. He had taken her hope with him to the grave.

As the wind lashed her down McCaul, she pulled up the collar of her wool coat, wrapped the silk scarf tighter around her neck. Winter was coming. Would she keep walking the four blocks back to her office every day in the freezing cold? She needed the exercise.

Baldwin Street. She barely peered sideways at the restaurants and shops, the couples, the groups of university students scouting out places for dinner. She made her way to D'Arcy, the next street south, empty in comparison, soothing with its old semi-detached houses sitting quietly in the dusky light. Only her own steps echoed softly on the pavement.

Even the wind was calmer as she approached Beverley Street. Then an agitated voice broke the silence. Or maybe it was Rebecca's silence and the woman had been speaking all along, only Rebecca had to get close enough to hear. An accent of some kind.

"... never were any good ... You're spoiled! You're stupid! You don't understand anything ... and you're dirty."

Rebecca slowed down. The voice seemed to be coming from a backyard enclosed by a six-foot-high hedge that smelled musty with autumn. Its leaves had fallen, but the gnarled old branches twisted upon one another in a complicated pattern that hid the yard from the street.

"You don't deserve to live. You're stupid, you're fat, you're ugly. You should be punished for what you did. You're a monster! You should've died like the rest of them."

Rebecca stopped. Was it a mother speaking to a child? The voice sounded older than that. Should she interfere?

"Why don't you wash yourself? Look at your face — anyone can see what you had for lunch. Join the human race. Try at least to look human because you aren't human, you're an animal. Even animals clean themselves. You should end it all now — it would be better for you and everyone else."

Even if it weren't a child, the threat of violence ... Though the voice was not shouting, rather it droned on. More chilling for that. Rebecca stepped with hesitation toward the back door of the house where the hedge began. If she could only see them, she might gauge the danger.

"Get a knife — that's not so hard — and push it in there, you know, where your heart is supposed to be. I can get you a knife right now and you can do it — save everyone a lot of trouble."

That was enough for Rebecca. She strode through the opening of the hedge and looked around the yard. Where were they?

"Excuse me!" Rebecca called out.

Inside the hedge now, Rebecca squinted in the dimming light. In front of a wooden shed in the back corner a small old woman sat straight up, alarmed, in a vinyl kitchen chair. A green woollen hat was pulled down over her head, grey hair straggling beneath. Her shoulders shook with terror in an oversized men's coat. Was she the victim? Rebecca looked around the yard. A child's wagon sat piled with bulging bags near the woman. Rebecca saw no one else.

"Do you need help?" Rebecca asked, still looking into the shadows of the yard.

The woman stared at her with large dark eyes but said nothing. Her body continued to shiver.

"Is someone trying to hurt you?"

The woman's face was blank. Her delicate features must have been pretty long ago. Maybe she was just cold.

"I can't help if you don't tell me what's wrong."

No reply.

At a loss, Rebecca turned to go.

"She has no heart," the woman said.

The same voice Rebecca had heard before. She had been talking to herself.

"Who?"

"She."

"Everyone has a heart," Rebecca said.

The woman looked down at her feet. "They come at night. Steal the tips off her shoelaces. Look, the plastic tips, they're gone."

She was speaking about herself in the third person. Okay. The woman's running shoes were so dirty, Rebecca couldn't tell if the tips were there or not. "Why would someone do that?"

The woman looked at her as if she ought to know. "So her shoelaces will come undone. And she'll trip and fall. And get dirty. They want her to be dirty so she'll get sick. And die."

Logical. "Who?"

The woman looked away and pointed half-heartedly to a tree. Rebecca wondered if the people who lived in the house knew they had a squatter in their yard. It would be hard not to notice her. All they had to do was look out their windows.

"My name's Rebecca. What's your name?"

"She's going to sleep now."

"Out here?"

The woman looked around herself as if for the first time.

"It's too cold to sleep outside," Rebecca said. "Would you like me to find you a warm place to sleep?"

"Here!" the woman shouted, agitated. "Stay here! She turns it on."

Rebecca followed the woman's eyes and saw a portable heater close to her feet. The filament was starting to turn red and she could feel the warmth from where she stood. An extension cord snaked from inside the shed.

"Okay," Rebecca said. "Look's like you're all set."

*Mind your own business next time*, Rebecca thought, as she continued back to her office. Even if she called social services, there weren't a lot of places for homeless women in the city. The old lady would end up in a psychiatric ward overnight, terror-stricken. Leave it alone. Bad end to a bad day.

Driving home later after her office hours, she felt her stomach grumble, anticipating the matzo ball soup, Greek salad, and potato skins with cheese and bacon that she would pick up from Yitz's delicatessen on Eglinton Avenue. Her favourites even if they didn't cover all the food groups. Why shouldn't she indulge herself now and then? She ate at the kitchen table while reading the *Globe and Mail* that had come that morning.

At nine o'clock her phone rang.

"Hi, sweetie, what's up?"

Her mother's voice always cheered her. "Just loafing in front of the TV."

"You know," said her father on the extension, "you lose IQ points for every hour you watch. Your mother's IQ is down to thirty-eight. She's addicted to *The Young and the Restless.*"

Rebecca smiled. Her mother hated soap operas.

"I love her anyway," her father said.

"Pshaw. How are you feeling?" Her mother always treaded softly around Rebecca's depression.

"I'm a little down. One of my patients died in hospital today. Just fifty-three."

"I'm so sorry. What from?"

"She had a stroke. I thought she'd pull through. I wasn't there when it happened."

"Shouldn't blame yourself, dear. You're not God."

Rebecca smiled. Her mother was trying to make her feel better, but inadvertently underscored a doctor's arrogance. "You still believe in God?"

A moment of hesitation. "Most of the time."

"If anyone cares, *I* still believe in God." Her father. "He's got a long white beard and lives on a mountain in Israel. He looks like Charlton Heston."

"Ignore him. He's in one of his *silly* moods."

Rebecca didn't remember when he wasn't. Which was fine by her.

"I want to make my brilliant girl smile."

"Thanks, Dad."

"Did you have dinner?" her mother asked.

"Yitz's matzo balls aren't as good as yours."

"Now you're making me feel guilty."

"You should be proud, Flo, you passed on a Jewish skill: how to make your family feel guilty."

"I don't want you to feel guilty," Rebecca said. "I want you to have fun." It was partly true. She wanted them to enjoy themselves, but she missed them. "You only have another two weeks."

"Did you speak to Susan?" Her mother's voice took on an edge.

"Not lately."

"I'm worried about her."

"Oh, Flo, you worry too much. She'll be fine."

"I told you, Mitch. I haven't seen her like this before. She's been pregnant three times and she's never been like this. What d'you think, Rebecca? Should we worry about your sister?"

Rebecca wondered: did they bring up touchy subjects when they were actually in the same room together, or only on the extension when they called her long-distance?

"Susan's pretty resilient," Rebecca said. "Her pregnancy's progressing normally. She just has to accept that she's having a fourth child. And she must be tired. Who wouldn't be?"

When Susan had discovered she was pregnant again, she'd called Rebecca from Montreal and wept into the phone. Her husband was an observant Jew; there was no question of an abortion.

"I was looking forward to saying 'my daughter the doctor and my daughter the lawyer,'" her father quipped for the hundredth time.

"Don't ever say that to Susan, Mitch. She's upset as it is."

Susan had finally applied for law school after years of waiting, and would have started that fall, but had to ask for a deferral to have the baby. How was she going to have the energy to start the next fall? The baby would be less than a year old and the three boys all under nine.

"I'll call her tomorrow and see how she is," Rebecca said.

"Good girl," said her father.

"Only wait until sundown," said her mother. "You know they don't pick up the phone on Saturday."

Rebecca spent the next hour tackling the clutter in her kitchen. Too many publications arrived automatically on her doorstep because of her obligatory membership in medical organizations: the *Canadian Medical Association Journal*, the journal of the Royal Society for Physicians and Surgeons, the *Ontario Medical Association Review*, the *Medical Post*, and on and on. It was one way to keep up with the constant flow of medical developments, but her house was filled with paper. All she could do was stack the journals on the bookshelf until they became outdated.

In fact, she had signed up for a day of lectures on Saturday, an update for general practitioners sponsored by a few drug companies. She unfolded the brochure and read off the list of titles: a new maintenance treatment in asthma; new procedures in obstetrics and gynecology; updates for treatment of depression and anxiety; new medications in pain management; developments in pediatrics.

In the middle of the centre page was a black and white photo of a man with intelligent eyes and a hint of a smile, his strong chin thrust forward. Dr. Mustafa Salim, Chairman of Hassan Pharmaceuticals. He was a special guest visiting from Egypt, apparently, where the founder of his company was a medical advisor to the government. A few days ago she had picked up the University of Toronto *Bulletin* near the coffee wagon in the hospital and found the same picture of Dr. Salim. He was giving several more lectures next week on pain medication research, one in the pharmacy building, one at the U of T bookstore: "New Investment in Egypt after the Peace Accord."

Then the phone rang. Nesha. Her heart lifted. He would be the only one calling after ten in the evening. San Francisco was three hours behind. He called on the weekends that he didn't fly in. She picked up the receiver.

"Rebecca?"

She smiled at the lilting sound of her name in his mouth. It suggested so many things: his lips on her neck, her leg wrapped around his, their bodies arching toward each other.

"Rebecca, is that you?"

"Sorry, I was preoccupied." She couldn't tell him his voice had transported her to the bedroom.

"Preoccupied with what?"

She looked down at the brochure. "Oh. Um, I'm going to some lectures tomorrow and they've snagged an interesting guest speaker for the luncheon. He's Egyptian. You follow Middle East affairs more than I do. He seems to be doing a lecture circuit. Something about promoting investment in Egypt after the peace accord with Israel."

"Investment in Egypt! That's a laugh. Sadat may be working on peace, but the radical elements in his country won't just sit by. Ever heard of the Muslim Brotherhood?"

"No."

He paused. "Never mind. How are you?"

"Fine." Could he tell she was barely fine? "Who're the Muslim Brotherhood?"

"You sure you want to know this? They're a grass-roots organization that puts out the equivalent of soup kitchens in Egypt. Sort of like the Salvation Army here. Except that the Salvation Army wants you to believe in Jesus and love your neighbour, while the Muslim Brotherhood wants you to kill your neighbour. They assassinated the Egyptian prime minister in the fifties because he was too tight with the British."

"Why do you know so much about Egypt?"

"The Middle East interests me. So much potential and so little progress. Long ago, Muslims were an advanced civilization. Inventive, tolerant. But they've been going backwards for centuries. When Jews were dying in pogroms in Poland and Russia in the 1800s, they realized they needed a homeland like everybody else. They wanted the tiny part of the desert that was theirs nearly two thousand years ago. But the Arabs didn't want them taking even a fraction of their desert, like there wasn't enough of it. Nothing's changed. They've taken over from the Nazis."

Nesha had seen his family murdered by the Nazis. He was sensitive about Jewish survival.

"None of the Arab countries are stable enough for investment," he said. "I wouldn't give them a penny."

"Don't worry. I'm not looking to invest. I'm just trying to learn some new medicine."

"Didn't mean to bend your ear. You're a conscientious doctor, keeping up like that. My hat's off to you."

"You don't wear a hat."

"I wore a baseball hat the first time we met."

"An aberration. I've never seen you in one since."

"I'm wearing one right now."

"No, you're not. What colour is it?"

"You don't know everything about me, you know."

"Well, I'd *like* to know everything about you."

"Well, I'd like to be there holding you in my arms right now."

"So what's stopping you?" she said, picturing his bow-shaped mouth close to the phone.

# *chapter two*

## Frederika

**Berlin, September 1927**

Frieda always knew it would come to this: bored to distraction, she stands in the dank factory over some operator whose thin fingers fly, feeding the fabric under the sewing machine needle. The affixed lamp steals a circle of light from the gloom. All the machines float in circles of light in the murk of the windowless workroom.

Frieda pretends to pay attention while her cousin, Greta, sews together the seams of yet another white shirt, her small, steady feet working the treadle. The heat from the warm September afternoon settles in the air around them like a cloud. The other machines whine and clatter, their din adding up to a noise Frieda thinks will make them all deaf before their time. She has read about the structure of the ear, the delicate hair cells within the cochlea, a tiny organ coiled upon itself like a snail shell. Sound is dependent on these hair cells, and the cells are fragile. In all her reading she is astounded to learn how vulnerable and dependent each part of the body is upon the others. And how fraught with danger life can be, depending on what traits one inherits and what century one is born into. And the state of the finances of one's family.

Her Vati insists on her learning all the different steps it takes to run the factory, from making the white shirts that are their staple to the new business of undergarments — long underwear for men, vests and underpants for women. And Vati is watching from his corner office. Not only her. From his vantage point her father can see the women standing at the long table cutting out the thick layers of cotton fabric around cardboard patterns with sharp knives. He can see the row of sewing machines with their young women operators bent over the material. The women glance up frequently from their work, coquettishly tilting their heads toward him.

Frieda cannot bear them, the silly girls who are so taken with her handsome Vati, a Jew who won the Iron Cross when he pulled his commanding officer to safety during the Great War. A rare thing for a Jew, the Iron Cross. It helps with the customers in the store in the front. Though Eisenbaum's faces Meinekestrasse, it is one store up from the corner at the Kurfürstendamm, the smartest thoroughfare in Berlin. Her brother, Wolfie, also rakish in his suit, serves the customers who come in to buy shirts and the latest style of undergarments, only a few feet away from Vati through that door with the round window that separates the store from the workroom. In this heat Vati wipes his brow with his handkerchief. Whenever he's needed, he opens the door to the store and enters that other world where he rearranges his face and transforms himself into a salesman.

Frieda sighs. Would she rather wait on customers like her father and brother, smiling politely while the women try to decide between the different fashions of bloomers? Maybe then she might have time to study. There is seldom a steady stream of customers. And now with the inflation coming back again, people are not buying much. That is not a good thing, Frieda knows; less money for their family. And yet she is strangely detached from the means by which they make a living. She wishes she could look again at the chemistry book her class began just before she left. The part where it says that chemistry is primarily the science of the transformations of substances into other substances. Not only could two substances combine to form a new substance, but a substance could decompose into other substances. Like the marvel that transformed two atoms of hydrogen paired with one of oxygen to make water. In fact, other changes took place that seemed impossible and inexplicable. Coal could transform into diamonds! That is what she wants, what she desperately needs: for the substance of her life to change into something else that is impossible — happiness.

To her surprise the door to the store creaks open and Wolfie sticks his head in. He says something to Vati that she cannot hear. But she knows it is about her because they both turn to look at her before Vati disappears into the store.

Frieda immediately leaves her post.

"I'm not finished," Greta says, pouting, as Frieda heads toward the round window in the door.

She stares through the glass in confusion. In the middle of the store stands Herr Doktor Kochmann, their family physician since she was a little girl. More than their doctor; their friend. And her confidant for some things that she cannot discuss with Vati. What can he possibly be doing here? Buying himself underwear?

She wants to go say hello, but something holds her back. The doctor is portly in his tweed jacket and short grey beard, his hair scant. Beside him Vati looks quite fashionable, agile in a grey suit. He still has all his hair and sports a thick brown moustache.

Wolfie spots her through the window and strolls to the back. He winks at her and opens the door a crack so she can hear.

"Herr Doktor, it's wonderful to see you! Are you buying your own shirts now, that you honour us with your presence?"

"Herr Eisenbaum, it's always a pleasure. Such a bright store, and so well laid out. Wolfie is looking well. I hope you don't mind me taking the liberty, but I felt I should talk to you about Frederika. She says you have taken her out of school, and she is so bright, first in her class, she tells me. She has such a facility with information — medical information, you understand."

"Herr Doktor, it is very kind of you to come, I am sure, but my first concern must be for the business. You must understand my position. The times are uncertain. I had to let two people go last month. Frederika is sixteen now. She must learn to work like all the other girls. If she were a boy …"

"Herr Eisenbaum, she is not just any girl. She has understanding far beyond her years. She learns so quickly. A fine mind is a rare thing."

"That is precisely why I want her to learn how to run the factory. She's smart — you think I don't know? I'm no fool, Herr Doktor. Even her older brother admits she's smarter." He glances back at Wolfie with a devilish smile, and Frieda ducks out of sight. "She will learn from the bottom up and one day she will take over the whole thing."

"I hesitate to interfere. But to take such a student out of school so soon …"

"But she's a girl. She doesn't need more schooling. She needs to learn the business. What is another year, more or less?"

"I am thinking of more than one year of school, Herr Eisenbaum. She has such a precocious intellect in one so young. Not only the intelligence, but the curiosity. I've given her some old medical books because she wants to learn, and she learns very quickly. She's mentioned to me the desire to become a doctor."

For once Vati is speechless. Frieda feels her heart swell with joy — that someone has so much faith in her. Also a pang of regret that Vati knows she has discussed her deepest desires with someone else, rather than with him. She wishes she could run into the store and beg Vati herself, but she knows that will do no good. He is a stubborn man who keeps his own counsel and rarely changes his mind about anything.

However, he defers to authority, in this case, the doctor, though Frieda knows it is only for form's sake. Vati will not be rude.

"I will speak to my wife," he says.

Herr Doktor Kochmann shakes Vati's hand, bows slightly, then leaves.


In the evenings after dinner, Frieda's mother usually sits at the window in the living room. She takes up this position every night, staring straight ahead. It isn't that she's drained from the day, because what does her day consist of? Walking across the street two or three times a week to the hairdresser, who will wash and wave her hair, manicure her nails. At least once a month ordering new clothes from the dressmaker, going for fittings. Irmgard, the maid, goes to the shops for groceries, and Frieda's grandmother cooks the meals. Which leaves Mutti time to stroll languidly down the Kurfürstendamm to the exclusive shop where the sales clerks have saved her size in the latest coats from Paris. She can also get lost in oversized books like *War and Peace*.

No, she doesn't stare out the window from fatigue, but to get away from them all. Especially Oma, who has had a hard life and never tires of reminding them of it. She and Opa came from Poland before the turn of the century. Once Opa found a job with a tailor, he brought his young wife in to do the fine finishing. They worked for many years before opening their own business, Oma working alongside her husband in the store.

Frieda doesn't remember much of Opa. She was six when he died. Oma came to live with them then, a small, fierce woman whose opinions were unshakeable. She feels the same way about the business as Vati, that it eclipses all other considerations. Frieda will find no ally in her. Oma's attention, at any rate, is taken up with Frieda's older sister, Luise.

"Ernst," she says to Vati, "you should've seen how Luise made the dough for the dumplings today. She stuffed them so carefully, every one is a little masterpiece, isn't it, my *liebling*?"

Though Oma can be stern, her white hair pinned tightly, perfectly, to the back of her head in a chignon, she gazes with adoration at her middle grandchild. Luise chomps dreamily on one of the little masterpieces, pale blue eyes resting briefly on the faces of her father, her mother, Frieda, for affirmation.

When none arrives from her parents, Frieda says, "They're delicious, Louie."

Luise lets out a snorty laugh. "They're delicious, Louie," she mimics.

"No, no," says Oma. "Ladies do not laugh like that. Quietly, Luise, ladylike." Oma is always immaculately turned out in a crisply starched white blouse and black wool skirt.

Luise's face goes blank. She bites a piece of potato filling off her fork and chews with her mouth open. Periodically, Oma wipes the food off the girl's lips with a napkin. She does this mechanically, as if it is the most natural thing in the world for a crust to form around the mouth of someone who is eating.

Frieda picks at her food, waiting for Vati to say something about Herr Doktor Kochmann.

Instead, he says to his mother, "Don't you think she's had enough? It won't help if she gets fat."

Every morning Oma braids Luise's light brown hair into two braids over her ears, as if she is ten and not eighteen. As if Oma can stall time and, by sheer will, keep the chasm from widening between the child's mind and the adult body.

"She's not fat! Are you, Luise-mouse?"

Luise smiles serenely and pokes her fork into some chicken.

"One day some nice young man will come and sweep her off her feet," says Oma.

Vati slams his hand down on the table. Everyone jumps. "Don't be ridiculous! That will never happen. Look at her!"

Everyone turns to look at Luise, whose plump white cheeks fill with more chicken. She smiles, pleased with the attention, her mouth open chewing the food.

"She's a beautiful girl," says Oma. "She looks like me when I was young. Only she doesn't have to work her fingers to the bone like I did. We came here for a better life and we found it."

Vati squares his jaw, controlling his anger. "I know you mean well," he says, "but I can't have her hoping for something she'll never have. She must face reality."

"She will learn, Ernst. I will work with her. But I need time, since I have no help. I, for one, refuse to give up." She looks pointedly at her daughter-in-law, who stares into the centre of the table as if the plates are dancing.

"No Jew in Berlin would marry a —" Vati begins.

"There are so many Jews coming now from the east," Oma goes on. "There must be a nice young man among them. It would be a raise in stature for them to marry into a German family —"

"*Ostjuden*? Are you mad? They're religious fanatics. Those Jews are our misfortune, with their caftans and forelocks. And their ridiculous superstitions. They don't even speak German!"

"We were *Ostjuden* once," Oma says. "You think it was easy when we came, that people welcomed us? You don't remember how many times you came running home with bruises or a bloody nose. I didn't make a fuss. I just pushed you back out. It was the only way to teach you."

"So I became German. *We* became German. We made an effort to fit in. We learned the language. But these *Ostjuden* — they speak that gibberish, that jargon, and bring the air of the ghetto with them. Now the papers rail against all of us because the new Jews draw attention to themselves. Did you see what the papers are saying now? That Jews are unpatriotic. That we stayed home during the war. That we didn't fight! Do people really believe them? It's only been nine years since the war ended and they think they can convince people with lies like this!"

Luise shrinks back in her chair, her head lowered.

"Don't be frightened, *liebchen*," Oma says, stroking Luise's head. "Vati is not angry with *you*." She looks at the flushed face of her son. "*Are* you, Ernst?"

Vati picks up his napkin and wipes his moustache with great care, patting it from one end to the other.

Frieda is getting restless. She feels time running out. Mutti sits across the table facing her, but her eyes are blank. She could be thinking anything. She could be thinking nothing.

"How many Jews were in your company, Vati?" Frieda has heard it all before but encourages her father to talk. If he's in a good mood, maybe he'll bring up the subject of Herr Doktor Kochmann's visit.

"Many, many Jews. They all fought bravely. Many died. We felt we had to prove we were proud Germans. You were born here, so there's no question of your being German. We've risen far since I was your age."

Dinner is almost over, and so far Vati has made no attempt to broach the question Frieda carries in her heart. She knows her mother is a fragile creature and must be approached with the utmost care. Once dinner is over she will retreat into herself and it will be impossible. Yet dinner is nearly over. The borscht is finished. The chicken. The time passes and Vati has not raised the subject of the visit. The maid has gone into the kitchen for the cooked fruit compote for their dessert.

Dinner is over. Frieda is crestfallen. Vati never intended to give her the chance. She watches her mother, desperation rising in her chest.

Mutti has taken up her position at the window. Frieda thinks she sits at the window so that it doesn't look so odd, her staring into space. Because she never really *looks* at anything. She has wandered into some other world where no one can follow her. During dinner Vati gives her the pills and potions the doctors have prescribed over the years for her problem. What the problem is depends on the doctor. Hysteria, one says. A weak constitution, says another. The disappointment of producing a backward child. Most of the time she sits immobile as if lost in some labyrinth in her mind. Frieda wonders at this beautiful creature that is her mother, her thick dark hair loosely bound at the nape of her slender neck.

Frieda will not live her life like this. She will not. Her chest throbs, throbs with the injustice of it. Vati is Vati, but she has a right to her life.

The distant figure sits in the stuffed chair reading the paper. He's following the preparations for the Olympics to take place in Amsterdam next year.

Frieda approaches as if through a tunnel. "Vati," she says.

He doesn't look up. "Look at this. A young Jewish girl is going to be on the fencing team. You realize this is our first Olympics since before the war? They wouldn't let Germany come in '24. And here's that rabble-rouser, Hitler, at it again …"

"Vati, I know Herr Doktor Kochmann came to see you today." She glances at Mutti, who stares, mesmerized, out the window.

"It is of no concern to you," Vati says, his eyes still on the paper.

"How can you say that? My whole life depends on it." She is astonished at her own temerity.

Vati glances up, his eyes narrowing in anger. "Don't be insolent. You have nothing to say in this regard. I need you in the store. That's final."

"You said you were going to speak to Mutti. You told Herr Doktor …"

Vati flicks his newspaper to another page.

She runs to her mother, kneels before her. "Mutti, Herr Doktor Kochmann came to see Vati in the store today. He says I'm an exceptional student — he says that I should stay in school. I want to be a doctor.

Mutti! Please help me. I want to stay in school. I want to go to university."

Mutti blinks, but her eyes are lost somewhere else.

"You're wasting your time, Frieda. If you weren't so selfish you would understand I need you in the business. Wolfie will never run the place. He's not as smart as you, not as serious. He's out there now, somewhere with his women, drinking and gambling. Who will run the store when I can't? Mutti? *Luise*? You're the only one."

"Greta's a smart girl. Why don't you train her? She's part of the family."

"She's my niece, not my daughter." A pause. "In my day I wouldn't have dared argue with my parents."

Frieda continues to kneel before her mother. "You haven't asked Mutti. If Mutti says no, I won't speak of it again." What possesses her to make this offer? The most she can hope for is that Mutti will say nothing.

Vati frowns at her. "Why do you put me in this position? You know how it is with your Mutti."

Vati stands to go. Then a small voice, muffled by years of silence, stretches into the air.

"Frieda is not like us."

Vati turns toward the beautiful woman in the chair, his mouth open with astonishment. Mutti looks up at him for a brief moment, her long neck arched, swanlike.

"Don't keep her from life." Then she turns back to the window and escapes once more into the tangle of her silence.

He takes her hand gently and brings it to his lips. "Karolina, my love."

# chapter three

Bizet's Pearl Fisher duet washed over Rebecca at 7:00 a.m. Saturday. She lay there spellbound, transported by the rousing voices of two tenors issuing from the radio and filling the room — she didn't know who they were, she didn't care; she just loved the music. Until it stopped and she remembered.

Even after a year, every time she woke up alone in her queen-size bed an ache bloomed in her chest. During the week she was too rushed to think. But on weekends, when she had the luxury of lying still upon waking, languorous beneath the covers, the first thing that filtered into her consciousness was the empty space beside her. She ran her hand along the cool, vacant expanse of sheet. *David*. Red hair, impish smile. Warm hand in the small of her back. His face rose in the air like the morning, like the music. *Go away*, she thought. No point loving a dead man. Rolling over, she turned off the radio.

At least she had something to do today. No more time to think. She stumbled into the shower and let the steady hum of the water take her over. Mindlessly, she massaged the shampoo into her dark mass of hair, which had grown too long. She hated going to the hairdresser.

While she was rinsing, she thought of Nesha, the only man she had let into her life since David had died. He was coming in a few weeks during the American Thanksgiving. Thursday to Sunday, he said. Then he had to fly to Boston to eat a holiday dinner Sunday evening with his son's girlfriend's family.

Their long-distance relationship suited Rebecca. He was on the same far edge of the continent as her parents. Any further and they'd fall off. Though he was in San Francisco and they were a long day's drive south in Santa Barbara, the winter haven of snowbirds who could afford it. Once a month he'd fly to Toronto, and they would spend happy long weekends together. She didn't know anyone else like him. He swaggered like a biker in his cracked leather jacket, but he was an accountant. They had a history together, meeting when his elderly cousin, Rebecca's patient, had been killed in the spring. They had each delved into her death separately. During the process of uncovering the layers of truth and memory, they had discovered each other. She had been astonished that she could still love someone. Perhaps it was Nesha's own wounded heart that drew her, the murder of his family during the war while he was a boy. She saw that boy in him still, despite the age difference between them. What was it — fifteen years?

She dressed carefully for the trip downtown. A day among her peers called for a skirt and pantyhose. She found a tweed jacket that made her look academic. And low-heeled pumps for the trek on public transit.

She got off the subway at Union Station, then crossed to the other side of Front Street where the Royal York lay in a regal pile. It was one of the series of luxurious hotels the Canadian Pacific Railway had built across the country in the late nineteenth and early twentieth centuries. Despite the nippy November morning, she remembered a summer long ago when she and David had vacationed in Alberta and stayed at another CP hotel, the Banff Springs. As they drove toward it, from the distance she thought they had stumbled into a fairy tale: glittering above the fir trees, a rambling many-storied and -peaked castle threw giant shadows on the backdrop of mountains. It was the second year they were married. When she thought they would go on forever. Only hotels, it seemed, went on forever.

She stepped up to the mezzanine level of the Royal York and followed the crowd into the conference room. By the doorway, a sign on a tripod read "Updates for General Practitioners," the logos of three drug companies set tastefully in the lower right corner.

Long, narrow tables covered with white cloths had been placed width-wise from front to back in the huge room, with an aisle down the middle. Several people stood near a lectern at the front.

She nodded and smiled at a few familiar faces, kept walking forward to the front and the only available seats. Picking up one of the many free pens scattered on the table, she read the plastic surface: "Vipranol: Hassan Pharmaceuticals," paired with the emblem of a snake. Vipranol. She had never heard of it. The lunch speaker would, no doubt, enlighten her.

At nine, one of the organizers spoke into the microphone, introducing the first speaker, a respirologist. In her notepad Rebecca wrote down the date and subject of the lecture.

The man began: "No doubt, you have all noticed in your practice the increased incidence of asthma among children. Whereas asthma was relatively rare a scant twenty years ago …"

By 11:45 a.m., she had heard three lectures and scribbled fifteen pages of notes, which she hoped she could decipher when she got home.

She followed the throng into the banquet hall and found a seat at one of the round tables.

Waiters served them a salad, a choice of chicken or fish, and a trifle for dessert. After the servers had come around with coffee and tea, a middle-aged man coughed into the microphone. The chatter in the room diminished to a low buzz.

"It is my great pleasure to introduce our guest speaker, Dr. Mustafa Salim, the chairman of Hassan Pharmaceuticals. His company has done brilliant, innovative work with snake venom, and he has come to North America to give a series of lectures on that research in the interest of scientific exchange. He's in Toronto to collaborate with Connaught Labs on a special project. The founder of Hassan Pharmaceuticals, Dr. Mohammed Hassan, is an advisor to the president of Egypt, Anwar Sadat, and was recently at Camp David with U.S. President Carter during the historic accord between Egypt and Israel. We're very lucky to have Dr. Salim here with us today. Let's give him a warm welcome. Dr. Mustafa Salim."

Polite applause. Dr. Salim stepped in front of the microphone and peered at his audience over reading glasses. Dark intelligent eyes. A high-coloured complexion, rather than brown. Not what she expected an Egyptian to look like. His brown hair lay in short waves, abundant for a man of maybe sixty.

"Thank you. Very kind. It's delightful to be here.

Canadians are such a reasonable, enlightened people, it's always a pleasure to come here."

She had never heard an Arab accent before. Nasal and guttural at the same time. Very cultivated. Also not what she expected. He spoke slowly and deliberately, sure of himself.

"When I say to you 'Egypt,' what do you think of? The pyramids. The Sphinx. The desert. They are miraculous, of course, and, God willing, they will last forever. *Inshallah* is what we say in my religion. 'If God is willing.' But I am a modern Egyptian, and as much as I love the pyramids, I want more for my country.

"And you will be much amused, gentlemen — and ladies — that my method is based on an ancient creature that has killed people in the desert for millennia. A mutant species of the genus *Vipera*, a kind of desert viper that is quite beautiful, an almost velvety sandy green colour. Beautiful but dangerous. Like some women."

The women glanced at each other; the men cleared their throats. He was a dinosaur, thought Rebecca. But a charming one.

"This desert viper produces venom that would kill an adult, if, God forbid, the adult were unfortunate enough to offer himself to be bitten. What exactly is snake venom? It's a toxic saliva made up of enzymes, mostly proteins. According to their principal clinical effects, the venoms are classified as either neurotoxic, that is, attacking nerve tissues and interfering with the transmission of nerve impulses, or haemotoxic, attacking the blood and circulation system. To date, venom has been used medicinally in the production of antivenom. But we have taken a giant leap ahead of that science and have produced a drug that has an analgesic effect on pain using the neurotoxic type of venom. We theorized that if neurotoxic venom interferes with the transmission of nerve impulses, then maybe we could manipulate minute amounts of venom to interfere with the transmission of pain along those nerve impulses.

"There were many hurdles along the way. Snakes do not create a lot of venom. For them, it's a precious commodity that requires energy and time to produce. Since they paralyze their prey with it, most snakes will not expend it needlessly. It's their principal means of obtaining food. Of course there are short-tempered varieties that will inject you with poison on principle — if they feel you've stepped into their territory, for instance. Not so different from some people."

Polite titters.

"Because of this conservation on their part, if you ever get bitten by a poisonous snake, the chances of actually getting injected with venom are only fifty percent.

"We have established a snake farm where the workers 'milk' the venom. Despite the term, milking a snake for venom bears no resemblance to the milking of a cow or a goat. It requires a highly specialized skill and experience. And very fast reflexes. It's not easy to find people to do this kind of work. But once they start, they see that snakes are all God's creatures and come to love them. One gram of dried venom requires the milking of fifteen snakes.

"One of the most rewarding experiences I've had was the summer I spent in a lab overlooking a harbour in Cape Cod where fishermen catch squid for the scientists there. You are all familiar with the squid nerves used in neurological research?"

He peered up, momentarily scanning the audience, some of whom nodded.

"The squid's nerve fibre, the giant axon, is much thicker than ours. It looks like a thick piece of fishing line. For that reason it offers unequalled opportunities for experimentation, even if all the work must be done before the axon dies, within two hours of dissection. We made great strides using the squid as a test paradigm for our venom.

"After years of hits and misses, trying to understand the basic process, we're encouraged by our latest results. Extensive findings show that our new drug, Vipranol, has an analgesic effect on pain caused by cancer, multiple sclerosis, and arthritis."

Everyone in the room was turned toward him, absorbed in the exotic details he offered in his emphatic yet lilting voice. He segued into specifics about the buffers they used in the lab and their methods of keeping the preparation stable. Though Rebecca found her attention drifting at the description of technique, she saw some of the doctors at her table taking notes.

When Dr. Salim stopped speaking, everyone applauded with enthusiasm. A few people stepped up to the podium to ask him questions.

Rebecca stood up on weary legs. She was having trouble sleeping at night, more so on weekends, and found her energy flagging by afternoon.

Two of the organizers stood chatting off to one side. As she pushed her chair in, she noticed a short elderly man, his grey-brown hair wind-tossed, pass her on his way to Dr. Salim, who was gathering his notes at the podium. The man stood out in his navy parka, as if he'd just come in off the street. The doctor towered over him.

The man didn't look like a colleague. She kept watching: he spoke too quietly for her to hear, but what he said must have caught Dr. Salim's attention, because his ruddy face turned pale. The doctor answered something Rebecca didn't understand, since it wasn't English. It wasn't Arabic either. *How unlikely*, she thought. It sounded like German.

Dr. Salim looked around suddenly as if to see whether anyone had heard him. His eyes fell on Rebecca.

She pretended to be searching for something in her handbag. When she looked up again he was still watching her, sideways now, at the same time conversing in low tones with the man. The doctor looked apprehensive, but she couldn't tell whether it was a reaction to the man or to what he was saying. Did he want her to approach and interrupt? Was that the meaning of the expression she saw on his face?

Then the other man noticed her. He handed Dr. Salim a business card, abruptly turned on his heels, and walked across the room to the exit.

Dr. Salim watched him, then walked away from the podium, notes in hand, and headed to a distant door. But he seemed to change his mind, glanced at her, and shifted direction, stepping toward her.

Shaking his head, he said, "In Egypt that would never happen. People can complain about armed guards, but at least they keep people like that out."

Surprised at being spoken to, but curious, she asked, "What did he want?"

"You didn't hear?" He watched her shrug. "Just someone off the street with an axe to grind. Not everyone likes doctors."

"Maybe you should report it to the hotel."

He smiled, observing her. "Well, you know, Dr. ⋯.."

"Rebecca Temple."

"I think, Dr. Temple, he just needed to get it off his chest."

His dark eyes watched her with an interest that flattered but puzzled her.

Suddenly the two organizers chatting in the corner bestirred themselves and rushed to their guest star. Rebecca excused herself and walked to the door, feeling the man's eyes upon her.

# *chapter four*

**January 30, 1933**

Every day the trip on the U-Bahn becomes harder, the passengers around Frieda more nervous and sullen. Today the tension is unbearable. They all sit in their winter coats and hats, staring straight ahead as the subterranean black slides by outside the windows of the train, a blackness mirrored in their eyes. She cannot look at them; their desperation threatens to overwhelm her. The occasional beggar makes it onto the train and manages to pocket a few *pfennig* before being thrown off. Frieda gets off the U-Bahn at her stop near the university.

It is not a good day. Rumours are flying about who will become chancellor. The Republic has gone to hell, and no one knows how to fix it. General von Schleicher lasted less than two months as chancellor before being dismissed by President von Hindenburg. Now the wind carries wild rumours that Storm Troopers will seize the

Wilhelmstrasse and the Presidential Palace. As leader of
the largest political party, Hitler is demanding the chan-
cellorship for himself. Yesterday, Sunday, one hundred
thousand workers jammed into the Lustgarten in the
middle of Berlin clamouring against Hitler. At least
there is hope.

Vati says their family has nothing to worry about.
Though Hitler is a rabid anti-Semite, at least he would
take care of the Communists who want to nationalize
all businesses. How would the family survive without
their business? At any rate, the Eisenbaums are proud
Germans. Hitler's ravings don't include Jews who
fought for the Fatherland in the Great War and were
awarded the Iron Cross.

Frieda climbs the stairs to street level, breathing the
January chill into her lungs. Turning to look behind her,
she gazes high up at the Quadriga, the four bronze
horses poised atop the Brandenburg Gate, the female
statue of Victory at the reins of the chariot. As a child,
Frieda insisted that Vati lift her onto his shoulders to get
a better look at the sweeping arches fashioned after a
Greek temple, the horses with their graceful heads
turned to one side, their bony legs lifted toward some
urgent destination. She cannot reproduce the awe of
those young years for this entranceway in the sky, nor
the security she once felt, the assurance that if she
worked prodigiously and absorbed all the medical
knowledge laid before her, the profession she loved so
deeply would embrace her.

She should be paying more attention, because turning
away from the horses in the sky, she finds herself caught
up in a crowd of angry men in dusty overalls and work
pants. Most of them are young, stinking of sweat and
cigarettes. At the front of the horde — the direction
they're moving in — two huge red banners snap in the

wind. Amid the confusion, she hears them shout, "To hell with you fascist pigs!"

She pushes her way through the bodies, only to be confronted by their adversaries — seething young thugs with clipped hair, wearing brown shirts. "Death to Bolshevik shit!" they shout into the air.

Faces on both sides twist in rage. At first she sees only fists pounding. Then she notices the clubs. One man swings at another's head. A booming *thwack* on the skull. Blood streams down his face. Many faces. Another club swings. A bone cracks. On one side, a knife flashes and slits open a man's cheek. Then someone pulls out a pistol and begins to fire. It all happens in a minute. Less than a minute.

Enough time to create pandemonium in the morning crowd. Everyone, including Frieda, scatters away from the echo of the gun in the wintry air.

She wishes she could soar over the street like the horses on the Brandenburg Gate. She runs, flees without looking back. It's the first time she has been this close to a skirmish. They used to happen in working-class districts between the Browns and the Reds. Now she hears them from her family's apartment in well-to-do Wilmersdorf, the screaming of the brown-shirted thugs, the smashing of truncheons over bones, the firecracker pop of pistols in the night.

She can't stop shaking as she makes her way up Wilhelmstrasse toward the Charité Hospital. So much has changed in Berlin in just a few years. Nothing has been the same since the stock market crashed in America. American investment was the backbone of Germany's economy, shaky since the war, and that investment has now dried up. Almost immediately, the *Beamtenbank*, the official bank, failed. Business after business died, throwing millions out of work. People have to live on compensation cards, the equivalent of food stamps. Millions of people hungry. The Weimar Republic offered no solution. President Hindenburg, at eighty-five, appears senile. Hitler rails against the Versailles Treaty that has humiliated the Germans with war reparations they can't pay. In the same breath he blames Marxists and Jewish war profiteers for their ills.

Frieda's intellectual friend, Leopold — the one who fancies her — says Hitler is a fool and cannot be taken seriously. But his National Socialist party gained ground in the 1931 election. She is impatient with politics, with anything that takes time away from her medical studies. But the "little Austrian corporal," as some call him, and his vicious followers are plunging Berlin into civil war.

As she walks, Wilhelmstrasse turns into Luisenstrasse, one of the streets that frames the rectangular area of eleven hectares covered by the Charité Hospital, an impressive complex of red brick buildings with brownstone trim and ornamental gables.

She steps through the door of the hospital, soothed by the order and sanity inside. Only now does she feel her blouse sticking to her skin beneath the coat. She hurries to her locker, changes into her white frock, and runs to join her fellow students at rounds.

Herr Doktor Rosenzweig, a tall, stocky man with black hair and bushy eyebrows, reaches for the chart at the foot of the patient's bed. While he peruses the sheets of paper, the plump, balding patient leans forward from his pillows, glances uneasily toward the group of students hovering in a semi-circle a polite distance away. He looks like he wishes he could be anywhere but here. The doctor is finally ready.

"Herr Werner is a fifty-one-year-old male who presented with jaundice. He has experienced nausea and vomiting unrelated to meals, accompanied by anorexia.

Ten days before being hospitalized he noted dark urine. Two days before admission he noted that his eyes were yellow. His vital signs: temperature ninety-nine degrees Fahrenheit, pulse ninety-six per minute, respiration sixteen per minute, blood pressure one-thirty over seventy. The liver edge is smooth, slightly tender, and palpable five centimetres below the costal margin. Here are the facts in chronological order: vague upper abdominal pain for one year; nausea and vomiting, anorexia, tachycardia, hepatomegaly, hemorrhoids, slight proteinuria, hyperbilirubinemia, bilirubinuria, increased serum transaminase concentration, increased serum alkaline phosphatase concentration." He peers around at the students. "So what do we do now? Fräulein Remke?"

Ilse Remke thinks a moment. "Surgical exploration?"

Herr Doktor Rosenzweig turns away. "What would we do before that?"

The large-boned Fräulein Remke blushes and lowers her eyes. Rosenzweig peruses the group. Frieda ventures to raise her hand. "Fräulein Eisenbaum."

"Evaluate which of these are most important. For instance, hemorrhoids are common, and tachycardia and mild proteinuria are non-specific findings in many types of illness. I would put hepatomegaly and jaundice first in order of importance, then hyperbilirubinemia and bilirubinuria next."

"Very good, Fräulein. Now you will find that even so, the accumulated facts are common to several diseases. So we must select a central feature of the illness around which we can orient the diagnostic analysis. A central feature such as fever, jaundice, hepatomegaly, renal failure, among others. It takes practice to correctly select a feature as the focal point of a diagnosis, years of experience and a wide knowledge of the natural course of diseases." He smiled paternally, his bushy eyebrows arching together. "God willing, you won't kill too many patients on your way down that road to experience. Now, Fräulein Eisenbaum has chosen hepatomegaly and jaundice as the central feature of the diagnosis. What are the diagnostic possibilities? Herr Wurzburg?"

A thin, fair-haired student snaps to attention. "Stone. Hepatitis. Carcinoma of the pancreas."

"Those are most likely. In this example, the past history of epigastric pain makes extrahepatic obstruction a reasonable possibility. It would be tempting to proceed directly to surgical exploration, as Fräulein Remke suggested."

Ilse Remke nods with a relieved smile, while the patient stares into the doctor's face with unalloyed fear.

"But if the jaundice were caused by hepatitis, surgery and anaesthesia might prove disastrous."

Frieda feels sorry for Ilse Remke, who has been embarrassed in front of her peers, and now keeps her eyes lowered.

"Thus the prudent physician first asks, 'Will further observation or examination help to distinguish between the diagnostic possibilities?' At the moment, I'm afraid they will not. But I've heard that someone in America is working on developing a needle biopsy for the liver. Until that happens, there is no option save for surgical exploration, which is planned for later this morning."

Rosenzweig smiles at Ilse Remke, not unkindly. "Fräulein Remke was right all along, but we must be able to think our decision through and understand how we got from here to there."

To Frieda's astonishment, Ilse Remke glowers at the doctor with what looks like contempt.

Later that day Leopold takes a break from his history studies at the university and meets Frieda in the hospital cafeteria. She is sitting at a table drinking tea with lemon when he rushes in, his face flushed behind the wire-rimmed glasses. He's a tall, lanky young man with dark blond hair already thinning in the front.

"The little corporal is chancellor!" he says, throwing his books on the table.

Her heart sinks. She hopes Vati is right about Hitler. "How?"

"Senile old Hindenburg appointed him. I'm sure Hitler was very persuasive. He must've blackmailed him with something. He's been appointed on the condition that he can put together a majority in the Reichstag."

Frieda is embarrassed at how little she knows about the workings of government. "And can he?"

"Impossible. As a party, only the Nationalists are like-minded, and even if they joined the Nazis, their vote wouldn't be large enough. If Hitler formed an alliance with the Catholic Centre party, he might get his majority. But they hate each other. It's impossible."

"I don't think that will stop him."

"Nothing will stop him. If he's gotten this far, he'll figure out a way. It's just a matter of time."

Gales of laughter and high-spirited voices turn everyone's attention to a corner of the cafeteria. Nurses and female clerks and helpers flock around a group of brown-shirted men wearing swastika armbands.

"The new heroes," Leopold sneers.

An older nurse at the next table says to the air, "Hitler will solve our problems. You'll see."

"I can come by to escort you home later," Leopold says. "What time are you finished?"

"I can take care of myself," she says, amused but touched.

Early that afternoon Frieda is walking down the hall toward a seminar when orderlies wheel in Herr Werner, today's rounds patient, from his surgery. She has a moment, and since no one is about she tiptoes into his room. He is still sleeping off the anaesthetic beneath the hospital blanket. Her curiosity gets the better of her. She wants to know the answer to the puzzle.

She picks up the chart from the foot of the bed. Her heart sinks for a man she doesn't know. During exploratory surgery, they found that plump, balding Herr Werner has carcinoma of the head of the pancreas. A death sentence.

On her way out of the hospital that evening, she spots Leopold waiting on the sidewalk.

"I worry about you," he says, taking her arm. "You're so small. Beautiful, but small."

Leopold is a head taller than she is. Not bad looking, a bit thin for her taste. But she has no time for a man. Not if she wants to pass her exams.

"Someone could scoop you up with no effort," he says, peering down at her with an absent smile. "And something is up tonight."

As they head toward the U-Bahn, crowds of excited people hurry past them in the same direction. Something is indeed up. Newspapers at the stand near the hospital catch her eye: "Reichstag Dissolved! New Election Called!"

She feels the earth shifting beneath her feet. A din rises in the distance. A roar like the ocean. When they turn the corner, thousands of men in uniform appear, phalanx upon phalanx carrying torches aloft. Tens of thousands of brown-shirted Storm Troopers and SS men in polished jackboots hold high a filament of flame as they march from the Tiergarten, passing under the Brandenburg Gate and down the Wilhelmstrasse to the thunder beat of drums.

Her heart strums wildly in her chest — she is glad of Leopold's arm as they keep moving. Her fear is irrational. What they are witnessing is a show of strength from the new leader of the country. Nothing more. Yet there *is* something. She feels it emanating in waves: the hatred in the faces of the soldiers.

# *chapter five*

Rebecca stooped along the snowy road — when had it snowed? She dug in with her shovel and lifted the snow, dug in and lifted, dug in and lifted. Mechanical, too fast, cartoon-like. All the while bullets flew over her head, someone shooting as she tried to shovel faster and faster. How long could she go on without getting hit? Her blood would be very red against the white snow. She had to shovel faster! Dig in and lift. Dig in and lift. Then she heard it. The bullet whizzed by her ear, making it ring. Her heart pounded in time to the ringing. The next one would hit its mark. The blood in the snow. Then the ringing!

Rebecca sat upright with a start and blinked awake. The newspaper rustled in her lap. Her heart thudded, thudded. But that wasn't the sound. Her bell was ringing. Someone was downstairs at her front door.

She descended the stairs slowly, still in a daze. Saturday night; she wasn't expecting anybody.

Turning on the outside light, she peered through the small square of glass in the front door. She rubbed her eyes, then threw wide the door and gaped at her sister.

Susan gave her a sheepish, half-hearted smile behind a curtain of blonde hair. "Hi, Rebecca."

Her leather jacket was far too small to enclose her pregnant belly. A backpack lay beside her on the stoop.

"What are you doing here? How did you get here?" Rebecca searched the empty air behind her for Susan's husband. "Where's Ben?"

"In Montreal."

Rebecca picked up the backpack and led her sister into the house. "Please tell me you didn't drive all the way by yourself."

Rebecca fell into the habit of scolding her sister because Susan was two years younger. But she was also taller and, despite appearing contrite, gazed down at Rebecca with the knowing look she had developed in childhood. Bemusement usually accompanied the look, but not this time.

"You're eight months pregnant. You shouldn't be driving for hours like that."

Susan lowered herself slowly into a kitchen chair. "I'd give anything not to be pregnant!"

"Susan!"

"Three children are enough," she said. "I didn't want another one. I was supposed to be in law school in September. This baby screwed everything up."

*It wasn't the baby who screwed*, Rebecca thought.

She took the plastic containers with last night's leftovers from the deli and put them on dishes to microwave. "There's some leftover matzo ball soup and potato skins. Here, have some salad. You must be starved."

They didn't look like sisters. Rebecca had always thought Susan was the good-looking one, tall and willowy, one wave of blonde hair falling over her face. She reminded Rebecca of Lassie, only less obedient. She had their father's long nose, but on her it looked elegant. She had also inherited his stubbornness.

"I can't eat. I'm never going to eat again."

Rebecca understood, but she was the big sister. "Does Ben know where you are?"

Her hazel eyes stared at Rebecca. "I couldn't take it anymore. Ben and the two oldest came home from *shul* today and I made them all lunch — grilled cheese sandwiches. Do you know how many slices of bread you need to make four grilled cheese sandwiches? Eight. And if Ben wants more, it's ten. That's almost half a loaf. Do you have any idea how many loaves of bread I buy in a week? How much time I spend shopping for groceries? The hours preparing food? Lunches for the kids? *Shabbat* dinners? Who *am* I? I'm a cook and a maid. I'm someone's wife and someone else's mother. When I look in the mirror I don't see myself anymore. I don't know who I am, Rebecca. I've *disappeared*, and this big fat nonentity has taken my place."

Rebecca got up and stood behind her sister, wrapping her arms around the front of her neck with affection. "You're not fat. You're pregnant. And you've got the best family." She felt a hollow in her chest at the word.

"I know I should be grateful for everything …"

Though she didn't say it, Rebecca knew they were both thinking it: *I have a family of my own and you don't.*

"But I — I hate my life. I can't do it anymore. I wanted so desperately to go to law school. Feel some respect for myself. I'd make a great lawyer, Rebecca. I'm passionate about justice and I'd …" She stopped and took a breath. "I finally got accepted and then bingo! Another triumph for Ben's sperm. I'm a bloody baby factory."

Rebecca stood beside her, a hand on her shoulder. "Do you want me to call him and tell him you're here?"

Susan shook her head. "I want him to worry. I want him to be stuck with the kids all by himself. He's going to have to get used to it because I'm not going back." Susan looked up at Rebecca with large, determined eyes. "I'm going to have this baby and hand it to him. Then I'm leaving. I'll get a job in the evenings and put myself through law school."

"But Susan ..." Rebecca knelt into a crouch beside her sister's chair. "You love your children."

"I've disappeared into the wallpaper, Rebecca. I'm just not *there*. You don't understand because you always had a career. You always knew who you were. I need to know who *I* am."

Rebecca wavered to her feet, sitting down in the chair beside her sister. "Susan, you're the most organized, competent woman I know. Law school is still waiting for you. Start *next* September. Get a nanny. Get a cleaning woman. You don't have to do everything yourself."

"We can't afford it. Mark's starting bar mitzvah lessons next year and with the Hebrew school tuitions for all of them ..."

"Mark doesn't need bar mitzvah lessons *and* Hebrew school. Send him to public school."

"Ben'll never go for it."

"Is there any money in investments you could use?"

"We're saving it for Mark's university."

Rebecca sighed. "Use it for *your* university. You'll earn the money for their tuition later."

Susan blinked back tears. "I think he's having an affair with one of his students."

Rebecca examined her sister, still beautiful despite her bloated middle. Were the inflated hormones of pregnancy making her irrational? Ben was the most solid, down-to-earth man Rebecca knew. "Do you have any proof?"

"It's a feeling. He's so distracted. He just comes home to sleep. He barely notices me. He'll notice when I'm gone, though." She closed her eyes. "I'm so tired."

Rebecca stood up. "You need some rest. Come upstairs to the guest bedroom."

Rebecca pulled out the sofa bed upstairs and put on fresh sheets and a quilt. She left Susan in her pyjamas trying to get comfortable, half-sitting, half-lying on her back, her belly large and round beneath the covers.

When Rebecca no longer heard any movement upstairs, she called Ben in Montreal.

"Oh, Rebecca! I was just going to call the police. Susan's missing. I took a nap after lunch with the boys —"

"Ben —"

"— and when I woke up she was gone! I'll have to call you back —"

"She's here, Ben."

A beat of silence, data processing. "She's in Toronto? But why? Did she drive? Is she crazy? Put her on the phone. I have to talk to her."

"She's sleeping, Ben. Did you notice she's been upset about the baby?"

"I know she's upset. Look, can I talk to her?"

"She's sleeping."

"I know you mean well, Rebecca, but this is between Susan and me. I know her, and she'll come round once the baby's born. She loves kids. She's just tired. Now put her on."

"Ben, I waited until she was asleep because she wouldn't call you. She's very angry."

A moment of deliberation. "I'll get my mother to look after the boys. I can be in Toronto by dawn."

"No, Ben!" How could she put it delicately? "She needs some time to herself. I'll try to get her to call you tomorrow when she wakes up. No promises."

Rebecca stared at her TV screen for a few hours, watched the news with the same distraction. Jimmy Carter walked across the White House lawn to meet some dignitary or other. In Ottawa, the gangly Joe Clark, their youngest ever prime minister, who had defeated Pierre Trudeau in the spring. "Joe Who," as the headlines dubbed him, had caused an uproar during the campaign when he promised to move the Canadian embassy in Israel from Tel Aviv to Jerusalem. He was still dealing with the fallout. A talking head on the news said the Arab states threatened an economic boycott of Canada. Why all the fuss about Israel? Was nothing else going on in the world? Yet another demonstration in Egypt protesting the pact with Israel. She thought of the venerable Dr. Salim. He couldn't be very popular among some circles in his own country. And all the other Arab nations that had ostracized Egypt because of the peace accord. Who could understand the antagonisms in that ancient part of the world? None of the flickering images interested her. Instead of looking for a late-night movie, she went to bed.

Rebecca was in the middle of a dream about her parents. She was visiting them in Santa Barbara, only her mother looked like Susan and she had three little kids running around the apartment.

"Rebecca! Come quick!"

Rebecca sat up in bed. She blinked at the clock: 3:50. Had she dreamt the voice?

"Rebecca! Wake up!"

She jumped out of bed and ran to the bedroom across the hall. Susan was lying in the bed, her covers thrown off. "My water broke! I'm having the baby."

"I'll call an ambulance."

"No time. It's coming now."

Rebecca took a breath. She turned on all the lights and brought in a goose-necked reading light from her bedroom, aiming it at Susan. She ran to gather towels and found a sterile disposable scalpel in her medical bag.

Susan groaned when Rebecca placed a clean folded sheet beneath her. "Take it easy, sweetie," Rebecca said. "It'll be fine."

She picked up the phone and dialed the operator. "This is an emergency. I'm a doctor and I'm going to be delivering a baby at home. I need you to call an ambulance." She gave the address to the startled woman operator and hung up.

"I don't want this baby," Susan moaned, her face mottled with effort. "I don't want this baby."

Rebecca lifted Susan's knees to examine her. She was fully dilated, and the baby's head began to appear.

"I don't believe it!" she said. "Susan, the baby's coming *now*..."

"I *told* you. I've had enough practice to know."

Susan's labour with the three other children had been mercifully short. A few hours and it was all over. She was made to have babies. However, this one was a month early.

When the head was partially visible Rebecca said, "Push! Bear down!"

Susan whimpered and groaned. A bit more of the head appeared.

"I don't want this baby!" Susan groaned again, and the rest of the head eased out. The shoulders were the harder part, but after three other babies, Susan's body knew the way.

Rebecca supported the little body, covered in mucus and blood, on its slow way out. Susan moaned a little, deep in her throat, but on the whole she was remarkably quiet through the ordeal.

"Doing great, sweetie. Push some more."

"I don't want this baby!" Susan screamed.

"It's coming whether you want it or not. So push and help it out."

From the size of the head, the baby was tiny; Rebecca prayed it would survive the trip to the preemie unit.

"Nearly there! Just a bit more. One more good push."

She held her hands beneath the miniature shoulders to support them on their way through the canal. Once they were out, the rest was easy. The slippery body slid into Rebecca's waiting hands.

"It's a girl!" she said. "A tiny, beautiful girl. She has all her fingers and all her toes."

No response from Susan. Rebecca cut the umbilical cord with the scalpel. She held the baby up until she whimpered and Rebecca knew she was breathing on her own. She needed to get to an incubator. Rebecca wrapped up the bundle in a clean towel.

She placed the baby beside Susan, who shook her head and closed her eyes, a tear squeezing through. "Watch her while I finish."

She tied off Susan's end of the cord and cleaned her up with more towels. Through the dark night a siren approached. It wasn't until the doorbell rang that she allowed herself a deep breath and finally acknowledged the pounding of her heart.

# *chapter six*

---

**April 1, 1933**

The first day of April should excite Frieda with the prospect of spring. Despite the chill, the morning air feels milder on her skin, the cold edge gone, as she leaves her family's apartment on Sächsische Strasse. But she cannot rejoice in the buds forming on the branches of the linden trees, or the sparrows flitting around the muddy lawns. Today, all the Jews in Germany, her family included, are in a kind of limbo. All week newspapers and radio broadcasts have announced the imposition of a boycott of Jewish businesses on April 1. The uncertainty of what will happen gnaws at her. Since Hitler became chancellor, the world has become a dangerous place. A Dutch Communist was accused of setting fire to the Reichstag in February. He was barely intelligible in court, a halfwit not competent enough to burn down an outhouse, never mind the parliament building. Nevertheless, the Nazis convicted and decapitated him. Then, using an emergency decree, they jailed opposition leaders, forced writers, scientists, and physicians into exile, and beat up anyone who spoke out.

Vati says things have gone badly for Jews before, that it is a phase that will pass and they must make the best of it. He is still privileged, with his Iron Cross, and can get on a first-class train car with only a second-class ticket. He gets a pension from the government as a war veteran. It will all pass.

Vati has already left for the store, three blocks away from their apartment. Saturday is their busiest day. Frieda walks with dread toward the fashionable stores of the Kurfürstendamm, the elegant street that runs perpendicular to Meinekestrasse, where Eisenbaum's is located. She will pass it on her way to the U-Bahn.

The only thing that keeps her going is the prospect of her medical studies. Yesterday at the hospital she delivered a baby on her own for the first time. No assistance, only a doctor's supervision. She felt elated for the first time in months. A healthy baby boy yowling at his sudden entry into the world. She smiles, remembering.

The smile dies on her face when she turns east onto the Kurfürstendamm. Brown-shirted ruffians stand guard in front of stores along the street. Only stores owned by Jews. She almost stops breathing as she passes them in their full uniforms, guns prominently displayed in their holsters, high polished leather boots up to the knee, arrogant legs spread apart.

The first Jewish store she passes, Schmidt's, where they sell sewing supplies, thread, imported trims, and buttons, is closed, the metal gates up. When she reads the sign posted on the gate, she understands why a business would keep closed on their busiest day.

"*Achtung Deutsche!* Attention, Germans! *Kauft nicht bei Juden.* Don't buy from Jews. These Jewish parasites are the gravediggers of German craftsmen. They pay German workers hunger wages. *Hungerlohne.* The proprietor is the Jew Herman Schmidt." The word *Jew* is printed in larger letters than the rest.

Frieda keeps walking, unable to help staring into the faces of the young brutes, searching for their eyes, which retreat into shadow beneath the peaks of their pillbox caps. They look like normal boys, some with pimpled cheeks, all with chins set in unquestioning resolve. She cannot fathom it. Is this the city she was born in, has lived in all her life?

Another sign, this time posted on a store whose owner has dared to open shop. "*Deutsches Volk!* Defend yourselves! Do not buy from Jews. The Jews of the whole world want to destroy Germany!"

An elderly woman tries to enter the store, which sells gloves and stockings.

The uniformed hooligan posted by the door jeers at her. "Go buy from real Germans, *Gnädige Frau.* Down the street, you'll find a store where the Jews don't steal your money."

"You have no right to tell me where to buy," the old woman says.

"Jewish cow!"

"I'm not Jewish! I don't have to be Jewish to go into a Jewish store."

The man smirks at her. Other women hang back and turn around.

Frieda's heart sinks as she approaches Eisenbaum's. A blank-faced ruffian stands guard by the door, ignoring Vati as he rages. There's a sign posted over the window that names him as the proprietor, "the Jew Ernst Eisenbaum."

"This is an affront, you understand. Not only is it an insult, but you've got the wrong place. Check your orders and you'll see there's been a mistake."

"You are not the Jew Eisenbaum?" The brute's voice drips with sarcasm. Frieda recognizes a nasal country accent.

"You have no idea who you're dealing with. Maybe this will clear things up."

Vati reaches inside his jacket and pulls out a leather box. Frieda can hardly watch, though she cannot turn her eyes away. The thug turns his head slightly, glancing down. Vati opens the box and holds the Iron Cross, the country's highest medal, in front of the man's face. The lips tense up, the eyes unknowable in shadow.

"I was fighting for this country while you were still wetting your bed."

A small crowd has formed around them, though Frieda hangs back.

"He has the Iron Cross. Leave him alone," one woman bystander says.

"Show some respect," another woman chimes in. "Get out of here."

The Brown Shirt lifts his face enough to bring his eyes out of the shadow. They flit around the group, assessing the situation. Frieda realizes he's younger than she, not more than eighteen. Less sure of himself, now; confused. He nods curtly and, nostrils flaring, stalks away.

Vati looks up and spots her, the pain in his eyes unbearable. Her throat fills with bile.

The whole ride on the U-Bahn, Frieda sits shaking. The rage and loathing she feels frightens her. She walks toward the hospital with a purpose she doesn't feel. It's her habit to walk briskly as if she knows where she is going. The self-assurance of her gait has encouraged younger students at the university to ask her for directions. But she feels no such confidence today.

Once inside the hospital with its clean white walls, its instruments to measure blood pressure and heartbeat, she is relieved. She is in her element and can immerse herself in the study of the human body, the only thing she understands anymore.

At least she can look forward to rounds with Herr Doktor Rosenzweig, her favourite professor. He has agreed to supervise her thesis, which all medical students must submit in order to earn the title of Doktor. Her topic is puerperal fever, the infection caused by streptococcus that still kills women after childbirth, sometimes taking their infants with them. These are the most heartbreaking deaths she has witnessed in the hospital. She can see the roundish cells of *streptococcus pyogenes* on slides of tissues under the microscope. The bacteria can live without oxygen but can also tolerate it, an admirable adaptive mechanism. Something to teach mankind. Normal individuals can harbour the bacteria without getting ill. But when organisms are introduced to vulnerable tissues, like tears in the vagina after childbirth, festering infection occurs.

Herr Doktor Rosenzweig gathers his group of medical students around a woman who just had her gallbladder removed. Frieda implicitly trusts his medical acumen; his bushy brown eyebrows are paternal and make him a comforting presence. His posture has a tentative quality today. Not the tall, straight-backed picture of confidence that is usual.

He has just started presenting the case when Ilse Remke marches up to him followed by Herr Doktor Kuhn, a junior physician with thick blond hair. Ilse proclaims in a loud voice, "We have a message for you from the faculty. You are no longer wanted in this hospital. You are to leave today."

His mouth falls open during a second of stunned silence. "How dare you!" he cries, his face turning red. "You are not allowed to speak to me like that. I'm a senior physician."

"Herr Doktor Kuhn is taking over." She turns to Kuhn, waiting.

Kuhn clears his throat. Rosenzweig was his advisor. "I regret ... Your services are no longer required," he mumbles.

Ilse, barely containing herself, shouts, "You are to leave at once!"

The paper in his hand starts to shake. "I take my orders from Herr Doktor Taubman," he says, teeth clenched.

Ilse's mouth tenses into a line. "We'll see about that." She turns on one foot and stomps away, Kuhn following.

They all stand there in shock, watching her back recede. The students turn back to Rosenzweig, who is pretending to study the patient's chart but who Frieda can see is staring rather than reading. The patient looks bewildered and engages one of the students in a discussion of how to relieve her pain.

In a few minutes Ilse returns with another senior physician, Herr Doktor Ledeker, a balding man with a round face and wire-rimmed glasses. He is shorter than Herr Doktor Rosenzweig and seems to be addressing his neck.

"Apparently you did not understand Fräulein Remke, who was relaying our message. Let me make it perfectly plain. Herr Doktor Rosenzweig, you are no longer welcome here. You must leave now. You have five minutes to gather your things and get out!"

The doctor's face has turned purple. "I've been at

this hospital for nearly twenty years. You don't have the authority to dismiss me! I'm going to Herr Doktor Taubman to see about this!"

A wicked smile plays around the edges of his lips. "Herr Doktor Taubman is no longer the head of the hospital. He has been dismissed. Along with all the other Jewish doctors who have taken the place of true Germans. Now we will finally have a real hospital."

Rosenzweig's head quivers, his jaw set. He is controlling himself, but Frieda sees the pulse beating in his neck, senses the disgust, the rage. He stares down at the shorter man, his mouth slightly open, as if he will say something. Instead, he turns to Frieda, avoiding her eyes.

"Don't forget the patient," he says to her hair. He turns and walks away. Two Jewish students look at each other, wordlessly follow him out of the room and down the hall.

Frieda cannot move. She wishes she could sink into the floor and disappear. Ilse Remke is glaring at her, but Herr Doktor Ledeker has moved toward the gallbladder patient and is beginning to present the case. Another Jewish student, Wurzburg, has also stayed. Frieda cannot hear the doctor through the buzz in her head. His outline has become fuzzy, the whole room waves and shimmers. Where is she? Surely not the familiar, sensible hospital she used to feel safe in. Who are these people? She cannot remember their names, though she knows she should. The man beside her (what is his name?) moves an elbow into her arm and brings her back. But is she back? Is this the same place? Everything looks different to her. The paint on the walls is a duller white and shines on a peculiar angle that sets shadows beneath everyone's eyes. She tries to focus on the patient, tries to remember why she is here.

Her mind is in turmoil for days after the dismissal of the Jewish doctors, who made up at least one-quarter of the total physicians in the hospital. How can she go on? How long will they let her? Her immediate concern is her thesis — how will she finish it without a supervisor?

By the end of the week she has decided to approach another professor, Herr Doktor Rausch, to supervise her thesis. He teaches her class laboratory techniques and is a down-to-earth, pleasant fellow.

One afternoon she knocks on his office door and is shown in. He sits down behind his desk, a chubby little man with curly brown hair framing a bald crown.

"What can I do for you, Fräulein Eisenbaum?"

He is not smiling now as he usually does in class, and her confidence fails. But she will not leave without trying.

She begins to speak quietly. "I have a problem since the dismissal of Herr Doktor Rosenzweig." Rausch begins to blink, and she looks away from his face before proceeding. "He was the supervisor for my medical thesis and now ... I am well into it and would like to be able to finish it. I was wondering if you ... if you would consider being my supervisor." She looks at him finally for his reaction.

It's his turn to stare into space. Finally he says, "I understand your position, Fräulein Eisenbaum, but you must understand mine. The atmosphere in the hospital ... It's very strict now ..." He finally looks into her eyes again and his resolve seems to go flat. "I will ask the administrator and let you know tomorrow in class."

For the first time she feels some hope.

The next day, they are seated on their benches in the lab when an unfamiliar man walks in wearing a white coat. "I am Herr Doktor Gebhardt," he says. "Your new laboratory instructor."

Some of the students exchange glances. Since Frieda's position in the class is precarious, she has stopped speaking out. But she is not the only one concerned. One of the other students asks, "Is Herr Doktor Rausch coming back?" Frieda suspects Rausch was his thesis supervisor.

"I understand he has retired from the hospital," says the new instructor.

An embarrassed silence descends on the room. Rausch was a well-liked teacher. Not only Jews, it seems, are "retiring."

While the class goes on, Frieda's heart sinks. The slide under the microscope is blurred and will not focus. It is all her fault. Because Rausch didn't have the heart to turn her down. Because he didn't toe the party line. He went to the administrator on her behalf and it cost him his job. Maybe all he did was ask if he could supervise a Jewish student's thesis. Maybe that was enough in this new system in the hospital, in the country, that did not acknowledge even the possibility of treating a Jew on an equal footing.

In the next few weeks the configuration of the classroom shifts. The first few rows are reserved for students wearing Nazi armbands who salute each other with "Heil Hitler!" on entering the room. Frieda finds herself sitting further and further away till she is in the last row along with the few other Jewish students whose fathers are decorated veterans of the war. Her face burns with shame and anger. If Jewish doctors are not "true" Germans, what are they? What is *she*?

The new rector of the university, a staunch Nazi, has introduced twenty-five new courses in racial science. Medical students must now learn about the ascendancy of the Aryan race in all facets of life, both physical and moral. One of her new texts is devoted to skull types.

One day Ilse Remke passes her on the way into a class and whispers in her ear, "The only reason you're still here is that your father bribed someone to give him the Iron Cross."

Frieda is reading an anatomy book while she waits for Leopold at a table in the corner of the hospital cafeteria. She no longer feels comfortable in the centre of the large hall. She tries to be as inconspicuous as possible, as one of the few remaining Jews still allowed to practise in the hospital. People watch her with resentment. Some with curiosity. Where is Leopold?

She wishes she could melt into the furniture. She ignores all of them studiously. Especially Hans Brenner, a medical intern a few years ahead of her, who sits at a table across the hall, speaking to a dark-complected man she has seen him with before. A foreign student stands out in the sea of pale faces and is not befriended by everyone. Brenner avoids eye contact with her, but every time she looks up, he's watching her. He's not unattractive, his brown hair thick and his eyes dark, but those eyes frighten her with their overweening ambition.

She keeps her face doggedly in her book, so that she doesn't see Leopold until he is standing in front of her.

"Sorry if I kept you waiting," he says, "but there was a bit of a family emergency."

He steps aside to reveal behind him a slender adolescent girl, her hair arranged in two pigtails.

"This is my sister, Hannelore," he says. "I'm looking after her today."

The girl is plain, with heavy black eyebrows and wide cheekbones. Nothing like Leopold, except that her dark eyes are intelligent and she smiles unsurely.

"Is today a school holiday?"

Hannelore lowers her head so that all Frieda can see is the white part down the middle of her crown dividing the thick hair.

Leopold glances around nervously but the tables near them are empty. He doesn't notice Hans Brenner across the hall. "Hanni's school no longer accepts Jews," he says quietly.

"Bastards!" Frieda mutters under her breath. The girl's eyes widen at this, then a shadow of a smile.

"Tomorrow she starts at a Jewish school," he says. "She has to go a little further, but it's a good school. A very good school. Today she has a holiday." He pats her head with affection.

Frieda wonders how many other Jewish children are having holidays in Berlin.

"What's your favourite subject?" Frieda asks her.

Hanni looks up and gives a half-hearted smile. "Sports."

Leopold smirks. "Hanni is an excellent athlete. Not so good in math or history. But she jumps very nicely."

Hanni blushes and glances at Frieda to see if she's listening. Frieda looks attentively into her eyes to encourage her. Hanni blurts out, "At my sports club, I'm the best high jumper."

"She's a rabbit," Leopold says, skirting the top of her head with his hand.

"Don't do that," she says. "I'm not a baby."

"How old are you?" Frieda asks.

"I'm fourteen. I'm going to train for the Olympics."

"The Olympics! Really!" She glances at Leopold, who nods distractedly.

"That's very ambitious. Good for you."

"I'll be seventeen when the Olympics come to Berlin. I'm going to be the best high jumper in girls."

"I'm sure you will," Frieda says, smiling uneasily at both of them. She is thrilled at such hope. Thrilled and appalled. When she looks across the hall, Hans Brenner and his friend have left.

In the coming weeks, the German Students Association announces an "Action against the Un-German spirit," which will climax in a cleansing, a purge by fire. They intend, they say, to burn books. Students with swastika armbands stand at the head of classrooms, in hallways, in the square of the university, shouting about the German revolution that will free them from the humiliation of the last war. In those fourteen years, the libraries became filled with Jewish filth. Poison-literature. Now the struggle begins against the un-German spirit and they will win. Shout hurrah! *Sieg Heil!*

The day of the purge Frieda can scarcely get close to the square on her way to the hospital. The trucks and vans that line the Opernplatz are being unloaded by brown- and black-shirted men. Their cargo is books.

Frieda works late that night so that she can observe the scheduled event. She admits it's morbid curiosity, but she wants to see it for herself, this primeval degradation of the German soul. One-third of the way through the twentieth century, the most cultured nation on earth is pedalling backward. How far will they go?

Leopold insists on coming to escort her home. A new distress is on his face when he greets her in front of the hospital. "They won't let me take my final exams." His skin is ashen, his eyes glazed behind the wire-rimmed glasses.

"I'm so sorry, Leopold," she says, the words hollow in her mouth.

"People I thought I knew ... people who used to be friends. And now ... I can't graduate." He rubs his eyes beneath his glasses.

She takes his arm to comfort him. She herself feels lucky for the moment, but how long will that moment last? How long will Vati's Iron Cross protect her?

They start to walk, a slow pace compared to the scores of people hurrying in the same direction.

"Can you go somewhere else to finish? I hear Prague has a decent university."

"I'd have to take my year over again." He keeps his voice low. "I've checked into Prague, Warsaw, even Paris. They don't have the same courses — history is taught differently everywhere — so naturally their exams are different. It's too late to do anything. The exams are next week. My career is gone. Everything I worked for. Everything I dreamt of."

He looks shorter, his lanky frame stooped over.

"You're young," she says, not knowing how to comfort him. "Can't you go an extra year?"

He stares blankly at the crowds of excited students passing them in their rush to the square where the pyre has been building all day.

"My father's business is not going well. Suddenly customers are finding fault with the brooms from the factory. The same brooms they've been ordering for years. How can I ask him to pay for an extra year? And living expenses in another city." He shakes his head. "My family needs me to *make* some money, not spend it."

They stop talking as they approach the back of a throng of people. Somewhere a band is playing martial music that is transported above the crowds by speakers set high off the ground. Frieda and Leopold are pushed forward by a sudden swell of students eager not to miss anything. When this group reaches the crowds already stationed around the square, each side shouts to the other, "Heil Hitler!"

Frieda and Leopold could try to extricate themselves from the mass of people — she feels his arm tugging her aside — but she can't take her eyes off the centre of the square, once so dignified and familiar with its sweeping porticoed buildings stationed around the perimeter. The Roman-style statues perch high at the edges of the roofs, watching over the wide plaza. The whole place has been transformed, unrecognizable in the beating dark, illuminated by the procession of torches and flags held high.

Frieda cannot pull herself away. In the centre a massive pyre of books has been built high over a base of logs. The darkness of the night deepens when torches are thrown from all directions onto the mountain of books, setting them alight. The flames are mirrored in the faces of those standing around her. Then a group of students steps forward, their arms filled with books. They shout a fire-oath: "We dedicate ourselves to the struggle against class warfare and materialism, for the community of the people and an idealistic way of life."

They fling the books onto the burning heap. Flames leap up. The air is filled with the pungent odour of burning words.

Another student group steps forward and shouts, "We dedicate ourselves to the struggle against the Jewish character of journalism alien to the nation." They throw their offering to the god of fire. The books include works by Karl Marx, Thomas Mann, Rainer Maria Remarque, Sigmund Freud, and, of all people, Helen Keller.

Whispers float through the crowd. *Dr. Goebbels is here. Dr. Goebbels. Look, there he is.*

On a makeshift stage, someone shouts above the din, introducing the Reichsminister, Dr. Josef Goebbels. He steps up to the makeshift microphone with a clumsy, uneven gait; one of his legs must be shorter than the other. Frieda shudders at the appearance of the strange, thin insect of a man, his round eyes bulging. The leaping flames throw shadows on his face. He begins to speak in a didactic voice.

"The age of an overly refined Jewish intellectualism has come to an end, and the German revolution has made the road clear again for the German character. This revolution came not from above; it broke out from below. It is therefore in the best sense of the word the fulfilment of the will of the people. Revolutions that are genuine do not stop anywhere. No area can remain untouched. As men are revolutionized, so are things revolutionized. For that reason, you do well, in these midnight hours, to consign the unclean spirit of the past to the flames. The old lies in the flames, but the new will arise from the flame of our own hearts."

Frieda is filled with disgust. And bewilderment. The man is eloquent in a base, primitive way that is terrifying. They are all listening so intently. They believe him. Leopold finally manages to pull her away while mobs of young people sing the Horst Wessel song and dance around the flames that reek of gasoline. *When Jewish blood spurts from the knife then all will be well.* Ashes float around the edges of the fire. What is left in the libraries, Frieda wonders. Nothing worth reading.

When they walk out of earshot of the crowd, Leopold says, "You know what Heine said? 'Where they start by burning books, they end by burning people.'"

# *chapter seven*

The maternity wing of Mount Sinai was the one section Rebecca could count on for an aura of optimism. It was the only place in the hospital where patients arrived for a hopeful event and not because they had kidney disease, heart congestion, or cancer. Her sister's case would be different, and Rebecca would somehow have to deal with that. In the afternoon she entered the strange world of the preemie unit, where incubators were laid out at random angles around the nurses' station. Rebecca had to pull on a hospital gown and scrub her hands in the sink inside the unit.

Her niece's tiny body lay naked in the incubator except for a diaper, her skin thin and translucent, the veins visible just beneath. An IV was inserted into the skin of her scalp. Wires taped to her little chest snaked through the porthole of the box to a heart monitor. Her miniature hand reached awkwardly into the air. What was going to happen to this little girl whose mother wouldn't look at her? She weighed in at three pounds, ten ounces, respectable for a preemie. But she would need more than the usual love and care, not less, in order to survive her early tumble into the world.

When Rebecca walked into her sister's room, Ben was already sitting at the foot of the bed, which was hidden behind a curtain. He got up to embrace her and, to her surprise, held her for a long, emotional moment. She had phoned him early that morning when they arrived at the hospital. She had also called her parents in California, who were thrilled at the news of the baby but less than thrilled at the prospect of a rushed packing to get home.

Ben finally pulled away, his narrow, unshaven face drawn with anxiety. His shape reminded Rebecca of her father, tall and lanky, but his curly hair was dark and crowned with a skullcap.

"She won't talk to me," he said with wonderment. "What did I do that was so terrible?"

In the semi-private room, Susan's bed near the window was completely encircled by the curtain. She had shut him out. Her roommate in the bed closer to the door had smiled a greeting when Rebecca walked in.

Rebecca pulled Ben toward the window and lowered her voice. "She's overwhelmed. You have to be patient and understanding. She's deeply disappointed about law school."

"Well, I had my doubts about that anyway."

"What d'you mean?"

"Kids are too young. They need their mother."

Rebecca examined him a moment, made sure she had his attention. "Their father could pull up the slack. You're an academic, Ben. Universities are more flexible than businesses."

"I'm overloaded at work. I can't do any more than I'm doing. If I get behind, there are five guys waiting for my position. What am I supposed to do?"

"Work something out that lets her get to law school in September. Does McGill have a day care centre? Do you have a neighbour who'll babysit?"

He leaned his head in one hand. "I didn't need this now. They just gave me more classes."

"You have to deal with this. It's not going away."

He looked up at the closed curtain. "She won't even talk to me. I don't know what to do. She won't go look at the baby. She's like a different person."

Rebecca gestured for him to sit down at the foot of the bed again. She drew the curtain aside just enough to step in, then pulled it behind her.

Susan was lying on her side with her eyes open, staring into space, her blonde hair dull on the pillow. Rebecca's heart contracted at her pain.

"Susan … how are you feeling?" Susan blinked but didn't answer.

"Would you like me to bring a wheelchair and take you to see the baby? She's gorgeous. Looks just like you."

Susan turned her head to look at Rebecca. "I don't want the baby. I don't want to see it. I don't want to touch it."

Her grey eyes told Rebecca to leave her alone, but Rebecca couldn't.

"I know the problems seem insurmountable right now …"

Eyes open but not listening.

"… and your mood is down after the delivery. You've had baby blues before. But you want to look beyond this. We can all sit down and talk about the options, sweetheart."

Eyes half closed, closing.

"With the right support, you should be able to start school next fall."

"It's just talk," Susan said, with closed eyes. "Nothing will change. I don't want the baby."

"Susan —"

Her sister turned over to face the other way, dismissing her. Rebecca felt like a traitor, but she was going to have to speak to the obstetrical resident about calling for a psych consult. *I should talk.*

Before she left, Rebecca again entered the otherworldly preemie unit. After scrubbing her hands once more, she stepped toward her niece's climate-controlled Isolette. The nurses had needed a name to put on the incubator, and Ben had suggested Miriam, his late grandmother's name. Rebecca put her hands through the two portholes that extended into gloves on the inside of the plastic box. It was the only way she could touch the tiny body. Little fists balled into the air as Rebecca gently placed her hands around Miriam's torso.

"You're a fighter, aren't you? Yes you are. You're going to be okay."

She left Ben an extra key to her house with the offer of the spare bedroom while he was in town. The same bedroom his tiny daughter had been born in. Cleaning it up hadn't been fun.

She was walking the four blocks back to her office to pick up her car, thinking that tomorrow would be a better day. Pamela Forbes, one of her classmates who had gone into psychiatry, would take a look at Susan tomorrow. Their parents would arrive back from California tomorrow. Her mother was always a soothing influence.

The sun was still shining late in the day, though the air was brisk. The streets were quiet on this Sunday afternoon as she walked along D'Arcy. Then she heard the voice.

"Where is it? Where is it? You can't have it! It's hers."

Rebecca approached the backyard encircled by the tangled hedge. In the bright daylight she could make out the old woman through breaks in the gnarled branches the twilight had veiled the other day. The woman was standing with her shoulders hunched in a defensive posture, arms crossed around her chest. In her circumscribed view through the hedge, Rebecca searched the yard. It was empty. The woman was still talking to herself. Suddenly, she began to march back and forth, back and forth.

Rebecca didn't know where the impulse came from, maybe because she felt so helpless with Susan, but she turned around and went into a sandwich shop on Baldwin Street a block away. She ordered a cheese and bacon sandwich and coffee with lots of cream and sugar, and returned to the house on D'Arcy.

She entered through the rear where the hedge began and was astonished to find the old woman still marching around in the backyard in her oversized man's coat. Three steps forward, turn, three steps back.

"Where is it?" she muttered. "Where is it? You can't have it!"

"Hello," Rebecca said.

The woman's head snapped back. "She's so tired."

"Well, why don't you stop and sit down? I've brought you a sandwich and some coffee." She held them in front of her.

"Mittverda."

"Excuse me?"

"Mittverda makes her do it."

"Who's that?"

"Mittverda."

"But there's no one here. You can stop and rest."

"Mittverda orders her. Can't stop."

"Where is Mittverda?"

She pointed to the house. "Leave her alone! She won't listen anymore. Go away!" She put her hands over her ears, shaking her head back and forth. Suddenly, she stooped to the ground, picked up a stone, and flung it at the house. Next, she picked up a book from her wagon and threw it in the same direction.

"Where is it? Where is it?" she yelled. "You can't have it!"

Rebecca, standing with the sandwich and coffee in her hand, turned to look at the house. Did a curtain move in the window? "Is there anything I can do to help?"

"She doesn't exist."

"Who?"

"The lady. Doesn't exist."

Rebecca was taken aback. The woman was talking about *her*. She had felt this often since David had died, but no one else had ever suggested it. "Can't you see me?"

"Only the teeth."

What was it like in this woman's head? "My name's Rebecca. What's yours?"

"BirdieBirdieBirdie."

"Is that your name?"

"Terrible smell."

Rebecca sniffed the air: nothing.

"Bad bad smell. Can't stand it!" She covered her nose with a dirty hand.

"What do you smell?"

"Worms underground. Dead." She pointed to the brown grass around them.

"Are you hungry? I brought you something to eat."

The woman scowled at the package Rebecca was holding out. She shook her head. "Poison. Can't fool her."

"Why would I want to poison you?"

"Mittverda orders."

"I don't know Mittverda." Rebecca opened the paper wrapping. "Ummm, this looks good. Do you mind if I take a bite?" She took a nibble off one corner. "It *is* good. Let's try this coffee." She took a sip. "Lots of cream and sugar, just the way I like it."

The woman watched her closely, her thin face streaked with dirt.

"Do you want to try some before I finish it?" Rebecca said, preparing to take another bite. She held out the other half.

The woman stared at the sandwich but didn't move. Rebecca took one step forward. The woman stiffened. Stepped back, put her arms around her stomach protectively.

"Where is it? Where is it? You can't have it! It's hers!"

Did she want it or didn't she?

The book the woman had thrown earlier lay between them. It looked like a children's picture book. *Aesop's Fables*. Rebecca placed the sandwich on top of it, the coffee on the ground beside. She flapped her hand in what she hoped was a friendly wave and took a step toward the exit.

"Precious!" said the woman in an urgent voice. "Keep Precious safe!"

The woman had taken a plastic shopping bag from inside her coat and stood leaning forward, as if she wanted to move toward Rebecca but someone had glued her to the spot.

"Lady. Precious keep safe!" Slowly, with much hesitation, the woman brought the bag forward until she held it in front like an offering. Her mouth was open, lips quivering. The bag appeared lightweight, its contents rounding out half of it. She lifted it higher at Rebecca.

Rebecca stepped back toward her. "You want me to take it?" The woman's fist clenched the top of the bag. Rebecca put out her hand to take it. The old woman held her ground this time, didn't fade back, intent on passing on the dirty thing. Rebecca tried to hold onto it with thumb and forefinger, as if it were a dead cat. Which it might be. At least there was no obvious smell. The woman fixed her eyes on the bag until Rebecca left the backyard. She would throw the filthy thing into the trunk of her car, hope nothing crawled out of it.

As Rebecca stepped toward McCaul Street, a man's voice boomed into the quiet.

"Birdie! Where's the little Birdie? Look what I got for you! It's a surprise!"

Rebecca turned around. A man wearing a dirty maroon ski jacket and a grey wool hat approached the corner yard she had just left. Behind him he pulled a collapsible trundle buggy filled with bags. He walked with a pronounced waddle, one arm held against a bulge in his jacket where he must have been hiding the surprise.

"I got some mousies for you!" he called out. "Lookit." He headed toward the entrance in the hedge.

Rebecca had never seen a man so ugly. His nose was so flat and disfigured, it appeared smashed into his weathered face. His lips caved in where his front teeth were probably missing. Not too much of a stretch to believe he was delivering mice.

At least the woman wasn't friendless after all, thought Rebecca.

Walking to the car, she pulled apart the handles of the plastic bag and peered inside. It looked like blue flannel. A dusty little flannel blanket wrapped around something. She pawed at the bundle until one end came away to reveal a vinyl arm. It was a doll. Okay. Everyone was entitled to their own "precious." She placed the bag in the trunk of her car, unwilling to throw it out just yet. It didn't smell. Let it sit there a while.

Somewhere in the distance, the phone rang. Rebecca startled awake. Where was she? The green bedspread. Her bedroom; the light on. Was it morning or evening? She was sitting up in bed, the newspaper across her lap. She reached for the receiver automatically and mumbled into it.

"Hi," said Nesha.

"Umm." Her mouth felt gummy.

"Did I wake you up?"

"I'm not sure I'm awake. What time is it?"

"Must be around ten your time. Did you have a long day?"

It all came back to her. "My long day started last night."

Silence on the other end. She better explain. "My sister, Susan, drove in from Montreal."

"Isn't she pregnant?"

"She was. She went into premature labour and I had to deliver her baby in the house."

"Good God! Did her husband help?"

"She came alone. She was running away from her family. Didn't want another child. Anyway, the baby's in an incubator in Mount Sinai. Too early to tell how she'll do. She's over three and a half pounds so she's a good-sized preemie, but all kinds of things can go wrong at this stage."

"Since I don't know what can go wrong, I can be doggedly optimistic. In that spirit of ignorance, I congratulate you."

How could *he* be optimistic after everything he'd been through?

"How's your sister?"

"Very depressed. I feel helpless. It's so heartbreaking seeing her reject her baby."

"You must be exhausted. I'll let you get back to sleep."

"Nesha? I've been thinking. Do you like children?"

Silence. "I must. I have one of my own."

"And Josh is a nice boy."

"Man. He's twenty-two."

"It's just that … I don't want to get too old before — before I start thinking about having a child."

"You're young yet. Lots of time."

"I'm thirty-three."

"Rebecca, I'm forty-eight. I've been through all that."

Her heart fell. Without realizing it, this was something she'd been worried about.

"I *am* tired," she said. "Good night."

"Rebecca?"

"Yes?"

"I'll see you in a couple of weeks."

# *chapter eight*

**April 1934**

Though Frieda must attend lectures every day, forcing herself to go to class becomes more and more difficult. Only two other Jewish students are still attending, young men whose fathers were decorated in the war. The three of them sit in the back row though there are empty seats in front of them. Even so, none of them wants the taint of the other, each sitting separately, with as many seats between them as possible.

She times her entrance to the last minute, so that most of the students are already seated in the lecture hall. Nevertheless, often one or two Aryan students walk in late before she has seated herself, and as they pass, they entertain themselves by jostling her and sending her flying into the back of a chair.

She has noticed a decline in the standards of lectures since the qualifications for teachers changed from possessing scientific knowledge to professing Nazi ideology. The basis for their medical studies is no longer rational science, but race and blood. Not blood in the objective sense, not the blood she recognizes under a microscope, but a mystical, magical blood that defies definition.

During a Racial Science lecture, the professor pulls down a chart of head shapes and expounds on the difference between Aryan and non-Aryan types. While he goes on with his pointer, the students in nearby seats, mostly young men, turn their heads to the back where Frieda and the two other Jews sit. They whisper to each other, staring at her breasts, snickering under their breaths in a way that sickens her. Contempt isn't enough. They've added lasciviousness, a coarse appraisal more appropriate for a streetwalker.

Somehow she must carry on. She must walk with her head high despite the daily degradation. She only has this year left, then she can write her exams. If they let her. Is she fooling herself into this preposterous hope?

She must also steel herself to work in the hospital every day. At rounds and in clinic groups, the attending physicians ask her no questions and she offers no answers. She struggles daily against the urge to miss rounds so that Ilse Remke and people like her cannot use her absence as ammunition: *See, Jewish doctors are lazy, unreliable.* Herr Doktor Hans Brenner still stares at her when they pass in the hall. She cannot interpret his gaze, blank as a curtain.

When she is in Emergency one day, Herr Doktor Nolling, the attending, assigns her to clean up a patient's vomit. She has become adept at positioning bedpans and cleaning incontinent patients with diarrhea. Next, she must examine a man complaining of hemorrhoids. She enters the curtain to find a stocky, grey-haired man waiting on a cot. She checks his chart.

One look at her and the man's face goes rigid. He yells at the top of his lungs, "I want a man doctor!"

"Now, now, Herr Braun, I'm Fräulein Eisenbaum and I'm going to examine you ..."

"And I don't want a Jew touching me!"

An impatient nurse yanks open the curtain, scowls at Frieda, and, with a brusque jerk of the head, dismisses her from the cubicle. Frieda's face goes hot as she creeps away and down the hall under the stares of the other nurses and students.

Late that afternoon on the way home, Frieda takes a detour. She crosses a small park she has often passed through, only this time she stops and stares at a bench. It was green the other day, but now it has been painted yellow. On the back, printed in large black letters: "Only for Jews." Her heart begins to race and she wonders if she's dreaming. Could such a bizarre thing happen in real life? Will she ever wake up? Her legs ache with exhaustion and she wants to sit down, but she is embarrassed to sit on such a bench. She continues on her way in a fog.

She touches the blue plaque attached to the door that signifies a *Krankenbehandler*, a caretaker of the sick. The plaque has replaced the sign of the doctor. She has been coming here since she was a little girl, a simpler time when doctors were called doctors and shown respect, no matter their religion.

She tries the door that used to be kept unlocked. No longer. She isn't surprised. There's no telling who might jump into your apartment these days.

Herr Doktor Kochmann answers the door himself. His head and face are still round, despite the weight loss. "How nice to see you, *liebling*. How are you? Any better?" He bends over to kiss her cheek, the grizzled hair of his trim beard grazing her skin.

She shakes her head, surprised when a tear begins to dance in her eye.

"Come. Sit."

He lumbers to one of the leather chairs in his office, and she can see he's not holding up so well himself. He was always a portly man, yet now, despite losing some of his paunch, he moves more slowly. The national health insurance will no longer pay for treatment by Jewish doctors, which means most of their patients have left them. She supposes all the portly doctors will be losing their bellies. They have less money for food, more time to reflect on their plight.

"I need some more," she says, eyes downcast. "I can't sleep." She looks up at his drawn face with apology.

He sighs, smiles sadly at her. "I understand."

Suddenly she sees herself sixteen years old again, the day he came to the store to persuade Vati to let her stay in school. What was it all for?

She pulls some bills from the pocket of her skirt and hands them to him.

"How are things at the hospital?" he asks, avoiding her eyes.

"All right," she lies. "Everything's fine. I just can't sleep."

"Why don't you leave Germany?" he says, reading between the lines. "You're young. Leave while you can."

She blinks at him. Everyone with their advice. How can she go against Vati?

"I'm surprised your father isn't trying to get your sister out. Isn't he afraid for her? She's fortunate the family takes care of her at home. If it ever comes to her going into an asylum ... you must've heard of the sterilization program for people like her?"

She is startled by the allegation against Vati. Vati wouldn't put them at risk.

"What about you?" she says.

He shakes his grey head. "We're too old, Helga and I. Not enough money to start over somewhere else. Too tired."

He gets up and plods to a cabinet in the corner. She stands up when he returns with the little tube of pink liquid. "Tell your Vati that it's time to go."

"Oh no," she says, smiling faintly. "Everything's all right. It's just that I can't sleep."

She slips the tube of phenobarbital into her pocket and kisses him goodbye. Maybe she can make it last for two weeks. She's having trouble getting up in the morning. Not just because she can't sleep. She used to get by on little sleep. But she has lost her way, her sense of purpose. What's the point of going to the hospital when every moment she's there she expects someone to come up to her and spit the cursed word in her face. "Jew! Get out! It's your turn now."

## October 1934

Working where she is not wanted has taken its toll on Frieda. The hospital has become an alien place where she must try to learn what she can, despite the hostility and scorn of the staff. She is there on sufferance, the only Jewish student left who has the stomach to face day after day of derision. The other two Jews have stopped coming. She has heard that one immigrated to Brazil and the other is teaching biology in a Jewish school. The daily strain has given her constant headaches and melted pounds from her body.

Early one morning a patient is admitted to her floor after an emergency appendectomy. Summoned by a surly nurse, Frieda heads toward the room, noting the back of a Nazi officer at the nursing station down the hall.

An elderly woman in the bed is stirring awake, her mouth open, her yellow-white hair tangled against the pillow. Her chart says, "Maria Brenner." She is babbling sounds that don't quite form words.

"You're all right, Frau Brenner," Frieda says, coming to the side of the bed and patting the woman's arm. "We took your appendix out. You'll be fine now, dear."

"Don't bother," says a voice behind her.

Frieda turns to find the Nazi officer standing in the doorway. Hans Brenner. Herr Doktor Hans Brenner.

"She doesn't understand. She hasn't for a long time." He steps toward the woman, at the same time removing his uniform cap. His brown hair has been cut short, military style, revealing a well-shaped head. He takes the patient's hand with no discernible emotion on his face. "My mother suffers from dementia, Fräulein Eisenbaum." He looks into Frieda's face pointedly. "But she is not to be reported. You understand?"

Her eyes are level with a scar around his mouth. She nods. The elderly feeble-minded, the demented who have had the bad fortune to land in an institution, are given "mercy" injections. Who knows how many have been dispatched that way already. Yes, she understands. He's a Nazi, but when it comes to his mother, he makes an exception.

"No, little Mutti, the student doctor will not report you." He pats the unresponsive hand. Turning his brown eyes on Frieda, he says, "It's the least you can do."

She doesn't dare ask why. He's a Nazi doctor and she's a lowly Jew. There doesn't need to be a *why*.

He turns back to the old woman in the bed, smoothing down the white hair. "Did you notice you're the only Jewish student left in the hospital?"

Frieda is uncomfortable with this discussion. It's the only time Hans Brenner has spoken to her.

"Why do you think that is?"

So there *is* a why. She feels strangely absent. Separate from her body, as if she is looking down on herself from the ceiling. "My father's war record."

"Your father's war record," he says with quiet irritation. "No. It's because I asked for you."

Frieda's mouth falls opens. She is astonished. "I don't understand."

"I don't understand it myself. But my dear mother always said when you want something, you must go after it."

She takes a sudden breath. The empty creature she has become cannot speak, only tries to hang on to her real self floating by a filament near the ceiling. Her real self looks down and sees that he is a handsome man, tall and wide-shouldered, with a strong nose and sculpted mouth.

"One could say you were in my debt." He turns away from his mother to observe Frieda more closely, his eyes travelling over her hair, her mouth, her breasts. "You're a shining light, Fräulein. Too bad you're Jewish."

## January 1935

The government has decreed that only Jewish doctors may set exams for Jewish medical students. Thus, in January, Frieda must find twelve Jewish physicians, one for each of her subjects. Former professors who used to teach at the medical school are easily persuaded away from their depressing clinics, where the level of anxiety among Jewish patients is unprecedented. Each of the professors makes up an exam for her in their area of expertise, some eagerly, some with bittersweet nostalgia for the days when setting exams was routine.

By March she has passed all her written and oral exams. The professors send her test results and their endorsements of her achievements to the administration office of the medical school. Then she waits.

But when the list of graduates comes out in April, her name is not on it. She must gather her courage to go to the registrar's office. She has not been to the university since the previous fall.

She stands before the secretary, a middle-aged woman, her thin, mousy hair pulled back behind each ear with pins.

"Yes?"

"I've come to get my certificate," Frieda says. She has resigned herself to her name being left off the graduating list, but she needs the certificate if she is to practise medicine.

"Name?"

"Frederika Eisenbaum."

The woman's neutral business face goes blank. She has stood up in preparation to go to some file and look, but now stops. "There is no certificate for you."

Frieda realizes the woman has recognized the name as Jewish. Her anger rises almost beyond control, but she must control it. "All the documents have been sent in. I passed all the exams."

"We received no documents."

"You haven't even looked."

"I know all the names. Yours isn't there." The woman's chest puffs out as if she is defending her home.

"I want to speak to the registrar."

The woman glares at her, then turns and disappears down a hallway. Frieda's heart thumps. All those years, all the training in the hospital, the dreams.

After a few minutes, the woman returns with a man in tow. To Frieda's shock, he is wearing a Nazi uniform. What else did she expect?

"I understand there's a problem," he says.

Behind him the woman holds her head high, one side of her mouth curled up in a smirk.

Frieda lifts her chin. She will not be intimidated. "I've come for my certificate. All the proper documents have been sent in. I passed all the required exams."

"Fräulein Hebmann cannot find your papers."

"All the documents were sent in. They have to be there."

"And yet they are not."

His eyes are a blank wall. They reflect nothing, not even her own wavering image.

She stumbles out of the building and squints into the April sun. Are these the same ancient stone-faced buildings she used to pass, day in, day out? Their facades wobble in the morning air as if the heat from the sun is colliding with her dream of what they used to be. She once loved the university more than any place on earth. The students still cross the square carrying rucksacks filled with books and discussing the latest theories with their classmates. But she has lost her place among them. She is a ghost they cannot see, don't want to see, refuse to see. She is disappearing, even to herself. She must stop herself from dissolving into the ground like snow in April.

She wanders across the square, only vaguely aware of the people she bumps into.

"Watch out!" someone says, from somewhere outside of her dream.

"What's the matter with her?" Another disembodied voice.

The sun reflects off the stone and fills her eyes with splinters of light. But when she closes them, she sees a man in a Nazi uniform with no hat. His brown hair is shorn, military style. She knows what she must do.

She enters the first building she comes to and finds a public phone. She dials the operator, asks for an address and phone number. Then she inserts a coin and dials.

"Surgery."

"Could you tell me what time Herr Doktor Brenner is finished seeing patients today?"

"Two o'clock. Would you like an appointment?"

"No. Thank you."

She wanders the streets for two hours, down Unter den Linden, past the Reichstag and the Brandenburg Gate, that symbol of childish joy when Vati carried her on his shoulders. Gone forever. Her eyes water from the bracing wind, and without a thought she walks into a café, ignoring the sign in the window, "No Jews Allowed." She sits there sipping coffee for another hour. In the washroom she combs her hair and applies lipstick, dabbing a bit on her cheeks for colour. Then she heads for his office, not far from the university.

His office is on the first floor of a well-kept building with grey marble in the hall. A pregnant woman walks out of the office, holding the hand of a little boy. Frieda waits for precisely two o'clock before opening the door.

The young blonde woman behind the counter looks up and says, "Surgery is closed for the day."

"I'm not here for the surgery," Frieda says. The woman watches her, waiting. Frieda forces herself to continue. "I'm a medical student. I need some advice from Herr Doktor Brenner."

The woman hesitates. "Your name?"

"Frederika Eisenbaum."

The woman stands up; the back of her head with its short blonde waves vanishes down the hall. Frieda hears her knocking, some words in low voices.

The woman reappears. "This way," she says, leading Frieda down the hall where a door is open, waiting.

She steps through. Hans Brenner, in a white jacket, sits behind a desk, writing. When he looks up, his intense brown eyes register recognition. But whether it is welcome or not, she cannot tell. He is an ambitious man and is adept at hiding his feelings, a trait that will serve him well. He lays down his pen and stands up, coming around the desk. He leads with a strong chin; his mouth seems ready to smile, but doesn't.

"Fräulein Eisenbaum, what a pleasant surprise." He gestures her to sit in the chair near the desk, then closes the door his assistant has left open.

He steps around her and perches on the edge of his desk, watching her. His hair is longer than she remembers, not as severe. One of his legs swings inordinately close to hers.

She is at a loss, doesn't know how to begin. "How is your mother?" she says, embarrassed.

His mouth lifts on an angle. "Deteriorating, as can be expected. It's not good to get old. But you're not here to talk about my mother."

She looks down at her hands, one folded politely in the other. "I'm having a problem getting my certificate," she says quietly. "I passed all my exams. All the documents were sent to the registrar — but they refuse to give me my certificate." The room feels very hot suddenly. "I don't know what to do. I'm at my wits' end."

She closes her eyes, leans her forehead on one hand to keep from falling over. "I'm sorry. I'm not feeling very well."

He gets off the desk to stand beside her. He puts out a cool palm to feel her forehead. "You're feverish. Come into the examining room."

He leads her next door where she stands stupidly. The sun has moved behind a cloud outside the window. What is she doing here? He steps behind her, his warm hands lifting off her coat, laying it down on a chair. He smells of antiseptic soap.

She lies down on the leather examining table, her heart racing. He presses his stethoscope to her chest just inside the collar of her blouse. He is listening to her heart thumping, thumping. Does he know what is in it? Does she?

His murky brown eyes stare down at her beneath the lashes. "What do you want me to do?" he says.

The intimacy of his question pulls the muscles of her stomach taut. She bites her lip. "I don't know."

He blinks, touches her mouth softly with his finger. "Shouldn't bite your lips."

She takes his hand in hers, holds it a moment, then moves it slowly to her breast. She hears the soft intake of his breath, the tiny sound in the back of his throat, more than a murmur, less than a groan. She recognizes his desire and rejoices.

A phone rings in the distance, a tinny, ordinary sound in this extraordinary moment. Then his assistant's sensible shoes stepping down the hall toward them. The spell is broken. Awkwardly, he moves his hand away.

She gets up, puts on her coat while he watches wordlessly. As she steps toward the door he grasps her arm with some urgency and pulls her to his chest. Their faces are so close together she can feel his breath on her cheek. His skin is very close-shaven; she wants to touch it.

But his assistant is knocking on the door. "Herr Doktor Brenner, the hospital is on the phone."

At the business-like voice, he lets Frieda's arm go as if it were a lit match.

She walks out of the office under the gaze of the blonde assistant.

The following week, her medical certificate is delivered to her apartment by special messenger.

# chapter nine

A tentative knock on the examining room door late Monday morning. Rebecca's assistant, Iris, said through the closed door, "Dr. Forbes is on the phone for you."

Rebecca excused herself to the mother and the little boy whose sore throat she was examining and stepped into her private office to take the call.

She pictured Pamela Forbes, the oversized glasses and wavy brown hair, unchanged since they'd been in school. When she was at her lowest, Rebecca had fleetingly considered calling her for the name of a psychiatrist. Fleetingly. But it was impossible. She was a doctor. She ought to be able to handle things on her own. She knew what to do. Didn't she? Her mother had told her since she was a child that she wore a crown on her head. Well, the crown was getting cumbersome.

"I've just seen your sister," said Pam. "She's depressed and angry, but not suicidal. On the contrary, the rejection of the baby is a defence mechanism. She's hardening her heart against the baby to protect herself. If she lets the baby in, she'll lose herself again the way she did with the other children. She feels she's lost her life to others and she's angry about it."

Rebecca took it in. "I can understand all that, but what about the baby? The baby needs her. Doesn't she care about that?"

"She knows the baby will be looked after. No one will look after *her* if she doesn't do it herself. She needs some time, Rebecca. She feels she's trying to save her life. Is the father capable of taking care of the child?"

"Ben's a good father, but he has three other kids at home. In Montreal."

"The baby will be in an incubator for at least a month anyway. Maybe that's a blessing in disguise. A lot of things can happen in a month. She needs support from the people around her. Moral and practical. I gave her a prescription for Elavil, but I don't think she wants to take it."

Susan never liked taking medication. She probably wouldn't touch antidepressants.

"I appreciate your seeing her so fast, Pamela."

"I'll send you a written report and check on her tomorrow. The social worker will probably be in to see her later."

When Rebecca dropped into the hospital to see Susan on her way home, her father was sitting in the chair at the foot of the bed. He did not look happy, but when he saw Rebecca, his tanned face lit up. He stood to embrace her.

"How was your flight?" she asked.

"Fine."

"Where's Mom?"

His head motioned toward the curtain, still pulled completely around Susan's bed. He whispered to her,

"What the hell happened to your sister? It's as if aliens swooped down to kidnap her and brought back the wrong Susan."

She couldn't help smiling, though sometimes her father's humour irritated her. It was the way he dealt with everything, including trouble. She suspected he didn't know any other way. But this time there was no mirth in his face, only confusion. When was the last time she'd seen him confused? When David died.

"Where's Ben?" she asked.

"Told him to go to the cafeteria for a bite. They've got some kosher stuff. He needed a break."

She took her father's arm and guided his tall, thin frame past Susan's roommate, who was finishing off her dinner from the hospital tray. Her husband perched on the edge of her bed, munching on some chips from a bag. Rebecca smiled and nodded at them as she pulled her father from the room.

"You're looking well," he said, making a point of examining her from top to bottom. "Are you feeling better?"

They both knew what he meant. She shrugged and managed a noncommittal smile.

"Still trim, I see."

She had lost weight after David died, though she didn't need to. Now she was on the thin side, which she knew was fashionable. But she didn't feel particularly healthy at this weight, as if she'd lost the fat that had insulated her from the vagaries of the weather, both outside and in.

"New sweater?" she said, eyeing the stylish grey cable-knit sweater her father wore over his shirt. It went nicely with his short grey hair.

"Your mother's favourite pastime when we're in California. Shopping for *schmatas*. After she buys a whole bunch of stuff for herself, she feels guilty and has to buy something for me."

They strolled arm in arm down the hall.

"Have you seen the baby?"

One side of his narrow mouth arched up. "She's a little *pitchek*! I stood beside the incubator and she looked up. I *swear*. I think she recognized me. Is she going to be all right?"

"She'd be a lot better if Susan ..." She glanced sheepishly at her father. "No, that's not fair. It's not Susan's fault. She's very distraught, Dad. She's going to need our help."

"I'll do whatever I can," he said without missing a beat.

She hoped it wasn't a knee-jerk reaction while everyone was upset. They were all going to have to pull their weight to get Susan out of the mire she'd found herself in.

Ben walked toward them from the elevators, his head down. He had shaved, but his hair looked straggly under the skullcap.

"How's the cafeteria food?" her father asked, getting Ben's attention before he passed by.

He stopped awkwardly, shrugged his narrow shoulders, more stooped than usual. "Not very hungry."

"Miriam's doing fine," Rebecca said.

*As well as could be expected,* the nurse had said. Rebecca understood the subtext: without a mother.

Ben nodded absently. They walked toward the preemie unit.

"I'm at the end of my rope," he said. "I don't know what to do. The doctor said Susan needs some time to herself. Dr. Forbes wouldn't tell me much since I seem to be the enemy. I don't get it. But that doesn't really matter. What about the baby? She needs a mother. And what about the boys in Montreal? They need a mother. I can't help feeling she's being selfish ..."

Rebecca held back her temper. "You're going to have to be more understanding. She's deeply depressed. She needs your help, not your disapproval."

He looked away, eyelids lowered, then nodded toward the door of the preemie unit. "That's who needs my help."

Rebecca pictured the skinny pink body in the incubator. She felt guilty for agreeing.


Tuesday morning Rebecca moved around quietly in her bedroom getting ready for work. She wasn't used to having company and didn't want to wake Ben in the spare room. He'd said he was going to the hospital later in the morning since there wasn't much for him to do there: Susan wouldn't talk to him and the baby slept most of the time. What would they do when Susan was discharged from the hospital tomorrow?

Rebecca did rounds, visiting two patients who had undergone surgery. She made her way to Susan's floor by eight. But on reaching the room, she became disoriented at the change. Susan's roommate stood in her housecoat looking out the large window, now open to view because the curtains around Susan's bed were pulled back all the way. The secret tops of buildings lay exposed in a panorama framed by the window. Susan's bed was made up, but there was no sign of her.

"Good morning," Rebecca said to the roommate, who turned around and smiled. "Have you seen my sister?"

The smile went flat. "She left. Really early. The nurse asked about her, too."

Rebecca opened the closet door. Susan's clothes were gone.

"You saw her go?"

The woman nodded. "I was half asleep, but I thought someone was picking her up."

"Why did you think that?"

"She made a phone call. She was telling someone a time. I just assumed ... I'm sorry, maybe I should've called the nurse."

Rebecca hurried to the nursing station. The night nurses were just finishing their shift and putting on their coats. She recognized a stout black nurse from the other day.

"Excuse me. My sister, Susan Cohen, the one with the preemie — did you see her leave?"

"She your sister? She getting me in trouble running out like that. No one see her go, she just up and leave while we looking the other way. She shoulda waited to be discharged. Something happen to her, we in trouble."

The nurse began to walk away, then turned back to Rebecca. "And she just leave her little baby? What's the matter with her?" She shook her head gravely, heading toward the elevators.

In case of an unlikely possibility, Rebecca ran back to the room to call her parents.

"What's up, dear?" said her mother. "Are you at the office?"

"Did Susan call you?" Rebecca asked.

"No. Why? Where are you?"

"It's nothing. Got to run. I'll call you later." No need to alarm them. Yet.

The roommate was sitting on the edge of her bed watching Rebecca.

"Did you hear anything my sister said on the phone? The name of the person she was talking to?"

The young woman stared into the air, thinking. "Like I said, I was half asleep. And she was talking really quietly. I think she said something like, 'It would be nice to see you again, after all this time.' And I heard her say something about the back of the hospital. I guessed she meant that was where she wanted to be picked up."

"What time was it?"

The woman looked at her watch. "It must've been five. Maybe five-thirty. I'm sure you'll find her. She wouldn't leave her baby."

Rebecca turned toward the window, away from the roommate. She called her own number and waited for Ben to answer.

"What's up, Rebecca?"

"I don't want to alarm you ... Susan's left the hospital."

"What do you mean? Where'd she go?"

"That's just it, I don't know."

"You don't know where she went? How's that possible?"

"No one really saw her leave."

"That's unbelievable! Doesn't anyone work at that hospital? Didn't they try to stop her? She just walked out? Unbelievable!" His voice wavered with anger.

"Did she keep in touch with any of her friends here? Is there someone she might've called?" When there was no response, she said, "Didn't she have a friend, Diane, in high school? She used to see her sometimes when she came into town."

No response.

"Ben?"

"I don't know. I can't think. Yeah, Diane."

"What was her last name?"

"Diane ... Diane ... Starts with an *L* I think. Can't remember. This is insane, Rebecca. How can she just walk away? What am I supposed to do? I can't stay here indefinitely. I've got to get home. The boys need me. We better call the police."

"The police?"

"She's missing, isn't she?"

"She left of her own free will, Ben. Nobody forced her. So the police won't get involved. As much as she's distressing us, she hasn't broken any laws."

Usually when Rebecca got to the office, she spent an hour before patients arrived doing the paperwork that was the bane of a doctor's life: workmen's compensation forms, insurance forms, notes for missed work, and on and on. This time, however, she called her parents' house. Her mother answered.

"Do you remember the name of Susan's friend from high school? Diane something?"

"That's a strange question at this time of the morning. Why don't you ask Susan?"

Rebecca took a breath. "She left the hospital."

"Left? What do you mean *left*?"

"Her roommate said she left early this morning."

"You don't know where she is?"

"I'm trying to figure that out."

"Oh God! I thought I made her feel a little better yesterday. I guess I saw what I wanted to see. Diane Lipman. It was Diane Lipman. From high school. But she's married now — her last name is Rolf. I'll look up her number for you."

Rebecca remembered Diane from high school, a short, pretty girl with big black hair and very white skin. She was in Susan's class, two years behind Rebecca, and sometimes came to the house.

"Hi, Rebecca, long time no see," said Diane when Rebecca called. "How are you?"

When she explained she was looking for Susan, the woman went quiet a moment. Not an awkward quiet; a thinking quiet.

Then she said, "I haven't seen her."

Rebecca didn't know if she had the patience to be diplomatic. "You two were good friends, I know that. She probably told you not to say anything. But her husband's very upset. She has three children in Montreal ..."

"I really haven't seen her. But she did call."

All right. "Do you know where she is?"

"I can guess. She asked me for a number. Someone we went to school with."

"Can you give me her name?"

"Look, I don't want to make any trouble for her. She called me in confidence."

"I understand. But I need to speak to her and find out if she's okay. She just had a baby and she's very depressed. I don't want anything to happen to her."

"She didn't sound good. I've never heard her like that before."

"What's the woman's name?"

Diane was thinking.

"Can I have her number?"

The woman thought another moment. "It's not a her. His name is Jeff."

Rebecca's stomach dropped. "Her old boyfriend?"

"Jeff Herman. I told her she could come here, but she insisted on calling him."

"Thanks, Diane."

Rebecca felt her anxiety rising as she dialed the next number. Her little sister. Falling apart.

"Is this Jeff Herman?"

"Yes?"

"I don't know if you remember me. It's Rebecca Temple, Susan's sister."

"Of course I remember. It's been a long time."

"Could I speak to Susan please?"

A beat went by. "You think Susan's here?" he asked, his voice playing at disbelief but with room for ambiguity.

The last Rebecca had heard he was in law school. A voice like that would serve him well in his chosen profession.

"I spoke to Diane Rolf," she said, hoping that would be enough.

"How is Diane?"

Obviously it wasn't. "Look, I know you're trying to protect Susan, but a lot of people are worried about her. She just had a baby and she may need help."

"Even if what you say is true, I'm perfectly capable of assessing that and taking care of any problems. I have a friend who's a doctor, too, if need be."

"I'm her sister. Could I just speak to her? Just so I know she's all right?"

A pause. "Hold on."

Rebecca could picture Susan shaking her blonde head and Jeff whispering to her just to say a few words to get her sister off the phone. Rebecca felt awkward suddenly, that this stranger had become their go-between. Evidently he wasn't a stranger to Susan.

"Hello, Rebecca," said Susan in a slow, tired voice.

"Susan! Are you all right?"

"As all right as I can be." She sounded exhausted.

"Give me the address there and I'll come and get you. You can stay at my place."

"No, Rebecca. Ben's there."

"He'll be at the hospital for the day. I'll get him a hotel for tonight."

"Then there'll be the next night, and the next. I'm staying here, Rebecca. Tell Mom and Dad not to worry. I'm fine."

"Susan, please …"

"I need time. More time. Please don't tell Ben where I am."

"That'll be easy, since I don't know where you are. Is it really the best thing, to stay with your old boyfriend? I can find you a room in a hotel if you really want to be alone."

"Stop treating me like a child. I'm here because I can talk to Jeff. He remembers me when I was a person, before I disappeared into motherhood. It's not like I can have sex or anything, Rebecca. What are you worrying about?"

"Look, you're depressed after having the baby. You're not yourself."

"Not myself. No, I'm not. I can't be that Susan anymore. But then, who am I? I'm lost, Rebecca. I turned around one day and I wasn't there. Please don't tell Ben where I am. You know what I mean."

Iris arrived while Rebecca was sitting at the front desk behind the counter, staring listlessly at the lab and X-ray results in front of her.

"Are you all right?" she asked, hanging up her coat in the closet.

Rebecca pretended to read one of the forms. "Family problems."

Iris, who knew Rebecca's family after being her assistant for seven years — more than an assistant, really — waited for more. Not obviously. She sat down at the paperwork on her side of the counter and wiggled her pen at it. Her short blonde hair swept up, taking some pounds off her generous frame as the eye followed the curve up and away. What would she do without Iris?

"It's Susan. You know — the baby blues."

Iris nodded. She'd had two children of her own several decades ago.

Rebecca went into automatic mode for the rest of the day, treating patient after patient, carefully making sure she didn't miss anything, distracted as she was. She was exhausted at the end; her only consolation was that she could call up Diane to get Jeff Herman's address if it came to that.

After her last patient, she stopped by the hospital. Ben was sitting in a gown beside Miriam's incubator, his hand through the porthole touching her face. Rebecca's heart contracted. What had he done to deserve this? Married a smart, beautiful woman who wanted more than he'd bargained for: herself. He was still relatively young. Maybe he could adjust.

When he saw her he came outside, throwing the hospital gown into the large laundry disposal.

"Did she call?" he said, without preliminaries.

"She's staying with a friend," Rebecca said. "She's all right."

"Friend? Who?" Relief and confusion fought in his face. "What's the address?"

"I don't know." For a change she was glad to be ignorant.

"What's the number? I want to talk to her."

"I'm sorry, Ben. She says she needs time. She doesn't want to talk to you yet."

He put his palm across his forehead as if taking his temperature. "What did I ever do to her? Why is it all my fault?"

Rebecca had no answers for him. He trudged away, his thin frame stooped, the black skullcap bobbing toward the elevators.

When she could no longer see him, she drew a hospital gown over her street clothes, then scrubbed her hands inside the preemie unit. She sat down in a chair beside Miriam's incubator and reached her hand through the porthole, laying it gently on the tiny face. The lights were low; a few other parents spoke to their fragile infants in whispers. It was a different world in here, everything else forgotten in the all-consuming drive to just get through the night. She understood that. She was on home turf.

"Hi, sweetheart," she murmured. "Auntie Rebecca's here. Tell me about your day."

# *chapter ten*

**September 15, 1935**

In the Sunday afternoon lull between lunch and dinner, Frieda pours tea for Leopold and Wolfie in the living room. Mutti is in her chair by the window reading *Middlemarch* in translation. Irmgard, the maid, is in the kitchen preparing some chicken soup and dumplings; Luise and Oma are taking their afternoon nap; Vati sits by the radio with his nose in the newspaper. The soothing strains of Mozart float through the air while Wolfie rattles on about fencing at his sports club.

Though Frieda loves her brother, she recognizes the wastrel in him. It is his insouciance and good looks, the dark, wavy hair that falls over one eye, that persuade people to overlook his annoying habit of asking them to lend him money. *He cannot help it*, his friends say, *and he's always so good-humoured that we forgive him.*

"I'm not happy with the new fencing instructor," he says to Leopold. "He knows the moves but has no style. What did you think of him?"

"Oh, he's all right," Leopold says. "Remember, he's had to come down from his last job."

All of them know without further comment that the instructor was dismissed from some Aryan sports club because he was Jewish. It isn't just the Jews in the civil service and most of the professions who have been let go. Jewish journalists, actors, artists, and athletes have now been purged, prompting them to take the positions that are being vacated by nervous Jews who are emigrating.

"Where did Steinberg go?" Leopold glances at Frieda. "The last instructor."

She nods her acknowledgement at being included in the conversation.

"England," Wolfie says. "He's probably sweeping floors there."

"That's more than he can do here," Leopold says. "It's all academic to me anyway. I won't be able to afford fencing lessons anymore." His pale complexion goes pink and he avoids Frieda's eyes. "Business is not good for my father. Nobody wants to buy brooms from a Jewish manufacturer anymore."

Wolfie leans over with solicitude. "I'm so sorry, Leo. Instructors be damned! *I'll* teach you. It always makes me feel good to do battle with you because I'm so much better than you." He hits Leopold's arm playfully.

Frieda hopes Leopold hasn't lent her brother any money.

"Hanni wanted me to be sure to ask you," he says to Frieda. "Next Sunday her class is competing in that big sporting event they hold every year in Grunewald. Her school has been training for months and she's very excited. Will you come?"

"Ah, the champion high jumper," she says.

She smiles noncommittally, not eager to make the long trip out to the forest preserve of Grunewald, on the western outskirt of Berlin, where the Jewish community has bought their own stadium.

"I, for one, would love to come," says Wolfie. "I love a sporting crowd, and all those young girls in their shorts! As long as it isn't too early in the morning."

Frieda bites into an almond biscuit to avoid a smirk. He rarely gets up before noon on Sunday, having stumbled into the house in the middle of the night before.

Suddenly, Mozart is interrupted. A crowd cheers across the airwaves, subsides, and a sharp, precise voice begins: "From Nuremberg we bring you the following announcement by the Deputy Führer, Rudolf Hoess."

A straightforward voice begins, with a lack of emotion that chills her blood: "Utterly convinced that the purity of German blood is essential for the further existence of the German people, in order to safeguard the future of the German nation, the Reichstag has unanimously resolved upon the following law, which is promulgated herewith:

"Section 1: Marriages between Jews and nationals of German or kindred blood are forbidden. Marriages concluded in defiance of this law are void, even if, for the purpose of evading this law, they are concluded abroad. Proceedings for annulment may be initiated only by the Public Prosecutor."

Frieda brings her hand up to her cheek as if she's been struck. She wishes Leopold were not there so she didn't have to put up a strong front.

"Section 2: Relations outside marriage between Jews and nationals of German or kindred blood are forbidden."

Frieda crushes the biscuit in her other hand. Is it still her hand? Can she be sitting here in the same living room she has always known when the world is turning upside down? She looks up. Leopold and Wolfie appear to have stopped breathing and stare into space. Vati has put down his paper and turned to look out the window, as if he cannot bear the view inside. Mutti has closed her book.

"Section 3: Jews will not be permitted to employ female nationals of German or kindred blood in their households."

Irmgard, their maid, has stepped into the room, wiping her hands on her apron. Her mouth falls open as the banal voice continues.

"Section 4: Jews are forbidden to display the Reich and national flag and to present the colours of the Reich. On the other hand, they are permitted to display the Jewish colours."

In a fog, Frieda tries to picture the photos she has seen of Nuremberg, the medieval walls, the charming timbered houses. Her throat has constricted, her stomach tensed into a knot. She will never think of the ancient city the same way again.

"Section 5: A person who acts contrary to the prohibition of Section 1 will be punished with hard labour. A person who acts contrary to the prohibition of Section 2 will be punished with imprisonment or with hard labour. A person who acts contrary to the provisions of Sections 3 or 4 will be punished with imprisonment up to a year and with a fine."

The radio cuts to the roar of a crowd. Oma stumbles from her room, awakened by some instinct of danger. The clamour on the radio stops as if on command, and Hoess, in the voice of a sleepwalker, begins again.

"The Reichstag has adopted by unanimous vote the following law, which is herewith promulgated: A citizen of the Reich may be only one who is of German or kindred blood, and who, through his behaviour, shows that he is both desirous and personally fit to serve loyally the German people and the Reich. The right to citizenship is obtained by the grant of Reich citizenship papers. Only the citizen of the Reich may enjoy full political rights in consonance with the provisions of the laws."

When Frieda looks up, everyone is staring at the radio, motionless, including Irmgard. "I don't understand, Frau Eisenbaum." She addresses Oma. "Does that mean me?"

Oma stands near the doorway, her palm to her cheek. Irmgard has been with them for fourteen years, since she was sixteen.

"But what am I to do?" Irmgard cries, her hands clasping and unclasping the bib of the white apron she wears over a black dress. "I've never worked anywhere else!" Her tears fall on the polished wooden floor. "How will I live?"

Mutti is playing the ostrich, her eyes closed. Vati, immobile in his chair, stares away, arms crossed over his chest, his face drained of colour.

Finally Oma has the presence of mind to pat Irmgard on the back and say, "You will find other work."

Leopold jumps up from the sofa. "I must go home. My family needs me." Then, raising his voice for Vati's benefit, he adds, "We are preparing our papers to leave Germany. It must be clear by now there's no future for us here."

Vati turns his head slowly toward him. "We have seen bad times before," he says, his voice firm despite the sorrow in his eyes. "If we only hang on, things will get back to normal again. Hitler hasn't been so bad, after all. More people are working now."

"With all due respect, sir," Leopold says, "most of the new jobs are in the armed forces. He's re-arming

Germany. That can mean only one thing. He's getting ready for war."

"Impossible!" Vati says. "He's preparing the army in case of attack."

Leopold's long legs cross the living room. He shakes his head. "These decrees, they make anti-Semitism legal. Things can only get worse before they get better. Your family is in danger, as are we all."

Vati's eyes narrow. "Are you implying that I would risk the safety of my family? What impudence! If I thought for one moment that they were in any danger, I would stand in line at the American Embassy myself to get papers. I'm a veteran of the war and have been accorded privileges. I'm sorry your family feels they must leave, but we are in a totally different position."

Frieda follows Leopold out of the living room. He leans down to kiss her cheek. "There's no future for us here," he says, his hazel eyes agitated behind his glasses. He peers behind her, as if still addressing her family in the distance. "None of us." He begins shyly. "I didn't think it would come to this."

She raises her finger in the air to stop him, glances behind herself into the apartment, but sees no one. She steps out into the hall with him, closing the door behind them.

"You heard me say my family is preparing to leave," he says. "How would you feel if I went with them?"

Her chest goes tight. "You must do what you think is best."

"That's not what I meant." He takes a gulp of air. "If you married me, you could get papers too. You'd be part of the family. You could leave."

She examines his face. He is serious. "You're proposing to me?"

She has wondered what she would do in such a case. She knows Leopold loves her. And yet she feels no delight in the question being raised, only wariness for how to answer. She is not ready to marry him. Or anyone. Is something wrong with her?

"I have an uncle in America who will sponsor us," he continues. "New Jersey." He pauses a moment. "My parents don't want to go without me." He takes her hand. "And I won't go without you."

She feels her throat constricting. "Leopold ... I ..."

"I'm sorry for being this forward. I know it's too fast, but ... circumstances are forcing my hand."

"I think you *should* go," she says. "Go while you have the chance. It's not so bad for us. My father is right — our circumstances are different. And I can't leave my family. They need me. I have responsibilities, patients to look after. But please, *please* don't stay on my account."

Frieda watches him walk down the street from an upstairs window. Her heart is clamouring in her chest. She is torn between Leopold's logic and faith in her father. Vati has seldom been wrong before. It is easier to believe in him than to fall prey to the dire predictions of Jews who have read Hitler's ravings in *Mein Kampf*. It is easier to go on with one's life than to turn it upside down. But when that life becomes precarious? This, then, is the issue. Are their lives precarious? Do they leave everything they love behind for a country where they don't speak the language, where their past achievements and position mean nothing, where they will be foreigners?

At least she has some medical work here. Not in the state hospitals, where Jews can no longer work. And not paid for by the state-sponsored medical insurance, which is also off-limits to Jews. But several Jewish hospitals have opened to fill the need for both patients and physicians. And though payment is meagre there, since most Jews have been denied the means by which to make a living, Frieda supplements this income with work at a Jewish school. It is not what she dreamt of, but it is something. What rankles her most is that she will never be addressed as Frau Doktor Eisenbaum, since she could not finish her medical thesis.

The next morning Frieda puts on her jacket and heads for the door.

"Where are you going?" Oma asks.

"Where are you going?" Luise mimics from the table, where she is eating breakfast.

Frieda is surprised at the question. "To the hospital. Same as every morning."

"Be careful," Oma says, her small head trembling. "Keep your wits about you. The streets can be dangerous."

"Aren't you going to the store?" Frieda asks. Vati has already left.

Oma shrugs. Frieda looks at her grandmother, the strongest person she knows. Her strength is disintegrating before Frieda's eyes. Oma's white blouse is tucked crookedly into her black skirt. It has been a while since Oma worried about *her*.

Frieda slips out the door.

The morning is cool and overcast as she leaves the apartment carrying her leather briefcase and walks north toward the Kurfürstendamm. The banal voice from yesterday will not be stilled in her head. She dreads going by the store. After the speech from Nuremberg yesterday, Vati said nothing to her, but in the evening she overheard him and Oma murmuring about the business, how they would continue. Things would be harder, they reasoned, but they had a viable business. Hadn't the government itself ordered undershirts for the army from Eisenbaum's, even after the boycott of Jewish stores? The government may hate the Jews, but it needs them.

She passes two stores owned by Jews, both closed, with the gates up. The door to a small neighbourhood café opens as a customer steps out. She catches sight of a sign posted inside the door: "We Don't Serve Jews." A little shock passes through her, buzzes in her head. She stands at the door as it closes, staring at the few tables where people are eating breakfast. A middle-aged waitress who has served her family sees her and rushes to open the door. "Fraulein, we are forced to put up this sign. Just ignore it. Please. Please come in."

Frieda tries to smile, but her face is too stiff. "Some other time. Thank you."

Numb with mortification, she approaches Eisenbaum's. What will she find there? Instead of opening the door, she stops by the window, looking in like a voyeur. Three young women in street clothes and hats lower their heads before Vati, touching handkerchiefs to their eyes, while he stands erect, arms folded across his chest, immobile. He looks like a monolith, but Frieda knows better. There's a confusion in his face she's never seen before.

It's not till she opens the door that Frieda recognizes the women from the shop in the back, sewing machine operators usually in aprons. Their voices are low; the walls have ears.

"This is the only job I ever had, Herr Eisenbaum. I will miss it awfully."

"I enjoyed working here, Herr Eisenbaum. You were always fair. It's a terrible shame."

When they see her, they bow slightly, take one last look at Vati, and file past her out the door. He stares after them, his face drained of blood, his eyes empty. She steps toward the round window of the back door that leads to the shop, to see if anyone is left. A young woman is arguing with Wolfie. His hand is on her arm, and she is shaking her head vehemently. Wolfie never lost an opportunity, and it seems one of his opportunities worked right in the shop. Now his playing field has shrunk and he will have to make do with Jewish girls.

At that moment the front door of the store opens and a young woman wearing a stylish beret is pushed inside by the tall, paunchy man behind her.

"My wife has come for her things, Herr Eisenbaum," the man says.

The woman, round of face and hips, looks down at the floor, avoiding her former employer's eyes. She disappears behind the door to the back.

"It's too bad about the store, Herr Eisenbaum," the man says, in a flat tone of voice that belies his words. "But it's not so bad for Kristine. She was always tired when she came home. You didn't pay enough for the work she did."

Vati watches the man beneath hooded eyes. In another time this conversation would have been impossible. "Frau Rheinhardt was paid the same as the others ..."

"You made a good profit on her back." The man looks around surveying the store. "A good profit. What does a store like this make in a week, eh?"

Papa stares at him dumbfounded.

"That much, eh?"

Kristine steps back into the store carrying a small bag. "Is that all you have?" says her husband. He turns to Vati. "Is there anything else you can give her?"

"I don't understand."

The man gestures at the goods with a sweep of his hand. "Is there anything else here you can give her? Underwear? *Something?*"

Vati takes a quiet breath and steps to the shelf piled high with women's panties. He scrutinizes the sizes and takes down two pair. Silently he moves to the counter, rolls the panties in tissue paper, and places them in a bag.

Kristine keeps her eyes more resolutely on the floor. The man takes the parcel from Vati's hand, clasps large fingers around the woman's arm, and leads her out the door.


For the next few days, they must eat leftovers and eggs for dinner because the kosher butchers are out of business and the other shopkeepers would not serve Oma when someone pointed her out as a Jew. Oma went straight to Irmgard, their former maid, and got a list of the stores she patronized while in their employ. Early the next morning, Oma visited those shops while they were still setting up their wares, before other customers arrived, and, after imploring the owners and invoking Irmgard's name, came away with the lesser parts of the cow, inferior potatoes, and a small bag of coarse flour.

One day Frieda finds she cannot force herself to go down the stairs to the U-Bahn. They are too steep, or the tunnel too confining, or the crowds too thick, she knows not what. She only knows that the panic rises in her throat when she thinks of descending to the underground.

She boards the streetcar travelling east to the hospital. It will take longer, but what difference does it make anymore. She takes the last seat, beside a middle-aged woman carrying a string shopping bag filled with parcels. Beneath fly-away red hair, she wears a dazed expression; a steady odour of sweat emanates.

*Die Electrische* sways along its tracks in a mellow rhythm, but Frieda cannot be soothed. She keeps her eyes straight ahead, trying not to attract anyone's attention. She is small but professional looking, with her black leather briefcase. She has caught her straight brown hair in the back with a clip and affects a haughty look in her hazel eyes. People will not guess she is Jewish. The woman next to her is staring at her, but Frieda suspects she would stare at anyone who sat beside her. There seems to be little awareness in her eyes.

When they are halfway to the hospital, a large group of people boards the bus, including a stout elderly woman in a dark flowered dress. She climbs the stairs of the tram, breathing heavily. Frieda glances at her and stares with horror: around her ample neck lies a gold necklace with a large Star of David. She is jostled in the aisle by the crowd, finally balancing in front of a young woman who immediately jumps up to offer her the seat.

But when the old woman sits down, the man in overalls standing in front of her shouts, "Look at her! What's she doing here defiling the bus? Get off, you dirty Jewess!"

The woman beside Frieda starts to breathe noisily and shifts in her seat with agitation.

"Get out!" a woman nearby cries. "You don't belong here with good Germans."

The man in overalls grabs one of the old woman's arms and lifts her from her seat, then pulls her to the door of the tram. Her white hair, tied in the back, starts to unravel. She opens her mouth to cry, but no sound comes out. The other passengers sit wordlessly; some look away. When the door of the tram slides open, the man pushes her off. The conductor watches nervously but says nothing. Through the window, Frieda sees her stumble and fall to the ground. Frieda's heart is racing; the muscles in her legs tense up. The red-haired woman beside her puts her hand on Frieda's knee as if to calm her. Frieda is startled by her kindness and flinches. All the passengers on that side of the car watch out their windows as the prone figure tries to get to her feet.

Frieda stares straight ahead as the tram pulls away. She is sickened by her own cowardice. Why didn't she help her? Isn't she supposed to help people?

She gets off at the next stop, though she must walk for nearly an hour to get to the hospital.

# *chapter eleven*

## Birdie

**Toronto, November 1979**

"Watch what you're doing with the soap, you stupid cow! Can't you even do that right?"

"Don't call her that. It's an insult to the cow."

"What was I thinking! At least a cow is useful. From a cow you can get milk."

"More than milk. If you're starving you can eat it. Yum, hamburger. Yum, brisket. Yum, spare ribs. Not like her. How can she possibly be useful? Look at her teats. Dried up like her. No flesh on her bones. Look at her skinny arms, her legs are worse. The meat would be stringy. Bah!"

"You're not doing the soap right, stupid cow! You're out of order again. Not the whole abdomen, just the left side. Always the left first. What the hell's the matter with you? How many times do I have to tell you? Start over!"

Birdie stopped the progression of the soap down her body. She looked down. The abdomen again. This was where she always went wrong. The abdomen was a circle. Her hand went around in a circle. She couldn't stop it. She peered through the spray of water: the hand below clutching the soap. Disconnected. Not hers. How could it be? If it were hers she could control it. They didn't understand that it wasn't hers. They couldn't see through the water. *She* could barely see, but she knew that someone switched it when she was in the shower. One minute it was hers, then the next time she looked down, it wasn't. It *looked* like hers, but it wasn't. She didn't mind. It was the price she paid for the surging stream of water that washed off her sweat as soon as it formed. And there was always sweat. She perspired like mad. Mad! Yes that was a good one. Did she sweat because she was mad or was she mad because she sweated and the bacteria hatched in the drops of water beading all over her skin? Millions of bacteria. Millions begat millions. No matter. Too late for conjecture. Only action counted. This water. The bacteria were swept away in the deluge, the bugs trying to kill her, no chance for them if she did this right. She must do it right. She must start again just like they said. They hated her, but they were right. She deserved to be hated.

The soap smelled clean. It would clean away all the dirt, the bacteria, the excrement the bacteria left behind, all the terrible things she'd done. Start at the left forehead, the left cheek, the left nostril, get every spot, every atom of skin. If you missed an iota of surface, the bacteria would seize it, make it their own, burrow into the pores where they would propagate and breed and multiply and fester until you're done for. It'll be over. Finally. Not so bad. Would it be so bad? Oblivion. The struggle would be over. No more war with the bugs. They would win. But she would win oblivion. She could forget. Finally. She would join all the tiny souls that she let loose so long ago. Yesterday. All those tiny, innocent, perfectly formed creatures that would never understand anything.

No, mustn't think about that. Mustn't think. They never suffered. Not like her. What choice did she have? Ever? And now The Controller has found her. Has come for her. She must protect her Precious and keep her safe.

*He* understood. He knew because he had been there. No one else. All gone, the others. He had seen what it was like, that she had no choice. Where was he? He must protect her from The Controller. He was the only one who could. Because she had protected him once. She did everything she could. Not much. But he kept his life (he must remember). Now The Controller wants hers. And now *he* must protect *her*. Because The Controller will come back. *Where is it? Where is it?* She won't give him her precious treasure. It's a piece of her and he can't have it. There are so few pieces left after everything they took. She has shrunk to nearly nothing. Soon she will *be* nothing.

Birdie looked out shyly past the curtain of water at the other women, coming and going. They were not like her; they showered for a moment at the nozzles along the tiled wall. Then they went swimming, or came back from swimming. She had seen the pool: it was blue, the colour of formaldehyde. Stunk of chlorine. She couldn't go near the pool. It would kill her. Kill her and preserve her at the same time. She would float like a perfectly preserved specimen in a giant bottle: *This*

*was how a wicked woman ended; examine the heart.*
*What? Can't find it? Well there's the problem. There*
*was no heart.*

There was, once. *He* remembered. He remembered
when she had a heart like everyone else. But it had
been broken. Like the rest of her. It didn't vanish without a fight. She had struggled, but they pulled it out of
her chest and tore it apart with their teeth. Not all at
once. Bit by bit. They were hungry. Like the bacteria
that gnawed at her body and chewed her up, left their
slime on her skin.

Where *was* he? He never came anymore. He hated
her too. No, maybe he was on the other side, the
men's side. He couldn't come here. Only women. Men
gave women babies, and men weren't allowed here.
But *he* couldn't make babies. Not ever again. She
wanted to see him. Where was he?

"You did the abdomen again, you stupid cow!"

Birdie stopped soaping. She looked down. Her
hand was circling her stomach again. Was it her hand?
No, they switched it again.

"Don't you ever learn, stupid cow? Only one side
at a time. How many times must you be told? *Gott in
Himmel.* Start over!"

Birdie let the rain of water rinse the lather off. Then
she lifted the soap to the left side of her forehead again.

Later she sat in a corner near the lockers. Eyes
down. Don't look at them and they'll leave you alone.
Wait till they go. Sit very still; play with the little key
around your neck. Hair still wet. Eyes down. Look! A
crack in the tile. Bigger than last time. Filthy. Swarming
with bacteria. Bugs breeding, swelling up, a city of
germs spawning till they flood over. Filth and more
filth. Look! The crack is growing! There! Can't they see
the floor moving? Creaking open with bugs. Like a

great yawning mouth. The floor is disappearing into the crack.

She jumped up. "Stop it! Stop it! Can't you see?"

The others cringed back, stared. She was used to it. Always her effect on people. They would be sorry when the bacteria got them.

Must get out. Oh sweet clean wind! Cold fresh scoops of it on the street. Swept over her still damp hair, scouring her skin from the bugs and their larvae, their rot and putrefaction.

Walk faster — no, slower. No, faster. If The Controller found her out here it would be the end of her. Finally, the yard. The Controller couldn't hurt her here. Open shed with the key. Pull out the wagon. Where's my Precious? I remember. Precious gone. I miss her. There, there, don't cry. Let's find the darling box. Feel the smooth metal with the dear little house, green trees. Open the lid. See the pretty mouse? Pat the pretty fur. Something long ago, darling and warm — when was it? Can only remember the braids. Sweet braids. Like a mouse tail, twisted and shiny. Feel my pretty braids. Where are they? Gone, all gone. The Controller took them. Like everything else. But he wasn't happy with every *thing*. He wanted her soul, too.

An image flew by in her head. Glass breaking. The Controller in a white coat, angry, shouting. What's in her hand? A pen? Lines on paper, like ladders. Like snakes. Inky little strokes between the snakes. Pen wriggling in her hand. She's turning into a snake. Can snakes be afraid? She's scared like the men waiting, but not the same scared. A different danger. Nothing compared to theirs. She wants to tell them it's all right, knowing it isn't. Their eyes watch; her pen jumps between the snakes, squiggles in ink. No people. Just numbers. Do numbers have eyes? Can they be scared?

Something was missing from the box. The numbers. The squiggles and snakes and numbers that used to have eyes. She pulled all the bits of paper and old pens and broken pencils out of the pretty box till she saw the bottom shining beneath. It was gone. What was gone? Can't remember. Her heart being eaten alive, that was what.

# chapter twelve

## October 1935

In the next few weeks Vati and Oma disappear early in the morning to go to the store. Though they have some stock of goods remaining, their supply is dwindling on the store shelves since there are no operators left to cut and sew after the Aryan women have departed. Greta has come in to help a few times but her family is preparing to immigrate to Argentina and she must do her part and stand in endless lines at the innumerable agencies that require documents to be signed. At any rate there's less money to pay her since business has fallen off.

So Oma must start sewing again, after all these years. The conversation at dinner goes like this:

Luise says, "Where were you all day? Why weren't you here? I looked all over for you but you weren't here."

Each day Oma replies in an exhausted voice, "I was in the store, *liebling*, because Vati needs me. Vati cuts patterns in the material and I sew the pieces together."

Oma and Vati are both pale with fatigue.

"Can I come too?" asks Luise.

Oma picks up a napkin with a tired hand and wipes food from around Luise's mouth. "No, *liebchen*. You must help Mutti at home."

A light goes on in Luise's face. "Look what I made today." She bends down to the floor at her feet and brings up a sheet of paper. "Mutti gave me a crayon and I drew myself. See?"

She holds the page with pride, first for Oma, then Frieda. A large head dominates a small torso with stick legs. Long squiggly lines hang from either side of the head, presumably braids. The eyes are two vertical strokes; the mouth is a large circle that seems to be asking, "Why?"

Frieda pictures her mother trying to get Luise out of her hair for a few minutes, sitting her down with some paper for amusement.

"Can I come with you tomorrow?" Luise asks, her mouth full of food. "Please, Oma?"

"I'm sorry, *liebling*. You must keep Mutti company. She's lonely when Berta goes to the shops to get food."

They have been lucky that their former maid, Irmgard, has an aunt, Berta, who, at forty-eight, is beyond the reach of the recently enacted laws disallowing Aryan women under forty-five from working for Jews. Unlike her niece, she is plain and unsmiling, flat-chested, her grey-brown hair pulled back severely into a knot. But she's efficient and does what she's told. Oma must show her how to cook the food the family likes, chicken soup, gefullte fish, and pierogies. Nevertheless the apartment starts to stink of sausage and sauerkraut, which she prepares for lunch for Mutti and Luise and herself. Though the sausage is pork, Oma says nothing and sometimes even takes left-overs for herself and Vati the next day for lunch. Frieda understands: it is too hard to fight everything.

Though Mutti has been saddled with Luise, she still manages to look beautiful. She must be taking the girl with her across the street while she gets her hair done by Ulrike, a woman who works out of her apartment. Mutti visits there twice a week for her hair, once a week for her manicure. She also manages to find time to read the classics of literature: *War and Peace*, *Moby Dick*, *Les Misérables*. She seems to like large dramas, as if getting lost in someone else's epic rescues her from the confines of her life.

Frieda knows how hard it must be for her mother to take care of Luise, who can barely feed and clothe herself. Luise is a chore Mutti was never good at. They had nannies when they were young and so Mutti knows little of the basics of child care. Though Wolfie was only two when Luise was born, he tells Frieda he remembers their mother crying softly at night. Mutti knew early on that there was something wrong with her new child. Once Frieda was old enough, she was called upon to help. *Frieda, please take your sister out of the bath and dress her.* Or, *Please help Luise eat lunch.* This when her sister was eight and Frieda six. Then, luckily for all of them, Oma decided the business no longer needed her and she began to stay home. She was the only one who had the infinite patience required to take care of Luise.

Now that the job has fallen to Mutti again, it shows. Luise's hair hangs in unwashed braids and her face is smudged. On particularly bad days, a crust of food forms around her mouth.

Frieda is exhausted after a day working in the hospital and the school. She covers for senior physicians who need a rest or are called away. But she is in competition with all the other Jewish doctors who have not emigrated and there is little money available. She wishes she could earn more for the family.

"Is there anything I can do to help?" she says, trying to keep the fatigue out of her voice.

"Be a good doctor," Vati says, dipping his spoon into the cabbage soup.

She attempts a smile, but her face muscles aren't up to it. His grey eyes are tired and focus on the food. He has aged in the last two years; she doesn't remember when his shoulders began to stoop or his hair turned grey.

At least twice a week, sometimes at dawn, sometimes during dinner, they are startled into silence by the thunder of boots running up the stairs just outside their door. Without fail, what follows is a banging on a door upstairs or downstairs, then otherworldly weeping, pleading. To no avail. Some hapless man is marched down the stairs into a waiting car, his wife and children lamenting at the door. The Eisenbaums all hold their breaths, heads down, unwilling to face the fear in each other's eyes.

Wolfie has started joining them for dinner, most likely to save the cost of a restaurant meal. But he stays only long enough to eat, then excuses himself, jumps up, and hurries out the door. Sometimes Oma reproaches him while he rushes to finish dinner.

"Every now and then, Wolfie, you might stay home and be with your family. And maybe you would come in on time to the store if you didn't stay out so late."

Then he has to make a point of going around the table to give Oma a kiss on the cheek before escaping. Vati remains curiously silent about Wolfie's evening activities, sometimes even throwing Oma a warning glance. Frieda wonders about this change in Vati's attitude, since he has never approved of the card games that keep Wolfie out till all hours of the night.

Then one morning she understands. As she walks out into the hall, she sees Vati step out of Wolfie's room holding some bills in his hand. He closes the door quietly behind him. When he sees Frieda, he stuffs the money into his pants pocket.

"Wolfie had some luck last night," he says without further explanation.

Frieda stifles her surprise, but realizes now that their future, her future, hangs by a slender thread.

Hoping for a day off from worry, Frieda sits at the back of the trolley with Leopold on one side, Wolfie on the other. Leopold is half a head taller than Wolfie, and though he's attractive, with dark blond hair brushed back in curly waves, it's Wolfie who stands out wherever he goes. Something about the way he holds himself, his head on a roguish angle, watching the world with brown eyes that know, yet are charged with curiosity. Eyes framed by long, boyish lashes. The three of them are riding to the end of the line to the Grunewald where the annual Sportsfest is taking place. Children from all the Jewish schools in Berlin are competing with each other in track and field. This morning the trolley is filled with people heading to the stadium. The air is nearly festive, but the excitement is subdued by the presence of non-Jews whose tolerance cannot be counted on, tempered by the general atmosphere of fear in the city.

Nevertheless, Frieda catches two young Aryan women casting furtive glances at her handsome brother. After the Nuremberg decrees there's little chance of any interaction. He plays at catching their eyes while deftly conversing with Leopold.

"Your sister better not disappoint me. If I'm coming all this way, she better win."

Leopold smiles sideways at Frieda. She's happy to forget everything for a few hours, grateful, for once, to Wolfie, who manages to put everyone into good humour.

"Well, will she win or not? What are the odds?"

Frieda kicks his leg with her shoe. "None of your gambling here, Wolfie," she says, only half joking. "This is a wholesome event and you're not to corrupt it."

"She *will* win," Leopold says, shrugging. "She always does."

At the end of the line, everyone gets off the trolley for the hike through a heavy wood. The autumn linden and oak smell musty, full of their approaching death. Frieda fills her lungs with their exhalation, pretends this autumn is like any other, a slide into the temporary sleep of winter. She lets the excitement of those around her buoy up her spirits.

They approach the front gates of the stadium amid a throng of people. They struggle to stay together. Leopold pulls Frieda and Wolfie to one side, where his parents, Herr and Frau Sussman, are waiting for them.

Frieda met them last spring at Passover when the Sussmans invited her to their Seder. Her family celebrates the holiday with a large dinner, but no ritual. The readings, the asking of the four questions by Hanni, the youngest, even the matzo, were foreign to her, whose family continued to eat bread, which was forbidden for the eight days of Passover.

Leopold introduces Wolfie.

"Ah, the brother of the doctor," says Herr Sussman, a tall round man.

Wolfie raises an amused eyebrow.

"Fräulein Eisenbaum." The equally tall but slim Frau Sussman smiles politely. Leopold gets his delicate features from her.

They all file into the stadium, an open-air structure, and take their seats on the rising tiers amid the noisy good cheer of the crowd.

Within ten minutes, the centre field is filled with groups of children, their schools distinguished by the different colours of their shorts: blue, green, red, orange, and all the shades between. At the signal, they all start to sing "Hatikvah," the Hebrew song that has become an anthem of hope.

Frieda's scalp tingles at the melodic din of thousands of voices lifting the Hebrew syllables into the air. She doesn't know the words — her parents neglected her Jewish education — but she hums the tune and surveys the singing throng with pride.

The field is divided into several areas where different events proceed. A group of boys of uneven height, mostly thin and gangly, line themselves up on the track. Someone announces on the public address system that junior boys will race the one-hundred-metre dash. After the report of the starter's pistol, the boys bolt down the track that runs along the perimeter of the field. The race is over almost before it begins. A moment later, they announce the winner, Friedrich Something; it's hard to make out the names over the loudspeaker, but the multitude cheers nonetheless. Meanwhile, a group of girls has replaced the boys on the track.

"There she is!" Herr Sussman cries and points. The girls are lined up at the starting point, each crouched down, one leg bent behind the other.

"Which one is she?" Wolfie asks.

Leopold points to a tall, lanky girl in red shorts. Frieda remembers the dark braids from two years earlier. Hanni's hair is now cut short into a face-framing bob.

The starter's pistol crackles: the girls charge out from their positions. Hanni runs with her head back, her mouth open, as if sucking in some purer level of air above. Her short hair flies behind while her arms crank her body forward. She spurts to the finish line first. Jubilation rises up from the stands like the muted roar of the sea.

"Is that *her*?" Wolfie says. Leopold nods vigorously while the throng cheers. Wolfie jumps up and shouts, "Hurray for Hanni! Hurray!"

Hanni stands panting, head down, her hands braced on her knees. She looks up into the bleachers searching the crowd.

Wolfie waves and cries, "Hurray!" again.

Frieda pulls him down, embarrassed.

He grins at her. "You have to encourage children."

The girls return to their respective teams, one of her competitors patting Hanni on the back as they walk.

The next event Hanni takes part in is the long jump. The group of young girls stands off to the side as each takes her turn at the sand pit. One by one each girl walks back to the starting point, takes a run at the take-off board, and leaps into the pit, legs flailing. Each gets three turns. One of the teachers measures the distance with a tape.

They all watch Hanni position herself well back from the pit. She stares at the sand calmly, unhurried in her concentration, oblivious, it seems, to the thousands of spectators. When she is ready, her body stiffens; she begins to stride rhythmically toward the pit, relaxed but accelerating, nine, ten, twelve strides before she plants a foot on the takeoff board, leaps into the air, takes flight, then slides into a landing in the sand. *A work of art*, thinks Frieda.

As she strolls away after her third turn, Wolfie says to Leopold, "She's magnificent! Look at those legs. They go all the way up to her neck."

Frieda sees Herr and Frau Sussman exchange nervous glances.

A shot put competition follows, then a gymnastic event in which girls somersault. Hanni finally appears again for the high jump. All the competitors take turns jumping over the bar, which is set low in the initial position. Each time the teachers raise the bar higher, more girls are disqualified for touching or knocking it down from its stand. Eventually, only Hanni in her red shorts and a taller girl in blue are left.

The teacher raises the bar another notch. Now it is over Hanni's head. Frieda doubts that anyone can jump that high and clear the bar.

The girl in blue takes a run at the bar, jumps sideways, bringing her legs up and over, but not quite enough. The bar rattles, teeters, and plummets to the ground. The audience gasps, then claps politely as she strides away, her head down.

Hanni waits in the distance, bent over, hands on her thighs, until the bar is replaced on its stand. Frieda sees her step to the starting position. Hanni focuses her eyes on the bar for a full minute. Her chest expands as she takes in some deep breaths. Everyone grows quiet in the bleachers. Then she begins to run, her head back, her body tearing toward the stand with the unreasonable bar set over her head. She runs hard until the final steps, then bounds with a cat's impossible grace, aiming her legs toward the sky. In that second, it's hard to tell if she has cleared the bar, her body is so close. But when she drops down into the sandy pit, the bar lies fixed in its place high over her head, untouched. The crowd roars.

By the time the games are over in the afternoon, Hanni is a star. She has received winner's ribbons in five different events.

The Sussmans are being congratulated by other parents as they all wait for their children outside the entrance of the stadium. Leopold stands next to Frieda, but doesn't take her hand as he usually does when they're alone.

Hanni arrives amid an entourage of girls, all flushed and giggling. Her face is ordinary, with heavy eyebrows and a longish nose, but she is lithe and taller than the others, the centre they all lean toward while they joke about the day. She smiles serenely, the ends of her dark hair damp and straggly from the shower.

"Here's our winner!" Herr Sussman says, embracing his daughter.

Her mother and Leopold kiss her in turn. "We're so proud of you," says Frau Sussman.

"You remember Frieda," Leopold says.

"Congratulations." Frieda shakes Hanni's hand. "You're an exceptional athlete."

Hanni gives her a wide smile. "Thank you."

Leopold introduces Wolfie. Hanni eyes him. "Are you the one who cheered?"

Wolfie's lashes drop boyishly and he grins. "I couldn't help myself. The heat of the moment. At that moment you were magnificent."

Hanni blushes to the roots of her hair.

They join the crowds of people tramping back through the woods to reach the trolley home. Everyone is tired but in good spirits.

While they wait in line, Frau Sussman turns to Frieda and Wolfie. "Please come back to our home — we'll have some coffee and cake. You can help us celebrate."

Hanni sighs. "I wish we could have real cake." Frau Sussman stiffens. "I'm sorry, Mutti," Hanni says, "but you know your cake isn't the same without butter."

"We will make do," says her mother, looking away.

*The dream of the day is over*, thinks Frieda. Oppressive reality falls back upon them like a curtain. The show is finished and they must return to their stress-filled lives. One of the smaller deprivations is the severe shortage of butter, which can no longer be used in baking. "Guns not butter" is the new slogan the government throws about in their push for re-armament. Sacrifices must be made for coal, steel, and oil, because Germany has enemies who want to wage war.

"You remember the chocolate pastries we used to get at Schmidt's?" says Hanni. "I dream about them. I can almost taste them."

"I'll get you some," Wolfie says. "Schmidt's is on the way home."

The Sussmans look at him with apprehension. "They don't allow Jews in Schmidt's anymore," says Herr Sussman.

"We can't take that seriously when we're desperate for chocolate pastries," Wolfie says, smiling at Hanni.

"Please don't do anything foolish," says Frau Sussman.

Hanni can barely take her eyes off him.

On the trolley, the older Sussmans take seats near a window while the young people take the long seat across the back. As she sits down next to Leopold, Hanni's skirt rides up, revealing a scrape on one knee painted with the telltale stain of iodine.

"You must be more careful with such lovely legs," Wolfie says, sitting beside Frieda.

Hanni shrugs but smiles shyly at the compliment, pulling down her skirt. "The track is made up of rough cinders. All the teachers carry bottles of iodine. Everybody's legs have spots by the end of the day."

"So how high did you jump?" Wolfie asks. He must bend his head to speak to Hanni on the opposite end of the bench.

She smiles. "One-point-six-five metres. As if that will mean something to you."

"I know excellence when I see it. Didn't they say you broke a record?"

"My jump is the best in women's."

"In Berlin?"

"In Germany."

Wolfie's eyebrows rise. "We have a champion here! She must get some chocolate pastries at the very least."

Frieda sees some girls turning around and pointing Hanni out to their parents.

"So what's next after this triumph?" Wolfie asks.

Hanni looks out the window nonchalantly. "I'm training for the Olympics."

Now Wolfie looks really impressed. He turns to Frieda with wide eyes, mouthing *The Olympics*.

"Why didn't you tell me she was that good?" Wolfie asks Leopold, who looks out the window as if he cannot bear the conversation

Leopold says, "I tried, but you wouldn't listen."

"I thought you were exaggerating."

"I don't exaggerate."

"So then it's Frieda's fault for not explaining that you don't exaggerate."

Leopold takes Frieda's hand. "Frieda is faultless."

"Of course," Wolfie says, rolling his eyes.

"Look," Leopold says quietly, avoiding Hanni's face, "there's talk about a boycott of the Olympics by the Americans. At least *they* can see the irony of the games being held here. After everything they've done to us, you think the government will allow Jewish athletes to compete?"

Hanni stares out the window. "I'm the best jumper they've got. They'd be stupid not to let me compete."

A silence falls over the group. The trolley sways eastward back through the city. Passengers embark and disembark, some of them glaring at the clusters of children with their parents.

"Please, let's just go back to the Sussmans' place," Frieda whispers to Wolfie.

He turns to the window, watching the streets fly by. "I'm getting off at Schmidt's. Who's coming with me?" He turns to the others, his gaze resting on Hanni.

"I'll come," she says.

Frieda sighs. "We'll all come."

Leopold taps his mother on the shoulder as they go by and says they will meet at home. As Frieda heads toward the trolley steps, she turns to wave goodbye to the Sussmans. Frau Sussman's face has turned pale as she watches her daughter step down from the car.

While they walk the block to the bakery, Wolfie takes Leopold aside, letting the two young women saunter ahead. Frieda glances over her shoulder and sees Leopold reaching into his pocket. *So like Wolfie*, she thinks with irritation. *He'll give you the earth as long as you pay for it.*

Wolfie stops on the corner, three stores away from the bakery. "Wait here. If something happens, you don't know me."

As he steps toward the bakery, Frieda follows him. When they are out of earshot, she pulls on his arm to stop him. "You don't have to do this to impress Hanni. She's already impressed."

Wolfie shines his smile on her, the one he pulls from his bag of magic tricks that makes him irresistible.

"You worry too much, little sister. Don't you know me yet? Would I walk into danger?"

"What about the 'If something happens you don't know me' business?"

"Just for show."

She watches him stroll into Schmidt's, insouciant, hands in his pockets, as if he's just decided he's in the mood for a pastry. Despite his warning, Frieda edges toward the front window of the bakery. Above the cake and pastry display, a sign reads, "We Don't Serve Jews." She will never get used to the sinking feeling in her stomach whenever she comes across that sign. Or the one that says, "Jews Not Wanted." She should be accustomed to them by now, since they've sprouted everywhere like poison mushrooms after a storm. But they always take her by surprise, as if each one is the first she has seen.

Through the window, she sees Wolfie leaning over the counter flirting with the middle-aged server, who nods and giggles while placing pastries in a large box.

All at once, loud voices rise behind Frieda. In the storefront window looms the reflection of two men in Nazi uniforms. They open the door of the bakery and swagger inside. She curses Wolfie for his careless bravado. He won't impress anyone at the police station. She grows hot with fear — she must not run, she must watch and try to help him.

The woman behind the counter stops smiling when the men approach. Frieda cannot see their expressions, but the Nazis stand behind Wolfie, one with his hand on his uniformed hip, waiting. Wolfie gives a polite nod, picks up his box of pastries, then smiles at the men. He's engaging them in conversation! Damn him! He's going too far. He points to the confections behind the counter and their eyes follow. What if they ask him for his papers? The jig will be up.

She glances over to the corner where Leopold and Hanni are waiting. Hanni stands rigid, her hand over her mouth. Though Leopold has his arm around her shoulders, he looks tentative, as if he is ready to run at a moment's notice. They search Frieda's face for clues. When she turns back to the store, Wolfie is stepping out the door.

Taking his arm firmly, she yanks him away. "Don't ever do that again," she mutters under her breath.

"I was just telling them the chocolate ones were best."

"You shouldn't press your luck," Frieda says. "One day it will run out."

"Everyone's luck runs out sooner or later."

Hanni beams him a dazzling smile.

Frieda looks over her shoulder at the bakery. "Let's go." She takes Leopold's arm and begins to walk away briskly.

As soon as she walks into the Sussmans' apartment, Frieda can see how much has changed for them. The apartment is half-empty; the large glass-fronted buffet that she saw in the dining room at Passover is gone. One of the long sofas is missing, and there is only one upholstered chair left in the living room. They've been selling their furniture, she concludes. The table in the dining room — not the huge mahogany one that was there before — is covered with a flowered cloth on top of which lie papers and books. A typewriter sits on one corner.

"You must excuse the table," Frau Sussman says to her guests. "We use it as a desk where we fill out papers for emigration."

The books were on travel to the United States and South America. One was a text on learning English.

Frau Sussman disappears into the kitchen with the box of pastries.

"You look surprised, Fräulein Eisenbaum," says Herr Sussman. "The factory will not be ours for much longer."

Frieda shoots a look at Leopold, who turns away.

"One of our suppliers is eyeing it for a takeover. Did I tell you, Leo, he came in on Friday and said, 'How many orders did you take in today?' He already thinks of it as his. A greedy man can go far when he joins the party."

"Will you get compensation?" she asks.

"If we're lucky we'll get ten percent. I have a cousin in a small town north of here. He got himself beaten up by the SS who was taking over his store when he suggested that there should be compensation. No, we will be lucky to get anything." Glancing at his son, he says, "Leo must've told you we're trying to get out of the country."

"Yes, of course," she murmurs.

"The papers must have the names of all the people who are applying. Four names for our family. I won't leave without my children, so all the papers have to be in four names. And then, of course, all of us have to go. Or none of us can go. There's only one problem." Herr Sussman puts his hand on the back of one of the chairs as if he needs steadying. "Leo won't go. He won't go because he's waiting for you. And what are you waiting for?"

Leo glares at him.

Frieda lowers her eyes from Herr Sussman's scowling face. "I have to stay with my family. My father ... my father is not prepared to leave."

"Doesn't he see what's going on around him? What do *you* think, Herr Eisenbaum? You're a sensible young man." He addresses himself to Wolfie who is next to Hanni on the sofa. "Can your father be persuaded to leave?"

"Vati is a decorated war hero," Wolfie says. "We Germans love our war heroes. He rescued his officer from certain death in the middle of a fierce battle. Does that sound like the kind of man who can be persuaded about anything? We'll be all right as long as the government remembers he's a war hero. You, on the other hand," Wolfie adds, "should run like crazy."

Everyone stops in stunned silence.

"I'm joking," he says finally.

They all let out a collective breath.

"Besides," he says, "Hanni has to stay for the Olympics. She's the best jumper in Germany." He looks down at her and grins.

She smiles shyly, her eyes turned to him sideways.

# chapter thirteen

On Wednesday Rebecca threw herself into her work at the office. An upswing of flu and strep throat was making the autumn rounds. Children, their mothers, and elderly women colonized her waiting room. By noon, Iris, usually fresh-faced and perky, was flushed from the endless caravan of cranky patients.

Iris usually took an hour for lunch at one of the local restaurants, but today she and Rebecca had brought sandwiches and ate in Rebecca's private office.

They left the door of the office suite unlocked so people could walk in and sit down, though no one was there to greet them. Iris never scheduled appointments between twelve and one, insisting they needed a break.

At 12:40, Iris sauntered to the washroom down the hall. A few minutes later she slunk back.

"You won't believe this. The waiting room's full. They must've come early for their appointments."

Rebecca finished her coffee and stood up. "It's a dangerous precedent, but let's start early."

Iris shook her blonde head in disapproval, but stood to follow Rebecca. "They'll think they can come in whenever they want."

The rest of the afternoon passed in a blur. Rebecca swabbed a lot of throats for culture and prescribed antibiotics for people with obvious infections.

When the last patient had left, she realized she hadn't called Susan all day, or spoken to Ben. She rummaged in her purse for her wallet and pulled out the slip of paper on which she'd scribbled Jeff Herman's number. What was the point of calling her? Rebecca doubted anything had changed since yesterday. Susan would still refuse to speak to Ben. Who would still not understand her anger or how to deal with it. Part of Rebecca thought her sister was ungrateful for what she had. Had she herself ever been that angry with David? They hadn't been married long enough. Theirs would always be a storybook marriage because her prince had died young. What would she give up to have David back again? Her career? Her self-esteem? Her right arm?

The anniversary of his death had passed in October, shortly before the Jewish New Year. She had lit the twenty-four-hour *Yahrzeit* candle in its glass base and placed it on the stovetop. For a few moments she'd stood clutching the edge of the counter, watching the flame flicker in the darkening kitchen. This was all that was left of him, then. Shadows on the enamel. Pain like a sword through the heart. And images that came unsummoned. David setting up his easel in the backyard and painting a tangle in the garden. A moody piece she had always loved. Down in the basement now along with all the other paintings she couldn't bear to look at.

She sat down near Iris at the adjoining desk behind the front counter. A mound of paperwork awaited them.

"How's the baby?" Iris asked while they both worked filling out forms.

"Holding her own. She's a fighter."

Iris smiled sideways at her and nodded, her blonde hair held up in stiff waves with what must have been impenetrable hair spray. Rebecca hoped she wouldn't ask any more questions and Iris complied, searching through patient files for what she needed.

Rebecca hadn't informed her about Susan going AWOL. She told herself it was private, but really she was embarrassed. She preferred to keep it to herself, a family failing that might seem inexcusable to an outsider. Not that *she* excused. But she knew what it was like to lose all hope, so how could she condemn Susan? All she could do was watch her sister's drama unfold. Listen as Ben let himself in the front door at eleven-thirty after spending the evening at the hospital. He was leaving Friday to drive back to Montreal and the three little boys who waited for him. How was he going to leave Miriam?

The paperwork wasn't finished, but by 6:45 her head felt heavy. She would come early tomorrow and finish it.

She threw on her coat and waved goodbye to Iris. "I'm going to visit Miriam."

Iris managed a tired smile over the paperwork, her hair holding up better than the rest of her. "Give her a kiss for me."

Rebecca opened the front door of the medical building and plunged into the cold evening air. One thing she hated about the slide toward winter was the encroaching darkness. In the middle of November it was dark at six o'clock. By the winter solstice, in another five weeks, night would fall before five. Her mother had taught her that every season had its own beauty. But her mother loved life and had managed to pass on that optimism temporarily to both her daughters when they were young. It was the tragic arc of Rebecca's life that had annihilated joy. Not the slow passage of time with its disappointments, but a spectacular shooting out of the sky of the magic optimism with which her life had begun. Everything had changed when David died. She could divide her life into B.D. and A.D. Before David and After David.

Even in this post-David era, she had to adjust to the weather. Her feet were cold. Time to give up shoes and haul out the leather boots.

She crossed Beverley Street to D'Arcy and approached the backyard encircled by the hedge. She had been too busy and distracted the last few days to stop by and check on the homeless woman. Not that it made a bit of difference. Another disaster for which she had no solution. The woman wouldn't even take the food she offered. Rebecca would just pop her head in and say hello.

The house was dark when she stepped around the hedge into the backyard.

"Excuse me," she said, not to alarm the woman by her sudden entrance.

The convoluted hedge obscured much of the street lamp's illumination. She headed for the glowing red element of the space heater near the shed.

"Hello?" she said. "Where are you?"

All at once a form separated from the shadows and jumped toward her. She caught her breath and dodged to the right, adrenaline pounding. But the form didn't stop. It kept running with an odd waddle out the opening of the hedge. A gust of sour perspiration floated past her. She leaped out of the yard and searched the street — the ugly homeless man from a few days ago was shuffling across Beverley Street toward Spadina as fast as his game legs could carry him.

She turned back toward the yard, her heart still racing. "Hello?"

Intently, she searched the shadows on the ground from where the man had vaulted. Why didn't the woman answer? A metal leg glinted: the kitchen chair lay turned over on its side. When she bent over to pick it up, her hand brushed against something firm in the shadowy mound next to it.

Her throat went dry. She put her hand out and felt a leg. Her fingers fumbled sorting out the person from the fabric. A skirt? A coat? Another coat? Her hands shaking, she found the woman's head. Her heart fell. The hair was matted with something sticky. Rebecca didn't need to see it to know it was blood. She bent her cheek close to the woman's mouth, feeling for breath. A tiny flutter. She found a limp hand. Was there a pulse? Very weak. The skin was cold, but that didn't mean much out here in the dropping temperature.

"Birdie!" she called out. "Birdie, can you hear me?"

Suddenly a light went on in the house and streamed into the yard. Rebecca looked down at the woman: her head was covered with blood.

"Help!" she cried toward the house. "Please help!"

A curtain moved aside in a back window.

"Call an ambulance!" Rebecca shouted.

Finally the back door opened and out stepped a middle-aged woman with short greying curly hair. "What's going on?"

"This woman's been hurt. Call an ambulance. I'm a doctor."

The woman ran over to stare at the figure sprawled on the ground. "My God!" she muttered.

"After you call for help, please get a blanket. And a flashlight."

The woman hurried back inside the house, leaving the door open. Rebecca could hear her on the phone.

She returned with a blanket, arranging it over the prone figure. "Is she still alive?"

"Barely."

"I told her not to stay out here," the woman whispered.

"You know her?"

"She's been here a while."

"You let her stay in the yard?"

Rebecca took the flashlight from her and lifted Birdie's eyelids. Her pupils were unresponsive. Bad sign.

"A sick old woman. Should've been in a special hospital, *you* know." She touched her head with her finger. "But she was very stubborn. I told her it was dangerous to stay out here at night. At least we got her the little heater. She wandered around. Who knows the kind of people she met? Crazy as her. But I didn't expect this."

The woman had a bit of an accent. Was it German?

"I saw someone running away," Rebecca said. "A homeless man. He was here before. Maroon ski jacket."

The woman nodded. "I've seen him. I can't believe it. I didn't think he'd do this."

They both stared at a rock that lay nearby, outlined in the light escaping the house.

"She had nothing. What was the point of attacking her? Who but a crazy person?"

"What's her name?"

The woman looked at Rebecca as if she had asked an unreasonable question. "They called her Birdie."

A siren approached in the night, its forlorn wail winding toward them.

The woman looked down again. "How will I tell him?"

"Who?"

"My husband."

"He'll be upset?"

She shrugged as if she had said too much. "He's sensitive."

The young paramedics beamed a light at the yard. "Who called for an ambulance?"

"I'm a doctor," Rebecca said. "Over here."

They moved toward her with their equipment.

Rebecca reported: "Elderly woman, around seventy, with evidence of head trauma. Breathing and pulse weak. Pupils fixed and dilated."

One of the men bent over Birdie with a stethoscope, shone a light in her eyes. "Let's get her out of here pronto!"

They fixed a brace around her neck, then lifted her carefully onto a board. The board went onto a gurney, which they placed in the back of the van. The woman climbed in and sat beside her but looked away from the mangled head. The paramedics were taking her to Toronto General.

"I'll walk up and meet you there," Rebecca said to the woman. "What's your name, so I'll know who to ask for?"

The woman looked dazed, kept her eyes off the body beside her. "Sentry," she said. "Johanna Sentry."

The ambulance pulled away, its siren startling in the night.

Rebecca sailed through the evening air along D'Arcy past McCaul Street, along Elm, to the wide boulevards of University Avenue. She hovered at the edge of the sidewalk waiting for the light to change, Mount Sinai behind her. The ancient monolith of Toronto General stretched along the other side of University, south from College Street. Downtown trauma cases were brought here.

The emergency waiting room was filled with downcast people waiting to be seen. Johanna Sentry sat in a corner, arms across her chest. They had taken the old woman into a trauma room right away. Mrs. Sentry looked up as Rebecca approached. Her grey-brown hair lay in short curls around a face severe with no makeup.

"You didn't have to come," she said curtly.

*Neither did you*, Rebecca wanted to say as she sat down in the seat beside her. "I wish I'd done more for her. I could've called social services."

"You were there in the yard before? You spoke to her?" Her dark eyes filled with recrimination, as if Rebecca had invaded her privacy. Which she had.

"I went in a few times. She said alarming things out loud. Violent things. I thought she needed help."

"Very public-spirited, I'm sure. But it wouldn't have made a difference. We tried to help her. She didn't listen. I'm not going to blame myself."

"No one's blaming you," Rebecca said.

"We both work. How much can we do?"

"What do you do?" Rebecca asked, trying to steer her away from guilt.

"I'm a teacher. People think teachers work till three-thirty. But I coach five days a week and don't get home till seven. My husband coaches in the evenings at the university. We're hard-working people. How much are we expected to do?"

Yes, it was a German accent. Rebecca always felt uneasy when she heard one. This woman was old enough to have seen the war.

"Nobody's blaming you. In fact, most people wouldn't have let her stay in their yard. You were very generous."

The woman's heavy eyebrows knit together in thought.

Every now and then a name was called out. After half an hour, a handsome man in his thirties walked into the waiting room. Mrs. Sentry raised her arm energetically as if she were in class.

"There's my son. I shouldn't have called him."

He stepped toward her, a dark wave of hair falling over one eye. He wore a navy wool pea jacket and leather boots. The seats were all taken so he stood in front of his mother.

"What happened?"

"You didn't have to come."

"Of course I came. How is she?"

"Someone hit her over the head. It's very bad."

When he glanced at Rebecca, Mrs. Sentry said, "This is the lady who found her. Dr. —"

"Rebecca Temple."

"This is my son, Dr. Sentry."

"Erich," he said, watching Rebecca with observant brown eyes. "It must've been a disturbing experience. Are you all right?"

His mother gave him a dirty look. "You didn't ask *me*."

Without missing a beat, he said, "Are you all right, Mother?"

"I'm upset."

"Of course you're upset. It's a horrible thing, finding her like that."

"I won't sleep all night."

"Take something. I know you don't like to, but this is a special circumstance."

He addressed Rebecca. "Do you practise near here?"

"Almost across from your parents' house. On Beverley Street."

"GP?"

She nodded.

"You should give my mother your card. Their doctor's moved north. Though they're both in excellent health," he gave his mother a guarded glance, "it's good to have someone close by in an emergency."

"They could call *you*," she said, digging in her purse for a card.

"I'm a pathologist at St. Mike's. Only used to corpses. Anyway, it's unwise to treat family."

Rebecca handed the woman her business card.

A male voice boomed out, "Johanna Sentry!"

They looked up. Two uniformed policemen, one tall, one average height, scanned the waiting room until Mrs. Sentry stood up.

"Follow us, please."

The woman glanced nervously at her son.

"Don't worry," said Erich. "Just a police report. It was a crime. You'll have to answer some questions, that's all. You should go too, doctor, since you found her."

His mother's eyes beckoned him. He followed them down a hallway out of view of the ER.

The young policemen stopped and turned toward them, one with pad and pencil in hand. "Who found her?" asked the tall one.

"I did," Rebecca said.

"Come with me."

He led her further down the hallway past a corner.

"Tell me what happened."

She explained how the week before she had come across the old woman talking to herself and had gone into the yard tonight to check on her. "On Sunday a man came to see her when I was leaving. The same man was in the yard when I found her. He ran away when I came in."

"Can you describe him?"

"He looked homeless. Weathered skin, broken nose. In his sixties at least. He was wearing a dirty maroon ski jacket and a woollen hat. Grey. He has some problem with his hips. A waddling kind of walk. Probably arthritic. And he was pulling along one of those bundle buggies."

"Did you catch a name?"

"No."

"Would you recognize him if you saw him again?"

"Yes. He had a very distinctive face. Extremely unpleasant. But he seemed to be her friend. He called out and said he was bringing her a present. Mrs. Sentry has seen him before."

"The woman who owns the house?"

"Yes."

"You say the injured woman was talking to herself. You think something's wrong with her — mentally?"

"I'm not a psychiatrist, but I'd guess schizophrenia. She seemed to be hearing voices."

"There are a number of those people on the street."

He took one of her cards for contact information and accompanied her back to the waiting room. A doctor with an operating room mask pulled down around his neck led Mrs. Sentry and her son into the ER, stopping close to the door. Rebecca stood watching through the glass pane. She had seen enough doctors conveying bad news to recognize the posture, the head angled downward, the veiled eyes.

Erich looked up, saw Rebecca and shook his head. He motioned for her to enter.

The OR doctor was saying, "… she had a fractured skull and lost too much blood. I'm sorry."

Johanna Sentry stared at the doctor, blinking, until he turned and walked away.

"I'll try to reach Dad," Erich said. "He'll want to come down." He put an awkward arm around his mother's shoulders, as if they were unused to such intimacy.

"I'm very sorry," Rebecca said, feeling clumsy, as usual, around death. "Did she have any family?"

Erich opened his mouth to say something, but his mother answered first. "We don't know."

He glanced at his mother but said nothing more.

Rebecca watched him, wondering if her adrenaline was working overtime. Were they hiding something?

"It was nice meeting you," Rebecca said. Mostly out of politeness, since the mother was a prickly sort.

Rebecca excused herself and headed for the exit to University Avenue, surprised not by the death, but how these strangers had reacted to it.

# chapter fourteen

**Spring 1936**

Leopold knows a cigar store vendor who still dares to keep foreign papers behind the counter for steady customers. Last fall, shortly after Hanni's triumph in the Grunewald, he began to bring Frieda copies of the *New York Times* — he hid them inside his jacket — to show her how different life is in America. She has kept them, and sometimes at night she brings them out and marvels that there's a place where people can voice conflicting opinions in a forum as public as a newspaper.

### BRUNDAGE FAVORS BERLIN OLYMPICS
#### Has Faith in Nazi Pledge

CHICAGO — Avery Brundage, president of the American Olympic Committee, asserted here today that he knew of no racial or religious reasons why the United States should consider withdrawal of its athletes from competition at the Olympic Games in Berlin next year.

He was responding to Jeremiah T. Mahoney, president of the Amateur Athletic Union, who was quoted as personally opposed to American participation because of German discrimination against Jewish athletes.

Brundage stated, "The AOC must not be involved in political, racial, or sociological disputes. The Nazi government has agreed to accept Olympic rules. A boycott would be a travesty for Olympism, for the American athlete would become needlessly involved in the present Jew-Nazi altercation and become a martyr to a cause not his own.

"It seems," he said, "that opponents of the Nazi regime, mainly Jews and Communists, are not satisfied with Olympic rules; that they really want a boycott to undermine Nazism; they mean to use the games as a political weapon. The Jews and Communists must keep their hands off American sports. We must stand our ground and not give in.

"Mr. Mahoney, on the other hand, has mayoral ambitions in New York and is wooing the Jewish vote."

In the end, the Americans, led by Avery Brundage, convinced themselves that Jewish athletes were being treated fairly and decided against the boycott. They made the decision in time to compete in the winter games held in Garmisch-Partenkirchen, which took place in full Nazi splendour in February.

Less than two weeks later, Hitler, perhaps encouraged by the success of those games, marched German troops into the Rhineland, an area demilitarized by the Treaty of Versailles. The river Rhine, Leopold maintains, is considered a natural border between Gaul and Germany, and after the war, France insisted that the east bank be removed from German control so that the *Boches* could not use it as a platform for attack again. According to Leopold, the student of history, the river has always been the boundary between Western civilization and something darker, more primitive. Hadn't Julius Caesar himself stopped at the Rhine, believing the murderous German tribes too barbaric to be absorbed into the Roman Empire?

The papers in March are filled with pictures of soldiers on horseback being cheered by the inhabitants lined up along the route. But afterwards, the whole country hold its breath, waiting for France to respond and send troops. Of course that would mean war, and no one, including France, wants this. Leopold is particularly on edge.

"Hitler's gambling," he says. "He's sent a small force to see what everyone will do. France could easily defeat him there now — they must not let him get away with it. According to the treaty, England is obliged to back them up. And America should protest and show him that he can't just do as he damned well pleases."

But one day goes by with no response from the world, then another. Nobody protests. Nobody sends troops. The German papers roar with jubilation. Hitler is a hero who will bring Germany back to the glory it so rightly deserves, which it has been denied so unjustly since 1918.

And if anyone thought the Rhineland incident would affect the coming of the games to Berlin in August, they were sadly mistaken. In June the anxious mood of the city lifts. Berlin has been dressed up like a tart going to the opera. Thousands of blood-red Nazi flags with their swastika centres flutter high above the streets, attached to building fronts in endless succession. Interspersed, but not as profuse, are the white Olympic flags with their insignia of five interlocking circles representing the continents. *Fellowship among continents is commendable*, Frieda thinks wryly, on her way to the hospital. Much easier than fellowship among countrymen.

Like sentinels, banners two storeys high have been erected along Unter den Linden. When the wind rises, all the flapping in the streets sounds like a flock of birds startled in formation.

By July, foreign visitors are strolling the sidewalks, gawking at the banners and buildings festooned with swastika flags row upon row. How can they know that for their benefit, all the signs forbidding Jews have been removed from the entranceways to shops, grocery stores, restaurants, parks, and swimming pools?

One evening Wolfie insists on taking Frieda to a neighbourhood ice cream parlour they frequented before the "No Jews Allowed" signs went up. Now that the signs have been removed, they stroll in, Frieda's head down as they pass the waitress. She is too busy to notice. They sit down and eat their favourite flavours of ice cream, smiling at each other like cats that have swallowed canaries.

Meanwhile, the German government has responded to international pressure over the past year and invited twenty-one Jews, including Hanni, to train at special Olympics centres. Since then, Leopold's skepticism has abated somewhat.

"She's the best woman jumper in Germany," he tells Frieda. "They'd be mad not to let her compete. In the pre-Olympic qualifying tryouts she came first with a jump of one-point-six metres, four centimetres higher than her closest rival."

But one Saturday afternoon in the middle of July, Frieda is called to the hospital telephone. "It's an emergency," Wolfie says. "Come to the store at once. Bring a sedative." He hangs up with no further information.

All the way home she is running over the different scenarios in her mind: Mutti has had a breakdown; overworked Oma has gone beserk; Vati is threatening to kill Wolfie for coming into the store late.

When she hurries into the store, Vati is sitting behind the counter.

"What's happened?" she asks.

He waves a dismissive hand at the door behind him that leads to the workroom.

She pushes it open and finds Oma at her usual place at her sewing machine.

Oma looks up from her work and points her nose to the office. "It's just the silly girl."

Frieda sees Wolfie sitting in a chair with Hanni curled on his lap, her head burrowed into his neck. She's sobbing quietly.

"What's happened?" Frieda says.

Wolfie removes his hand from Hanni's back to reach for a letter on the desk. "Read this crap."

Frieda steps forward and takes the letter from him. It is from Reich Sports Office Director Hans von Tschammer und Osten, who regrets to inform Hannelore Sussman that she will not be considered for the German Olympic team because of her mediocre achievements.

*Mediocre achievements*, Frieda thinks with disgust. Even such a blatant lie must have cut the poor girl to the quick. All the patriotic banners and interlocking circles flapping cheerily in the breeze mean nothing to those who no longer have a place in the life of their country. She looks up at Hanni, hiding her face in Wolfie's neck, and silently forgives him for summoning her with the "emergency" message.

She scans the rest of the letter, in which von Tschammer und Osten says that Hannelore must understand that standards must be kept high and therefore only the best can be included on the team. He thanks her for her efforts and has included for her use two tickets for standing room only for the high jump event. Standing room only! The insult is clear.

Wolfie tries to stir, shifting Hanni's weight. "Look who's here, Hanni!" he says, moving his head so that Hanni must lift hers.

She blinks up at Frieda, her face bloated from weeping.

"I'm sorry," Frieda says. "This is terrible for you ... so unfair ..."

"They're idiots," says Wolfie. "She's the best jumper they've got and they won't let her compete. They'd rather lose than let a Jew play."

Hanni's mouth sets. "They have three spots on the team and they're only using two. I was supposed to be the third one. Why are they doing this?"

"Look," says Wolfie, "let's find a British reporter — or a French one — and tell them what they've done. Embarrass the bastards in the foreign papers, the ones they're so intent on impressing."

"No!" says Frieda vehemently as Hanni watches him with interest. "It's too dangerous. Once the reporters are gone, who will protect her? Or her family? Do you want them to end up in Dachau?"

Wolfie stares at her, annoyed.

"All right," he says, "when the Americans arrive, find them and tell them you want to go to the United States. Tell them you're the best jumper in Germany and they'll get you over there. And then you can compete for them."

Frieda shakes her head.

Hanni sniffs a few times, stifling tears. "But how can I go without you?"

Wolfie glances with embarrassment at Frieda, who looks away, astonished at their intimacy.

"Look," he says, "I was going to surprise you, but what the hell — you need a present now. You won't believe what I've got." He reaches into his jacket pocket and pulls out some tickets. He holds them in front of Hanni, who wipes her eyes as she examines them.

"Four tickets to the fencing match. August 5. How did you get these?"

"I have my ways."

She shakes her head rhythmically. "No," she says, head back and forth. "How can I go after this? How can I show my face?"

"You *must* go. Show them you're better than them."

"I'm too embarrassed. I can't. Look at what it says in the letter. *Mediocre achievements!*"

"But you know it's a lie. Don't let them win. Remember, you're the champion. You have no reason to be embarrassed. *They* should be embarrassed. You will wear your best dress and take my arm when we walk in. You will be the most beautiful woman there."

Her chest heaves in a sigh.

"Frieda has something that will make you feel better. Don't you, Frieda?"

Frieda remembers the tube of sedative and pulls it from her purse. She goes to the little washroom in the corner to find a spoon and a glass.

Later, when they're alone, Frieda asks him, "How could you afford four tickets to the Olympics? They must've cost a fortune."

Wolfie chuckles. "I won them at cards. I was going to sell them — they would've brought in a lot of money — but I had to do something for her, she's had such a shock. She deserves to go. Promise you won't tell."

"And you'd love to go," Frieda says. "Who are the other two tickets for?"

He smiles at her mischievously.

Oma insists on making Frieda a snappy little jacket from some off-white linen she picked up at a shop that was closing out. She nips it in at the waist to show off Frieda's figure.

"It's not every day you go to the Olympic Games," says Oma.

Frieda wears the new jacket over a soft cream-coloured blouse tucked into a narrow maroon skirt with a slit up the side. She angles a wide-brimmed straw hat over one eye, her hair wound inside. She hasn't been this dressed up since she graduated from high school.

Wolfie whistles as she steps through the front door ahead of him. They are meeting Leopold and Hanni at the U-Bahn. If they wanted to go to the Zoo station stop, they could join the crowds and watch the Olympic events broadcast on a giant screen. "Our great German technology leads the world!" the newspapers crow. Wolfie describes how he stood there amid the mob on the opening day (Saturday, when he should have been in the store) and watched the torch bearer mount the stairs on screen to light the Olympic flame. The Zeppelin *Hindenburg* floated high above the athletes marching in the new stadium, filled to capacity, while the spectators cheered and gave the Nazi salute.

At the U-Bahn, Leopold smiles sadly when Frieda approaches. "You look beautiful," he says, bending to kiss her cheek.

The Sussmans have moved into a smaller apartment after the takeover of their factory. She dares not ask him how they are living, refuses to let him pay for anything.

Hanni is sulky in a white cotton dress that skims her tall, boyish frame, arms crossed over her chest. Wolfie beams at the sight of her. He holds her at arm's length, examines her scrubbed face with no makeup, the chin-length brown hair in soft waves around her unhappy face.

"Beautiful," he pronounces, kissing her on both cheeks. "My favourite high jumper." He takes her arm and loops it through his.

Frieda can't remember when she has seen so many elegantly dressed people as those queuing up to go into the fencing hall. Thanks to Oma she can hold her own here in her maroon and cream outfit. The men in Nazi uniforms make her nervous, though they stand and joke with their companions like everyone else.

Once they have reached their seats, Frieda sits down beside Hanni, the two men on the outside. She takes in the huge expanse of the room where natural daylight streams in through a wall of glass running along the whole perimeter above the tiered seating. Forty-foot-high banners cover either side of the hall, the swastika insignia glowering in the middle. She reads in the program they have received that they will be watching the women's individual foil competition.

Teams of women fencers march in. All of them wear heavy white jackets over white breeches and white knee-high stockings.

Wolfie leans over to Hanni. "There's Helene Mayer," he whispers. "She won the gold medal in 1928 in Amsterdam. She's the only Jew competing for Germany." Giving Hanni a meaningful look, he adds, "In *any* event." He turns back toward the players. "And she's only half-Jewish. Most of the Hungarian team are half-Jewish too."

Frieda looks at the German team and Helene Mayer. She's tall and icy-calm, her blonde hair coiled in braids around her ears. The most Aryan-looking of all of them.

The first two fencers, an Italian and a Hungarian, salute each other, lifting the handle of their foils close to their mouths, then sweeping the foil down to the ground.

With their free hand, they each pull the large wire mesh mask over their heads.

An official says, "*Êtes-vous prêtes? Êtes-vous prêtes? En garde! Allez!*"

The bout begins. Frieda cannot follow the action, it goes so fast.

"I don't understand," she whispers to Leopold.

He points to the four men hovering near the two fencers as they move back and forth. "There are two judges on either side of each fencer. The objective is to hit your opponent's chest with the tip of your blade. Only the chest, nowhere else. When a judge sees a hit, he raises his hand and the president calls out to halt. The first player to score five hits against her opponent wins the bout."

Suddenly the spectators around them jump up and cheer. The Hungarian fencer has scored the fifth hit on her opponent. The bout is over. A new bout begins.

Three bouts go by before Frieda begins to recognize the players on the different teams. Finally Helene Mayer steps up, a blonde Amazon. Her opponent is American.

Wolfie bends over. "I've heard Helene doesn't wear a chest protector beneath her jacket like the other women. Interferes with her movement."

Hanni rolls her eyes. Frieda sees her embarrassment and wonders how long Wolfie's infatuation with this young girl will last.

The two fencers salute each other. After that it's all downhill for the American. Helene Mayer shouts with exuberance at each lunge she makes toward her hapless opponent. Within short order she has scored five hits. The crowd jumps to their feet, applauding and shouting their approval.

After everyone has sat down, Frieda's eye is drawn to a figure still half-standing off to the side below them.

The man in the Nazi uniform is staring at her, his hand touching his cap in greeting. Her heart drops in her chest. Is he really looking at her? The dark, familiar eyes … She catches her breath. It's Hans Brenner. She hasn't seen him since that day in his office. Though she has thought of him often.

She nods, then turns away. No one else has noticed. The next bout has begun and Leopold is engrossed in it.

She avoids looking in Brenner's direction for a few minutes, but when the bout is finished and the audience is clapping, she glances over and finds him watching her. She feels warm, too warm.

After watching a dozen bouts, Frieda can sometimes spot when a fencer touches her opponent for a hit. Usually they move too quickly for her to follow, but she strives to concentrate. She turns her body toward Leopold, away from Brenner. Every now and then, when the audience is applauding, she turns slightly to find Brenner in her peripheral vision. For the moment his attention has been captured by the fencers.

After several hours, all of the Italian, French, and American fencers have been eliminated. The three women left — among them Helene Mayer — are medallists, but now they must play each other to see who wins the gold, silver, and bronze. The audience, whose attention has been flagging after the hours of competition, comes back to life.

The official announces, "The next players are Ilona Elek of Hungary and Ellen Preiss of Austria.

Wolfie leans closer to Frieda and whispers, "Both half-Jews."

Everything depends on these final bouts. Excitement hangs in the air. The spectators follow every move and murmur at every hit called out. The scoreboard rises quickly from 1 to 4 under each name. Otherwise the great hall is silent except for the thin, ringing sounds of metal upon metal and the shuffling of the fencers' feet. Ilona Elek scores a final hit against her opponent. The crowd jumps to their feet, applauding. When she returns to her place, the Hungarian coach, a middle-aged man in a brown suit, pats her on the arm with glee.

Wolfie leans over and says, "This means the Hungarian can win the gold but the Austrian can't go higher than the silver. It all depends on the next two rounds."

The official calls out, "The next players will be Helene Mayer of Germany and Ellen Preiss of Austria."

The two women step to the centre strip and salute each other. Merely by her size and majestic bearing, the blonde braids wound over her ears, Helene must be a daunting opponent. The brown-haired Preiss is of medium height and ordinary appearance in comparison. They pull on their masks and start.

"Whoever loses this round gets the bronze," Wolfie whispers.

Foil clangs against foil. Preiss holds her own against the Amazon, but just barely. Helene cries out with vigour at each hit, both for her and against her. The audience loves her and claps each time she scores a hit against Preiss. When the score is 4–4, the spectators lean forward with rapt attention.

Though Frieda watches closely, she misses the winning hit. When the official declares the hit against Preiss, the crowd stands up and cheers. Helene's teammates pat her on the back while the German coach, all smiles, shakes her hand vigorously.

Wolfie's eyes shine with excitement. "This is it. Preiss gets the bronze. Now what everyone's been waiting for. These two will fight for the gold."

During a short break one of Helene's teammates massages her shoulders. Another hands her a glass of water. Her coach leans beside her, lips moving silently close to her ear.

Finally the official calls into the microphone, "In the final bout the players are Ilona Elek of Hungary and Helene Mayer of Germany."

The two women salute each other. Helene Mayer has met her match in the Hungarian fencer, who is nearly as tall, if not as handsome. They both must be nervous, Frieda thinks, yet their faces show no emotion. They pull on their masks and stand *en garde*.

"*Êtes-vous prêtes? Êtes-vous prêtes? En garde! Allez!*"

The audience leans forward to catch every move. Wolfie is beside himself with excitement, fidgeting in his seat.

They dance back and forth at each other, lunging, feinting, their foils aimed to strike. The two best players in the world manage to avoid each other's foils for a time, then suddenly a hit from one side, and in quick succession a hit from the other side. The audience claps loudly with each strike.

Frieda finally realizes why she is so ambivalent about Helene Mayer. She's a Jewish athlete who is playing for a country that hates Jews. Why should Frieda want her country to win when it is no longer her country?

The audience begins to clap: she has missed another hit. In two more minutes, the score reaches 4–4. The one who scores next will win the gold medal.

Frieda holds her breath. Everyone in the audience, it seems, is holding their breath. The two fencers are sparring back and forth, foils clashing, when a judge's hand goes up. Frieda has missed it again, but she sees who the strike is against: Helene Mayer. There's a flurry of activity between the judges and the president, their heads bobbing together.

Finally the official announces, "The gold medal goes to Ilona Elek of Hungary!"

The spectators leap to their feet. A roar rises up from them, a tumult, as if they had wanted the Hungarian to win all the time. The Hungarian team dances around the winner, embracing her left and right. Two of them lift her into the air. Their coach is weeping tears of joy.

"Damn!" says Wolfie, clapping and scowling at the same time. "I could've made a lot of money if Helene'd won." He has to shout to be heard above the cheers.

"You made a bet on this?" Frieda hisses. She shakes her head with disgust. Hanni, however, is smiling at him.

Frieda stands up, glad to be able to stretch her feet. She looks for Brenner but has lost sight of him in the crowd. People have begun to leave, and three or four men in Nazi uniform move along the aisle of the row ahead; without warning one of them breaks away and stops in front of her.

"Fräulein Eisenbaum," says Hans Brenner directly before her, touching his cap. "It's nice to see you again." His companions watch her from ten feet away, their faces blank. "My friends and I are going out to celebrate. Would you care to join us?" He glances back at the group of men, whose faces have turned stony. "No, no, of course not."

He observes her as if they are alone, his eyes wandering to her breasts and legs. He can't take his eyes off her, and she is thrilled. "Do you see patients?" he asks. "Are you practising?"

Leopold sits stiffly beside her, staring into the distance.

"I work at a hospital, covering for some physicians." One of his friends is clearing his throat, trying to get Brenner's attention. They've had enough of this illicit interchange between the Aryan and the Jewess.

She lowers her voice. "I never thanked you for your help with my certificate."

He stares at her, and she can see in his eyes the image of her body lying on his examining table, his hand on her breast. But he waves the suggestion away — which one, she wonders, her thanks or the memory? "Not necessary ..." he mumbles.

"Nevertheless," she says softly.

He gives a slight nod, then walks away, followed by his companions, who stare straight ahead without giving them a glance.

Once they're out of earshot, Wolfie mutters, "You surprise me, little sister. Maybe you could arrange a little game for us. I could make a bundle there."

She silences him with a nasty look.

# *chapter fifteen*

E arly Thursday morning Rebecca trudged up the stairs to her office. She was exhausted. Despite the ordeal of the previous night, she'd kept up her routine of visiting patients at the hospital before her office hours. She tried to shut out the picture, but she kept seeing the man jumping past her in the yard, the woman covered in blood. Her medical training had kicked in while they waited for help, but she was unprepared to deal with violent death. Or the helplessness of watching someone die.

She was getting out her keys when footsteps sounded behind her. She jumped, still on edge, hurrying to unlock the door. While she fidgeted, two neatly groomed men in dark wool coats headed up the stairs after her, one tall and bulky, the other average size.

"We're looking for Dr. Rebecca Temple," the bulky one said. He held up his police identity badge for her to examine. His sparse black hair was combed forward, his bulbous nose a patchy red.

She was glad he was on *her* side. "Come in." She led them into the empty waiting room and stopped in the middle.

"I'm Detective Fitzroy and this is Detective Bellwood. Would you mind answering some questions about what happened last night?"

They sat down in the waiting room while she repeated what she had told the constable the evening before in the hospital. Fitzroy listened intently, taking notes in a small pad, while Bellwood looked around at the office.

"So you think the dead woman knew this man who looked like a vagrant?" Fitzroy asked.

"He called her Birdie. Said he'd brought her something. He was trying to please her."

Bellwood suddenly came to life. "Did she call him Stanley?"

"I left when he went into the yard. I didn't hear anything after that."

"If it's who we're thinking," Fitzroy said, "we've had trouble with him before. He's a tough guy. Not usually with women. But he's been known to hit out when he's not happy. Maybe Birdie did something he didn't like."

The morning flew by, with no time for a break between patients. A few minutes before noon, Iris knocked on the door of Rebecca's examining room. "Phone call for you. A Dr. Sentry."

Rebecca was just handing over a requisition form for physiotherapy to a woman with a whiplash injury.

"I'll be right there," she said. Maybe he had some news about the murder.

She stepped into her private office and picked up the receiver. "Rebecca Temple."

"It's Erich Sentry here. I hope you don't mind me calling your office."

"It's fine. We break for lunch at noon."

"That's what I was hoping. I was wondering if you'd like to have dinner tonight."

She sank into her leather chair and stared out the window at the tops of the spruce trees across the street. His mother's German accent echoed in her head. Should she blame the son?

"Um, certainly. That would be nice." Would it be?

"What time do you finish at the office?" he asked.

"Around six-thirty."

"How about I pick you up at seven? You're in the white brick building on the corner across from my parents' house?"

Iris had already left when Rebecca heard Erich climbing the stairs in the empty building. She gave her dark mass of hair a last brush in the mirror of the small bathroom. A touch of lipstick. She was going on a date? What would Nesha think? It was just dinner. He would want her to eat.

When she stepped out into the waiting room, Erich was standing in the middle in his pea jacket, surveying the office. He was a bit taller than average, handsome in a boyish way. A strand of brown hair fell over his forehead. He smiled when she appeared, intelligent eyes taking her in.

"I always wondered what it would be like to have live patients."

She grinned. "They're more trouble when they're alive. The trick is to keep them that way."

He took her coat from her arm and helped her on with it. A light whiff of aftershave as he stood behind her. What did she expect? Formaldehyde?

She turned off the lights and locked the office door behind them. Leading him down the stairs, she asked, "Did you have a place in mind for dinner?"

They stood inside the front door of the building. She had her hand on the switch to turn off the hall light when he said, "I'm sorry if I didn't make myself clear." He was suddenly embarrassed. "We're going to my parents' house. They wanted you to come for dinner."

"Oh," she said, hiding her disappointment in her sweep out the front door.

He took her elbow when they crossed Beverley Street. The Sentry house stood on the opposite corner, its entrance actually on Beverley; only the backyard faced D'Arcy. They had the requisite scrap of front lawn typical of houses downtown. The porch needed painting but was at least clean and uncluttered, unlike its attached neighbour, whose veranda contained bikes, old lawn chairs, and newspapers piled in a box.

Erich opened the door and led her inside. The fragrance of roast chicken softened her regret. She followed him into the living room on the right, where the clean lines of the Scandinavian sofa and chairs vied for space with bookcases, hi-fi equipment, a shelf full of audiotapes, and a floor lamp wearing a fringed orange shade. Above the fireplace hung a long, tarnished sword that looked antique. A striped orange and cream rug lay on top of the brown broadloom. A long leather gear bag leaned into a corner. There were no religious symbols. No swastikas.

A slight archway separated the dining from the living room. The table was set for four on off-white linen beneath a simple chandelier of translucent glass globes. She spied movement in the kitchen, which led off the dining room.

"What can I get you to drink? Wine?"

"Thanks." She smiled weakly. What had she gotten herself into? An evening with the dour mother. Would the father be equally dour?

On the wooden mantel over the fireplace stood several photos, most of Erich when he was younger. One, however, was a more formal photo taken with a much younger Mr. and Mrs. Sentry standing behind a chair where a pretty woman sat holding a young child on her lap. Erich resembled his father when he was young. His mother was slightly taller than his father and not much changed over the years, though her short hair was darker and more abundant then. The wide-eyed child must have been Erich. None of them looked happy, but the couple half-smiled for the camera. The small-boned, pretty woman in front made no effort to smile; her eyes emanated pain.

Erich returned with two glasses of white wine, an older, much shorter man on his heels.

"This is my father, Will Sentry. This is Rebecca Temple."

The older Sentry put out his hand and smiled with confidence at her.

She proffered her hand, speechless, staring at the face she had seen the previous Saturday in the Royal York. The windblown man who had crashed the conference and engaged Dr. Salim in an acrimonious exchange after lunch. In German.

"Delighted to meet you," he said, his German accent nasal but not unpleasant. He was perfectly polite now, his dark, greying hair combed neatly.

"Erich tells me you're a doctor, too?"

She nodded, trying to make sense of things. It would be rude to bring up the incident.

Mrs. Sentry appeared from the kitchen, wiping her hands on a dish towel. "Hello, doctor. Glad you could make it. Come sit down."

Her face had softened since last evening, almost aglow in her husband's presence. Rebecca recognized it with a pang: the difference love made.

On her way into the dining room Rebecca noticed some framed photos propped up on a teak sideboard. In one, a dashing Will Sentry stood dressed in white protective fencing gear, a sword held jauntily in front, his mask under an arm. Rebecca's mind plunged back fifteen years to her first year in university when she had chosen fencing as her athletic option. All undergrads had to spend a year mastering the sports activity of their choice. Not especially athletic, she'd avoided team sports like volleyball. That year she'd learned to fence with a foil, surprised at the sport's complexity and energy level. But her main problem had been her lack of aggression, an insurmountable defect in fencing, since, during a bout with an opponent, the first fencer to establish a threat had priority and any hit from the fencer with priority took precedence over a hit from the other. It was called right of way. She'd rarely won a bout. The next year she'd met David and other interests had taken hold.

"You're a fencer," she said, gesturing at the photo.

"I coach the varsity team at the university."

"I took fencing as an undergrad," she said. "I was pretty awful, but I have fond memories."

He observed her with new interest. "You must have some European blood."

"My mother was born in Poland, but came here as a child."

He watched her for an uneasy moment. She knew there was no love lost between Germany and Poland. The Nazis had murdered millions of Poles in the last war. Apart from the Jews. Maybe it suddenly occurred to him that she was Jewish. Had he been a soldier? What was he remembering?

Finally he said, "You should try it again. I can teach anybody to fence. Want some lessons?"

Erich lifted an eyebrow on his way to the kitchen to help his mother.

"I'd be hopeless. Really. But thanks for the offer."

"Nonsense! Anyone can do it as long as they're reasonably healthy. You didn't have a good teacher."

Erich helped his mother bring in four steaming bowls of barley bean soup. They passed around a basket of rye bread.

"Why don't you come to our tournament Saturday? We're playing the teams from Western and Queen's. It's the last one at Hart House before we move into a new building. So it's special."

"Dad ..."

"Well, she's fenced before. She was interested once, maybe we can persuade her again. And if *she* comes, maybe *you'll* come?" He lowered the spoon into his soup. "It starts at one but come at three. The weaker players will be eliminated by then. I know how valuable a doctor's time is. You two can arrange to meet at Hart House." He smiled pointedly at Erich. "Maybe you can spare a few hours away from the corpses."

"This is delicious," Rebecca said, trying to change the subject. "It reminds me of my mother's soup."

Erich snickered sideways at her. "Maybe your mother buys her soup from Daiter's too."

Daiter's was a Jewish delicatessen in Kensington Market.

"I bought some on my way over," he said. "My mother doesn't have much time to cook."

"You're giving away all our secrets," said Mrs. Sentry, sending him a half-smile.

"I wanted to thank you for your trouble last night," Will Sentry said to Rebecca. "It must've been a terrible experience."

"It was very upsetting," she answered, letting her spoon rest in the bowl. "For all of us, I'm sure."

"Yes," said Mrs. Sentry. "Very upsetting." She pushed away her unfinished bowl. "I had trouble concentrating all day. I'm afraid to be in the house alone in case that man comes back. He knows our backyard. If he killed once, he can kill again."

"Maybe the police have found him," Rebecca said.

Mrs. Sentry shook her head. "A detective called. What was his name?" She looked at her husband.

"Fitzroy."

"He said they were still looking for him. They were checking the men's shelters but hadn't found him yet. I'm afraid I'm going to walk in one day and he's going to be inside the house."

"Oh, honey," said her husband, smiling fondly at her. "With your muscles, you could knock him down with one good punch."

"Well, you may laugh," she said, moving her spoon around in her soup. "But I come home to a dark empty house and I'm nervous. You didn't see what she looked like, all bloody, her head knocked in."

The smile died on his face. "Is that necessary?" he said softly.

"I'm sorry." She looked penitent for a moment, eyes downcast. "But really, doctor, shouldn't I be frightened?"

How could Rebecca answer that? "The man looked tough, like he'd been in some fights." The broken nose. "But he ran when I came into the yard — he didn't attack me."

"What about the college boys renting next door?" Will Sentry said to his wife. "I'll ask one of them to come into the house with you when you get home."

She nodded into her soup.

He addressed Rebecca again. "My wife said you visited the poor woman often."

"I just saw her twice. All in the past week."

He leaned forward on his elbows, eyes waiting for more. He was still a handsome man, playfulness in his dark eyes.

"She said some disturbing things when I was walking by. I was concerned for her. How long was she there?"

He sat back, arms across his chest. "She moved around a lot," he said. "We've known her for years. People tried to put her into hospital, and she'd run away. Then she'd turn up in an alley. Or in our back-yard. We never knew how long she'd stay. She refused to live indoors. It was too dangerous, she said. People always stole things from her, she said. And always dragging that stupid wagon wherever she went. All her earthly possessions."

Erich and his mother brought plates of food from the kitchen: a chicken that had been barbecued in some restaurant, baked potatoes in foil jackets, presumably from the same establishment, coleslaw (from Daiter's, Rebecca guessed), and a bowl of green beans from a can.

"You're a doctor," Will Sentry said. "What do you think she had?"

She glanced at Erich. He must have ventured a diagnosis.

When the dish of chicken came by, she speared a slice of breast with her fork and placed it on her plate next to the potato.

"Her speech was rambling — it was hard to follow her train of thought. I'd say she might've been schizophrenic."

Erich threw his father an impatient look as if to say, *We've been over this before.*

"But she did talk to you?"

Rebecca nodded, spooning some sour cream onto her potato.

"She didn't talk to everybody, you know. You must've touched her somehow. Do you remember anything she said?"

She looked at her host, who was cutting up his chicken, along with the skin, and placing neat little pieces into his mouth. Why did he care what the woman had said to her?

"They were strange things. Probably not things you want to talk about at a dinner table."

"Don't worry, doctor, we're not squeamish here."

"Speak for yourself, Dad."

His father looked at Erich. "The squeamish pathologist. It's a good thing all your patients are dead."

"Ouch." Erich chewed on some potato.

"Really, doctor. I'd like to know what she said to you. Did she talk about people? Anyone she knew? Or us, even. We knew her a long time, you see."

Was this why she had been invited? To find out if the old woman had said something?

*All right*, thought Rebecca. "Her speech was very disjointed — it was hard to follow. She seemed to think people were controlling her. Threatening her. She indicated your house once."

"Did she say any names?"

He was persistent. "Only a nonsense name. Started with an *M*. 'Mit' something. Mit — Mitverba, I think."

The couple stopped eating and looked at each other.

"Does it mean something?" Rebecca asked.

Will Sentry put down his fork. "Mittverda. It's from the war. The concentration camp."

"She was in a camp?"

"We were all in a camp."

Rebecca looked at them with new eyes.

"So ... you knew her that long?"

He nodded, staring off into the air.

"I thought she was a stranger," Rebecca said, trying to keep accusation out of her voice.

"She became a stranger," he said. "Originally she was my cousin."

Erich glanced at him, then down at the table.

"A very dear cousin," the elder Sentry added.

Rebecca put her fork down. Suddenly everything had changed.

"It's a shock, isn't it?" he said. "Once she was a beautiful, intelligent woman. This is the way of the world. It crushes us all, one way or another."

The pretty woman in the photo. Impossible.

"Your accents, are they German?"

"We're German Jews. A miracle that we survived. More or less intact. Except for my cousin. Luckily it wasn't obvious when we were questioned by Canadian immigration after the war. She got worse after we came here. Delayed reaction, I guess. Some people bottle things up, then it's too much and eventually they collapse. The war was too much for her. She saw too much."

*They were* Jews. *They hid it well,* Rebecca thought. "We're so sheltered in this country," she said. "I can't imagine what you went through."

"It's nice to be sheltered from such things. Maybe that's why Canadians are so decent. You were right. This isn't good dinner conversation." He picked up his fork and launched into his food.

They all began to eat again.

"And yet," he chewed on the chicken and the words, "I'm still curious if she said anything you wondered about. Perhaps the police have asked?"

Something niggling was trying to surface in her memory. "I wondered about a lot of things. But the last time I saw her she kept repeating the same words.

'Where is it? Where is it? You can't have it.' I guess it makes sense if she thought people were stealing from her."

The elder Sentry stared through her to some distant point.

"That's enough, Dad," Erich said, before his father could ask any more. "The post-mortem is over."

# *chapter sixteen*

Cairo, October 1936

My dearest Hans,

I was overjoyed to receive your letter with its eloquent description of Berlin and the Olympics. If only life arranged itself according to our wishes! I would so much have loved to stay for the games, but I could not justify the extra year to my family. I didn't realize how fond I had become of the city until I returned home. Though I dearly love the city of my birth, the same climate that sustains jasmine and hyacinth vines encourages the growth of cockroaches the size of Berlin mice. No matter how often we clean them out (I think the poison makes them stronger!), before we turn around there they are again, sharing our food. I sorely miss the order and cleanliness of a northern place. A few cold days and all your insects are gone. Though I do not miss the brawls in the street.

I don't know how you feel about this, but I will only say it is too bad that your "Revolution" has eliminated some of the best doctors from the hospital.

Now that I am home, I am becoming impatient with the attitude here that Egyptians can succeed only at business in cotton or beet sugar or carpets. Though my father boasts about his "doctor son" to his friends, he insists I join him in the cotton business. He longs to add "and Son" to the Hassan Cotton Company. He says a medical degree gets you position in the community, but not enough money to make a comfortable living. I didn't study medicine for the position!

My father has forgotten how he disobeyed his own father during the European war by going to Turkey with his stocks of cotton and loading them on a ship to Germany. He made his fortune in contraband cotton. His contacts in Turkey later found a German nanny for me — what status! I thank her for my familiarity with the language.

You may remember my fascination with snakes (how many times did I apologize for scaring you with that harmless little devil?). Egypt is home to some of the deadliest. Yet their venom may be employed to help mankind. I cannot think of a better way to spend my life than to work at turning poison into medicine that helps people. But my father rules the family with an iron hand and I shall have to convince him the venture can be profitable. Research with venom requires patience and many small animals for subjects. There is no shortage of small animals, but the transfer of results to human patients will be a tricky business. It will be difficult to develop a drug without harming the people who try it in the early stages. It will take all my powers of persuasion to convince my father that money can be made in snake venom. He has given me a year to prove myself and show him I have some sense. For now I have joined the medical clinic of a cousin who allows me two days to see my own patients.

Despite the upheaval that has taken over your country, the people are far better off than in Egypt. You would not believe the poverty and filth the majority live in. There is no work for them so they live on the edge of starvation. They certainly cannot afford a doctor when they get sick. And yet it is the poor who need medical attention the most. It is enough to break one's heart. In the city it is an effort to remember that Egypt was a superior culture four thousand years ago, though evidence of it lies just beyond, in the desert. I am still mesmerized by the vision of the three pyramids on the plateau of Giza as you drive southwest of Cairo. There also lies the Great Sphinx with the head of a man and body of a lion, symbols of wisdom and strength. Where is that wisdom and strength now? By the way — you know the famous profile? The nose was shot off by Napoleon's soldiers for target practice. I'm afraid this is our experience with European "civilization."

But enough of that — tell me about your medical practice and how things have changed in the hospital — and the city — since I was there. I long to hear about the place I called home for five happy years. And I implore you to remember you always have a place to stay when you visit — and I can promise my mother will treat you like a prince. I know it is a long way to come, but please consider it for my sake.

Your affectionate friend,
Mohammed

P.S. How is your dear mother? I know her illness must weigh on your mind.

Berlin, December 1936

Dearest Mohammed,

Your letter reminded me how much I enjoyed your company during our training. I am only sorry you had to return to your homeland where I am sure you are much needed by your parents.

As to the letting go of the Jewish doctors from the hospitals, yes, some were good, but they took up too many spaces, squeezing out Aryan doctors who had every right to practise. Of course, some people will suffer, but there is a purpose in the end. The system was not working, and now, despite the hardship for some, things have become balanced and German doctors can practise medicine the way we were meant to.

I long ago forgave you about the incident with the snake. I must admit, after I settled down and stopped shaking, the little fellow began to interest me. Your idea about transforming venom into medicine is exciting, and I am sure your father will come round. I hope you will write and let me know how your plan develops.

Thank you for asking about my mother. Sadly, her illness is progressing and she does not recognize me. Her memory is gone — she doesn't even remember who *she* is, never mind me. What must it be like, to forget *everything*? One becomes an empty vessel and the question arises — who *are* we if we cannot remember? It has made me realize we are our memories, for without them we are nothing. I'm sorry if this depresses you, but I rarely speak of her to anyone.

Since I was a boy I've dreamt of seeing the pyramids and the Sphinx. As much as I would love to make the trip and visit you (and all the insects you complain about) I cannot see a time in the near future as my practice is extremely busy. The political situation is also uncertain and makes travel difficult. Perhaps when you have got your snakes together and need someone to scare — a year or two? — things will be more settled here. It is Christmas now and rather lonely with just my brother to celebrate with.

Fond regards,
Hans


Cairo, February 1937

My dearest friend,

In all my years of training to be a physician I never imagined I would see such suffering. I keep it from my father — he would disapprove mightily — but I will confide in you. One day a week I spend treating the paupers who live in the northern cemetery. It is but one of a group of vast cemeteries stretching along the base of the Moquattam Hills. Tourists call the place "City of the Dead." You must understand Egyptian cemeteries are not like European ones, but are a labyrinth of room-like tombs and mausoleums. The poor who live there left their villages in search of work. They earn a few pennies here and there, never enough to pay rent in the overcrowded city. Thus they end up squatting in tombs or in hovels where tombs used to be.

After fourteen hours of seeing patients suffering from the most devastating diseases — and who could never afford a doctor — I cannot see straight, and stumble home. Some of my German professors thought I should be concerned with the tropical diseases I would find in my homeland. What romantics! Those are nothing compared to the pervasive infectious diseases arising from the overcrowding and general filth that breeds vermin of all kinds! The feces in the streets (both animal and human), the smell of urine in surprising places, like public buildings where men relieve themselves in the stairwells.

To all this, add the backwardness of folk remedies that defy all logic. Mothers of infants with diarrhea stop feeding them altogether because of some misguided "traditional" advice from their mothers and aunts. What a calamity! When I tell them to give their babies as much liquid as they will take, they shake their heads in puzzlement and tell me I was educated in the West where human bodies must be different. They hang amulets around the child's neck and say, "Allah will cure her." And then they are horrified when their children die! I cannot tell you how demoralized I am after such a day. Yet they need my services infinitely more than the middle-class patients who come to my clinic with colds and stomach ailments.

There is an organization, the Muslim Brotherhood, trying to help, set up ten years ago by a devout Muslim schoolteacher named Hasan al-Banna. They send people to deliver food to the poor, set up schools for the children, and organize prayer meetings. Al-Banna is a great admirer of your Adolf Hitler and has written to him many times. He has strong anti-British feelings, as do many here. Though our country has formally been granted independence under King Farouk, in reality the English still control everything here. They are in the barracks, the police, the army, and one is hard-pressed to find an Egyptian irrigation inspector or judge.

Germany is constantly in the news. Tell me how things are for you and whether there is still violence in the streets.

Your friend,
Mohammed

Berlin, April 1937

Dearest Mohammed,

It pains me that you are so upset by the conditions in
your city. Though it shows you have a generous heart, I
must say I agree with what your father would say, once
you tell him, that your time would be more usefully
spent on other things. Establishing yourself in a practice,
for one. The snake venom idea, for another.

Ministering to the poor is very idealistic, I'm sure,
but best left to the religious orders. I'm afraid I feel
the effort is fruitless for someone in your position.
Before you call me heartless, hear me out. The poor,
as people say, will always be with us. You can relieve
their suffering for the moment, but if their living conditions are rife with disease, they will not stay well for
long. It is like trying to make water run uphill. You
may succeed for an instant, but then gravity takes
over and all the effort is wasted. You have too much
talent for such folly. You must be more selfish and
look at the broader picture.

I hope this doesn't offend you — I consider you
one of my few friends and am only concerned for your
future. What happened to your snake venom propos-
al? I am personally very interested in the idea of
researching the venom. Perhaps we could collaborate
in some way. I find seeing patients all day rather
tedious. An old classmate of mine works in a laboratory
at the university and has offered me space. Would the
venom withstand shipping? I would, of course, pay for
all costs. Please think about it.

My country has grown strong in the years since
Hitler became führer. We have recently won back,
without force, the Rhineland, a strip of land along the

Rhine, which was demilitarized at Versailles at France's insistence. We are not children, to be told where we can and cannot go! And by those self-righteous fops, the French!

Fondest regards,
Hans


Cairo, January 1938

Dearest friend,

I'm sorry for not writing sooner, but I must lie low. Since I started working with the Muslim Brotherhood, the police are after me — the government kowtows to the English (known here as a government of pimps). They fear us because we provide services they should but don't. We're winning the hearts of the people so the English worry about insurrection. As well they should. All these years they've lorded it over us and expect our gratitude for the "superior" culture they've thrust upon us. But they've taken from us more than they've given. Most of the people are starving and disease-ridden. You would not believe how many children die because they are malnourished. *Inshallah*, God willing, our efforts will help to save some.

In the meantime I have started raising a kind of viper that the Bedouins have shown me, since it is native to the desert. The work itself — milking venom from the vipers' fangs — is painstaking and results in but a tiny amount of clear liquid. Only a tiny amount can be used at any rate, if we intend not to kill the animal subjects. I pay people for cats and dogs from the street and we inject them with minute quantities of venom. It's hard to adjust the dose not to kill them. I have begun to mix the venom with saline for better control. We have given the snakes English names — Edward, Victoria, and George after the most recent monarchs, though I feel more affection for the snakes.

May Allah grant you health and strength.
Your friend,
Mohammed

# *chapter seventeen*

By four o'clock on Friday, Rebecca had finished with her last patient. Every few weeks Iris persuaded her that they both needed some time off before the Sabbath. Though neither of them actually observed the Sabbath, they closed the office early and Iris invited her two grown children home for dinner on those Fridays. She intended to harangue them, she said, about their exasperating single status. When was she going to be a grandmother?

She had already said goodbye and hurried out the door. While putting on her coat, Rebecca stood at the window overlooking Beverley Street. She had never paid attention before, but she could see the front of the Sentry house from there. Her stomach turned at the memory of the other night.

She flicked out the lights in the office and locked the door. On her way down the stairs she remembered that Ben would be back in Montreal by now. This morning, newly shaven but haggard, he had stiffly touched his cheek to hers before leaving to drive back. A perfunctory embrace. He was angry that she wouldn't tell him where Susan was. Rebecca could hardly blame him. She insisted she didn't know. Technically speaking, that was true.

Downstairs, Rebecca glanced at the closed door of the first-floor office. Lila Arons, the other physician who practised in the building, stopped work at two on Fridays. All these women who had to take care of their families, thought Rebecca, envy squeezing her heart.

She wasn't due at her parents' house until seven. Lots of time to go visit Miriam at the hospital.

She opened the front door of the building and stepped outside into the chilly air. A weak sun had struggled to brighten the sky earlier but now gave in to November and receded into late afternoon clouds. Her father had said he would visit Miriam in the hospital while Flo was cooking, so she wouldn't be alone.

Rebecca crossed Beverley Street and walked toward the Sentry house on the opposite corner of D'Arcy. It was odd, being familiar now with a house she used to pass so often before without thinking. Like a loss of innocence — she'd never be able to walk past it again without feeling heartsick about Birdie.

Yellow police tape still flapped across the entry to the backyard where the hedge opened. She stopped to gaze into the yard, now stripped of the old woman's things. No wagon, no chair, no shopping bags. The police must have removed everything for investigation.

As she walked on, she peered through the tangle of hedge, remembering that night, the body drowning in shadow and blood. Nearly past the hedge, she stopped. What was that? Something wedged in the intricate branches just above the ground. She bent down to have a look. It was the cover of a small children's book. A cheerful little mouse in green breeches and red jacket jumped over a candlestick. The police must have missed it when they searched the yard. Or they didn't think it was important. It probably wasn't. She prodded the thick cardboard cover gently through its nest of branches and held it in her hand. *Mother Goose Nursery Rhymes*. In one corner of the cover, a sticker read, "Toronto Public Library," then below, "City Hall." This wasn't the book Rebecca had put Birdie's sandwich on that day in the yard. That was *Aesop's Fables*. Would the library lend out books to a woman who could barely give out basic information like her name?

Maybe she just took it. Or maybe it wasn't hers at all. What had the homeless man said before disappearing into the yard? He had a surprise for her: *some mousies*. A few pages still clung to the cardboard cover. Only one nursery rhyme had survived:

> Wee Willy Winkie runs through the town,
> Upstairs and downstairs, in his nightgown;
> Rapping at the window, crying through the lock,
> "Are the children all in bed, for now it's eight o'clock?"

A little mouse wearing a red gown and striped blue cap ran through the square of an old town, shaking his lantern high over his head. The ancient buildings threw blue shadows on the civic-minded mouse as he leaped to his duty, one beady eye and pink-edged ear in profile, thin brown tail curved behind him.

So this was the mouse. She pulled a tissue from her purse and wrapped the remains of the book in it, depositing it gingerly in her bag.

Instead of heading to the hospital, Rebecca turned south when she got to University Avenue. City Hall was less than a fifteen-minute walk away. She could satisfy her curiosity and get some exercise at the same time. She

walked east along Queen Street, ogling the Osgoode
Hall courthouse, a rambling nineteenth-century structure in the Palladian style (she had read in her book on
Toronto history) surrounded by large grounds and set
well back from the street. Separating the grounds from
the sidewalk, an ornate black iron fence stretched the
entire block of the property from University Avenue to
City Hall. She had read the narrow iron gates were
designed to keep livestock out of the grounds, since it
had been common practice to herd cattle down Queen
Street during the nineteenth century.

Passing the old gates, she stepped out of one century
and into the next. In front of her, the extensive square
rolled on and on, a carpet of concrete named after
Nathan Phillips, the mayor who had thrown open the
design for the new city hall to an international contest. A
Finnish architect had won with a design that some people
compared to a flying saucer. Rebecca found it quite beautiful in a futuristic way: the saucer-like building in the
centre seemed to float between two office towers that
soared skyward and, at the same time, curved toward it
like wings.

Up close it was a building fronted by lots of glass. She
pulled open one of the heavy wooden front doors. Just
inside, a tour group stood obediently around a guide
pointing out some aspect of the building. The library
entrance was down a short hall to the right.

She stepped past the counter where librarians were
checking out books for people waiting in a short queue.
Busy place for a Friday afternoon, she thought.

She strode down one aisle of books after another.
Past the children's section. Past the reference section.
The light drew her to the back of the library, where a
ceiling-high wall of glass looked onto the square. A
popular spot, judging from all the occupied chairs set

behind a ledge facing the glass. Since the building was round, the glass curved around the bend, but the straight wall of the library bisected it, leaving an oddly shaped bit of extra space. This was where she found him, the last chair in the row.

His distinctive profile gave him away, the crooked nose, the weathered skin. Wisps of white hair stood straight up from his head — probably static electricity from the wool hat, which lay at his feet along with the maroon jacket. He looked much older with his white hair exposed. The trundle buggy stood nearby, a reminder, in this shelter, of the outside, where there was little. He sat staring out at the square, a newspaper in his lap.

He must have sensed her standing there, because he turned and watched her with rheumy eyes. She wanted to ask him about Birdie, but what if he became violent? What if he ran? She could outrun him, but could she hold him before the police were called?

"Pretty soon they'll put up the skating rink out there." He pointed to the square. "For Christmas. It'll be real pretty, with lots of lights."

She nodded absently, then retreated to the front of the library.

"There's a man here who's wanted by the police," she said quietly to one of the librarians behind the counter.

The middle-aged woman observed her skeptically, her brown hair pulled back in a ponytail. "Oh? Who is it?" she asked, her eyes blank, as if Rebecca were making it up.

"The homeless man in the corner. The police called him Stanley."

The librarian blinked with a flutter of recognition. "What's he done?"

"He may've killed someone."

She shook her head. "He wouldn't have done that."

"I need to use your phone."

She looked at Rebecca as if she had just demanded some esoteric information, like the population of Tanzania.

"He's just a poor old guy who wants out of the cold." With an officious, stiff posture, she led Rebecca behind the counter into the office.

Detective Fitzroy was unavailable. A Sergeant Morelli asked Rebecca question after question about the incident in the backyard until she worried the old man might leave in the meantime. Finally the sergeant agreed to send some officers to check out her story.

With the police on the way, Rebecca knew it might be her only chance to talk to the man. His dented nose turned to her again as she approached.

"I know you?" he said.

"Is your name Stanley?"

He screwed up his rheumy eyes as if trying to remember her.

"I was a friend of Birdie's too."

He looked away again, his face contorted. "Oh, Christ."

"Have you seen this before?" She pulled the book cover from her bag, removing the tissue. The mouse in the green breeches still hung in the air over the candle stick.

The old man smiled wistfully. "She really liked them mice." Then a thought floated over his face like a shadow. "That there's a libary discard. They was gettin' rid of it 'cause it was in piss-poor shape. Libarian give it to me. I didn't steal it."

"I wasn't suggesting you did." She paused a moment. "She liked mice?"

"Couldn't get enough of 'em. Only time she smiled."

"You were there when she died, weren't you?"

He closed his eyes, shaking his head. "All my fault. You know she was difficult."

"Did something happen when you saw her last?"

"My hearing ain't so good no more and she didn't make no sense. I told her to slow down, talk sensible, but she wouldn't. Got me mad as hell."

He looked like he could deliver a good blow, armed with a rock.

"What did you do, when you got mad?"

He shrugged. "I got real mad. When I get mad, I'm bad. I can take on five big guys. They'll be sorry."

"Did you hurt her?"

He shook his head. "It's all my fault. I didn't believe her. She's dead, you know."

"Believe her about what?"

He screwed up his eyes again, recognition falling away. "I know you?"

In less than ten minutes, two constables walked into the library. Rebecca identified herself as the caller and led them to the wall of glass. The librarian followed, her arms crossed firmly over her chest. Patrons of the library began to look up as the police uniforms passed by. The old man had turned toward them as well. The two cops stopped beside him.

"Hello, Stanley," one of the young constables said. "Got yourself into real trouble this time, eh?"

The old man grimaced, his mouth caving in at the gums in front. "I didn't do nothing. What d'you guys want?"

"Come down to the station. We'll talk about it."

"Oh well, the libary'll be closing soon anyhow. You got donuts?" he asked. "You cops always got donuts."

"Sure, down at the station. Coffee and donuts. Come on, Stanley. Car's waiting."

The other constable held handcuffs at the ready.

"No! Don't go!" a young man bleated from the next chair.

A companion? Certainly another denizen of the streets, betrayed by the torn sweatshirt and deep tan. His blond hair shot up from his head in unruly corkscrew curls. Anxiety in his otherwise blank blue eyes.

"Leave him alone!" he said. "He's just an old guy."

The constable, not much older than the heckler, chewed the inside of his mouth. "You don't want to get into trouble, do you?"

"You threatening me?" The boy sat up tall, ready to roll. He couldn't have been more than eighteen.

"Shut up, Nigel," said the old man.

"It's police brutality. Don't let them take you, Stan. Please stay here. Please!"

"You don't know when to shut up, Nigel. Get you into trouble one day."

"Excuse me," Rebecca said, trying to distract them. "I don't think you need the handcuffs, officer."

Stanley was clumsily gathering the trundle buggy and putting on his jacket. The cop shrugged and returned the handcuffs to his belt. The young companion backed off, but his eyes smouldered.

"You better treat him right, man. Stan's a friend of mine, see. Nothing better happen to him." The boy raised his voice to make sure everyone could hear.

"*Stanley!*" the old guy said, throwing the boy a belligerent look. "Don't call me nothing but Stanley."

"Sure, sure. Stanley. Okay." Then a light went on in his eyes. "No, look, guys. You know, I'm gonna come with him since he don't feel so well. Do you, Stanley?" He stared into his face, willing the old man to agree. "You feel sick, don'tcha, Stanley? Need me to come with you."

"He's fine," the cop said. "You're staying here. But Dr. Temple," the cop turned to her, "Detective Fitzroy asked if you could come to the station too. It's just around the corner."

# *chapter eighteen*

---

**December 1936**

The euphoria of the Olympics dissolves when the signs forbidding Jews reappear in the windows of shops, groceries, hotels, restaurants, and theatres. Any notions that the government will soften its stand wither with the re-posting of the inflammatory pages of *Der Stürmer* on information pillars throughout Berlin. Frieda passes by the assembly of people standing in front of the kiosks, their heads lifted, chuckling at the grotesque drawings of fat, hook-nosed Jews who the propaganda minister, Goebbels, insists have grown rich by stealing from good Germans.

The Nazis have attached a sign to the storefront window of Eisenbaum's, identifying it as a Jewish shop. Nevertheless, at the beginning of December people start shopping for Christmas, and some old customers come in to buy presents. People remember that Eisenbaum's underwear is the best in Berlin. And it doesn't hurt that Vati has drastically reduced his prices.

Though Oma and Vati must work harder than before, Frieda notices at dinner that they are in better spirits with the increase in business.

Then one evening, Frieda comes home from the hospital to find Vati sitting on the living room sofa, his arm around Oma's shoulder while she weeps quietly into a handkerchief. Frieda doesn't remember ever seeing Oma cry before. It frightens her.

"What's happened?" she asks.

Vati purses his lips with distaste. "That lout, the husband of Frau Rheinhardt — she used to work for me, remember? — he came into the store today wearing a Nazi uniform and demanded money. He just went to the till and helped himself. There must've been fifty marks. He just took it."

"Did you call the police?"

Oma wipes her eyes with the handkerchief. "Don't be naive, Frieda. Where are the police when Nazi hooligans break the windows of Jewish stores and steal everything inside? The police are helpless against the Nazis."

"But what's to stop him coming in whenever he wants and taking the money?" Frieda says, alarmed.

Oma shakes her head. "We must be shrewder. I've been thinking, Ernst. We will have another place to put the money. We'll leave a little in the till. But every hour I'll come empty the cash register and take it to the back. I'll keep it in the drawer of my sewing machine."

"He won't be fooled so easily. He sees the customers buying before Christmas."

Vati pats her shoulder and stands to go into the dining room.

At dinner that night Luise is uncharacteristically quiet, not mimicking everyone's sentences the way she usually does. Berta, the maid, is bringing out the chicken and potatoes, setting them down on the table, when Frieda notices tears streaming down the woman's face.

Oma follows Frieda's gaze. "Why, Berta! Whatever is the matter?" Oma stands up and puts her arm around the thin woman's shoulders. Berta is usually silently efficient with no readable emotion on her face.

"Oh, Frau Eisenbaum, it wasn't my fault!" She weeps in earnest, now that she's allowed.

"Don't fret," Oma says, looking sideways at Vati, who hands over his handkerchief. "Just tell us what happened."

Berta sniffs into the handkerchief. "Me and Luise were at the greengrocer's today and I was buying some cabbage and you know the way Luise repeats everything ..." Berta looks around at everyone's faces. Luise and Wolfie are the only ones eating.

She continues. "The woman behind me in line, she says, 'That girl's not normal. She should ...'" Berta swallows. "'She should be in an asylum.' She asked our names, so I grabbed Luise and I just ran. She doesn't know our names so she can't find us. She can't do anything."

"It's all right, Berta," Oma says. "You did the right thing. Go to bed and rest now. Frieda and I will serve the rest of the meal."

Berta's shoulders stoop as she shuffles back to the kitchen.

"Luise mustn't go out anymore," Frieda says. "For her own safety, she must stay home with Mutti."

All eyes turn to Luise, who has been absorbed in eating some bread. Finding herself the centre of attention, she beams a broad, happy smile, her mouth full of food.

Mutti's eyes are filled with reproach when she lifts them to Frieda, but Frieda doesn't care. They all know about the sterilization program the Nazis have initiated for the "feeble-minded." It has been in the papers. The Nazis make no secret of it. Hundreds of thousands of inmates in asylums have been sterilized against their will after "failing" the highly subjective tests created by Nazi doctors. Questions that were designed to test not only intelligence but moral and social outlook. Questions like: What is loyalty, respect, modesty? What constitutes a satisfactory answer depends on the questioner. And poor Luise can answer only the simplest questions, like her name and address.

Frieda watches her sister eat happily. When she was still in medical school, the professor in her Racial Science class distributed a handout titled *The Law for the Prevention of Progeny with Hereditary Diseases*. It began:

(1) i. Anyone who has a hereditary illness can be rendered sterile by surgical operation if, according to the experience of medical science, there is a strong probability that his/her progeny will suffer from serious hereditary defects of a physical or mental nature.

   ii. Anyone is hereditarily ill within the meaning of the law who suffers from one of the following illnesses:

   Congenital feeble-mindedness
   Schizophrenia
   Manic depression
   Hereditary epilepsy
   Hereditary blindness
   Hereditary deafness

Oma smiles sadly at Luise. "Your sister is right, *liebling*. You must stay home."

"You must stay home," Luise repeats, lifting a piece of chicken with her hands.

Meanwhile, Jews are continually being arrested into "protective custody." In the building where the Eisenbaums live, sometimes whole families are taken away, their apartments sealed with tape by the Gestapo so the goods inside will not be looted by locals, but rather by the authorities, who can arrive at their leisure. There's an apartment like that on their floor, with tape across the door. Frieda avoids looking at it each time she walks by to get to her apartment. The Mundts, a middle-aged couple whose two sons managed to leave for Israel last year. One dawn a few weeks ago Frieda awoke to the stomping of Nazi boots on the stairs, the unrelenting banging on a door. Her heart hammered wildly until she realized the brutes were not pounding at *their* door, but on one down the hall. She stood with her ear to the front door listening to the Gestapo shouting for the people to get dressed, hurry up, throw the necessities into a small bag, only hurry up, you swine. A moan from Frau Mundt as she was ripped from her home, then a strumming of boots and shoes down the stairs as the couple was escorted out. Then nothing. Silence. Where are they now, Herr and Frau Mundt?

Several weeks later the Eisenbaums have retired to the living room after dinner. Vati turns the radio to some Christmas music, then unfurls his newspaper. Angelic voices fill the air with "Silent Night." Mutti is reading Dickens' *A Christmas Carol* in her favourite chair. Frieda is leafing through her internal medicine book, when a sudden rapping sounds at the door. Everyone jumps, though the knock is subdued, not like the insistent banging of the SS.

Vati approaches the door, but Oma whispers hoarsely, "No! Go to the bedroom. They always come for the men."

Vati stares at her with disbelief, but retreats while she goes to the door. Wolfie has gone out long ago and is hopefully out of danger.

When the door opens, there is no uniform, but only Irmgard, their former maid, peering behind her.

"Why, Irmgard!" Oma says. "What a nice surprise. Come in."

Irmgard jumps inside, relieved, it seems, to be out of the hall. She's wearing a woollen winter coat and a coloured kerchief over her hair. Oma embraces her; Irmgard wriggles out of her arms with embarrassment.

She blushes and stammers, "I'm sorry to come so late, but I was waiting outside until no one could see me come into the building. People kept going by. The streets are busy before Christmas, I guess."

Vati has come back into the living room and nods curtly at her while Luise runs to her to take her hand.

"I'm sorry, but you know how it is. I'll be in trouble if someone finds out that I've come to see Jews. That's the way it is now."

Oma takes a deep breath. "Come, I'll make some tea."

"No, thank you. I can't stay. I've come for Berta."

"What do you mean?"

"She can't work here anymore." Irmgard takes a gulp of air; her eyes dart around the living room. "The Gestapo is bothering us. They keep coming to my employer and saying, 'Don't you know her aunt works for Jews?' The family I work for is nervous. They say if the Gestapo won't stop coming, they'll have to let me go. They say they'll find Berta a job if I just come and get her."

She takes her hand out of Luise's grip and looks down. "I'm sorry, but I need my job."

There is a long, awkward silence. Finally Oma says, "Berta's in the kitchen cleaning up."

Irmgard nods and steps away from Oma and Luise, avoiding Frieda's eyes as she heads for the kitchen.

The family can hear Berta's exclamation at the sight of her niece. Then things go quiet for a moment before voices are raised, first from one woman, then the other. When the kitchen goes completely still, Frieda knows they have gone to Berta's room and are packing her belongings. Things will be very different now in the Eisenbaum household.

With Berta gone, the duties in the family must be redistributed. At one time it would have been Vati who made such decisions, but he has lost that self-assurance that made his word law. The downward spiral of events in his beloved country has softened his voice and brought doubt into his once certain eyes. He seems relieved when Oma and Frieda decide how things must change: Mutti is the only one left who can go to the shops for food. Oma will leave the store earlier to cook dinner and instruct Mutti, who will have to learn the basics of food preparation. (Besides, Oma reasons, what is the point of working her fingers to the bone to turn out more bloomers when Rheinhardt strides into the shop at least once a week in his Nazi uniform and steals the money from the till?) Frieda will help serve dinner and clean up after. Luise will have to stay home and keep out of trouble.

It is bad enough that it falls to Mutti to find food for the family. As it is, Jews are not allowed to shop for food during regular hours. They must scrounge for scraps at the end of the day when the produce has been picked over. Even at the best of times, Mutti would not be good at this job. She is not ingratiating enough to the shopkeepers Berta used to buy from, nor to the grocers who might have saved some vegetables for a hand-

some woman if she could exchange some pleasantries,
maybe show some appreciation. Mutti is not capable of
any of that; she would rather live in a book, and so
their meals suffer.

Lucky for them, Oma works miracles with what little they can get. Some old cabbage leaves cooked with
onions and thickened with a little flour stretch into a
satisfying soup. Pancakes are mixed with sliced crabap-
ples from the small stash that was salvaged from the
park in the fall and that is keeping company in their
section of the cool basement with old turnips, carrots,
and potatoes growing graceful little tendrils.

From the articles in the Jewish paper Vati has started
reading, it appears that there are a lot of German Jewish
women who do not know their way around a kitchen.
Frieda notices headlines like "Everyone learns to cook"
and "Even Peter cooks." She doubts that such encouragement will persuade Vati to pick up a mixing spoon.

## February 1937

One day in the middle of winter Frieda comes home from
the hospital in the evening to find everyone packing. The
household has been turned upside down — the drawers
of the buffet stand open, some of their contents on the
dining table in the process of being bundled up. Pots and
dishes clatter in the kitchen as they are moved about.

When Frieda steps into the dining room, Oma
looks up from the box into which she is placing some
candlesticks.

"What's happened?" Frieda asks, bewildered.

"We have to move," Oma says as if it were self-
evident.

Frieda has never lived anywhere else. This apartment is the only home she has ever known. She stands transfixed, watching her grandmother.

"We're moving into the back of the store," Oma says, reaching for some plates already wrapped in paper. "Don't look so surprised. You can't remember this, but we lived there before you were born. We can do it again. If we're out of here by the middle of the month, the landlord is willing to charge only half the rent. That only gives us five days to get out."

Frieda begins to sweat. Still in her winter coat, she shivers and her body begins to shake. "I don't understand. Why do we have to move?"

Oma licks her lips and keeps piling objects wrapped in paper into the box. "The store ... the store is not in our hands. The Nazi Rheinhardt — *Scharführer* Rheinhardt — came in today ..." She lowers her voice and glances at the doorway leading to the hall. "He just came in, swaggering without shame, and sat down at the cash register as if he owned the place. 'This is it,' he said. 'I'm out of patience.' Just like that. He told your father we were lucky. That he wanted Vati to still be the boss and run everything, since he was a war veteran, and the brute would give him a pension. A ridiculous amount that won't even pay for groceries. He said he thought that was reasonable! He didn't want to be unreasonable!"

Oma's head shakes uncontrollably. Her hands fly around the box. "We worked so hard to build this business. So many years. And for what?" She looks up to make sure no one is listening. Nevertheless she whispers in a hoarse voice, her hands flying, "Don't say anything to your father. He's very upset."

"But how can he do that, just walk in and take over?"

Oma looks at her with irritation. "Who's going to stop him? The police? There is no help."

Frieda ought to know better. Jewish businesses all over Berlin are being confiscated. The broom factory Leopold's family owned was taken over by a Nazi who used to be a supplier. She, like Vati, had counted on his war record for more protection.

A chill skips down her spine. "But how can we live?"

Oma doesn't look up. "We must sell everything we don't need. That'll keep us for a while. There will be no room where we're going anyway. The problem is getting a decent price for our things. People know we're desperate and won't give us what our belongings are worth. Can't be helped. We have to take what we can get. There are lots of people in the same boat."

Oma finally looks up at her, eyes filled with pain. "You have to be strong. Gather together anything you have that might be of value. People will be coming by tomorrow. We all have to do our part."

"I'm sorry I don't make more money," Frieda says.

Oma lowers her eyes again, wrapping some teacups in paper.


Frieda can't bear to watch Oma and Mutti going through their closets, choosing clothes they can live without. In her room, she fastens a bed sheet over her bookcase so that it hangs down, covering all her medical books. On a piece of paper she scrawls out "Not For Sale" and pins it to the sheet. Frieda makes sure all her medical instruments are in her leather case and walks out the door.

She walks blindly down the familiar streets, through the park where frost glistens on the junipers and brown grass. She has walked this way so many times, always with the knowledge of home in her heart, the safety of going home.

The doctor's street hasn't changed. Only she has changed. The very air is vivid, as if her mind is recording it for posterity.

Yes, something *has* changed. On the front door of the building, someone has written crude letters in white paint: "*Jude Raus!*"

Inside, she rings the bell near the *Krankenbehandler* plaque. Herr Doktor Kochmann answers the door with an expression on his face she hasn't seen there before.

"*Liebling*," he says, without the usual affection, peering behind her with anxiety.

"I'm sorry if I startled you," she says.

"I'm easily startled these days," he says. "I am waiting for that last knock on the door."

"No, Herr Doktor. You mustn't." Does she mean he mustn't think such thoughts, or that he mustn't wait? She doesn't know. She has never had to give comfort to her old benefactor. It has always been him comforting her. That is why she is here now.

He peers down at the medical bag in her hand. "Are you on your way to a patient?"

"I'm the patient," she says.

As he leads her inside she sees he has lost more weight, his old brown wool suit hanging loosely on his shrunken frame. She surprises them both when she begins to weep and tell him how they have lost the store. The pension proposed by the Nazi will not go far to support a family of six.

"It's over," she says finally. "We barely have enough to live on. They're selling everything in the apartment."

He sits down beside her on the sofa, taking her hand. "I'm sorry, *liebchen*. I'm very sorry."

"Who would've thought ... Remember all those years ago when you came to the store to persuade Vati I should stay in school?"

Kochmann smiles wistfully, nodding.

"Who would've thought it would end like this."

"We are all in the same boat, *liebling*. At least you are young. You have a chance. Helga and I ..." He shakes his head, glances over to a photo of his wife on the table. A much younger Helga, small and slender, smiles prettily into the camera, her hair gathered in a roll over each ear. "I can hardly get her out of bed anymore."

His eyes are unbearably sad. She throws herself into his arms to comfort him, feeling no comfort herself.

Vati and Wolfie spread the word among their customers and other shopkeepers that the Eisenbaums will be selling their belongings. Like so many others, they have to unburden themselves of their possessions and move to smaller premises.

For the next three days people wander through the apartment examining the furniture, the vases, the curtains with a critical eye.

"Is that a real Persian rug?" asks a woman in a coat with a fox collar.

"Of course," Oma says.

"I'll give you forty marks."

"Outrageous." Oma shakes her head.

*Vulture*, thinks Frieda from the other side of the room. The prospect of acquiring cheap valuables has put a sparkle in the woman's eyes.

"What about the curtains?" The woman forges on, ignoring Oma's response. "Are they for sale?"

Oma looks up at the velvet curtains and nods. Frieda has never paid much attention to them before but remembers Oma sewing them.

"They're too long. If you take the hem up, and throw in that painting, I'll give you eighty marks. Together with the rug, of course."

Frieda glances at the painting of mountains that has hung on the wall ever since she can remember.

In the dining room Wolfie is negotiating with a customer about some books. "Add a few more to this pile and I'll take it," says the stout man with glasses.

He seems to be buying books by the kilo. Not such a bad idea, since there are boxes and boxes of them: books on German history, literature, grammar, books by Goethe and Heine. Mutti has relinquished much of her library, keeping only those books she can't bear to part with. Unfortunately, these include large volumes like *Don Quixote* and *Oliver Twist*, which take up an inordinate amount of room, but there is so little that Mutti cares about that Vati has allowed them. Frieda has told Oma she will part with her clothes before she sells her medical books, concealed behind the sheet hung over her bookcase.

In three days they have managed to sell all the heavy furniture in the dining room, living room, and bedrooms. People come and go in the apartment, removing one stick of furniture at a time, until finally all that's left is a sofa, the kitchen table, a few chairs, the beds, some small chests of drawers, and their radio, which they have hidden in a closet behind some boxes so that no one can accuse them of listening to foreign broadcasts.

The evening before they are to move out, Frieda feels a weight on her chest as she folds her clothes into a suitcase. Luise comes into her room carrying a blouse by one sleeve, the rest of it hanging to the floor.

"Help me," she whines, pulling Frieda into the room she shares with Oma. "I can't ..." Luise says, pouting at the suitcase lying open on her bed. Her clothes, which Oma always folds carefully before placing them in a drawer or hanging them up, lie jumbled all over the bed. Like the chaos of their lives.

"Luise! What's the matter with you?"

Luise's face crumples and tears pour down her face.

Frieda's heart contracts with remorse as she takes her sister in her arms. "Oh, Luise, don't cry! I'm sorry, I didn't mean it." She wipes Luise's eyes with a handkerchief.

"Here, look." She takes a blouse and demonstrates how to fold it, one sleeve, then the other. "Now you try."

Luise's forehead creases with effort and she manages to fold a blouse, if lopsidedly.

"Good!" says Frieda. "Then put it in here." She places both pieces in the suitcase to demonstrate.

"Don't want to go," Luise says. "Stay here." Despite the defiant words, her eyes are large and frightened.

Frieda doesn't know how to protect her. That sense of helplessness brings on a surge of self-pity that surprises, then sickens her. Frieda's eyes begin to fill with tears until they brim over and slide down her cheek.

Luise's face grows calm. "Oh, Frieda-mouse, don't cry." She takes Frieda in her arms and pats her back. "I'm sorry. I didn't mean it."

# *chapter nineteen*

Rebecca arrived late for dinner at her parents' house Friday evening. Detective Fitzroy had kept her waiting for over an hour at Fifty-Two Division on Dundas near University, two blocks from the library where she had found Stanley. Instead of thanking her, the detective had scolded her for not handing the book cover to the police right away so that they could do their work. After satisfying himself she wasn't holding anything else back, he'd let her go.

Uncle Henry, her mother's brother, usually a guest at Friday night dinner, became very animated on hearing about the killing of the homeless woman across from his niece's office.

"Rebecca, you're a doctor, for God's sake! How do you get to lead such a crazy, exciting life? Haven't you come across three dead bodies in the past six months?"

"Don't be ridiculous, Henry," her mother said, bringing a bowl of sautéed mushrooms and onions to the table. "Doctors have to deal with dead bodies all the time. It's part of the job."

"Yes, but —"

"For heaven's sake, Henry!" her father said. "You're a history teacher. It doesn't take much to get you excited. Queen Victoria farted in bed? Oooh! That's exciting."

"Mitch!" Her mother waved a fork at him.

"Actually, Uncle Henry, I have a historical question for you."

Henry leaned forward with interest, his short, fuzzy hair a halo beneath the chandelier.

"Have you heard of a place called Mittverda? Something to do with a concentration camp?" She speared a piece of roast potato with her fork and brought it to her mouth.

"Mittverda? Can't say I have. Odd name. I thought I knew all the camps. Do you know where it was? Germany? Poland?"

She shook her head. "Sorry."

"May I know your interest?"

She shook her head some more. "Maybe later."

"Okay, okay. So I'm a nosy parker. Tell you what. I'll look it up in my little library when I get home."

Uncle Henry was a student of history and indulged himself by collecting all the books he could find on the subject. When he said "little library" he was being modest. One of the rooms in his small bungalow was lined with bookshelves to the ceiling. Her mother said it was because he had never married and had to do *something* to occupy his time.

"Have you heard from Susan?" Her mother asked this casually, but Rebecca heard the concern between the words.

"I tried calling her around lunch today," Rebecca said, "but no one answered."

Actually, she had gotten Jeff Herman's answering machine, but she wasn't going to say that in front of Uncle Henry, who probably didn't know Susan's situation. She couldn't imagine her mother telling her bachelor brother that his niece had abandoned her new baby. Her mother licked her lips and looked away.

"Flo, this chicken is outstanding," said Rebecca's father, chewing.

Had he been sensitive enough to change the subject?

Her mother watched him with expectation.

"What?" he said. "I can't compliment your cooking without you waiting for a joke?"

"I'll get some more mushrooms," she said, taking the empty bowl to the kitchen.

Rebecca's father took that moment to lean conspiratorially toward the table. "If a man speaks in a forest and there's no woman to hear him, is he still wrong?"

"I heard that, Mitch," said her mother from the kitchen.

After Uncle Henry had gone home and Mitch was ensconced in front of the TV, Rebecca sat in the kitchen with her mother. They were nursing their second cup of tea.

"Any plans for the weekend?"

Her mother routinely asked this question. Rebecca rarely had anything to tell her.

"I've been invited to a fencing tournament."

"A fencing tournament? Well, that should be interesting since you used to fence in university."

"My mistake was to mention that."

"To whom?"

"A fencing instructor."

"Young and handsome?"

"Old and handsome. But his son is young and handsome."

Her mother's eyebrows went up in a question. When Rebecca didn't embellish on the son, her mother asked, "When's Nesha coming?"

"Two weeks." She knew her mother thought Nesha was too old for her at forty-eight.

"Well, it sounds like fun. I say go for it."

Rebecca smiled at her mother's vernacular, but noticed the half moons, darker than usual, beneath her eyes.

"Do you want me to pick up some soup from Daiter's next week? Less for you to cook. It's too much to do, week after week."

"There's nothing like homemade. I thought you liked my soup."

"I do. But you look tired, and it would be one less thing you'd have to make."

"I'm more worried than tired. I can't sleep thinking about Susan."

Her sister had told Rebecca not to give anyone else Jeff's home number, but now Rebecca felt guilty.

"Do you want to speak to her?"

Her mother's eyes lit up.

Rebecca retrieved the number from her purse and dialed the wall phone in the kitchen. Susan picked up on the first ring.

"Hi, it's Rebecca. How are you feeling?"

A pause. "You know how."

"I called during the day to see if you wanted to come up to Mom and Dad's for dinner, but nobody answered."

"I don't answer the phone."

"I'm still here —"

"I'm really not ready to go anywhere."

"Mom would like to talk to you." Without waiting for a reply, she handed the phone to her mother.

Flo smiled with gratitude and took the receiver. "Hi, sweetie. I've been worried about you. How're you feeling?"

As Rebecca watched, her mother's face went from joyful anticipation to puzzlement to despair.

"Sweetheart, don't. Please. Stop crying."

Flo wiped a tear from her eye, then put her hand over the mouthpiece. "I don't know what she's saying. I don't know what she wants." She handed the receiver back to Rebecca.

Rebecca heard a few words between sobs. "... alone ... went out ... weekend ..."

"Susan! I can't hear you. Calm down and tell me what's happening."

Susan sniffed and wept. "He went out. To get his son. I'm alone. Always alone."

"Give me the address and I'll come and get you. Ben's gone back to Montreal so you can stay at my place."

Silence. Thinking. Breathing into the phone. Then Susan said, "51 Thomas Valley. In Rosedale."


Rebecca drove south on Bayview from her parents' suburban home. They had watched her rush out the door and made her promise to call them later no matter the hour.

Rosedale was the WASP enclave of upper-crust Toronto. A Jewish lawyer who bought an expensive home here was making a statement, claiming a kinship with the captains of industry, the leaders of the country. Who said a Jewish boy couldn't make good?

Though it was more than a month before Christmas, holiday lights were already winking through the greenery in some front gardens. Tastefully strung across a tall spruce here, a few bushes there. Nothing gaudy.

She parked in front of Jeff Herman's house, a solid two-storey brick affair lit up by strategically placed spotlights.

She marched up the front steps and was immediately impressed by the heavy door, an architectural work of art comprised of vertical slats of honey-coloured oak. Something you'd find at the entrance of a stately Anglican church.

She rang the bell. Chimes echoed inside. *Where are you, Susan?*

Finally the door opened. Susan, her eyes red from crying, made a sad attempt at a smile. She wore ivory silk lounging pyjamas.

Rebecca stepped inside a large vestibule rising to a cathedral ceiling. She embraced her sister. Susan didn't hug her back but felt limp as a doll.

"Where's Jeff?" The honey oak floors glittered too brightly beneath the chandelier.

"He went out to get his son. He's got him for the weekend. Joint custody. He'll be back any minute."

"Do you want to wait till he comes back to say goodbye?"

Susan looked off, thinking. "No. I'll get my things. Give me a minute." She stepped up the stairs with visible effort, her energy gone.

Rebecca had time to admire the dining room suite on one side of the hall. An oval oak table sat surrounded by barrel-like chairs with rounded oat slats for backs. Probably the same architect who designed the door. Everything screamed money.

While Susan still moved around upstairs, the front door opened. A boy of seven or eight stepped in, followed by Jeff Herman. He stopped in his tracks when he saw Rebecca.

"Hi. Remember me?" she said blithely, to disguise her embarrassment. "Rebecca. I came to see my sister."

"Yes, of course. Long time no see. You haven't changed that much since high school. Maybe your hair." He angled his head for a better look. "Is it curlier?"

She lifted a self-conscious hand to her hair. "Maybe."

Jeff, a lanky teenager, had improved with age. His shoulders had filled out and his unruly hair had been tamed. And tinted? It looked blonder than she remembered. He had a fine aquiline nose. Almost aristocratic.

"Tyler, take your coat and boots upstairs to your room."

Little Tyler, in a ski jacket and cap, peered up at Rebecca, who smiled. He didn't smile back, but sat down on the floor to take off his boots. Jeff watched with dispassion as the boy tried unsuccessfully to unzip his jacket.

"It's stuck," he said, looking up at his father with resentful eyes.

"Then I guess you'll have to sleep in it."

Rebecca stepped forward despite feeling Jeff's eyes on her. "I can help." With a quick flip, she unsnagged the zipper and helped him wriggle out of the jacket.

"Children need to learn to do things for themselves," Jeff said, ice in his voice.

"They'll learn if they're shown how," she said. Where was Susan?

"Go upstairs, Tyler."

The little boy ran up the wide staircase carrying his boots and jacket, one sleeve dragging on the floor.

"Pick up the jacket!" Jeff called out. Then to her, "You don't have children yourself, do you?"

It wasn't a question. He probably knew her story from Susan. He was appraising her beneath lowered lids, his regal nose sniffing. If he compared her to Susan, she would be found wanting.

"Why don't you take off your coat?" he said, suddenly playing at host as they stood awkwardly in the grand hall.

"She can't stay," said Susan from the top of the stairs.

Rebecca stared up at her, puzzled. She was still in her lounging pyjamas, no more ready than when she had gone up.

"Susan ..." Rebecca tried to find the right words. "Do you have your things?"

Jeff looked from one to the other. "What does she mean, Susan?"

This was an actual question, spoken in a soft voice, not the peremptory tone he had used earlier.

"I'm going to stay with Rebecca for a while, Jeff. I have to sort things out."

"Susan, please ..." The glacier in his eyes melted and threatened to flood over. "Please don't go. You know how I feel about you. Tyler's only here till Sunday. Then it'll just be the two of us. I'll take some time off work."

Rebecca observed her sister at the top of the stairs. She was still striking, a week after giving birth, a wave of long blonde hair falling over one cheek. But her eyes gave her away; her eyes mourned.

"She needs some time to herself," Rebecca said. "She has to consider all her options, including the baby in the hospital."

"She can do that here," Jeff said, the peremptory voice back. "If she goes with you, she won't come back."

"She has a new baby! Who needs her more?"

"*I* do!" he said. "You don't understand. I need her most."

"Excuse me," Susan spit out, "but I'm right here. Don't talk about me in the third person as if I'm somewhere else. Why does everyone treat me like an idiot?"

"Susan!" said Jeff, stepping to the foot of the stairs. "I've got your law school application in my briefcase. Remember what we were talking about? I'm going to speak to my friend Brian Metcalfe about your application. He's a prof in the faculty — it's always good to know someone on the inside."

Susan's eyes brightened a bit.

Rebecca had a sinking feeling: Jeff knew his strategy.

"You're a very bright woman." He lifted a foot onto the first stair. "You'll make a great lawyer." Then, as if remembering she was still there, he turned his head sideways to Rebecca. "She's staying here tonight," he said quietly.

Rebecca looked up to where her sister stood transfixed. "Susan?"

Susan's face grew calm as she watched Jeff place another foot on the stairs. She turned to Rebecca. "I can't," she said. "I'll call you in a few days."

Tyler stuck his little head out of one of the rooms upstairs.

"Go to sleep, Tyler!" his father boomed out.

"Jeffrey," Susan said, reproach in her voice.

Rebecca watched Jeff blink with a submission that would ruin him in court.

"If you change into your pyjamas quickly," he said to his son, "I'll read you a story."

Susan gave him a crooked half-smile of approval.

Without another word, Rebecca turned around and let herself out.

# *chapter twenty*

**February 1937**

The two windows in the back wall of the
Eisenbaums' workroom bring in little light. They
face west into a courtyard shared by other buildings that
abut Eisenbaum's and that preclude the presence of any
other windows. The absence of light drives Frieda to
despair — it will be difficult to read without constantly
burning a lamp. A few weeks in this half-light and she
will feel like a mole.

Under Oma's direction she helped Wolfie and Leopold
carry in the beds and chests of drawers, while Vati tended
to customers out front in the store. The diminished workroom has been moved off to one side: the two sewing
machines that Oma and Vati still use are there, as well as
a smaller cutting table. The huge one has since been sold,
along with Vati's desk. White cotton fabric is piled in one
corner beside a tailor's dummy. The Eisenbaum household

has sprouted in the remaining space like a flower in the wrong garden. The familiarity depresses Frieda, sucks her back to when she was fifteen and required to learn to sew so that she could one day take over the business. She sits on her narrow bed, listening to the hum of Oma's sewing machine. She fled the business to become a doctor. Nothing, it seems, has turned out the way she planned. Not the business, not her career.

Oma has organized the cramped space with a judicious placing of curtains to separate designated areas: the workroom on the side where the door leads to the store, Vati and Mutti's bedroom, and the room where Oma and Luise will share a bed and where Frieda will sleep on a cot. This leaves the large old stove at the back where they will cook their meals and eat at their kitchen table; here, too, they've placed the sofa where Wolfie will sleep. The small washroom has a toilet and sink. The washtub they brought from their apartment will have to do double duty for bathing.

Frieda's hospital earnings diminish as the Jews remaining in Berlin grow poorer. A Jewish agency distributes small amounts of money so the physicians can keep treating patients. She sees more and more people brought in who have attempted suicide and failed: a woman who didn't keep her head in the oven long enough; a man who jumped from a second-storey window only to break his legs and three ribs; a man who tried to hang himself with a sheet that unwound.

A smartly dressed young mother whose husband was taken away comes in with her two children and asks for poison pills. Frieda looks at the two little girls, aged four and six, their blonde hair in curls around their heads.

"Have you tried to emigrate?" Frieda asks.

"I have no one to sponsor me." She looks at the floor. "I have no one."

It is one thing to try to save oneself, quite another to try to save oneself with small children. "Do you know anyone who will take the children?" Frieda asks.

The woman looks up angrily. "I will not give away my children. We'll die together."

Frieda looks into the large blue eyes filled with pain. What good is she, with her stethoscope and her medical books? "I'm sorry," she says. "I wish I could help you."


Late in October, when the days are growing shorter, the Eisenbaums have just sat down to supper around the kitchen table. It's pleasantly warm near the large tiled stove on the back wall of the apartment, despite the cool evening air leaking in around the door that leads out to the courtyard. Oma has concocted a stew of turnips, beans, and potatoes that Frieda has become fond of.

She has just complimented Oma on the stew. All at once a thunderous banging explodes in the store. They all jump in their seats and stare at the door that separates them from the storefront. The enraged knocking continues on the street door of Eisenbaum's. Frieda stumbles out of her chair, her head filled with noise.

Wolfie jumps up almost instantly. "Vati! We've got to get out of here! They've come for us." He grabs his jacket from the hook on the wall and runs to the back door.

Vati shakes his head dolefully. "I can't. You go! It's me they want."

Wolfie's wild eyes take in his family while he stoops by the door, his hand on the knob.

"Go!" cries Oma.

He opens the back door warily, peers into the empty courtyard, then jumps out, disappearing into the dark.

The banging on the front door has gotten louder, angrier. Men are shouting, "Open up, you damned Jews!"

Oma gets up and heads into the store to open the door.

Her head pounding with alarm, Frieda notices Wolfie's bowl filled with stew. She empties it into the serving dish and places his bowl beneath hers.

She hears Oma saying, "We were in the back."

Boots stomp heavily behind Oma as she leads them past the workroom and the curtains dividing the bedrooms to reach the kitchen. Two burly Gestapo wearing black leather coats glare at the family.

"The Jews Ernst Eisenbaum and Wolfgang Eisenbaum must come with us!" one of the men shouts, as if they are not in a confined space.

"I am Ernst Eisenbaum," Vati says, standing up. "My son is not at home."

Luise has gotten up to crouch beside Frieda's chair like a frightened dog.

The other man moves through the apartment in spurts, pulling the curtains open with furious energy. There is nowhere for anyone to hide.

He opens the back door. "Where does this go?" he spits out.

"Nowhere," Oma says. "The courtyard."

He glances at the sixth chair, the empty spot at the table. "Tell him he must come to our station at Grosse Hamburgerstrasse tomorrow morning."

Mutti has turned white and stares at Vati with huge eyes. Frieda gets up to stand near Oma as she hands Vati his coat. Will she ever see him again?

He says goodbye to them with his eyes as each man takes him by one arm. They lead him out through the store.

Oma sits down at the table, puts her head down on her arms, and begins to weep.

For the next few days Herr Rheinhardt sits in the store, cheerfully greeting customers. He seems to be in an excellent mood. When he can't find what he's looking for in the stock, he calls Oma to find it. His wife, Kristine, the former sewing machine operator, has come back to help Oma sew together underwear and keep up production.

Wolfie returns under cover of night and stays out of sight. Oma has arranged blankets under Mutti's bed for him. The curtains separating the rooms are not enough to hide him, with Kristine sitting in the workroom all day. The Rheinhardts mustn't see him or they will inform the Gestapo. After a day, the strain is too much for everybody, and early the next morning, Wolfie leaves to go to the Sussmans'.

Vati has been gone three days. Five days. They all move around like ghosts, only Luise occasionally chattering. They don't dare say it: is Vati still alive?

Frieda sleepwalks at the hospital, going through the motions of her job. Where is Vati, in an unheated, grubby cell? Are they beating him? Is he still alive? She is tortured by the visions that rise, unbidden, in her head.

Oma has stopped eating. Her sewing has slowed to a trickle. Frieda must do something.

She prepares a small basket of food: some bread and cheese, a Thermos of warm cocoa, and some biscuits. Oma insists on coming.

They take the tram to the building on Grosse Hamburgerstrasse that used to be an old folks' home but is now Gestapo headquarters. Frieda has put on more makeup than usual and has worn her narrow maroon skirt with the slit on the side. She makes sure Oma hides her unkempt hair inside her hat and puts on some lipstick.

Frieda hesitates in front of the building with its flapping swastika banner. How many people have entered here, never to come out again? Before Frieda can stop her, Oma heads through the door.

By the time Frieda catches up to her, Oma is walking toward the Nazi sitting behind a desk in the lobby.

"Oma!" she whispers, wobbling on heels higher than she is used to. "Wait."

The man is writing at his desk, paying no attention to them. Two men in uniform look Frieda over on their way to the staircase. One raises an eyebrow with interest.

Frieda stops in front of the desk, Oma at her side.

Finally, the man looks up, irritated. "Yes?"

"My father was brought here six days ago. Ernst Eisenbaum. My grandmother and I … we would like … we request permission to visit him if he's still here. We've brought him some food …"

"Jewish?"

She nods.

"No visitors!" the man exclaims in a peremptory voice. "Where do you think you are?"

The Nazi who hesitated on the staircase now continues climbing up. She can read his mind: *Too bad. Just another Jewess come for her father.*

The man at the desk glowers at them, his blue eyes livid, but Oma steps forward. "Please," she says, "is he all right? We've just brought him a little bread and cheese."

He stares at her, incredulous; his blue eyes go blank. "Leave the basket."

Oma is not satisfied. "Is he all right?"

The man's eyes narrow. "He's alive. For now."

Frieda takes in a sudden breath. He's alive! She leads Oma away, the man's words echoing in her head: *For now*.

Early the next morning, before Frieda has left for work and before the Rheinhardts arrive, Vati walks into the apartment.

"Thank God!" Oma cries and rushes to embrace him.

He sways on his feet while both Oma and Frieda wrap their arms around him. He looks thin and frail and ten years older. His stubble of beard is suddenly grey, his cheeks sunken. Mutti emerges from the bedroom in her nightgown and blinks. She runs to embrace him.

"Sit down and I'll make you some porridge," Oma says.

He obeys, sitting down carefully at the table, as if not to touch a tender spot. He watches them with bloodshot eyes. Frieda sits on one side of him and takes his hand, Mutti on the other.

"They made me stand for hours every day, hour after hour, and they just went on with their business like I was a stick of furniture. Because I said the store was worth one hundred thousand marks. Isn't it worth one hundred thousand marks?" He blinks at Oma.

"Of course it is," she says, stirring the pot of porridge. "A couple of years ago it would've been worth more."

His hand is cold in Frieda's.

"They wouldn't let me sit down. I had to beg for water. One of the men who worked there ... he punched me whenever he went by. *Here*." He put his arm over his stomach. "They said Jews inflate prices so they can get more money for their property. They said ... they said Rheinhardt would pay me what they felt the store was worth. Ten thousand marks."

Oma stops stirring the pot and looks at him. The pause expands in the room until she says, "He's buying the store for ten thousand marks?"

His head droops forward, landing in his hand. "They said they would keep me there until I signed the documents. Or until Wolfie came into the station."

Wolfie? Frieda cringes. At least Wolfie is safe. *For now.*

"And then they showed me the basket you brought in. They let me have a bite of cheese, and all I could do was weep, I missed you all so much." He closes his eyes. "So I signed. The store belongs to Rheinhardt now. It's all legal."

## January 1938

The Eisenbaums must move again. Herr and Frau Rheinhardt now own the store, so the family has no business living in the back. Frau Rheinhardt says they plan to restore the workroom to its former size. Frieda can see the woman can't bear the sight of them. Perhaps there's a spark of a guilty conscience in there somewhere, although it will never find its way to the light.

The family finds a small cold-water apartment in a rundown building in the suburb of Friedenau, literally, the "meadow of peace," where Leopold's family has lived for the past few months. Other dispossessed Jews have moved into this working-class district infested with rats and cockroaches. A Gothic-style synagogue sits like a reproach on a nearby corner. Frieda can barely look at it. The only good thing about the place is that Wolfie can move back with them.

Oma has taken her ancient sewing machine with her, the one she used decades before they bought the industrial ones for the store, which of course had to be left behind. She concealed some of the white cotton fabric from the workroom in a suitcase beneath her clothes when they left. In the new apartment, she sets the machine on a small table near the bed she shares with Luise and begins to sew new underwear. When Frieda isn't out working, she helps Oma and Vati cut patterns on the kitchen table.

Once they have a small supply of underpants and vests, Vati and Wolfie fold them into rucksacks, which they throw on their backs. Together, they trudge out to visit outlying areas of the city where there are few stores and such merchandise is hard to come by. They spend the winter peddling their wares door to door, returning each evening haggard and half-frozen with barely enough money to buy food for the family. After a nap, Wolfie goes out for the night, still supplementing their income with his winnings at cards.

Leopold once again asks Frieda to marry him. Doesn't she want to be with him? he asks. Doesn't she love him? And she does, but not the way he loves her. Not the way she loves her family. It is a flaw in her, she knows, an empty place in her heart that should be filled with joy. She has tried to fill it with her medical career, all the knowledge and wisdom she can glean from her books and her teachers.

Before his family moved to cramped quarters, Leopold brought her to their apartment one afternoon when everyone had gone out. He presented her with an amethyst ring, the tiny stones arranged in a pretty flower. His family would be leaving soon and he with them, but he said this token of love would bind them while they were apart. She felt very tender toward him then, especially with the prospect of his departure, and they made love in his bed. It was the first time they had been intimate, and what surprised her the most was the joylessness. Despite her affection for Leopold, she couldn't keep Hans Brenner's shadow from passing between them. Yet for a brief interlude, she forgot about the wretched world outside and thought, *This must be happiness.*

Then why has that empty space in her heart not been filled with ecstasy? It is a lacuna she cannot explain, a defect when her heart was forming in her mother's uterus, maybe the flaw in her mother transplanting itself into her body and leaving a hole where emotion should live.

The Sussmans finally have all their papers in order and are only waiting for their American quota. After months of anxiety, their number finally comes up and they are allowed to leave for America. They are packing when Herr Sussman suffers a heart attack. It is all the stress, his doctor says. While he languishes in the hospital, their place is quickly filled by another panic-stricken family and the Sussmans are pushed to the back of the line. Who knows when their number will come up again?

# chapter twenty-one

"Is it too early to call?" Uncle Henry asked. "I hoped you'd be up."

It was 10:00 a.m. Rebecca was nursing a cup of coffee at her kitchen table, reading the Saturday *Globe*.

"I found your Mittverda. It took some digging. I checked all the books I had on concentration camps, but it wasn't in any of the indexes at the back — that would've been too easy. Well, I'm a stubborn old geezer so I started reading. And reading, and reading. You sure you want to hear this? It's pretty disturbing."

She put down her coffee. "Go on."

"Well, I'll summarize and save you the more upsetting parts. Mittverda's not indexed because it wasn't a real camp. It was supposed to be part of Ravensbrück — that was a camp for women. The Nazis gathered sick and weak prisoners at Ravensbrück and told them they were going to a sub-camp for young people nearby called Mittverda, where life would be easier. They actually called it *Schonungslager Mittverda,* which translates into 'indulgence camp Mittverda.' The Nazis were clever. They knew they'd have less resistance this way. Then they loaded the prisoners onto a truck and drove them a short distance to where they'd built a gas chamber. It only took a half-hour or so for the trucks to come back empty, except for the clothes of the dead inmates. Pretty soon the other prisoners realized what was going on. Mittverda was a code name for the gas chamber."

Rebecca pictured the old woman's face in the yard, thin and scared. *Mittverda says to poison me.* What had Birdie suffered?

"Where was Ravensbrück?" Rebecca asked.

"About fifty miles north of Berlin. The only camp the Nazis built specifically for women. It was one of the bad ones. But see, people would've believed them about the youth camp. There were other sub-camps, so at the beginning there was no reason to suspect."

Uncle Henry rarely got worked up about anything, but his voice had taken on a higher pitch. "What kind of animal tells prisoners headed for the gas chamber they're going to a special place where they'll be safe? I thought I'd read it all. This takes the cake."

"I'm sorry I asked you to do this. It sounds gruesome."

"No, no. I learned something. I'm a history teacher, and I should know the details of what happened. That's how you get to understand. What good is it if I can list all the events of the Second World War, the dates, the generals' names? That may make a neat and tidy high school exam, but to really understand history, you have to know what happened to people. And if it upsets me, well, that means I'm really getting into it. Or maybe it's like your dad says, I'm a big bore and my life *is* that dull."

Rebecca smiled.

"So, what does my niece with the exciting life have planned for today?"

"Your niece leads the most unexciting life imaginable. Otherwise she wouldn't be going to a fencing tournament this afternoon."

"A what?"

Rebecca walked past the round field of brown grass in the centre of King's College Circle where young men were kicking around a soccer ball. North toward the Soldiers' Tower, a memorial to those who had perished in the Great War. Before people could comprehend there would be a greater war to rival it. How many men like those playing soccer now had been killed before their lives began?

Hart House stretched along the other side of the tower, a handsome neo-Gothic structure in limestone donated by the Massey family, who had made their fortune manufacturing farm equipment. On one of the cement steps leading up to the ponderous wooden doors, Erich Sentry stood smoking. His brown hair was mussed from the wind. He looked accustomed to standing around with a cigarette in his hand. She didn't know a lot of doctors who smoked.

"Waiting long?" she asked, stepping up the stairs.

"Got here early so I'd have time." He lifted his hand with the cigarette, watching her with eyes narrowed from the smoke. "What, no reprimand from the doctor?"

"You're an adult."

He looked off toward the soccer players. "He's very hard to please."

"Your father?" He was nervous. "You're not competing today."

"I'm always competing. With real doctors. You know, the kind who treat live people."

"It's not what he thinks that's important. It's what you think."

"In that case I'm in real trouble." He flicked an ash into the air.

"Have they told you the results of the autopsy?" she asked.

"Sub-arachnoid hemorrhage from a fractured skull."

"I'm sorry. How well did you know her?"

He took a drag on his cigarette. "She was my crazy aunt. The only other relative I ever had."

"Aunt? Not cousin?"

He squinted at her. "Women thirty-five years older than you are automatically aunts. My first vague memory of her is when she had her breakdown. I was four. It happened while she was looking after me."

"Looking *after* you?" Rebecca echoed in disbelief.

"She wasn't always like that. I don't remember, but my parents talked to me about her sometimes. And there's a picture of her with me on her lap. She was beautiful. It scares the hell out of me, what happened to her. So while she was still okay, she took care of me when my parents worked. The day it happened, all I remember is her sitting staring at the floor like a statue. There was no bomb going off. Just silence. Like some monster had swooped down and sucked her soul out of her body. I remember crying my eyes out because I was hungry and scared. My aunt had disappeared inside this statue that wouldn't talk to me or move."

"What happened to her then?"

"My parents tried to find places for her to live. Institutions. It never worked. She hated every place, and none of them could deal with her. She'd go on her meds, seem to get better, then insist on leaving. Then, of course, once she got out, she'd go off the meds and be back to square one. Every now and then, my parents would bring her to the house, see if she could live with us. She'd be okay for a week, then she'd wander off and they'd have to get the police to look for her."

"Must've been a terrible burden on your parents."

"They didn't complain. My father loved her. And you know, I didn't expect it to affect me. But I feel it ..." He made a fist with his free hand and hit it against his chest.

She knew that feeling. "It's natural. You're in mourning."

He put out his cigarette and opened the massive oak door of Hart House, standing aside for her to enter. "Not a word to my father."

The time-worn stone stairs took them down to the basement. Their running shoes made no sound along the linoleum of the long hallway. She felt closer to Erich, now that he had confided in her. Maybe they could be friends after all.

"You know, when I was an undergrad," she said, trying to keep the dialogue going, "women weren't allowed in Hart House for sports. We didn't mind — it was a musty old place, even then. The university felt guilty and built us the Benson Building. It was spanking new when I took fencing there." She didn't say so, but from the looks of the cement block walls of the dingy basement, the men were moving out of Hart House just in time. And ironically starting in the Benson Building. She looked sideways at Erich. He made eye contact with her, but distractedly, with no feigned interest in her undergrad days. They strolled toward the subdued clamour of a crowd.

She followed him into the *salle* — the routine use of French in fencing lent the sport a cachet that had always given her guilty pleasure at the snobbery. The referee was called the president and, in keeping with the lofty title, wore a suit and tie.

Three fencing bouts were progressing at the same time, each with their coterie of hangers-on seated in the first few rows of the bleachers. Everyone's attention was fixed on the fencers, old-world debonair in their white padded jackets and breeches, with wire mesh masks to protect their faces. Pockets of spectators sat scattered higher up. Along the sidelines of each bout stood fencers-in-waiting, also in white uniforms, their faces intent on the action. A section of bleachers was taken up by the storage of carelessly deposited winter jackets, briefcases, and gear bags. Three blue-lettered signs were displayed on the highest seats at the back: University of Toronto, Queen's University, and University of Western Ontario.

Erich began to lead Rebecca along the perimeter of the wooden floor to one of the strips where a bout was taking place. The room echoed with the clashing of steel. Two fencers assailed each other with swords on a regulation *piste,* a rectangle of floor mapped out with tape that defined the limits of the bout. The elder Sentry, in navy sweatpants and jacket, stood at the side, arms across his chest, engrossed in the duel. On either side of him a young fencer, dressed all in white, had planted himself in the same posture with the same absorption on his face. Though shorter than his students, Sentry stood out. He had a presence, a rare intensity in his eyes below the mass of dark, greying hair that appeared to rise from the bounds of a haphazard morning brush. Despite the energy he exuded, Rebecca noted the strong shoulders were rounded with a fatigue the students wouldn't know for decades. The young men leaned toward him, listening while he spoke. Yes, she could see why he continued to coach past what was probably retirement age.

She had always found it difficult to follow a bout when others were fencing. In foil, unlike saber, a hit only counted if delivered on the torso. Yet each time a foil touched the opponent, the president would shout, "*Halte!*" The judges, positioned behind each fencer, notified the president of every legitimate hit. Most often the hit didn't count because it was on a leg or an arm, but the action went by so quickly, Rebecca barely saw them. It was all very civilized, but hardly a spectator sport, she thought.

"Good hit!" Sentry called out. "Keep it up!"

Erich hung back, several yards away from his father, watching the bout. Finally one of the fencers delivered a fifth hit on his opponent, the bell rang, and the bout was over. Will Sentry turned a moment and spied his son. He smiled broadly, strolling over to embrace him and shake hands with Rebecca.

"You're just in time. It's the quarter-finals." He gestured to the young men to approach. "Laszlo! Pawel! This is my son, Dr. Erich Sentry, and his friend, Dr. Rebecca Temple."

Erich looked at her sideways, embarrassed. She wondered if his father always introduced him as Dr. Erich Sentry.

They all nodded politely at each other. "Laszlo is up next, then Pawel. They've done very well today. Maybe they'll take home some medals." He beamed at them with pride.

"Good luck," Erich said, his face blank.

"Vlad!" Sentry motioned a reprimand to a young man talking to friends. To Rebecca he said, "I don't let them spend time between matches fooling around. They should be watching the next opponent to learn his idiosyncrasies. Something they can use when their turn comes."

"Sorry, Maestro!"

Vlad, tall and blond, took Laszlo's place beside
Sentry. Laszlo, a wiry young man with neatly trimmed
brown hair, stepped onto the *piste* facing his opponent
from the Queen's team. They saluted each other, a gallant
gesture Rebecca remembered with fondness. Each fencer
stood with his mask in his left hand, sword-arm
extended, the point of the weapon several inches from
the ground. The sword was raised gracefully till the
guard was chin level, the blade pointing up. A pause,
then the sword swept down again on an angle. The
whole thing took a few seconds. Salute the opponent,
then the president and judges, and the coach. So civilized.
One could almost forget it was a sport derived from
combat, a sport in which people tried to kill each other,
metaphorically. Finally each fencer drew his mask over
his head, starting with the chin.

The president said, "*Prêts? En garde! Allez!*"

Each fencer stood with feet at right angles, knees
slightly bent. One shoulder pointed toward the opponent, sword raised; the unarmed hand lifted behind the
head in a fluid arch for balance. The body turned sideways to the opponent to offer less surface area to hit.

Laszlo extended his sword and lunged at his
opponent, who parried and began his own return
thrust. They took turns lunging at each other. After a
few minutes the Queen's opponent scored a hit on
Laszlo. After the third hit by each player, they
changed sides. A momentary pause in the action.

Enough time for Rebecca to look up and spot a
figure in the auditorium entrance that astonished her.
Imposing in a calf-length grey cashmere coat, Dr.
Mustafa Salim, square-jawed, his dark eyes grim. He
stood searching the room as Erich had stood and
searched it moments before. And like Erich, his eyes
stopped on Will Sentry.

# chapter twenty-two

**March 15, 1938**

"Don't tell them I'm a doctor," Frieda murmurs to Hanni as they hurry along the crowded street, still blocks from the British Embassy.

"Why ever not? If I were going to hire a maid, I'd rather get someone who knew something. If they pick me they'll get a strong worker, but I need to be fed. I wish we'd stopped at that bakery back there. I'm starving."

"Didn't you have breakfast?"

Hanni shrugs.

Frieda imagines they look a strange pair marching together along the sidewalk; Hanni, a young Amazon, tall and athletically thin, her curly dark hair cut chin length. Frieda, prettier and daintier in her beret, is a half-foot shorter and has to take two steps for every one of Hanni's.

They slow down as they pass the newsstands. Heavy black headlines in all the papers shout, "*Anschluss!*

Victory in Austria!" German soldiers have crossed the border after the Austrian chancellor decided to hold a plebiscite about union with Germany. Photos show Austrians cheering as the *Wehrmacht* rides by on their horses. Women throwing flowers, throwing kisses. Leopold had shaken his head with a profound fatigue that evening as they listened to the radio broadcasts. The Austrian chancellor should've known Hitler would never take that chance, Leopold said. "How could Hitler trust a free vote where Nazis weren't in control of the polling booths?" Now Austria is part of the Reich.

Frieda comes to a halt at a photo on one of the front pages: grinning Nazi soldiers, their guns holstered, lean casually over a row of men and women on their knees scrubbing the sidewalk, while in the background civilians stand smiling. The caption reads, "Jews clean Vienna streets."

Two men are buying papers nearby. Frieda overhears one of them exclaim with excitement, "Austria! And not a shot fired!"

Hanni pulls on Frieda's arm and they continue on their way. A couple behind them discusses the new addition to their country. "The Austrians know which side their bread is buttered on," the woman is saying. "Vienna should be cheaper this year," says the man. "And the Viennese not so high and mighty."

Frieda is so occupied by the conversation that she is startled by the sudden roar of engines beside them. From nowhere two policemen on motorbikes jump the sidewalk and cut in front of the path of two men who are walking ahead of them.

"Papers!" shouts one of the policemen.

The two men look like ordinary businessmen in their wool coats and felt hats, carrying the requisite briefcases. Jews, Frieda assumes from their terrified faces. She pulls Hanni away, crossing the street while the men are ordered to open their briefcases.

The women continue on their way to the embassy, startled again by the sudden thunder of the two motorcycles winding down the street ahead of them; one of the unlucky Jewish men occupies the sidecar of one of the police vehicles.

When Frieda and Hanni turn a corner, they are confronted by a long, irregular line of women snaking three blocks all the way to the door of the embassy. Britain has made the humanitarian gesture of allowing Jewish women to enter the country to work as housemaids.

"Every Jewish girl in Berlin must be here," Hanni mutters taking her place in line. "It'll take hours."

So many Jews want to leave Germany that every civilized country in the world has tightened its immigration policy to keep them out. Frieda has tired of reading the German papers that revel in the negative responses from the countries in Western Europe, Central and South America, Canada, Australia. The English don't want to anger the Arabs so they strictly control immigration to British-held Palestine. Frieda knows from the Sussmans' frustrating efforts that the United States has stringent quotas for Jews and requires guarantees from an American citizen, usually a relative, willing to sign papers agreeing to support the immigrant. Since Herr Sussman's heart attack, they have lost their place in line and must wait again.

Frieda and Vati have already stood in line at the Argentine embassy to fill out forms. Mutti's brother, cousin Greta's father, has written several times comparing Buenos Aires to Paris. They are adjusting there, he writes, and urges Mutti to join them. The Eisenbaums might have a chance in Argentina, since they already have relatives who settled there. Frieda and Vati have also spent days, weeks, standing in line for Brazil, Venezuela, Australia, and Canada. She painstakingly fills out the forms on the typewriter on their kitchen table but, like Wolfie, she pictures the office clerks pitching the precious papers into the garbage as soon as they come in.

She folds her arms across her chest for warmth and resigns herself to a long wait. The air is still cold in March but not frigid like it would have been a month earlier.

"Save my place," Hanni says. "I'm going to run back to that bakery."

Before Frieda can respond, Hanni disappears into the crowd that has already formed behind them. Where she gets her appetite from Frieda doesn't know. Was *she* as hungry at nineteen? Well, the line isn't moving very fast.

Twenty minutes later, Hanni returns carrying a paper cone. She strolls right by Frieda, who is overshadowed by the taller women around her.

"Hanni!" she shouts.

The girl turns at her name and steps into the line. "I got you some *Abfall*," she says, handing Frieda the cone.

Because people are so poor these days, bakeries have begun to sell leftover crumbs from bread and cake trays. She has seen the clerks twist a sheet of white paper into a glass for support and tap the metal tray, shaking the crumbs into a cone that sells for ten *pfennig*.

"That's very nice of you," Frieda says, hoping Hanni had enough money to treat herself to a pastry.

After a few licks of the crumbs on top — donut pieces, some grated nuts — Frieda feels Hanni watching her sideways. "I'm not very hungry," she says, handing the cone back to Hanni. "You have it."

"Well, if you're not hungry," says Hanni, shrugging. She takes the cone and sticks her tongue down to dislodge the assorted mixture. "Hmm," she says, her head on an angle. "Shaved chocolate and a bit of rye bread, I think."

The line moves very slowly toward the embassy. Girls nearby who were chattering earlier are quiet now, hugging themselves for warmth. A small Asian man in a well-cut black coat and hat has approached some girls behind them. He is talking to them in a voice too low for Frieda to hear. In a few minutes he steps toward Hanni. He bows and smiles at them with yellow teeth. Frieda stiffens as he looks Hanni over with approval.

"Good morning, young ladies," he says in a heavy accent, his mouth struggling with the German syllables. "Perhaps you tired waiting in line to leave country. I represent agency seek for lovely ladies like you. Interesting work in China. Many cities, you choose. We make necessary arrangements — you no concern for passport or transport. You have lodging when arrive. Could be out Germany tomorrow." He smiles with prominent teeth, his eyes drinking in Hanni. "My car there." He points to the corner.

"Could our families come too?" Hanni asks.

The little man shrugs noncommittally.

Frieda loops her arm through Hanni's and interjects in a harsh voice, "We're not interested."

The man's smile vanishes and he moves down the line.

"Why did you say that?" Hanni asks, watching the man leave. "I'd love to see China."

"How much do you think you'd see from a brothel?"

Hanni's brown eyes go large and blink. "You think …"

They both turn and, after a moment, watch him escort a pretty young woman away from the line, across the street, presumably to a waiting car. The woman walks with her eyes lowered, perhaps embarrassed, but resigned.

Frieda takes a deep sigh. "If you want to go to China, go stand at the embassy. I hear they're letting Jews into Shanghai without a visa."

"So why are we standing *here*?"

"We can't afford the tickets. The fare's a fortune. And there was fighting there, but it's calmed down now." Frieda pulls her arm out of Hanni's and hugs herself for warmth. "Besides, I can't imagine going to China. It's so far. It's so foreign. It would be like going to the moon."

Once they get into the building, they must fill out a form and drop it into a deep box on top of all the others. Frieda pictures an English butler lifting each sheet out with an immaculate gloved hand and dropping it into a fire. They never hear from the embassy one way or the other. Yet another silence.

In April the government sends Jewish families forms on which they must list all their valuables. After dinner that night, instead of scouring through the books on Ecuador, Peru, and South Africa, less appealing countries but ones they haven't tried yet, Vati begins to write down the articles on a piece of paper, starting with their silver candlesticks and cutlery.

"There's only one reason why they'd need a list like that," Wolfie says, putting on his jacket to go out.

Vati keeps writing without looking up. "Of course. But we have no choice."

Wolfie sneers. "Soon the swine will come here and collect it all. You'd be better off selling it — at least you'd get some money for it."

"I have to put down something. We'll hide what we can. But each of us must hand over something. We don't want to give them an excuse to search the apartment."

Frieda sees Mutti place her hand over the ring on her finger, next to her wedding band.

"Don't put down my ring," Wolfie says. "I'm going to sell it."

Frieda remembers the gold ring engraved with his initials that her parents presented him when he was sixteen.

Wolfie slams the door behind him. Frieda turns the amethyst ring on her finger round and round. Leopold gave it to her when he thought his family was leaving for America.

"Don't put down my amethyst ring either," she says to Vati.

Without looking up he says, "I'll put down the amber one." Her parents' gift when she was sixteen.

Within a month policemen come to the door armed with the lists that the families themselves have filled out. Government-sanctioned theft, Frieda knows, but Jews are not going to risk their lives by making a fuss about silverware or jewellery. She doesn't know what Wolfie did with his ring, but she has hidden hers in a drawer among her underwear.

One morning, Luise disappears. Oma shrieks her name into every corner of the tiny apartment and searches under the beds. In all the commotion, Frieda hears a timid tap at the front door and opens it.

Frau Thaler, their elderly neighbour down the hall, is smiling sheepishly at them, while Luise stands beside her, holding her hand. Luise's other hand is engaged in stuffing a pancake into her mouth.

"I'm sorry, Frau Eisenbaum," the woman says to Oma, who stands with her lips firm in anger and relief. "But she came to my door when I was bringing in the milk."

Milk is no longer delivered to Jewish households. They must buy it on the black market at inflated prices, hence they have very little of it.

"I didn't think there was any harm giving her some. She drank it down so fast, dear girl." Frau Thaler wears a frumpy brown dress beneath a flowered apron tied around her stout waist. She turns adoring eyes at Luise.

"She's such a sweet girl. I'm happy for the company. I'm all alone, you know. My poor Gerhard died three years ago and we had no children."

When Luise starts licking her fingers, Frau Thaler brings out a handkerchief from her apron pocket. "There, dear, you can wipe your hands with that."

"It's very kind of you," Oma begins, "but she's ..."

Frieda holds her breath. The neighbour must see what Luise is, but Oma must not put it into words that can be repeated, even unintentionally. The Gestapo has informers everywhere.

"The Lord Jesus loves all his children, Frau Eisenbaum," says the neighbour. "She's welcome to come over whenever she likes. Send her over for breakfast in the morning. It'll give me someone to cook for."

During the summer Frieda is asked to fill in periodically for a physician who works at the Jewish hospital. She remembers him as a sought-after doctor with a busy practice. Now he ekes out a living tending to Jewish patients who have little means of paying him after being forced out of their occupations and businesses. Even he must take time off once a week or so, and Frieda has been recommended by Herr Doktor Kochmann. The senior physician pays her from his earnings, a meagre amount, with apologies.

The government has even decreed that Jews can no longer be travelling salesmen, so Vati and Wolfie must stop their selling jaunts in the suburbs. Oma has taken in alterations for Jews whose bodies are shrinking and who are still vain enough to want their clothes to fit. She shares the work with Vati, who otherwise mopes around the apartment, afraid to go out. Sometimes Frieda sees him sitting in a chair, staring at nothing.

A week doesn't go by without a decree issued from the government. In July, the edict comes down that all Jews must carry identity cards with their photos and fingerprints. Along with all the other Jews in Germany, the Eisenbaums must troop to their local police precinct and get fingerprinted. They decide to go individually or in pairs; in case one of them is "detained," at least the others will be safe. Vati goes with Mutti one morning.

"It is humiliating," he says, "but there seems to be no danger."

The next day, Oma escorts Luise with explicit instructions for her not to open her mouth. Frieda and Wolfie go separately at different times.

In the station Frieda watches the heavy, middle-aged policeman place her left index finger carefully into the ink pad then press the black tip onto her identity card. In a daze, she feels his cool, business-like hand repeat the process with her right index finger. Without looking at her, he wipes the black ink off her fingers with a cloth quite delicately, almost apologetically.

In August, the Nazi government outdoes itself: it issues a decree that all Jewish males must add the name "Israel" to their names, and all Jewish females "Sara." These new middle names must go on the new identity cards. The first time she sees "Frederika Sara Eisenbaum" on her new card, it is a shock. The names must also be included in signatures. When Frieda writes out a prescription she must remember to sign it with her new middle name. She is enraged that the government revels in its humiliation of the Jewish population even after it has stripped them of everything they owned and the means by which they might earn enough to live like human beings.

One evening everyone has gone to sleep, Luise snoring softly in the bed she shares with Oma. Nearby Frieda shifts restlessly on her cot. Maybe she should take something, but barbiturates are costly and she is saving the few she has for a serious case of nerves. She has no doubt she will need them.

She hears a soft rustling of fabric and sees Oma's shadow approaching in the dark. "Are you awake?" Oma asks.

Frieda pushes herself up on one elbow. "What's wrong?"

Oma lowers herself carefully to sit on the edge of the cot. "I have to ask you to do something for me, Frieda. It's very important."

The bed creaks as Luise turns over.

"What is it?"

"I want you to get me some pills. Enough to put me to sleep."

Frieda swallows hard. Is she really awake? Can she possibly have heard right? "I have some here if you can't sleep."

"You know what I mean. For when I can't go on. Enough pills to make me sleep for good."

Frieda feels her stomach sinking. What is she supposed to say: Don't be silly, Oma, everything will be all right? She knows it won't be all right, ever again.

She finds her grandmother's hand in the dark. It's soft but cold as she holds it in her own. "Oma." She doesn't know what to say. She doesn't want to lose her grandmother, who has always been the strong one in the family. "Is this really what you want?"

Frieda feels a tear drop on her hand. She pulls her grandmother into her arms.

Now that Austria has joined the Reich, Hitler has turned his gaze further afield, toward the Sudetenland, an area in Czechoslovakia where the people speak German. Leopold says that the region has mountains, and so is a natural defence for Czechoslovakia. But if Hitler takes it ... Every day Frieda reads the papers and cringes at the enraged voice on the radio as Hitler rails against the Versailles Treaty: this treacherous piece of paper created Czechoslovakia at the end of the war and tore the Sudeten Germans from the bosom of their rightful country. Frieda notices with alarm headlines like, "Pregnant Sudeten mother pushed off bicycle by Czech subhuman in Ostrava!" Or, "How long must our patient German brethren yield to such humiliating atrocities?"

By September, Hitler is making speeches on the radio about going to war over the Sudetenland to save the German population there: "The German people, united as one behind their Leader, can wait no longer ..."

There's a heightened anxiety in the air, not just among Jews. Frieda sees it in the faces of people on the street during the much publicized conference when the leaders of France, England, and Italy meet with Hitler in Munich to try to avoid war. If it wasn't clear before, it is now — Hitler must have Czechoslovakia; even if it means igniting a world war, he will not back down. Are France and England willing to go to war over a strip of land in an insignificant country like Czechoslovakia? In one of Leopold's *New York Times*, Frieda reads that British Prime Minister Neville Chamberlain calls the crisis "a quarrel in a faraway country between people of whom we know nothing."

The Eisenbaums have no papers yet, and Frieda knows imminent war will make it even harder to acquire them. Embassies, even borders, will be closed and it will be impossible to leave.

During the conference, Goering speaks at the Nuremburg Party rally, which is broadcast live. Frieda and Vati sit staring at the radio while Oma stitches the hem of a skirt that lies in a heap on her lap.

"A petty segment of Europe is harassing the human race …"

Czechoslovakia was the most recent enemy of the Reich. The Nazis are so transparent; why can't people see?

"This miserable pygmy race is oppressing a cultural people and behind it is Moscow and the eternal mask of the Jew devil."

"Why do you listen to this crap?" Wolfie jumps up and heads for the door.

"We have to know what's going on," Vati says quietly, without conviction.

Everyone in Germany holds their breath, Jew and Gentile alike. On a crowded bus, Frieda is standing over two women when she overhears one of them whisper to her companion, "I don't want my son going to fight for Czechoslovakia."

When the conference ends, the news is dismal. At least it's dismal for the Jews, though good for everyone else. Aren't all things relative these days? Hitler has won back the Sudetenland and in exchange has promised peace. He never wanted war, he says, only what rightly belonged to Germany. All the papers carry photos of Chamberlain, with his little pencil moustache, waving a sheet of paper in the air and proclaiming, "Peace in our time!"

"He didn't have the backbone to stand up to Hitler," Wolfie says, slapping the newspaper down on the table. "So much for England coming to save us. They've just shown him they're weak and can be pushed around. He's not going to stop with the Sudetenland."

**November 7, 1938**

While Frieda is stitching up a young boy's knee at the Jewish hospital, a nurse sticks her head in the doorway. "A German diplomat was shot in Paris. By a Jew."

"Why did he do it?" Frieda asks.

"His parents were on that transport to Poland in October. He was angry."

Frieda blanches. A few weeks ago, fifteen thousand Polish-born Jews who lived in Germany were taken from their homes at dawn and pushed into boxcars heading toward the Polish border. Some lived in Germany for decades; their children were born here. None of that mattered; now they are "Polish citizens." The Eisenbaums should have been on that transport, but Vati's Iron Cross saved them one more time.

"Stupid young pup," the nurse continues. "If the diplomat dies, *we'll* pay for it." She continues down the hall, spreading the news.

For the next two days, the condition of the young diplomat, Ernst Vom Rath, occupies the headlines. While he lies near death, the Nazis rub their hands: the world conspiracy of Jews has clearly shown its hand. Something must be done to punish them. All the Jews in Berlin are whispering among themselves, "If only he doesn't die."

Then, on the evening of November 9, regular radio programming is interrupted. "After a brave struggle, Ernst Vom Rath, third secretary in the German Embassy in Paris, has succumbed to his injuries. The Jew, Herschel Grynszpan, has been arrested and charged with his murder."

When Frieda looks up, Oma's stitching lies in her lap. "God help us all," she says.

Herr Doktor Kochmann, Hans Brenner, Ilse Remke, and Frieda are standing around a woman screaming in childbirth. They wear the usual white coats, except for Frieda, who wears one in bright yellow.

"This is killing me!" the woman cries. "Can't you give me something for the pain?"

Brenner says, "You must push the baby out, Luise, then we can give you something for the pain."

Frieda assumes it's another Luise, but when she looks down at the patient's face, it's her sister. Luise screams out again and Ilse slaps her on the side of the head. The slap is so loud it sounds like glass breaking.

Frieda startles awake. Oma is standing at the window in her nightdress; Luise is sitting up in bed, her eyes large with fear. Frieda hears noises outside and jumps from her cot to look out the window. Is she still dreaming? A chest of drawers is being thrown out the window of a nearby apartment. Then a stuffed chair, brown cushions flying. Then an accordion that clanks out a strident death rattle as it drops. Lamps, tables, books all plunge into the courtyard with a horrifying clatter.

Frieda runs into her parents' bedroom. Vati is standing in his nightshirt by the window while Mutti cowers in bed. Voices of men laugh and shriek all around outside, upstairs, downstairs. The shattering sound of china breaking, lots of china.

Then it's their turn: fists begin to hammer at their door. Incessant fists, then boots.

Vati, his face flooded with terror, looks at Frieda, then steps slowly toward the front door. He puts his hand out to unlock it, turns to look at Frieda once more, as if she is his last comfort, then undoes the latch.

The door flies open as a group of men in civilian dress storm in with axes and hammers, their faces contorted with hatred. Are they really men? Are they human?

One of them, a tall young man with clipped blond hair, lashes out in his rage and hits Vati in the face, knocking him to the floor. Frieda rushes to his side as the fiends run to destroy everything in their path. They pull the dishes from the small cabinet in the kitchen and throw them to the floor in a frenzy of destruction.

Frieda dabs at Vati's bleeding nose with her handkerchief, helps him sit up amid the deafening noise of their lives being reduced to rubble. Mutti runs from the bedroom in her nightdress and crouches near Vati. Oma leads Luise toward them.

In an abrupt moment of panic Frieda remembers her medical bag — it's sitting near her cot in the bedroom.

As she steps away from her family, Oma grabs her arm. "No," she says, but Frieda pulls away and creeps to their bedroom, where the men are slashing away with their axes and knives at the featherbeds and mirrors. Feathers fly everywhere. As she watches, one of the men picks up the black medical bag and lifts out the stethoscope.

"Please," she says.

He looks up, eyes puffy with rage. He steps toward her, lips curling at an ugly angle. She steps back.

"Those are medical instruments," she says. "I can help people with them."

"Look, Heinz," says the young man with the cruel lips. "This Jewish cow thinks she can help people."

Another man stops his rampage through the dresser drawers for an instant. "Shit on her," says the other man. "Just do what you're supposed to."

The first man picks up a hammer, glowers at her with loathing in his eyes. She thinks she's going to die. Maybe it would be better than this. Instead, he throws the stethoscope down on a night table they've neglected to pitch out the window and smashes down hard with the hammer: her beloved instrument is in pieces. Her audioscope is next, then the blood pressure cuff. All destroyed.

She stumbles back to her family in time to hear one of the men bark an order at Vati to get dressed.

"You're making a mistake," Vati says quietly. "I have the Iron Cross."

One of the men slaps him across the face, his eyes full of disgust. "Another Jew with the Iron Cross. How much did this one cost? It won't protect you anymore, you piece of shit."

Oma says, "Where are you taking him?" The men pay her no attention as they continue to break whatever they find.

When Vati has put his clothes on, Mutti clings to him, but two of the men pull her away. They are taking him out the door.

Frieda cries out, "Vati!" He looks back at her with mournful eyes, then vanishes down the stairs. As she stands at the door, stunned, Frau Thaler opens her door a crack, then quickly closes it shut.

Once the men have gone, the family leap to the front window to see Vati being pushed into a truck filled with other men. He's holding the bloody handkerchief in his hand. The truck pulls away out of sight. Frieda is numb. Her head spins with the racing of her heart. Will she ever see her father again? They let him go the last time, but that was different. They got what they wanted from him then, the business. This time there's nothing left to give them. Only blood.

Through her shock she hears Luise wailing. Oma is too distraught to comfort her and stares out the window, tears rolling down her cheeks. Mutti is whimpering in the corner. What will they do now, Frieda thinks, when they have nothing left? Everything is gone. She looks out the window to see a hellish orange glow in the distance. Something is on fire. Their whole world is going up in flames.

# *chapter twenty-three*

S alim bent his head on a resolute angle as he made his way along the perimeter of the *salle*. Rebecca would have liked to warn Erich, now that they were on friendly terms. But warn him about what? Possible fireworks in German? The Egyptian gave her no opportunity, in any case, striding toward them swiftly, elegant waves of brown hair falling over his forehead. The coach, his attention fixed on the bout, which his fencer was losing, turned in time to find Salim towering over him. Sentry went white.

"You're early," he said, blinking away his surprise.

"I couldn't resist," Salim said, smiling with his mouth, not his eyes. "It isn't every day I can see people pretending to try to kill each other."

Sentry turned stiffly back to the bout.

"You two know each other?" Rebecca said, partly to diffuse the tension, partly out of confusion. Last week at the hotel the two men seemed to be strangers.

Salim looked at her with interest. Did he remember her? "Won't you introduce us," he said to Sentry.

"Excuse me," said the coach. "I must attend to this." Watching Laszlo struggling in the bout, Sentry pulled the two waiting fencers a few steps away and began to whisper what looked like strategy.

Erich tried to breach the lapse in civility. "I'm his son, Erich. This is Rebecca Temple."

"Did you say 'son'?" He surveyed Erich with guarded eyes. "You see, you never know about people. Your father didn't seem the type for children."

Erich stared at Salim, interested now. "How do you know my father?"

Sentry's body stayed focused on the bout, but his head inclined slightly toward this last question.

"We knew each other long ago. Then we were both young and foolish. Now we are old and foolish."

He seemed younger than Sentry, though maybe he was just better preserved. He had an energetic way of speaking and only a few grey hairs among the dark waves. A full lower lip balanced the thin upper line, which was firmly set, giving his face authority.

He turned to Rebecca, closing the subject of him and Sentry. "Have we met?" he asked her.

Erich glanced from Salim to her, appearing confused.

"Briefly," she said. "At the medical conference where you spoke."

His eyes narrowed. "Yes, of course. The pretty young doctor."

Did he remember she had seen him and Sentry quarrelling? That, at the time, he had given no hint that he knew Sentry?

The bell rang, signalling the end of the bout. Sentry turned distracted eyes to Laszlo, who was saluting his opponent. Rebecca had been too preoccupied with

Salim's arrival to follow the match. If Sentry had been equally sidetracked, Laszlo's downcast face said all they needed to know about the outcome of the bout.

Pawel turned an expectant face toward their coach, waiting for enlightenment, some strategy he could use in his upcoming match with the same opponent who had just defeated Laszlo. But Sentry had lost his focus and seemed to be struggling between the task at hand and his unwanted guest.

Salim turned toward Erich. "We should let your father carry on. Perhaps we can all go sit down and watch from a respectable distance."

Following Salim, they climbed up into the bleachers and sat down in an unoccupied row, Rebecca in the middle. When she began to wiggle out of her wool jacket, both men gave her a hand. Salim pulled his arms out of the sleeves of his coat, revealing a thick white cotton shirt, presumably Egyptian. Erich wore a black T-shirt beneath his pea jacket. Along with the jeans he looked like a teenager.

"So what is your occupation, Mr. Sentry?" Salim bent forward to ask.

Rebecca noted his wide creased forehead, the substantial but refined nose.

"I'm a pathologist."

"A physician?" Erich nodded. "*Dr.* Sentry. So the three of us are doctors. What a happy coincidence." Then he seemed satisfied to let the subject drop while the next bout began.

In short order Pawel scored a hit against Laszlo's opponent. Sentry's face relaxed a little, then he looked up and waved imperiously at them. Rebecca was mystified by the gesture, but Erich understood that his father required his presence. He excused himself and stepped down through the bleachers. Sentry pulled him aside and seemed to be giving him instructions. She could tell Erich was controlling himself, his face a mask.

"Have you and the young man known each other long?" Salim asked, glancing at her with a casual suggestiveness.

"We only met a few days ago," Rebecca said. "Under unfortunate circumstances, I'm afraid. My office is across from the Sentrys' house. I found a woman injured in their yard. I met Erich's mother then."

Salim stared at her, nodding. She couldn't help feeling he wasn't really interested, just making conversation.

"Lucky for the woman you found her. What was wrong with her?"

"She had a fractured skull. I'm afraid she died in hospital."

"I'm sorry. Did you know her?"

"I'd spoken to her before. She was a street person. They let her stay in the backyard." It wasn't her place to divulge the woman's relationship to the family.

He arched up one prominent eyebrow. "Charitable. Then how did she fracture her skull?"

"Someone hit her."

"Ghastly. I can't imagine that such a thing is common in Toronto?"

"No." She saw Erich heading back, his jaw set.

"Was she able to tell you anything before she died?" Salim asked.

"She was unconscious. But before when we spoke, what she said made no sense, so I'm not sure it would've made any difference. I think she was schizophrenic. It was always hard to tell what she meant or what she wanted."

Without speaking, Erich edged past them to sit down.

"A problem?" Salim asked politely.

"Family matters."

"We were just speaking about the woman who was killed in your yard."

"My parents' yard."

"Ah. I was just going to say it's very complicated trying to have a conversation with a schizophrenic. I come across many in my country. There's usually no rhyme or reason to them."

Rebecca winced. Now that Erich had returned, they were no longer speaking about the murder of a stranger. "That may be true," she said, "but sometimes I felt that I understood. The last time I saw her, I think she was trying to tell me something. I just can't figure out what it was. Maybe it'll come to me one day. She pushed a shopping bag into my hands and I knew she wanted me to take it. She was very frightened about something."

Salim stared at her, now engrossed in her story. "Extraordinary. What was in the bag?"

"Nothing important. Just an old doll. It's still in the trunk of my car — I forgot about it."

He shook his head morosely, as if pondering the fragility of life. They turned back to the fencing. Pawel had scored two hits against his opponent.

"Are you staying in Toronto long?" she asked.

"A little while longer." Salim watched the fencers below, pensive.

"Dr. Salim is from Egypt," she said to Erich on her other side.

"Are you here for business or pleasure?" Erich asked.

"I'm giving some talks on a pain medication my company's developing."

"From snake venom," Rebecca added.

"You went to the lecture," Erich said, nodding. "I guess there's always room for a new drug for pain. But I wouldn't know, since people are beyond pain by the time they reach me."

Salim bent forward to address Erich. "Then the corpses in your country have something in common with the impoverished people in my country: neither will get relief from the pain medications available now. Most Egyptians can't afford drugs — they barely have enough money to eat. They've learned to bear their suffering and thank Allah for it. At the free clinics for the poor, they're lucky to get Aspirin. But our company is planning to give a portion of the new drug to the poor for free, once, God willing, it's out on the market. My brother-in-law is deeply affected by the misery they suffer in our country."

"Your brother-in-law?" Rebecca said.

"Mohammed Hassan, the founder of Hassan Pharmaceuticals."

One of the sponsors of the medical conference she had attended.

"I married the boss's sister."

"Good career move," Erich said.

"Yes, I've done well," he said, smiling modestly.

"Isn't he the one involved in the peace accord with Israel?" Rebecca asked.

"As in Camp David and Jimmy Carter?" Erich said.

"Yes, he went to Camp David. He's an advisor to Anwar Sadat."

"Have you met Sadat?" she asked.

"Several times. A remarkable man. Great presence. And he's very brave pushing for peace with Israel. There are Egyptians who want to kill him for it."

"The news on TV shows people demonstrating in the streets," Rebecca said.

"There's a large group of angry people who feel Sadat has betrayed Islam. That he cares only about ancient Egypt and the pharaohs, but nothing for the poor, or for solving today's problems."

She remembered her conversation with Nesha. "Is that the Muslim Brotherhood?"

Salim observed her with interest. "You know something about my country, I see."

"Very little, I'm afraid. If he's in danger, what drives him to make peace?"

"He wants the Sinai Peninsula back, which the Israelis have promised to return. But also, he's a forward thinker. He looks toward the West. He hopes the Americans will fill the aid gap left by Britain and, more lately, Russia. He's practical. He knows the Americans can give more than the Russians."

"But there will be a price," said Erich.

"There's always a price."

"What do the Americans want in return for their support?" Erich asked.

"You should go into foreign service, doctor. Mostly they want influence. An Arab country they can trust and work through. Most Arab countries are anti-Western. To a devout Muslim, the American way of life is corrupt and immoral. The idea of accepting help from such a country is anathema."

"Is Egypt different, then?"

Salim shrugged. "Much of Egypt wants to embrace the West. Perhaps it's a carryover from British rule. The irony is that while they resented British influence, at the same time they imbibed the culture. A dominant culture seeps through one's pores, whether one wishes it to or not. The Brotherhood is extremely opposed to all outside influence. They want to turn the country into an Islamic state. It will be a struggle, of that there is no doubt." Pressing his lips together in mock distress, he said, "They're very angry with Canadians at the moment. That business of your inexperienced new prime minister — I'm sorry, I don't remember his name

— he promised to move your embassy in Israel to Jerusalem. That would give legitimacy to Israel's claim on it when the Palestinians are claiming it as their own. The Brotherhood couldn't have found Canada on the map before. Now they know where you are."

"Joe Clark," Rebecca said. "The new prime minister." She had heard him pledge to move the embassy during his campaign, but hadn't given it any thought.

The bell rang, signalling the end of the bout. Pawel had won five to four. While Sentry patted his cheek, grinning, his teammates slapped him on the back.

For the next ninety minutes, Rebecca sat flanked by her new companions, watching the final stages of the tournament. Each team was down to three players, one in foil, one in epée, and one in saber — a total of nine men left. The three fencers in each category fought each other in consecutive matches. By this point they were all tired, their faces high-coloured with exertion. After each bout, the players removed their masks and wiped their brows with the backs of their hands.

Western was leading with four bouts. U of T had won three, while Queens lagged behind with one. Tension mounted. The Western team clapped with enthusiasm every time one of theirs scored. The two other teams were more subdued. If Western won the next bout, the games were over. If U of T won and tied with Western, then there would be some last-minute calculations, according to Erich, and the winner would be determined by the total number of hits scored minus the total number of touches against. There was still hope.

Sentry was whispering in the ear of a lanky young man before sending him out on the *piste*. The two fencers saluted each other, then the officials. Everyone in the room stopped talking.

Rebecca tried to follow but missed the first three hits each fencer delivered against the other. Sentry stood rigid, one hand on a hip, his face a mask of apprehension. The Western fencer landed another hit against U of T. The score was 4–3 for Western. The next hit was crucial. The clashing of swords was the only sound in the room. Then even Rebecca saw the Western fencer's foil bend into a curve against the University of Toronto chest. The president called out "*Halte*!" and conferred with the judges to determine if the last hit was valid. There seemed to be some disagreement about who had the right of way.

Will Sentry stood among his team, arms locked against his chest, waiting.

"I don't know about you two," Salim said under his breath, "but I prefer a more straightforward game. Like cricket, or soccer, where there's no question of who's won."

"That's very British," said Rebecca. "But your accent isn't British. I've been trying to place it."

Salim smiled sideways, disarming her with his charm. "I'm a citizen of the *world*," he said, stretching out the O in "world," suggesting undreamt-of expanse. "We have a villa in Spain. Perhaps I've picked up some of their pronunciations."

After a minute, the president returned. He spoke into the microphone. "The hit against the University of Toronto is valid. The score is five to three in favour of the University of Western Ontario."

Cheers rose from the Western side of the *salle*. Some students whistled, but on the whole, the ovation was subdued compared to the excitement she imagined on the football field or hockey rink.

The official waited for silence. "I'd like to congratulate the University of Western Ontario on their win in today's tournament."

This time the whole room applauded, including the U of T team. Polite, rather than enthusiastic. The official waited.

"The score was very close. All teams were worthy opponents and played exceedingly well."

This time the U of T side cheered more eagerly.

"As you all know, this is our last fencing event in Hart House. Next semester we move to the Benson Building in the new Athletic Centre at Harbord and Spadina. The Physical Education Department would like to invite everyone to an informal reception in the lounge upstairs to bid Hart House a fond farewell. We celebrate those years and at the same time look forward to the future in a new, state-of-the-art facility. Refreshments will be served."

People stood up and started filing out of the bleachers.

"Well," said Salim. "Shall we drown our sorrows in some wine?" He was closest to the aisle and stood up.

He led them down the stairs of the bleachers, heading for the gloomy U of T team, which was gathering together its gear. Will Sentry was gesticulating a fencing move with one of his team — perhaps some correction of an error in technique — when he saw them approach.

The head with the theatrical mass of hair tilted at them. "Of course, all the preparation in the world won't help if you get jinxed," he said to the fencer, raising his voice for them to hear. "We were winning up to the quarter-finals. And then something changed. Like an evil presence." He was staring at Salim.

"That's very petulant," said Salim, blinking his eyelids down slowly. "What happened to 'It's not who wins but how you play the game'?"

Sentry's jaw fell. "*Game*! It's an *art*, not a game."

"You know what I mean. It's not the end of the world, man. Get some perspective."

Erich turned his face away from his father, hiding a smile.

Salim led their escape out of the auditorium, muttering, "Don't they have those little rubber tips on the ends of their swords?"

They joined a small crowd in the reception room, hovering around three round tables that held platters of finger sandwiches surrounded by vegetable sticks. Small slices of rye bread and pumpernickel were spread with liver pâté, semi-ripe cheese, or cream cheese. A fruit tray held chunks of melon, pineapple, and clusters of grapes.

Rebecca and Erich waited politely in line, placing a few canapés on their respective Styrofoam plates. They stood patiently at another table to retrieve some fruit. When they emerged from the crowds around the tables, Rebecca saw Salim standing off to one side busily chewing through the rich assortment of canapés and fruit he had assembled on his plate.

"You're good at this," she said, stopping beside him.

He swallowed before answering. "In my position I've been invited to a lot of these things. I've had to develop survival skills. You'd be surprised at what you can learn. For example, I know there's a coffee urn behind that cluster of people in the corner. But, alas, no wine. Perhaps you won't miss the wine, if you brought your car and have to drive home?"

"I walked," she said.

He gave her a brief nod, then looked at Erich. "Subway," said Erich.

"Then it's certainly a pity about the wine, because I took a cab."

Despite his patter, she realized he had positioned himself to face the large entryway of the room and kept it in view while chatting to them. A cheer went up when the three fencing teams entered. They all headed for the food. All but Sentry. Rebecca saw him spot Salim through the crowd. Each fixed his eyes on the other.

Salim put a half-eaten canapé back on his plate and said, "Excuse me. I'm going to find some coffee."

He headed for the reputed coffee corner, then turned abruptly to make his way toward Sentry. They both disappeared outside the room.

"Would you like me to get you some coffee?" she asked Erich.

He looked mildly surprised, but said, "Thanks."

She moved in the direction of the coffee, then veered off toward the doorway. Peeking out, she saw the two men at the end of the long hall. They were arguing. Sentry leaned aggressively toward Salim with his hands on his hips, while the taller, stately Salim raised his hands palm up, reasonable by comparison. What could these two ever have had in common? Where could they have been old friends, as Salim had implied? The noise in the lounge behind her drowned out their dialogue, keeping the distant tableau a pantomime. But Sentry's posture as he straightened up, his hands dropping to his sides, told her that Salim was mollifying him, convincing him of something.

Then Salim shrugged. Sentry folded his arms across his chest, unappeased. Nothing appeared settled, only postponed. She was curious in an abstract way, but she didn't really want to know. She sensed a darkness between them, some unholy connection in the past.

All at once Salim turned away from Sentry and marched back toward the lounge. Before she could pull away from the door, he swerved down a stairwell and disappeared. He must have been upset to leave without saying goodbye to her.

By the time she found the coffee urn, Sentry had joined his team in the lounge. She could feel his eyes on her as she made her way back to Erich, balancing two cups of coffee on their saucers.

# *chapter twenty-four*

November 1938

For the next few days, the Eisenbaums sweep away the broken shards of dishes, mirrors, windows, and lamps. Frieda and Mutti do most of the work while Oma sits down every ten minutes holding her head in her hands. Every now and then Frieda hears her whispering, "Ernst" as she rocks back and forth. Luise sits beside her on one of the salvaged kitchen chairs, her arm around Oma's shoulder.

"Poor Oma-mouse," she says. "Don't cry."

All their chairs were smashed apart, but Oma has managed to lash some legs and seats together with strips of torn fabric, so that three of them can be sat upon with care.

In the bedroom Frieda collects the shattered bits of her medical instruments. Tears slide down her cheeks as she deposits the precious debris into a paper bag.

One day when the post comes, a package is delivered for Frieda: a narrow foot-long box wrapped in brown paper with no return address. Oma and Mutti watch as she rips off the paper and opens the plain cardboard box beneath. Inside lie a stethoscope and blood pressure cuff, used, but in good condition. She unfolds the accompanying note.

> My dearest Frieda,
>
> If I had a daughter I would want her to be just like you. Sorry to hear about your instruments. Perhaps you can use these. They have served me well. I wish I had more to offer you. Even hope is not in my power to give you. Warm regards to your family.
>
> R. Kochmann

How had he managed to save them? He is obviously cleverer about hiding things than she is. She puts one instrument in each of her coat pockets. Then she goes out.

People are cleaning up everywhere. Broken glass has been swept into heaps in front of buildings. Unrecognizable pieces of wood and upholstery that used to be furniture have been moved to one side.

As she walks, the smell of burning wood drifts on the November air. Something is missing on the corner she is approaching. The rising Gothic shape of the synagogue that usually draws her eye — where is it? For the first time in her life no roof blocks the sky, the blueness of which makes her blink. Only charred walls remain. A blackened chandelier sits amid the ashes of wooden seats and Torah scrolls. This was the orange glow she saw from her window that godforsaken night. How many more across the city like this?

She continues on her way, filled with loathing. She can't get out of her mind the image of Vati being shoved into the truck, his face pale and bloody. People have started talking about transports to the east, work in labour camps. She hopes if he is taken to a camp, it will be in Germany. Is he strong enough to work?

She reaches Herr Doktor Kochmann's building and steps inside. On her way down the hall she stops. Something is wrong: the door to his office is wide open.

She creeps to the door and looks in. The desk is broken in half and books lie scattered on the floor, the wooden shelves in pieces. She hears someone moving about in the apartment behind the office where Kochmann lives with his wife. If it were the Gestapo, they would be shrieking curses and orders. She steps inside, tiptoeing to the apartment, where the door is also open.

A rustling sound is coming from down the hall; the bedroom, she thinks. She has been in the apartment only once, when she was young and visiting with Oma.

When she reaches the room, two men dressed in shabby black suits and skullcaps are bent over the bed, fastening string around two forms wrapped in rubber sheeting. She gasps as if someone has punched her in the stomach.

One of the men looks up and stops what he is doing. "Are you their daughter?"

She stares at him, numb to her feet.

"I'm sorry," he says. "You didn't know ..."

He straightens up from the bed, and she sees that the form he has been preparing is larger than the other one.

"They didn't suffer," he says, folding his hands in front of him. The stance of an undertaker. "I'm sure it was quick. And painless."

Her head is shaking; it won't stop. "Was it …? How did they …?"

"Pills." He points to a small bottle on the night table. "Believe me, they were the lucky ones. I've seen some that do it, much worse. It's better this way, at their age. They're well out of it."

The other man steps to the foot of the bed and lifts the feet of the larger body. The first man begins to put his hands beneath the shoulder area to raise it off the bed.

"Wait!" she says. "Please. Can I see him?"

The two men look at her, then at each other. The man near the top loosens the string around the head and moves to the other body. In a practised movement, they lift the smaller form off the bed and carry it out.

She steps toward the side of the bed on wobbly legs, a pounding inside her head. Touches the black rubber. Unravels the string. She pulls down the top, revealing the pale grey face, the high forehead with its scant hair, the mouth open, like every corpse. It is no longer her beloved doctor but a shell of matter that will disintegrate in a few days. Where did he go, the gentle man who cared enough about her to change the course of her life? The picture of him in Vati's store all those years ago rises before her eyes like a chimera. How unhappy she was then, working in the shop. If not for him, she would never have known anything else.

She bends down and kisses the cold forehead.


Frieda has been warned to stay away from Gestapo headquarters at Grosse Hamburgerstrasse, despite her anxiety for Vati. Two different patients have passed on cautionary tales about relatives who insisted on inquiring about missing loved ones and never came back.

At least when she is treating patients, Frieda has to focus on work and Vati is pushed to the background. But when she returns home, the apartment is full of his absence. Oma and Mutti are downcast, pecking at their food. Luise has stopped chattering, and Wolfie stays out as long as he can.

Then one day shortly after Christmas, a postcard comes from Vati.

"Thank God!" Oma cries.

They all crowd around Frieda, who holds the card in her hand.

She reads it aloud. "My dearest Karolina and family, I miss you all very much. I am working hard but you mustn't worry. Hope you are well. All my love, Ernst."

It was posted from Buchenwald. Literally, "forest of beech trees." Frieda has heard about the camp there, that it is filled with "undesirables," many of whom are never seen again. She stares at the words, trying to pry meaning from them.

"He doesn't *say* anything," Wolfie exclaims.

"He says he's *alive*," says Oma, smiling for the first time in months.

Frieda has little time to use her mentor's stethoscope and blood pressure cuff before the government decrees that all Jewish physicians are to be decertified. Their certificates have become null and void and they can no longer practise medicine. Only a small number of the most senior doctors are allowed to keep tending to the Jewish community. Frieda can no longer treat patients at the hospital but continues to go to the Jewish school for part of the day, now in the capacity of nurse. She joins all the other Jewish doctors in the country in their slide toward poverty. The Eisenbaums rely more and more on

Wolfie's winnings at cards. When he loses, they have less to eat. Luise spends more time across the hall with Frau Thaler, who happily feeds her and sometimes sends her home with extra bread or potatoes.

Since his father's heart attack, Leopold has had to take on a new job to help support the family. He has begun to sell black market cigarettes, Gauloises from France, a more lucrative income than teaching history to impoverished Jewish students. On his forays into the small cigar shops, he wears a large overcoat with deep pockets sewn on the inside, filled with packs of cigarettes.

Several times a week, Frieda stops by their apartment on her way home to check on Herr Sussman. Though physically recovered, he is depressed and has lost weight. She has learned from Leopold and takes the chance of carrying her stethoscope and blood pressure cuff in a pocket she has sewn inside her coat. If she is stopped, she will say she is trying to sell them.

Frau Sussman has served her some ersatz coffee when Leopold comes home accompanied by Hanni, both wearing large coats. They look sheepish in front of her.

When Frau Sussman leaves the table to get more cups, Frieda whispers to Leopold, "Did you take Hanni with you to sell cigarettes?"

Hanni stares daggers at her, but Leopold blushes. "She wanted to. We need the money."

"It's dangerous," Frieda whispers. "What if you get caught?"

Hanni lifts her chin. "I'm not a child. It's really not your business."

**March 1939**

One morning in March when the air is milder and Frieda thinks they might survive the winter, Hanni storms into their apartment. Her curly hair stands out around her head; her coat is open.

"Where's Wolfie?" she cries.

"What's happened?" Frieda asks, afraid to know.

"I need Wolfie!" Hanni shouts, her face swollen from tears.

He has been home barely two hours after his usual night at cards, but Wolfie rushes out, a robe thrown over his nightclothes.

She throws herself into his arms. "They've taken them away! My father and Leopold! They're gone! They just pushed them onto a truck."

Frieda's heart contracts. She backs into a chair and sits heavily.

"My father won't survive! He's too weak." She looks at Frieda. "It's *her* fault!"

"You're upset, Hanni," Wolfie mutters. "Stop it."

She pulls away from him. "I blame you!" she shouts at Frieda. "If you'd married him, if you'd thought of someone besides yourself, we'd all be out of here. He wouldn't go without you. And now he'll die because of you. We'll all die!"

Frieda is breathless at this attack. She cannot speak as Wolfie pulls Hanni away. *It's true*, Frieda thinks, *it's all true*.

She feels Oma watching her. "She's hysterical," Oma says. "Don't listen."

But Frieda can't shut out the voice in her head that repeats the words.

That week, the Nazi juggernaut rolls into Czechoslovakia, the country that Hitler said he didn't want. Unlike the citizens of Austria, the Czechs do not welcome the conquerors but mourn the loss of their country. They are pictured in the newspapers, lining the streets of Prague, weeping while tanks roll past. What would Leopold say if he were here, Frieda wonders. That maybe now, England and France must realize there is no appeasing Hitler? The Jews in Germany have known that for years.

She misses Leopold's pronouncements on the events of the day. She misses the security of having him on her arm. She misses his freckled face with the intelligent eyes observing the world behind wire-rimmed spectacles. She misses him, she misses him. She dares not think of what's happened to him, whether he'll ever come back.

She must build up her courage to visit Frau Sussman. When she arrives at the door of the apartment, she taps lightly, not to frighten them.

"It's Frieda," she says quietly to the closed door. "Please let me in." She glances down the dingy hall, hoping no one else will notice her.

Finally the door opens. Frau Sussman hovers before her, hair unclasped and lying limp to her shoulders, eyes vacant. Hanni stands in the background, angry arms crossed over her chest.

"I'm sorry if I've disturbed you," Frieda begins. "I wanted to tell you how sorry I was ..."

Frau Sussman moves away from the door without a word, but leaves it open. Frieda follows, her heart shrinking at the sight of the other's pain. She nods at Hanni, who looks away without acknowledging her. She expected that. Frau Sussman begins mechanically to put the kettle on and to take out teacups and saucers.

"It isn't necessary," Frieda says. "I don't want to bother you."

"It gives me something to do," Frau Sussman says, not looking at her.

Hanni disappears into another room. The two women sit in the too-quiet apartment sipping at their teacups, neither saying anything that matters to them. They mumble platitudes about Czechoslovakia rather than mention the two men close to their hearts. It is a safer topic. Finally Frieda ventures into that minefield.

"I wonder what Leopold would say about Czechoslovakia?" she says.

Frau Sussman glares at her, and Frieda is sorry she has said his name.

But then the older woman gazes away into the distance, her eyes misting over. "He had an opinion on everything, didn't he?"

Frieda notices she has used the past tense.

The life of the Eisenbaums becomes even more circumscribed. It's not that they care to go swimming or to visit a café, or museum, or the zoo like normal people. They are too busy trying to feed themselves to remember what it was like to live a civilized life. Jews are only allowed to shop for one hour at the end of the day when there is little left in the shops worth buying. That's just as well, thinks Frieda on her excursion to the greengrocer, since they have little money to spend. The stores have to be within reasonable walking distance because Jews are no longer allowed to take public transportation. No more S-Bahns or streetcars for her. She never thought she'd be nostalgic for the tram. Some former patients beg her to come when a loved one gets sick. They give her what they can in payment, sometimes a meal shared with the family.

One day she gets tired of their meagre diet and tries to buy some cheese in a store. Another customer, a stout woman in a kerchief, inspects her and announces to everyone who can hear that Jews are not allowed to buy cheese. Frieda creeps away, mortified that someone can tell at a glance that she is Jewish. Later, when she has time to reflect on it, she realizes the woman sniffed her out because Frieda was better dressed, though her clothes are growing shabby with time. She also realizes she is lucky that nobody called a policeman.

Oma gives their friendly neighbour, Frau Thaler, money so that she can buy them some items they are forbidden to buy themselves: milk, cottage cheese, beans. If anyone found out and denounced her, she would be sent to a camp, but Frau Thaler never refuses. She begins to say she has a niece visiting, in order to explain the increase in groceries.

Frieda is asked to come to a neighbour's apartment building to treat a sick child. The older brother, who has come to fetch her, tells her along the way that their family has been summoned to Gestapo headquarters the following day, like so many others who have been rounded up for transport.

When Frieda arrives, the family is in turmoil trying to decide what to take, what they can live without. The child has a fever; the mother wrings her hands while Frieda listens to the little chest.

"How can he travel like this?" the mother cries. "Why are they doing this to us?"

Frieda leaves, shaken. She can do nothing to help. She doesn't even have any Aspirin.


## August 1939

She has begun to recognize the Nazi rhetoric. It has been months since the clamouring for the Sudetenland in Hitler's speeches, followed by the gift of appeasement from Chamberlain. If the method works, try it again. Less than six months later, the absurd propaganda hit all the papers in preparation for the invasion of Czechoslovakia. Vicious subhuman Czechs were attacking the blameless Germans among them, mainly women and children.

Now it is Poland's turn. The papers bristle with incidents of depraved Poles — they may as well have horns, she thinks — rising up against the honest, decent Germans along their borders. How dare they? How can peace-loving Germans go on without acting? They must protect their people. It is so predictable it is funny, if only Frieda could laugh.

At the beginning of August a light blinks at the end of the tunnel. The Eisenbaums get a letter informing them they have been accepted for immigration to Argentina. They will receive their papers within three weeks. Frieda feels a great sigh escaping her body, while Wolfie shouts with joy at the news. Certainly they are all greatly relieved, but how can they rejoice? They will have to leave without Vati and Leopold. They must also get permission to travel from the German government.

Frieda risks going on the S-Bahn and gets off at the Oranienburgerstrasse, the heart of the old Jewish quarter where impoverished Jews lived among the prostitutes in the seventeenth century. Above the rooftops, in the distance she spots the so-called New Synagogue, an exotic building crowned by a golden cupola and two Moorish towers glowing in the sun. This, she muses, is the danger of ever calling something new — the structure was built around 1860, but the name was never changed. Heading toward Grosse Hamburgerstrasse, she passes the grounds of the little Monbijou Palace, built for Queen Dorothea, mother of Frederick the Great. On her right lies an old Jewish cemetery, a fitting juxtaposition, considering the old folks' home the near-by building used to house. Even more fitting now that it's Gestapo headquarters.

She enters the building on Grosse Hamburgerstrasse that she has avoided up till now, heeding the stories of torture in the basement.

Holding the papers in front of her, eyes down, she waits for the man at the reception desk to look up. He is smoking a cigarette since he is only waiting on Jews. She allows herself a split-second glimpse to take in the clipped blond hair and acne scars.

He scowls at her. "Jew?"

She nods.

"Room Four." Without looking at her, he jerks his head to the right.

She walks down a hall and finds number four. She knocks, but there's no answer. After a moment, she timidly opens the door. The large room is filled with people standing in a line winding toward a desk where one official is leisurely checking a man's documents.

"This affidavit has not been stamped properly!" the official retorts.

"But sir, I was just there yesterday. They told me —"

"Next!"

The man slinks away, eyes downcast. Nobody looks at him; in fact, some of the people turn their bodies to avoid him.

Though everyone stands close together, they do not engage each other in conversation. Frieda understands. Nobody wants to tell his story; what is the point, since all the stories are the same, with minor variations. The room is so quiet Frieda can hear people breathing. It becomes unbearably hot as she stands in line. She closes her eyes, trying to think of something else: the little park near their old apartment, the linden trees shading the benches. But after two hours she is perspiring. Finally she reaches the desk.

The youngish man looks her over behind wire glasses while taking her papers. She waits for him to find something missing, but instead he snaps, "Come back in two weeks. Door Number Five."

She hesitates; he has all their documents. "May I please have a receipt?" she murmurs, looking past his face at the wall. Jews are not allowed to look into the eyes of the master race.

Without answering, he scribbles on a sheet of paper and throws it at her.

"Next!"

They don't have much left of value to pack. They long ago sold their lovely things — their cherry wood dining table, their damask sofa, their oak bedsteads, their carpets, their paintings. The silver and jewellery, even the watches have been confiscated. Anything remotely valuable after that, including their radio, was destroyed on the night of the broken glass, as it has come to be known. A few of Frieda's precious medical books escaped the flight out the window, and several more were salvageable even after the drop to the ground. She stacks these saved books into a box.

For many months now, each of them has kept a suitcase packed with the bare necessities under the bed, like every Jew in Berlin. One never knows when the Gestapo will come to the door and drag them from their homes.

A few days before Frieda is to pick up their papers from Gestapo headquarters, rumours circle the city: war is brewing. Voices on the street recount instances of Polish aggression. People crowd around newspapers where inexplicable stories abound of Polish mobs attacking German children. Frieda passes two women on the sidewalk. One says to her friend, "Poland has our territory. The Slavs will attack and murder us in our beds! Mark my words, it's only a matter of time." The Nazi rhetoric is still working.

Frieda can feel their opportunity slipping away. If war breaks out, the borders will close and no one will be allowed to travel, despite their papers. They will be trapped, like all the other Jews in the country.

On September 1, the day she is set to go to the Gestapo, Wolfie runs into the apartment shortly after dawn and shouts for them all to wake up. He has just come home after a night of gambling. Someone had a radio on during the game.

"The Nazis have attacked Poland!" he cries. "Oh, they say Poland provoked them and attacked first, but everyone knows that's a lie. Poland hasn't got a chance! You know how they defended themselves against German tanks? With *swords* for God's sake!"

The Eisenbaums spend the day by the radio that Wolfie won at cards, listening to the solemn pronouncements: if the Germans don't retreat from Poland immediately, Britain and France threaten unjustly that they will declare war. Imagine, a colonial empire telling us we cannot restore our own territory.

Frieda mulls it over for a while; finally, she puts on her jacket to go out.

Oma looks up from the radio. "Where are you going?"

"Our papers are supposed to be ready today."

Oma stares at her in disbelief. "Sit down, child. You can't go out today. It's too dangerous."

"If we wait till they declare war, it'll be too late."

Oma stands up, takes Frieda's elbow, and propels her to the room where Wolfie is sleeping. "Wolfie, wake up! Talk some sense into your sister."

Wolfie lifts his head from the pillow, his thick brown hair rumpled from sleep. "Umm ...?"

"Tell your sister she mustn't go to the Gestapo today."

He blinks awake. "Gestapo? Are you crazy?"

"Our papers will be ready today," Frieda says. "They'll declare war soon, then it'll be too late for us to leave."

Wolfie sits up, his eyes heavy with sleep. "It's already too late for that."

The next day, England and France declare war against Germany. The Eisenbaums are trapped.

# chapter twenty-five

It was nearly eight when Rebecca pulled up her jacket collar against the evening chill, walking south through the campus. Brown maple and oak leaves lay curled everywhere, scattered by the wind. The streetlamps illuminated the sidewalks but didn't penetrate the large grass round of King's College Circle, its centre murky in the dark. Like the Sentrys. Even Erich, who was nice enough but had impenetrable dark spots. Understandable, considering his parents' history. And his *father!* Something was missing there. By design. They withheld things, she was sure, on principle. It seemed to be a way of life for them. Could she blame them? She couldn't imagine what they had suffered. They had been through the unspeakable. She wasn't going to judge them. But she wouldn't go out of her way to seek them out either.

She had been disappointed when Erich didn't suggest going out for a bite. Unlike Salim, she and Erich hadn't eaten enough for a meal at the reception and she was peckish. She would have been happy to suggest a restaurant herself, but saw the impatience, his weight shifting from one foot to the other as they stood before Hart House. He said the nearby Bloor subway would take him directly home to his house on the Danforth. *How nice for you*, she thought. She also thought of the string of Greek restaurants arrayed like pearls along the Danforth, but said nothing as she waved goodbye.

Miriam would be lonely around now, she thought, heading across College Street, down McCaul, toward the rear of Mount Sinai. The wind blew her into the Murray Street entrance, where she pulled a tissue from her purse to blow her nose. Winter was looming.

She always felt like she was coming home when she set foot into the hospital. She had interned here, slept in the staff lounge when she was on call, delivered babies on the maternity floor, and after graduation worked in the Emerg to develop a patient base. She wasn't usually here on a Saturday night. Few people were around as she stepped down the stairs to the basement cafeteria, where she bought a slice of pizza.

Upstairs, on the preemie unit, she pulled on a hospital gown and scrubbed her hands with disinfectant soap. Here and there parents sat whispering solemnly beside their babies' incubators. Sound and lighting levels were kept low to avoid overstimulating the fragile infants, but she realized the soft quiet also acted like a soporific on the nerves.

She smiled at the sight of Miriam inside her incubator. The baby lay on her stomach fast asleep, face scrunched to one side, her tiny mouth pursed like a flower. Rebecca brought a chair over to the Isolette and sat down. So her little niece wasn't hankering for company either.

After forty minutes, Miriam had barely moved. She was out for the night. Rebecca blew her a silent kiss and reluctantly left.

She exited the hospital at Murray Street and walked the half-block to Elm, where the hospital residence for married interns stood. Her year there with David rose around her like an exquisite cloud, the bittersweet details of their tiny apartment distracting her on the way to McCaul. She sensed rather than noticed a car rolling along the street behind her. In the hospital district, cars often crept along looking for parking, so it didn't alarm her. She crossed to the south side of Elm and continued down McCaul for half a block, then stopped, ready to cross to D'Arcy on the other side. She looked both ways down the quiet residential street before stepping off the sidewalk.

She was nearly halfway across, feeling lonely on a Saturday night. All at once tires screeched to her right. A car roared out of a shadowy parking spot. A dark sedan was barrelling down on her! Her brain froze, but instinct took over — she leaped for the other sidewalk faster than she thought possible. She landed on one knee and crouched there, stunned. The car zoomed away. Just like that. Her heart raced in her mouth; she could barely breathe. What had just happened? She stood up slowly, her knee throbbing.

She thought she knew D'Arcy Street. It had never stretched this long before. *Hurry up*, she thought. Her knee hurt and she began to limp, though it didn't slow her down. She'd have a good bruise there tomorrow. She wouldn't cross another street without looking for the sedan. As long as she was on the sidewalk, she was safe.

She rushed, limping, past the semi-detached houses, their stamp-sized front lawns separated by steel fences, picket fences, waist-high hedges. Ignoring the pain, she dashed through the piles of leaves fallen from the towering maples and chestnuts.

Then she heard it behind her. A thud. Tires rolling along something not meant for tires. She turned her neck. Headlights aimed at her. The sedan had mounted the sidewalk and was rushing toward her angled like a drunk, one tire on, one tire off the curb. Her breath caught in her throat. She lurched forward, hemmed in by the hedges and fences of the lawns. She only had a few seconds! If she dashed into the street, he could run her down there. If she turned into one of the houses, he could probably trample down a hedge with his car. What about a fence?

The sedan bore down on her. Praying it wasn't locked, she swung open a steel gate and pitched herself through it, falling hard onto the leaf-strewn concrete walk. The tires squealed to a halt. His headlights, a few yards away, burned through the dark. She heard the car door open. Lifting herself up on her forearms, she craned her neck to see where he was. A dark-haired man hovered near the hood watching her. He looked ready to fly, his eyes darting up and down the street. An ordinary brown-skinned man, receding hairline, thin moustache. Then he took a step forward.

*Can't stay here! Get up!* Leaves flying, she scrambled onto her hands and knees. Clambered up the stoop. Flung herself at the door, pounding on it. *Please be home! Please, someone!* In her fog she knew the driver was waiting. She breathed through her mouth until the front door opened. A bewildered Latino man appeared in the doorway.

"Police!" she cried. "Call the police! He's trying to kill me!" She sagged into the door frame, shaking. Behind her, she could hear the car backing up, hurtling away. *Thank you, Whoever rules the universe, thank you.*

The man in the house tilted his head to peer around her. "*Qué pasa?*"

"*Quién es?*" a woman's voice called out.

A small woman in her thirties appeared beside him. She assessed Rebecca for a split second, then pulled her inside the door. Music played on a TV somewhere.

She gave her husband instructions in Spanish, then asked Rebecca, "Wha' happen?"

"A man tried to run me down with his car. Please call the police."

Her husband returned with a fleece blanket and a damp handkerchief. The woman wrapped Rebecca in the blanket and led her to an upholstered chair in the small living room where three young children sat watching TV on a sofa. Julie Andrews was singing, "The hills are alive with the sound of music." The children, all with straight black hair and broad cheekbones like their parents, stared wide-eyed at Rebecca. The woman picked a leaf out of Rebecca's hair, then bent over her, dabbing the handkerchief at her cheek. She pulled it away, red with blood.

Rebecca swallowed when she saw it. "Thank you."

"Your husband try to kill you before?"

"My husband! No! I don't know who it was. Please, where's your phone? I have to call the police." She could see their reluctance about the police and recognized the fear of immigrants. In some countries, the police were the ones to dread.

When she realized she had dropped her purse outside on the sidewalk, the husband went to retrieve it for her. Her hand was still shaking as she dialed the number on the card Fitzroy had given her. He was off that night, but the sergeant who answered said he would send someone.

While she waited, Rebecca sat wrapped in the blanket over her jacket, sipping from a mug of hot chocolate the woman had handed her. The husband pulled in a chair from the kitchen for himself — they had probably given her his — while his wife sat ensconced among her children on the couch. Two little girls and a boy smiled shyly at Rebecca. They all turned to the TV, where Julie Andrews was teaching the children of the Von Trapp family a new song amid the splendour of the Austrian Alps. Music filled the room. The scene seemed surreal. Maybe she had gone into shock and was hallucinating. She looked down at the mug of hot chocolate: it shook in her hand. No, she was awake. She rested it on the wooden arm of the chair and stared vacantly at the TV.

In twenty minutes, a decisive knock sounded at the door. Huddled in her blanket, she followed behind the husband, who opened the door to two young police constables, one dark-skinned and Asian-looking, the other fair with pale eyes.

"We're looking for Dr. Rebecca Temple. She called the station."

The man's eyes widened. "*Doctor?*"

Rebecca smiled weakly. "I called."

"May we come in?"

The man stood aside, eyes lowered.

Rebecca said to him, "It's all right. It'll be fine." To the constables, she said distinctly, "These people rescued me. They've been very kind."

During the commercial of *The Sound of Music*, they had exchanged tidbits of information and she'd found out they were from Guatemala.

The two men filled the hallway in their thick police-issue winter jackets and peaked caps. She described how she had been walking home when the black sedan had come after her and tried to run her down. The one with the pale eyes scribbled in a small notepad.

"Did you see the make of the car?" asked the dark one, his hair a shiny black. "A licence number?"

"It might've been a Dodge, I'm not sure. I was too busy running to catch the licence number."

"Could you describe the driver?"

"Young brown-skinned male. Could be Mediterranean. Or Indian. Maybe Middle Eastern."

"And you never saw him before?"

She shook her head.

"Any idea what's going on here? Why this guy comes out of the blue trying to run you down?"

"I'm completely baffled."

"Could it be a prankster out on a Saturday night?"

"He wasn't fooling around. He was trying to kill me."

"Are you hurt? Apart from the cut on your face?"

She put her palm gingerly to her cheek. "I hurt my knee when I fell."

"We'd like to take you to the hospital. Get you checked out."

It was probably protocol. But she knew she would wait hours for an X-ray in the ER. "That's all right, officer. Nothing's broken. Just cuts and bruises. I'd rather go home and take a bath."

"We'd feel better if you got yourself checked out. Got that cut looked at."

She pulled the blanket from around her shoulders and folded it up. No more looking like a patient. "I'll put disinfectant on it when I get home. Look, tell Fitzroy I refused to go. You'll be off the hook and I'll get a peaceful night's sleep."

"You know Fitzroy?" The dark-haired constable exchanged glances with his partner. Some signal made him put his notepad away.

"He's looking into the death of the homeless woman killed here last week," she said. "I found her. Just across the street."

The two men looked at each other again. "That's kind of a coincidence," said the fair-haired one.

"That's what I'm thinking. Though they arrested someone for it," she said. "A street person. Stanley something. I thought he killed her, but I'm not sure of anything anymore. You better tell Fitzroy to call me."

"If you're not going to the hospital, we'd like you to come down to the station and give a statement. While everything's fresh in your mind."

After she had described the incident at the station, the car, the driver, his bold pursuit of her on the sidewalk down D'Arcy, a woman police constable drove her home.

Her whole body ached as she lifted herself from the bath and crawled into bed. Just as she was falling asleep, the phone rang.

"Hello."

"Rebecca? What's the matter?"

How could he tell from "hello"? "I've had an accident. Well, not really an accident. Someone tried to run me down. But I'm all right."

An intake of breath. "Someone tried to kill you?"

"I'm all right. Really. Just shaken."

"What happened?"

"I left the hospital after visiting the baby. And a car started chasing me. He came out of nowhere, he just came at me ..."

"Did you see who it was?"

"A Mediterranean-looking man. Never saw him before."

"Did the police catch him?"

"No."

"What about the car? Did you give the cops a description?"

She sighed. "I didn't see much. I was running for my life."

"Christ! I thought Toronto was supposed to be a safe place. First this woman gets killed. Now someone's after you ... There's no connection, is there? I mean, why would someone try to ... What did the cops say?"

Now she was sorry she'd told him about Birdie when he'd called the other night.

"The beat cops who came out didn't like that it was a coincidence. But I haven't spoken to the detective yet. Look, don't worry. They've got the guy who probably killed her." What was the point of alarming him with speculation?

"You sound tired. Did I wake you up?"

"Kind of."

"I'm sorry. Look, get some sleep. I'll talk to you tomorrow."


She didn't get up the next morning. All her muscles ached. She lay on her back in bed listening to music by Schubert and Mahler on CBC. By noon she got hungry and crept out of bed in her pyjamas. She poured milk over some muesli in a bowl and sat down carefully at the kitchen table. After half an hour, she decided she needed to lie down more than she needed coffee and limped back into bed.

Beneath her half-drawn blind — she didn't like the room completely dark even at night — she could see the day was overcast. She thought she was still looking out the window at the leafless branches of the linden tree out front when the doorbell startled her awake. What time was it? Her clock radio read 2:20 p.m.

She wasn't expecting anyone. Could someone with evil intentions find out where she lived? She wasn't listed in the phone book. If they had followed the police car home last night, they wouldn't have waited till now, would they? It would be rather clever.

She lifted herself slowly and put on her silk robe, wincing. Stepped down the stairs one at a time, her knee singing out in pain. First stop, the kitchen. She pulled a steak knife from the drawer and held it behind her back as she approached the front. She couldn't see anyone through the small square of glass in the door. Either the person was a dwarf or they were hiding off to one side. She was going to call the police ...

All at once a figure moved into her line of vision in the glass of the door. Someone with a sheepish grin on his face. Nesha.

She swung open the door. He stood with his head bent, looking up at her like a supplicant. The fervor in his eyes belied the hands stuffed casually into the pockets of his cracked leather jacket.

"How did you get here so fast?"

"I have my ways. Is it all right?"

She had fallen for the melancholy in his eyes when they first met. She couldn't bear to add to it now. Put him out of his misery. She put down the knife and held out her hand. He took it and let her pull him inside. He swept her into her arms, smelling of leather and soap.

"Have I slept right through? Is this Thursday?"

"I changed my ticket. I told them I had urgent business in Toronto and they put me on a flight first thing in the morning."

"Urgent business?"

"I thought you needed a bodyguard." His head motioned to the knife on the hall table.

"You want to guard my body?"

"I'd love to guard your body." He pushed her back to arm's length. Fine, wavy brown hair framed his face. He wore a lopsided grin, examining the bandage on her cheek. "I better guard your face too. If I catch this guy, I'll kill him."

# chapter twenty-six

**January 1940**

Then, finally, what they have all been dreading. The colour drains from Oma's face as she reads the official document. All their names are listed: Eva Eisenbaum, Frederika Eisenbaum, Karolina Eisenbaum, Luise Eisenbaum, and Wolfgang Eisenbaum. They must report to the Gestapo at Grosse Hamburgerstrasse the following morning. They are allowed one small suitcase apiece.

"I'm not going!" Wolfie cries. "They're not going to get me that easy!" He strides back and forth across the small room, gritting his teeth together.

"What choice do we have?" Frieda asks.

"Have you heard of 'submarines'? People who go underground? I know a few the Gestapo would love to get their hands on. I won't go without a fight."

Frieda crosses her arms over her chest. "Where will you go?"

"I have friends." Rage has become deliberation. "When you play cards, you get to know people. Gentiles. One of them already offered me a place. It was just a matter of time before I took him up on it."

He looks at her pointedly. "You must hide too."

She glances at the other women: Oma, whose strength she has counted on more than she realized; Mutti, her face shrunken from hunger and worry; Luise, innocent, uncomprehending. "I can't. I won't leave them. We'll stay together."

He stares at his mother and grandmother. "I'm sorry, I'm sorry ... but I won't just let them kill me."

Oma strokes his face with her hand. "Never apologize for surviving. Don't look back. Of course you must save yourself."

He takes her hand and kisses it.

"We will fight in our own way," Oma says, turning on her heels and stepping into the room she shares with Luise and Frieda.

She returns carrying Luise's suitcase, which has been packed for weeks. The girl stands watching her, mouth open in confusion.

Oma takes her by the hand — neither is more than five feet tall — and, while the others look on, leads her out the door and across the hall. She waits a moment in front of the neighbour's door, hesitant. Her shoulders square back, then she knocks.

Frau Thaler opens her door. Frieda cannot see the expression on her face: by now she must have seen the suitcase. Oma mumbles something Frieda can't hear, pauses while the other woman speaks. Then slowly, with great fatigue, Oma puts the suitcase into Luise's clumsy hand and prods her into the apartment. Oma stands on the threshold looking inside, her eyes large with the knowledge of separation, the knowledge of death in her heart. Then she closes the door behind them and walks back down the hall.

"Oma!" Luise's voice cries from behind the door. "Where is Oma!"

Oma walks back to her own apartment, tears spilling down her small face. After she steps inside, Frieda closes their door quietly, then follows her to the bedroom.

Oma sits down on the bed, turning dark eyes on Frieda. "It's time," she says.

She reaches her hand under the head of the mattress and pulls out the vial of phenobarbital Frieda brought her last year.

"Please help me," she says, spilling the pills into the palm of her hand. "How many do I need to take?"

While Frieda stares at the pills, Wolfie says, "Take them with this."

The two women look up at the doorway where Wolfie is standing holding a bottle of schnapps he won at cards. Frieda feels a falling in the pit of her stomach. She sits down beside her grandmother and counts out enough pills, putting the rest back into the bottle.

Wolfie sits down on the other side of Oma. He pours some schnapps into the glass on her night table.

She looks into his eyes, strokes his hair. "My handsome boy."

He embraces her for a long moment.

She turns to Frieda, whose eyes burn with held-back tears. "It's for the best," she says. "I'm too old. I haven't got the strength to go on."

Frieda embraces her, sobbing.

"You must be brave and survive. My only regret is I couldn't see your father one last time."

Oma notices Mutti hovering in the doorway. "We must say goodbye, Karolina," she says, gesturing for her to come forward.

Mutti bends down awkwardly to kiss Oma on the cheek. "Take care of yourself," Oma murmurs. "Be brave."

A tear slides down Mutti's face as she stumbles from the room.

Oma takes a deep sigh. She looks at the little grouping of pills in her hand, then brings them to her mouth. She reaches for the glass, takes a gulp of schnapps. Swallows. Takes another gulp. Swallows. Frieda on one side and Wolfie on the other each support her with an arm around her back.

"I've had a good life," Oma says. "Don't mourn for me. Save yourselves."

Frieda feels her grandmother disappearing. She can almost hear the rhythm of her heart losing speed. Oma's body becomes heavy between them. When she slumps over, they each take a side and lay her on the bed, smoothing down her skirt.

Frieda sits on the bed, watching her grandmother's chest rise and fall, rise and fall. Slower. Slower. Slower. Stop. She holds the small hand until it begins to turn cold.

The undertakers come early in the afternoon. Though they are overburdened with dead Jews, they are organized to bury a body within twenty-four hours as is the custom.

Wolfie embraces Mutti, then Frieda, holding her at arm's length as if waiting for her to change her mind and say she will run too. She squeezes his arm and watches him leave for the apartment of the friend who has offered him shelter. He has not told her the name in case the Gestapo question her.


The following morning Frieda and her mother, each carrying her one suitcase, enter the sprawling gymnasium at Grosse Hamburgerstrasse. The place is already filled with people sitting on the floor, their luggage next to them. Frieda finds a small spot and pulls her mother down beside her. Though they are both wearing their good coats, Mutti has not combed her hair, which lies in a curly greying mass around her head.

After several hours the guards herd them into open trucks. A convoy of trucks heads west. As she passes through the city she was born in — for the last time? — Frieda is astonished at how beautiful it is. She sees the familiar streets and buildings in a new light: they are enveloped in a rosy haze that fixes them in an earlier memory, a time of absurd innocence. Can there have been such a time, when Jews were people just like everyone else?

She realizes after a while that they are heading for the Grunewald. The suburban scene of Hanni's triumph, so long ago it seems like another lifetime. They drive past the entrance to the sports arena, now taken over by the Nazis, and finally stop in a railway yard.

"*Raus! Schnell!*" the soldiers scream, pulling them from the trucks.

They strike at the women with wooden truncheons and whips to hurry them up. Mutti stumbles, falls getting off the truck. Frieda helps her up. A soldier swings with a whip, lashing her arm. Frieda cries out despite herself.

"*Schnell!*" he screeches, shoving them toward the waiting train.

More soldiers are shrieking and pushing to get them into the boxcars that were made to transport cattle. Frieda manages to scramble up into the high opening and helps her mother climb up. They are surrounded by women squashed together so tightly that there is no room to sit down. A soldier closes the door of the car.

The light disappears, then the air. A small ventilation shaft at the top of the door lets in a tiny amount of both.

Women moan throughout the car: "I can't breathe." "Get off my foot." "Get your hair out of my face."

The boxcar stands in place for hours.

"I'm so thirsty," someone says.

"Thirst is worse than hunger," says another.

Voices agree all over the car. They spend some time debating what is the most satisfying drink when one is parched with thirst. The distraction helps pass the time.

Finally a hum, a vibration works its way through the floor. Then a jolt. Then they are moving. "Thank God!" a chorus of voices rings out.

The train is not in a hurry, it seems, but rolls along slowly for hours. There are no sanitary facilities in the car, only a bucket in a corner for them to relieve themselves. Soon it is overflowing, raising an unbearable stench. Women who cannot reach it urinate where they stand.

Bodies press on all sides of Frieda, squeezing out her life. A coffin of bodies. She must find her way out. She closes her eyes and tries to transport herself to the park near their old apartment. Before the benches were painted yellow and marked "For Jews Only." She must relocate herself not only in place, but in time.

The effort occupies her for a while. She cannot say how long — she has lost all sense of time. All sense of everything is gone, except thirst.

Then, finally, while faint daylight still creeps through the narrow shaft in the door, the train slows down and comes to a halt.

"Thank God!" voices intone here and there.

*Don't thank him so quickly*, Frieda thinks. Where have they come to?

The door of the train is suddenly pulled wide open. Though the sun is feeble in the grey sky, the light hurts her eyes after all the hours spent in the dark. People in the front begin jumping out. At the same time that relief floods over her, Frieda feels herself falling from the sudden lack of support. By the time she reaches the opening, she is on her hands and knees lowering herself down to the ground. Where is Mutti?

She joins the other women who stand and stare at the astonishing blue lake in front of them. On the far shore, sycamores surround a church steeple. Is it possible this is the place she was so afraid of?

The soldiers arrange the women into ragged columns. Frieda finds Mutti and stays with her as they march along the road that follows the shore of the lake. Mutti trips over stones in the road and Frieda must keep steadying her. They pass a few villagers who turn away at their approach, unwilling to catch their eyes. After about a mile, the columns climb a hill. When they reach the top they see where they have arrived: acres of low grey barracks hemmed in by concrete walls mounted with guard towers. In the middle stands a square smokestack discharging a film of vapour.

Frieda hears a woman whisper in horror, "Ravensbrück!"

The word spreads down the column like a hiss.

# chapter twenty-seven

H er dusty red Jaguar was still sitting, lonely, behind the medical building as Nesha dropped her off Monday morning. He was one of those men who couldn't be without a car and had rented a Pontiac at the airport.

"You sure you'll be all right?"

She had spent most of Sunday in bed with a heating pad and Aspirin every four hours. "I feel better today."

He had made her a succession of cups of tea with lemon, which he claimed were better for her than coffee. Lying in his arms didn't hurt either.

"Doctors have a right to recovery time like everyone else," he said, putting his hand on the back of her car seat, drinking her in with his eyes.

"I'll be fine. I've got a full day of patients who need me." She leaned over to kiss him. He hadn't shaven yet, and a fine grey stubble scratched her cheek. She liked the intimacy of him before he was ready for the rest of the world.

"If you find it's too much for you," he said softly in her ear, "call me and I'll come get you."

He waited in the car, his window down, while she walked to the front door. She could see his breath turn visible and wisp into the cold morning air. Waving goodbye, she unlocked the door and stepped inside.

She started up the stairs, then stopped, remembering something. Turning back down again, she flicked the light on in the back hall and stepped toward the rear door. Outside, Nesha's car had already disappeared down D'Arcy. She unlocked the trunk of her Jag and opened it, picking up the dirty shopping bag that Birdie had thrust at her.

Holding it with her thumb and forefinger, she carried it upstairs. She deposited the bag on the paper liner laid out on the examining table in one of the treatment rooms. Iris prepared each room the evening before by ripping the used liners off the leather tables, then pulling fresh paper down. She wasn't due for another forty minutes.

A musty odour escaped the bag. Maybe she shouldn't have brought it upstairs. She took a pair of latex gloves from a dispenser near the sink and pulled them on. Instead of catching up on her paperwork, she was dissecting garbage. Precious, Birdie had said. Opening the top of the bag, she pulled out a blue cotton blanket wrapped in a bundle. She unravelled the mass impatiently until it lay revealed: an old plastic doll with one arm and one leg. Naked and bald but for a few tufts of blonde hair. One eyelid moved up and down over a marble-green eye, the other stayed closed. The mouth startled her. Though it shouldn't have, since it was a typical doll mouth, pursed together like a flower. As if it had just exclaimed *Oh!* Miriam wouldn't be saying *Oh!* for a while, but she had the same mouth.

What was that around the doll's jointed neck? It looked like a hospital ID bracelet. She lifted the doll sideways to read it. "Eisenbaum." The date and name of the hospital had been cut off and string had been attached to the holes in the plastic bracelet. She heard footsteps coming up the stairs. Iris was early. She rewrapped the doll in the baby blanket and placed the whole thing back into the plastic bag. Let the police deal with it.

She walked down the hall to the counter expecting to see Iris. In the middle of the waiting room stood the young homeless man she had seen in the library.

"What are you doing here?" she demanded.

He looked around, in no hurry, his blond hair in corkscrew curls. "This is a doctor's office, isn't it?"

"We open at nine. Call the secretary and make an appointment."

"But I'm sick now. You gonna turn away a sick person?"

"If you're really ill, go to Emergency."

"It's not an emergency. I'm just sick."

He would have been a handsome young man if his hair were washed and his ski jacket and jeans were clean.

"What are your symptoms?"

"I got pains."

"Where?"

"Here." He pointed to his throat. "And here." His head.

His watery blue eyes watched her sullenly. He made her nervous, but he wasn't the one who had tried to run her down.

"How did you find me?"

"You gave the librarian your card."

"And she gave it to *you*?" she asked, incredulous.

"She doesn't like you." He grinned. "She likes me. She left it on the counter where I could get it."

"Unbelievable," she muttered under her breath. Then to him, "Are you really sick?" Not the best bedside manner.

He tilted his head. "Pain's killing me."

"I don't suppose you have a health card? Never mind. What's your name?"

"Nigel."

"Wait here, Nigel." She imagined his proud mother naming him Nigel when he was born. When had that promise of childhood died?

Too suspicious to let him come into a treatment room, she went down the hall to collect some supplies and bring them back to the waiting area. Stethoscope around her neck, carrying tongue depressors, an ophthalmoscope, and an audioscope, she turned to step out of the exam room. There he stood in the door, blocking her way out. He was taller than she'd thought. If he wanted to, he could overpower her. Her hands began to sweat.

"Hey, your old man knock you around some?" He pointed to the bandage on her cheek.

"I fell. Not that it's your business."

He smirked.

She had to stay authoritative, show no fear. "Take off your jacket and sit down."

He obeyed, but the odour of sweat radiating from him made her turn away. She reached for a wooden tongue depressor. At least she felt more in control now that he was sitting.

"Open wide." She held down his tongue to look inside his throat. Listened to his chest with the stethoscope. Looked in his ears. Felt his forehead with her hand.

"Nothing here," she said. "You're not sick, are you?"

He shrugged.

"Why are you really here?"

"I want my friend back."

"Stanley?"

"They wouldn't let me go to the station with him. Hard-asses. Don't have no one else."

"I'm sorry. But what does it have to do with me?"

"It was your fault they got him. You called the cops."

Now she understood. "But he probably killed that woman."

"That stupid old broad? No, he didn't. Never. He liked her. Though she was a loser. Never knew what he saw in her."

"You were jealous."

"Jealous?"

"She took him away from you. He spent time with her."

His blond eyebrows rose. "Guess so."

"Did you kill her?"

He scowled. "I dunno. Don't remember. Can't always remember so good. Might've been high that day. Wouldn't remember if I was high."

"You wouldn't remember killing her?"

He thought a moment. "Would I get to stay in jail with Stanley?"

Footsteps sounded on the stair. Iris. Finally.

They both listened as Iris's heels clicked on the tile in the waiting area, then proceeded down the hall.

"Rebecca?"

"Who's that?" he hissed, jumping down from the table.

"It's all right. Just my secretary." She called out, "In here, Iris!"

Perfectly groomed in a navy wool suit, Iris stopped short when she reached the exam room. Her usually relaxed face froze. "What happened to your face? Are you okay? Should I call someone?"

"Everything's —"

She turned to reassure Iris when a large, unyielding arm swung her backwards with dizzying speed and landed around her neck. He held her facing Iris, his arm cutting off her air circulation.

"Leave her alone!" Iris cried. "You're hurting her! What do you want?"

"I want you to shut up! That's what I want! What's with you old broads anyhow? Can't you shut up?"

Iris put up her hands in acquiescence. "Okay. Calm down. Just tell me what you want and I'll get it."

Rebecca had both hands dug into his arm trying to pull it loose. It was a log.

"Stanley. I want Stanley."

"Who?" She looked at Rebecca, her eyes large with confusion, alarm. "Who's Stanley?"

Rebecca didn't know how long she could keep breathing.

"The doc here called the cops on Stanley. Shouldn't've done it. She can't just get away with that. He's my friend. I want him back."

"So, Stanley's in jail? And you want him out?"

"You got it." He paused a second. "I just thought of something. I'll trade the doc for Stanley! It's, like, a hostage situation."

"You've been watching too much TV."

"How'd you know?"

"Okay," said Iris, glancing nervously at Rebecca. "First loosen your hold on her neck, because you want her alive."

He seemed to think about this, then he relaxed his arm slightly. She could breathe again. Her lungs filled with air. *Thank you, Iris.*

"What's your name?"

"Nigel."

"*Nigel?*"

Rebecca prayed she wouldn't say something flip like, *What was your mother thinking?*

"Okay, Nigel. It's like this. If the police have your friend, you have to negotiate with *them*. Would you like me to call them and set it up?"

"Call the cops?"

"You want to trade your friend for the doctor, right? She's your hostage?"

"Yeah. The bitch called the cops on Stanley."

"Well, then, it's the cops you have to talk to."

"I get it. Sure. Okay. Call 'em."

Iris hesitated in her triumph. "You won't hurt her while I'm gone?"

"What, do I look stupid?"

Rebecca heard Iris on the phone in the front office, where they couldn't make out what she was saying. Rebecca couldn't distinguish words, only the panic Iris had kept beneath the surface with Nigel.

She reappeared at the door. "Police are on their way. Why don't you let her go now?"

"She's my hostage."

"You won't go anywhere, will you?" Iris addressed Rebecca.

She croaked out, "No."

"You broads think I'm stupid."

When they heard the police entering the office, he tightened his grip on Rebecca's neck. The air was squeezed out again. Her eyes began to water.

Two constables stood behind Detective Fitzroy in the doorway of the exam room. Rebecca was profoundly relieved to see him, his tall, authoritarian bulk reassuring. Yet she wondered if he could keep Nigel from choking her to death.

"Let her go, Nigel," Fitzroy said, massive beneath his wool coat, his bulbous nose glowing. "We'll talk better alone, without the women. Just us guys."

"I want Stanley back."

"I know. Let's talk about it."

"She's my hostage. It's her fault he's in the can."

"Okay. But you can let her go now because we're here. You did your job and got us here, now let's talk."

"Negotiate?"

"Yeah, we'll negotiate."

"How much do you want her? I want something to let her go. Drugs."

"Nigel, Nigel. We're getting away from the real issue here."

"Uppers and downers. Docs get free stuff from drug companies. Everyone knows that. She's probably got stuff right here."

Rebecca was all out of air. She had to do something or she'd pass out. She brought one hand down from where it was unsuccessfully tugging at his arm. Squeezing her hand between her back and his front, she located his groin in the baggy jeans and grabbed his testicles in her fist, crushing them like walnuts.

"Aowww!" Nigel groaned in pain. "Bitch!"

He shoved her forward, away from him. She stumbled, air filling her lungs again.

Fitzroy caught her. "Nice work." A satisfied smile lit up his blotchy face as he handed her quickly to the constable behind him.

Nigel didn't have a chance. In one step, Fitzroy reached him and seized one of his arms. The big man wrenched it behind his back, pulled the other one in tandem, and locked his wrists into handcuffs.

"You've done it now, Nigel. You're in real trouble."

"She deserved it!" he shouted. "She ratted on Stanley! I want to see Stanley!"

"Oh, you'll see Stanley, all right."

In the hall the constable said to Rebecca, "Are you okay? Do you want to go to the hospital?"

She stroked her neck with her fingers, feeling fragile as a bird. "I'll be fine."

"I'll cancel today's patients," Iris said. "You should go home."

Rebecca kept taking deep breaths. Just because she could. "No. I'd rather be busy. We'll just finish early. Don't book anyone past four."

The constables sandwiched Nigel from either side and shuffled him out through the waiting room, his hands cuffed behind him. A woman patient entered the office as they were marching to the door.

"What're you lookin' at?" Nigel spit out.

The woman stood in place, mouth open.

"Office isn't open yet," said Iris.

"Could I just wait in here?" the woman asked, peering after the constables. When Iris shrugged, she found a seat in the waiting room.

Iris led Rebecca to her private office and sat her down in her black leather chair. "Relax in here for a while. No hurry to start."

Rebecca leaned her head back and closed her eyes, but Nigel's arm kept squeezing her neck. After a few minutes there was a quiet rap at the door.

Detective Fitzroy poked in his large, round head with the scant hair. "Did he hurt you? Do you need a doctor?"

She sat up. "I'm okay. Just shaken up. What's going to happen to him?"

"He'll be charged. You'll have to make a statement."

"He may've killed the old woman."

"Oh yeah? He say so?"

"He said he couldn't remember. Said he was high on something."

"That's no help."

She leaned her elbows on her desk. "You think Stanley did it?"

"He denies it."

"You don't believe him?"

"Most of these guys wouldn't know the truth if it came up behind them and bit them on the ass. You should go home, doc."

"Too much work to do." Then she remembered. "I've got something for you."

She stood up and came round the desk unsteadily.

"Take the day off," he said. "I'll write you a note."

She gave him a wry smile as she pulled on a fresh pair of latex gloves. His eyebrow went up. She retrieved the dirty shopping bag from her closet. After leading him into one of the exam rooms, she deposited the bag on the paper-lined exam table.

"Birdie gave this to me the last time I saw her." She unravelled the baby blanket to reveal the broken doll.

"It looks like something she got out of the trash."

"There's an old hospital ID bracelet around its neck." She held it sideways so he could read it.

"Eisenbaum," he said, shrugging.

"Doesn't that strike you as odd?"

"Not really," he said. "That was her name."

"Her name was Eisenbaum?" She felt her heart contract. Sentry was such an English name, it invoked no feeling in her. But Eisenbaum. The woman might have been a Jewish grandmother.

Rebecca threw herself into the day's work. At lunch, Iris brought her some egg drop soup from a local Chinese restaurant, along with some General Tso chicken and rice. These kept her going. By the time she finished her last patient at four-thirty, she was exhausted.

Iris looked up sheepishly from her desk when Rebecca brought her the last patient's files. "I'm sorry, dear, but your neighbour from across the street just walked in and begged me to let her see you."

"Mrs. Sentry?"

# chapter twenty-eight

**February 1940**

"*Appel! Appel! Raus! Schnell!*"

Four o'clock in the morning. Everyone jumps from their flea-infested bunks. Frieda seizes Mutti's hand while the female guards storm them from the barracks along with the hundreds of other women. The guards rain blows on their backs with clubs as they fly past the dead bodies in the bunks, on the floor. Shrieks of pain. Howls. Outside in lines. Sub-zero. Floodlights shine in Frieda's eyes.

The muscles in her legs cramp after two hours of standing for roll call. The guards have been counting the thousands of women since 4:00 a.m. in their obsession with accuracy. The prisoners all wear striped dresses with long knickers, kerchiefs, and aprons, but no stockings. All in the same posture of arms across their breasts to keep in what small measure of warmth is left. All shivering, shivering.

Frieda is beyond numb and can only glance at Mutti beside her. Her mother's eyes are closed: perhaps she has managed to send herself into one of her books. *Ivanhoe? Jane Eyre?* As long as her body remains to be counted, that is all the guards care about, night after night. Their numbers must add up; the bodies of those who have died in the night — the death toll is staggering — are dragged out of the barracks to be included in the lineups.

She wonders how long Mutti will survive the work details during their twelve-hour days. Her grey hair has turned white. Exhaustion is shrivelling her face with each day. The work would be bad enough, but the guards take great pleasure in beating the prisoners whether they work or not. Truncheons, whips, resounding slaps with an open hand. She has seen her mother beaten on the head with a club by a woman guard just passing by. Mutti is all she has left, the only familiar face in a sea of faces. They have grown close, these few weeks in the camp, sharing a bunk with two other women. Mutti's face lights up when she sees Frieda.

Like most middle-aged women, her mother's waistline has thickened over the years. But the thin soup and piece of dry bread that passes for their main meal, the black ersatz coffee twice a day, have eroded their bodies. Frieda can feel the outline of the bones in Mutti's body beside her in the bunk.

Some of the sick and elderly, the children too young to work, have been put on a truck and taken to a nearby youth camp they are told will be less harsh. A coddling camp named Mittverda, it is said, where conditions are easier and the food is better. Everyone wants to go. At first Frieda considers asking the block leader to put Mutti's name on the list. Then the rumours begin to spread: there *is* no camp, or if there is, it's being used as a killing ground for prisoners. Someone saw one of the trucks come back within the hour, loaded with the clothes that the "coddled" were wearing. How could they have thought otherwise?

A layer of thick grey cloud hangs above their snow shovelling detail. Their group has been assigned to clear the road between the barracks. Though she told the camp authorities she was a doctor when they questioned her on arrival, they have not seen fit to use her medical skills. Instead, she lifts the heavy snow one shovelful at a time, the muscles in her back complaining with each movement. She is unused to physical labour and hopes her youth will make up for it. But what about Mutti?

She glances sideways at her mother, who pushes her shovel along but manages to lift very little snow off the road.

"You!" barks a woman guard. "What d'you think you're doing!"

Frieda is the only one who looks up to see the whip lash out at her mother. The others keep working. Instead of trying harder, Mutti drops the shovel to the ground. *Clink.* The sound breaks Frieda's heart.

She wants to shout at her mother, *Pick it up — shovel harder!* But the words die in her throat as the guard begins to bawl out obscenities.

"I've been watching you, you Jewish whore! That's it for the likes of you!"

She grabs Mutti's arm, wrenching her elbow. Mutti groans with pain. The guard pulls her away from the group.

"You'll see what we do with people who won't work!"

As she is dragged away, Mutti turns large eyes on Frieda one last time. Their eyes lock for a moment.

"Mutti!" Frieda says, stepping toward her. The one face left that she loves and that loves her moves further and further away till it vanishes around the corner of the barracks. She is so angry — not at the guard but at Mutti. Why couldn't she keep working? She didn't even try — she wanted to die. She didn't care if she left Frieda alone.

"Keep working!" a guard shouts, lashing her whip at Frieda, who is in a daze.

The pain stings her body, but her body has separated from her and drifted off somewhere. Where has it gone? She is barely there, feels nothing. Who is she? *Come back!* she thinks to herself frantically. *Don't leave me!* Whose voice is she hearing? Her own or Mutti's? Mutti. Then she remembers: they've taken Mutti away.

*What will they do with her?* Frieda thinks wildly, as she digs her shovel under the snow again. What does she *think* they would do? Mutti is too old. She won't work and she's too old. Fifty-two. They have a cement corridor where they take "asocial" women. Frieda has passed by it and seen the blood. People have heard the shooting. She will not picture her mother in the corridor. She will *not*. Though she is shovelling snow faster and faster, Mutti's eyes haunt her. She will see those eyes long after Mutti is gone.

Weeks go by, and Frieda loses track of time. The other women in the bunk, Lola and Herta, consoled her after Mutti was taken away. But there was another transport and two more women now share their bunk. Six in a bunk meant for two. In their misery and exhaustion, they have forgotten Mutti. Except when they say she was the smart one, choosing death. Frieda has not forgiven her mother for leaving her and tells her so in her dreams. Sometimes Mutti comes to visit in the barracks at night when no one but Frieda can see her.

The days are not quite as cold, but the nights still freeze them as they stand for *appel*, the roll call, night after night, hour after hour, to be counted.

One day as she is lifting bags of sand to carry them from one spot to another, she hears a strange sound. Yet eerily familiar. Birdsong. A bird is whistling in a tree somewhere, maybe near that picturesque lake beyond the cement walls of the camp. How can that be, in this place? The gentleness of the song amid the barking of the guards confuses her. The truncheons beating on women's heads, backs — how can the birds sing here?

The week the birds start singing, Frieda is in a detail digging an area of ground that will be a garden. The guard sits on a rock with the sun on her face, her eyes closed as if she's on a beach. Frieda looks up to see a line of prisoners passing by. The same striped dresses with aprons, kerchiefs on their heads. Wait! A face in the line pops out at her.

"Hanni!" she cries.

The guard looks up. Frieda doesn't care.

Hanni's face turns, her mouth opens when she sees Frieda.

"What barracks are you in?" Frieda says, trying to keep her voice down. The guard is staring at her.

Hanni points to the distance in front of her. "The end."

"I'll find you," Frieda says quietly.

The line passes. Hanni turns her head as far as it will go to take Frieda in one more time.

Frieda digs into the soil with renewed strength. The guard lifts her face to the sun again and closes her eyes.

When their shift is over that evening, Frieda's detail walks back to their barracks. Frieda slips away and heads past her building, past one barracks after another, no small distance. The full face of the moon shines in the black sky, outlining the women lingering in the open air like ghosts taking in their last fresh breath of spring.

As she passes Frieda hears someone murmur, "Pesach." So, it is Passover. Yes, she remembers the full moon during the holiday. They were not religious, but they celebrated the deliverance from bondage in Egypt with a special dinner, matzo ball soup, potato kugel, a fluffy sponge cake. They would eat matzo that night and relapse the next day to eating bread. They could have denied themselves bread for the week and eaten matzo, the bread of affliction, as was the custom. But like many German Jews, they didn't. Were they being punished for it now? Was God punishing them for not worshipping him enough? Frieda has thought about this at length during the months of incarceration while her body has gone through the motions of shovelling and lifting and digging. Such a God would be unworthy. More likely they are alone in the universe and God has been dreamt up by people asking unanswerable questions.

Frieda reaches the last barracks. She asks some women standing in groups if they know Hanni Sussman.

A figure bolts toward her and launches herself into her arms. Frieda feels her heart lift for the first time in months. Hanni's body is lean but muscular, still healthy.

"When did you get here?" she asks, holding Hanni at arm's length, trying to see the dark eyes, the dark unruly hair in the moonlight.

"Two days ago."

Frieda hesitates but has to ask. "With your mother?"

Hanni looks away. "They took her. Almost as soon as we got here. They put her on a truck to the youth camp, and I thought they were saving her. Then people told me ..."

Frieda puts an arm around her shoulder.

"And your mother?" Hanni asks.

Frieda shakes her head, her eyes down.

Hanni says no more but swallows in the silent dark. They don't speak for a while.

"At least Wolfie is all right," she says finally. "I was with him the day before they took us. He's still in hiding."

"Wolfie." Frieda turns the name over on her tongue as if it is candy, a taste from another life. She smiles at the memory of the handsome face.

During the hot months Frieda helps trim the trees and bushes, tend the marigolds, carnations, and chrysanthemums in the ornamental gardens that give the camp a deceptively benign look. Her back aches picking the tomatoes and beans on the low vines, the cucumbers on the ground that will go to the kitchen for the guards' dinners. This, she decides, is the cruellest job. She is being driven insane by constant hunger, yet she dares not put anything in her mouth. If she is seen chewing, they can shoot her. She wonders how long she can keep a bean in her mouth without chewing. Whether she can swallow it whole without moving her jaw. She is too much of a coward to try.

She meets Hanni every evening during the general milling about before bed, both of them exhausted but grateful for the presence of the other. Hanni has been building a wall with bricks; since they must use their bare hands, Hanni's, like the others in the detail, are chapped and bleeding. Frieda uses the underside of her own skirt where it is cleanest to wipe the dirt and blood from Hanni's hands. She has no water, no soothing cream. But Hanni is young and strong and she will survive this.

In September someone says it is Rosh Hashanah, the New Year. Frieda remembers the honey cake Oma used to bake, golden brown and sticky sweet. Sweet things for a sweet year. There will never be a sweet year again. Oma's face rises up into the air, grey hair pulled back into a tidy bun, lips smiling. *Frieda-mouse,* she says.

"Oma!"

The sound of her own voice brings her back. She is bent over a garden of roses, pulling the weeds out with her hands, sweating from the direct sun. Her hands are clammy, and her back aches. When she tries to straighten up, her arm catches on a thorn. Drops of blood rise to the surface and trickle down her skin. She wipes them away with a leafy weed.

Then to her right, she hears a groan, a thud.

"Frieda!" someone calls softly. "Help her."

The women around her know she's a doctor and have come to call on her in their times of need. The guards lean against a fence in the shade, talking and smoking.

Frieda creeps to the figure lying among the roses. Olga. She turns her over and bends her head down to the woman's chest. Puts a finger on the pulse.

"What d'you think you're doing?"

Frieda looks up. A guard.

"She's a doctor," one of the women dares to say. "The woman fainted."

"Well?" the guard says, smirking at Frieda. She looks drunk. "What can a doctor do for a dead person?"

"She's not dead," Frieda says quietly. "She has heat stroke. She needs water."

"Maybe she'd like some schnapps," the guard snarls, taking a flask from her skirt pocket and taking a swig. "Pull her out of there and get back to work."

It is also in September that Frieda notices Hanni's dress fits differently, though she has moved her apron higher to disguise it. She cannot be getting fat in the camp, so it can be only one thing. Frieda is barely able to contain her anger in the dusky evening by the side of the barracks.

"Why didn't you tell me right away? I could've gotten rid of it for you. Now it's too dangerous for you. You'll have to have it. What were you thinking?"

Tears slip down Hanni's bony cheeks. Frieda takes a deep breath.

"I'm sorry, Hanni. Was it Wolfie?"

She nods.

"He should've known better."

"Each time we saw each other we thought it would be the last. And then it was."

"When is it due?"

"End of December."

"Like Jesus," Frieda says, scowling.

One morning late in November, before work starts, the block leader shouts out, "Number 43709! Get your things and come with me!"

Frieda repeats the number to herself. It's her! She's going to die. They've found out what she's been doing and now she's going to pay with her life. She deserves no less. Ah, well. It wasn't much of a life. If she believed in God, she would pray. If she believed in God, she might not have *played* God. In His absence, she did what she had to.

The other women stare in pity as she walks past them carrying her soup tin and a comb, payment for tending to a woman with a broken wrist.

She follows the block leader to a building near the entrance of the camp. "Find some clothes in there," she snaps, pointing to a room piled high with clothes. "Hurry up!"

Frieda is confused. At least she wasn't sent to the corridor. They don't seem to be planning to shoot her. Amid the detritus of stolen lives, she finds a grey tweed skirt, an off-white blouse, and a black wool jacket. And in one pile, a heavy woollen coat! She pulls the comb through her tattered hair, then steps out. She feels human again.

She shares the back of an enclosed truck with five other women. None knows where they are going or what is in store for them. After about a half-hour, the truck stops and the five women are led off. Sitting by herself, all she can see out the window of the back door are trees with their bare branches.

The truck drives on. Twenty minutes later, it stops again. The back door opens, and the guard motions for her to get out.

She makes out a stone block building surrounded by pine. The forest smell revives her; when she dies, she would like it to be amid the smell of pine. The building looks like it might have been a hospital once, though the vegetation is encroaching.

The guard takes her inside and gives the uniformed man at the desk her papers.

"Fräulein Eisenbaum," says the man, perusing her documents.

She is surprised to hear her name spoken after so long being a number.

"Come with me."

She follows him down a hallway of closed doors to the back of the building. Finally he leads her into a room with counters and cupboards and a sink near a window. A laboratory. A young blond man is washing glass tubes at the sink. The sound of running water amazes Frieda.

"Where's the doctor?" the escort says to a man at a desk off to one side.

"He went out, Herr Scharfuhrer."

"You take care of her, then." He turns and leaves.

The youngish man at the desk stands and proffers a hand.

Nobody has asked to shake her hand for a long time. But this man is a prisoner like her; he wears a green triangle on his jacket, the sign of an asocial or criminal prisoner. She slowly gives him her hand. He sits down and reads her documents.

Asocial usually meant beggars in the street or gypsies. His sallow skin could be gypsy. He doesn't look like a criminal, but then who do the Nazis consider criminal? Thieves? Kidnappers? Murderers? The irony would make her smile, if she still could.

"What do they do here?" she asks.

The water stops running, the room suddenly quiet. The blond man must be standing at the counter behind Frieda.

"Medical experiments," says the man at the desk. His tone is matter-of-fact, as if it is a normal activity. "You're a doctor." It's not a question. He has her papers before him.

She nods. "What kind of experiments?" Not that long ago she would have been horrified. In this new universe, horror is the new normal. It is the everyday, where all things are possible.

"All kinds. Surgery. Drugs. All kinds."

"Why am I here?"

"Oh, didn't they tell you? Herr Doktor Brenner asked for you."

Herr Doktor Brenner. A name from another life.

"He said you were important for his work. It wasn't easy, let me tell you, getting a Jewess reassigned." He seems compelled to explain. The shock must be visible on her face. "It was convenient for him. You happened to be assigned to the same camp. You're lucky. This is a satellite camp of Ravensbrück. You understand?"

She stares at him, not understanding. Or maybe understanding too well. The black and white tiles mesmerize her; she wants to lie down and not get up. A small white spot on a black tile begins to pull her in. She wants it to suck her in and make her disappear.

The man bends forward. "Don't worry. It'll be better than where you were before. And you may find the work scientifically interesting."

She looks at him as if he's dropped from the moon. *Scientifically interesting*. Once this might have meant something to her. But now she has only one interest: staying alive. When she loses that interest, nothing will help her.

# chapter twenty-nine

The new patient sat in the treatment room with her coat still on. Rebecca stepped in wearing what she hoped was a reassuring smile, despite her fatigue.

"Mrs. Sentry. What can I do for you?"

She nodded, unsmiling, her complexion pasty. "I can't sleep. I don't think I've slept since … since she was killed. She didn't deserve it. I hated her once. But she suffered, and I forgave her. And now — I keep seeing her like that. The blood …" She looked away. "I hate pills. I never take anything. But I don't know what else to do. Can you give me something to make me sleep?"

The woman watched her with listless eyes, her shoulders hunched.

"I'll need to examine you. Could you take off your coat, please, and sit up here?" She motioned to the examining table.

Rebecca listened to her heart, checked her eyes and ears, took her blood pressure. The woman was fifty-nine but very fit and looked ten years younger. Apparently she had taught phys. ed. but now only coached. According to a routine medical history, there was some heart trouble in the family.

"It's hard to know much, you see, since most of them were killed in the war."

Rebecca nodded, but didn't understand. How could she?

"Your blood pressure is slightly elevated. You should monitor that. I'll give you a prescription for some Valium. It's a muscle relaxant that will help you sleep. You could try half a tablet to begin with and see if it helps. If not, take a whole one."

"Thank you, doctor." All at once the woman's lower lip trembled and she began to sob. "Everything's upside down since she died. Someone broke into the house today and threw everything around. They didn't take anything, but it was a terrible mess."

Rebecca stopped writing the prescription. She stood up and placed her hand gently on the woman's back. "That's very upsetting. What did the police say?"

She stopped crying. Hesitated. "My husband didn't want me to call them. He said he knew who did it — a student of his — and he'd deal with it."

"So, nothing to do with your cousin's death?"

She shook her head, appeared to recover.

Rebecca would tell Fitzroy anyway.

Mrs. Sentry stepped down from the examining table and began putting on her three-quarter-length coat.

"By the way, your cousin gave me something a few days before she died."

The woman stopped buttoning her coat.

"It was a broken doll in a shopping bag."

"A doll?"

"It had her name on it."

"What name?"

"Eisenbaum."

The blood drained from Mrs. Sentry's face. She sank into a chair near Rebecca, shaking her head. "It never ends." She sat a moment staring at the floor.

"Are you all right?"

She bent over, leaning her forehead into her hand. Rebecca couldn't see her eyes. "We were in the same camp during the war. She was the only one left who knew my secret because she was there. I've kept it from my husband all these years." She looked up and observed Rebecca, perhaps to see the effect of her words. "And if I tell you, you must promise never to say it to him."

"Anything you tell me is confidential." Rebecca didn't really want to know.

"I need to tell someone, now that she's gone."

Rebecca nodded reluctantly.

The woman lifted her head, squinting at Rebecca. She took a few breaths; a tear rolled down from one eye. "I was pregnant when I was sent to the camp. By my husband, of course, though we weren't married then. I didn't see him for three years during the war. You have to understand. To have a child in the camp was a death sentence. Even if you could hide your pregnancy — we were so thin it wasn't unusual for the Germans not to know — even so, once the baby came, that was it. Kaput! You can't hide a baby. A mother with a baby can't work. And they're angry that you've reproduced. More Jews. They throw you both in the gas chamber. But there was a doctor there, a Jewish woman, who saved those of us who had babies. We all begged for the same thing when she delivered us. Can you guess?" She blinked at Rebecca, almost defiantly.

Rebecca shook her head, not wanting to hear.

"We begged her to kill our babies." Tears welled in her eyes.

Rebecca held her breath. Why should she keep breathing?

"Here, now, in this country, it doesn't seem possible. But we wanted to *live*. It was the only way."

"A *doctor* killed the babies? A Jewish doctor?"

"She saved many women this way. She delivered the baby in secret. She'd say a prayer. Then she'd put her hand over the little mouth. It wasn't very hard, she said. They were so little. She saved us at the expense of her own soul." She closed her eyes. "My husband thinks our daughter died naturally; she was a few weeks premature. I told him it was a blessing."

A girl. "I'm so sorry."

The woman sobbed quietly into her hand. Rebecca handed her a box of tissues, then drew her chair closer. She put an arm around her patient's heaving shoulders.

When Mrs. Sentry stopped weeping, Rebecca said, "Your cousin kept the doll like a baby. She must've remembered. "

The woman wiped her eyes with a tissue. "She showed it to me once. It was horrible."

She stood up, taking a deep, cleansing breath. "I feel better, telling someone. Like a burden is lifted. I can tell you've suffered in your life. You understand."

Rebecca walked her to the front of the office. While Mrs. Sentry seemed taller now, resuming her erect posture, Rebecca had shrunk in proportion, encumbered. This was a role she hadn't counted on: the shifting of burdens from patient to doctor. How many burdens before her heart plummeted under the weight?

"Let me know how you're doing. I'd like you to come back for an appointment next week."

"I appreciate it, doctor, but I really don't have time. I don't like coming to doctors." Before she turned to leave, she whispered, "Remember, my husband must never know."

Iris was preparing the examining rooms for the next day. Rebecca sat down behind the front counter, gazing at the X-ray and blood test results that had come in. They blurred before her eyes. She couldn't get the picture of Birdie out of her mind. The small, dirty face filled with fears, real and imagined. The nonsensical babble. The beautiful woman in the photo had disappeared into this creature who lived so deep inside herself, no one could reach her.

All at once, tires squealed out front. Rebecca jumped up and ran to the window overlooking Beverley Street. Her stomach turned inside her. In the deepening twilight, Mrs. Sentry lay sprawled on her side in the curb lane in front of her house.

"Iris!" shouted Rebecca. "Call an ambulance!"

She grabbed a blanket and some bandages and ran downstairs.

Two young men had put down their book bags. They crouched over the woman. One of her legs splayed out at an unnatural angle on the asphalt.

"I'm a doctor," she said, kneeling beside them. "Is she conscious? Did she say anything?"

"She's out cold," said one.

Rebecca threw the blanket over her, then placed her stethoscope inside the woman's clothes. Her heart was still beating. She was breathing.

"Mrs. Sentry, can you hear me?" she said loudly. "Johanna?"

No response. Blood smeared one side of her head. Possible skull fracture, Rebecca thought mechanically.

One of the students took off his jacket and stooped over as if to lift her head. "Don't move her!" Rebecca said. "The ambulance will be here in a few minutes. Did you see what happened?"

"A guy ran her down. Not like a hit and run. It was like he was aiming at her."

Rebecca fell back on her haunches, feeling weak. It could have been her.

"I got the licence number," he said.

"Good work. Did you write it down?"

He pulled a scrap of paper from his pocket and showed it to her.

Iris crossed the street and ran over, bringing Rebecca her coat. "Anything I can do?"

For the second time in less than a week, an ambulance siren keened through the evening air, on its way to the same corner. It blocked the northbound lane of Beverley. Attendants jumped out and checked Mrs. Sentry's vital signs while Rebecca briefed them. Carefully they installed a brace around her neck and lifted her onto a gurney.

Two constables had arrived in a patrol car and were speaking to the students. Once the ambulance had pulled away, the same dark-skinned constable from the other night looked over at Rebecca.

"Is it the doctor?" he asked, stepping toward her. "Didn't we just see you on the weekend? A car tried to run you down?"

She nodded tiredly.

"What's your connection to this woman?"

"Mrs. Sentry's my patient. She just left my office."

"Was it the same car?" he asked.

"I didn't see it."

"These students say it looked like a Dodge. Isn't that what you said?"

She nodded again, feeling sick to her stomach.

"I don't like the sound of this, doctor. You better come to the station and speak to Detective Fitzroy." He gestured to the patrol car.

"I'd like to go to the hospital with Mrs. Sentry."

"You can do that later, doctor. Do you happen to know the next of kin?"

She told him where he could find the victim's husband and son. He wrote down the names in his notepad. Then he opened the rear door of the police cruiser to let her in.

Detective Fitzroy sat across from her in a small room at the Fifty-Second Precinct, the one she was getting to know too well, near City Hall.

"Nothing personal, doc, but I don't like seeing you this often."

"Feeling's mutual, but your constable insisted."

"He was concerned for your safety. So am I. Tell me exactly what happened."

"Mrs. Sentry came to my office. She said she couldn't sleep since her cousin was killed, and I prescribed something for her. A few minutes after she left I heard tires squealing. When I looked out the window she was lying on the road. My secretary called for an ambulance and I ran down." The personal details were confidential. And irrelevant.

"You didn't see the car?"

"It was long gone."

"You have any idea who was behind the wheel? Or why?"

"You'd be the first person I'd tell."

He tapped his pencil on the table. "How well do you know Mrs. Sentry?"

"I just met her the night the old woman was killed. Last week."

"So the connection is the old woman. What do you know about her?"

"Probably the same thing the family told you. She was in a concentration camp with Mrs. Sentry, her cousin, during the war. She was too sensitive to forget what she saw there and had a breakdown after they came to Canada."

"Her cousin?"

"Didn't they tell you?"

He nodded absently. "Would you mind taking a look at a box we found in the backyard? See if anything rings a bell?"

He reached for a large paper bag on his desk, pulling out a gold-coloured cookie tin. The top was illustrated with a fairy-tale cottage surrounded by coral and green flower beds. He removed the lid. Inside lay a glossy little drawing of a mouse in a pink dress with a collar, her long, thin tail curved gracefully behind. Beatrix Potter, if Rebecca was right. A dainty cap sat between the mouse's pink shell-like ears as she surveyed the tiny teacups with intelligent eyes. The fondness for mice, Rebecca recalled. Beneath the drawing lay a jumble of odds and ends: bottle caps, broken pencils, erasers, safety pins, a cork, and a corner of faded green cardboard that might have split off a notebook cover.

"Nothing leaps out at me. Have you spoken to Sentry?"

"Not getting a whole lot of information from him."

*What a surprise*, she thought. "Did he tell you their house was broken into today?"

Fitzroy's eyebrow shot up. "They didn't call the cops?"

"Mrs. Sentry said her husband knew it was a student of his and he would deal with it."

"Hmm. We'll get to the bottom of that. Meanwhile we'll find the driver of that car now that we have a licence plate. We'll look for paint on the victim's clothes and try to match the car. It's just a matter of time."

A squad car dropped her off at Toronto General. She called Nesha from the lobby to tell him about Mrs. Sentry.

"It's a long story. I'll tell you when I get back."

He offered to pick her up from the hospital when she was through. She didn't mention the incident with Nigel. No use getting him all wrought up.

Johanna Sentry was in surgery to relieve the pressure in her brain from the head injury. Rebecca found father and son in the surgery waiting room.

Erich nodded a desultory greeting, but his father appeared stunned, staring vacantly into space with feverish eyes.

"Any word?" she said, sitting down.

"Still in surgery." He looked at her as if appraising the bandage on her cheek, but didn't ask. "It'll be a while," he continued. "Apart from her head injury, she has a fractured pelvis, a fractured radius and ulna, and her bladder is perforated."

"I'm sorry."

"Apparently the car didn't have much space to pick up speed before he hit her. It could've been worse."

Yes, of course, she thought. His mother could be dead.

"The coward!" Will Sentry spat. "If I ever get my hands on who did it ..." He ran his fingers through his unruly hair. "She's a strong girl," he said, quieter now. "She can come through this."

Erich looked at his father, his eyes suddenly desolate.

She waited for ten minutes, then left. The surgery could go on for hours. She gave Erich her home number and asked him to call when he knew something.

The cool open air was a relief after the closeness of the waiting room. She thought of Nesha at home, waiting for her to phone. Instead of calling, she crossed University Avenue and walked briskly toward her office. She wasn't used to being chauffeured. She would rather drive herself home so that he wouldn't have to bring her back in the morning. To play it safe, she stayed on busy University Avenue and walked south to Dundas. She could wave at the precinct from here. Then west to Beverley. Traffic always rolled along Dundas, though the small Chinese shops were closed now. The Art Gallery of Ontario lay quietly on the south side, lit up but empty.

She felt more secure, now that the police were going after the driver with concrete information. So why was she so jumpy? She peered around herself in all directions, as she sprinted across Beverley. A dark sedan drove south toward her. Her heart pounded in her chest, but when the car drove past, she saw it wasn't a Dodge.

Her little Jag sat waiting patiently for her, shining beneath the street lamp on the corner behind the medical building.

She walked in the door of her house at eight o'clock. The smell of home cooking wafted through the air.

"How's Mrs. Sentry?" asked Nesha, helping her off with her coat.

"Won't know till she's out of surgery."

He put his arm around her waist and led her to the dining room He had set the table for two, candles lit in the middle.

"This is a lovely surprise," she said, somewhat embarrassed at the trouble he had gone to.

He handed her a glass of red wine. "*L'Chaim!*" he said, clinking her glass.

How appropriate. To life. She thought of all the newborns who hadn't survived the camps. "*L'Chaim.*"

He insisted she sit while he served the soup. Dainty pieces of mushroom and potato floated in a light broth.

"I hope you can hold your liquor. There's sherry in the soup, wine in the flank steak, and rum in the squash."

She smiled and tasted the soup. "It's delicious. But you may have to carry me up to bed."

"Just say the word."

The flank steak was a bit overdone, but she supposed that was because she was late. He had baked two halves of an acorn squash with butter, sugar, and rum in the cavity.

"You're going to spoil me," she said

"That's the plan."

"I didn't know you could cook like this."

Sometimes he had made her eggs for breakfast on the weekends he visited, but they had always gone out for dinner.

"I like to fool around in the kitchen. But I rarely have someone to cook for."

She was hungry and finished everything on her plate. His brown eyes had overcome the melancholy that usually lurked there and watched her with affection as she wiped the last bit of sauce from her dish with a piece of French bread.

An overwhelming sense of warmth rose in her. "Can you carry me up to bed now?" she said.

He grinned. He came around the table and stood in front of her. Taking her face in both hands, he bent to kiss her, his warm lips enveloping hers.

"Now, we'll see," he said, placing one arm beneath her knees, the other supporting her back. He lifted her with effort, against her protests.

"I didn't mean literally!" she said, laughing. He used to be a competitive swimmer and he seemed fit, but she didn't want to be responsible for any hernias.

She led him up the stairs to her bedroom. Not turning on a lamp, she let the hall light guide them.

He laid her down on the bed in the shadowy room and undressed her, kissing her body where each piece of clothing came off. He removed his own things and climbed into bed beside her. His warm skin tingled on hers, the strength of his arms, his firm shoulders. He was pulling her to him, she was disappearing, finally, the pressure of his body anchoring her, melding into hers.

Beside her ear, the phone began to ring. She sighed in frustration. His head hung motionless in the dark a moment, then he pulled back from her.

She sighed again and picked up the phone.

"Dr. Temple? Fitzroy here. Thought you'd like to know we got the guy who's registered to the car in the hit and run."

"That's a relief. What's his name?"

"Ahmed Mansour. Ring any bells?"

"No."

"We're going to put him in a lineup tomorrow morning. I'd appreciate it if you could come down, see if you can identify him."

"I'll try, but I just saw him for a second."

When she got off the phone, Nesha lay on his side propped up on an elbow. "They got him?"

"Looks like."

"And I got you."

She smiled in the shadows.


At eight-thirty the next morning, Rebecca sat behind a one-way mirror at Fifty-Two Division, waiting for the lineup. Detective Lapointe, a heavy bald man she hadn't met before, sat beside her.

"Okay." He gave the signal to someone.

Six men trudged into the enclosed room and turned to stand facing her in front of a wall marked off with black height lines. All the men had brown complexions and wore dark jackets with jeans. They all had dark hair and moustaches. She was impressed that the police had paid so much attention to detail.

She tried to picture the man in the car that night. She had just jumped through the gate of the house on D'Arcy and fallen on the walk amid the leaves. She could still smell their mustiness. The car door had opened — she turned to see the man get out and stand near the hood, searching for her with relentless eyes. Her brain had taken a snapshot of the receding hairline, the thin moustache. Then the door of the house opened and the man jumped back into the car and drove off.

"Number three," she said, surprising herself.

"Number three, step forward," the detective said into a speaker.

The man lowered his eyelids with disdain and took a step, anger spreading his nostrils.

"Take your time," said the detective.

The man seemed to stare at her through the mirror. She knew that was impossible, but the elemental fear of seeing him again gripped her.

"It's him."

When she left the room, the two students from the night before were waiting to go in and take their turn.

She had called Iris from home to tell her she was going to be late. When Rebecca arrived at her office, the waiting room was full of people.

"Yay!" cried a little boy. "The doctor's here!"

His young mother shushed him, blushing.

Rebecca smiled at them. "Sorry for the delay. It was unavoidable. We'll get right to work." She nodded at the familiar faces on her way to her inner office.

At one o'clock, Rebecca was still up to her elbows in patients when Iris tapped on the exam room door. "Dr. Erich Sentry on the phone."

Rebecca excused herself from her patient, whose underarms had erupted in eczema.

"Rebecca? I just wanted to let you know my mother will make it."

"That's great news. I'm so glad. The surgery went well, then?"

"The swelling in her brain is down. They put screws in to hold her pelvis together. She's in good shape for her age, but it'll be work getting back on her feet. And they repaired her bladder."

The woman was lucky to be alive. She might be incontinent, but only time would tell.

"Give her my best. By the way, did Fitzroy tell you they got the guy?"

"He brought a picture of him to the hospital to show me. I've never seen him before. You didn't tell me the guy went after you first."

"It didn't seem like the right time, with your mother in surgery."

"I'm going back to the hospital later," he said. "Would you like to grab a bite to eat after work?"

"Oh." How could she phrase it? "I'd love to another time, but I have a friend visiting from the States this week."

"Another time, then."

# chapter thirty

Early Tuesday morning Rebecca brought Nesha to the hospital to meet Miriam. He had been reluctant but had let himself be persuaded. The baby needed all the attention she could get. The nurses took care of her physical needs but couldn't give her the affection of family and friends. Flo and Mitch were coming in the afternoon, but till then Miriam would be alone. Rebecca could only stay for twenty minutes before leaving for her office.

"I don't know what to do with a baby," he said, putting a hospital gown over his clothes in the preemie unit.

After they had scrubbed their hands, she led him to Miriam's incubator.

"Oh, good morning, doctor!" nurse Alicia trilled in her East Indian accent. "Night nurse said baby slept very well last night, not much fussing. She's awake now."

Nesha narrowed his eyes in concern. "What does she have on her head?"

Miriam lay quietly on her back, an IV in her scalp held down by tape.

"It's an IV to keep up fluids. Sugar and electrolytes. I know it looks strange, but scalp veins are easy to find and she's less likely to dislodge the IV there."

The baby's dark blue eyes gazed into the air, unfocused. Rebecca checked the chart. The baby's weight had gone up two ounces. Not great. Better than nothing.

"Doctor said yesterday she can come out so you can hold her."

Rebecca grinned while the nurse opened the incubator and gingerly gathered Miriam in two hands, the monitor wires following.

"Which one?" she said, looking from Rebecca to Nesha.

He pointed to Rebecca.

"Sit down," Alicia said. "She's going to lie on you."

"You're next," Rebecca said to him, thrilled when Alicia placed the baby on her chest.

The nurse covered her with a little cotton blanket. For a second Rebecca saw the blanket Birdie had wrapped around her doll, the pathetic broken toy. To replace the doomed baby Mrs. Sentry had borne. Also premature, but with no chance of survival. How many babies had died that way? Silently, barely gulping down a breath before the tortured hand lovingly stopped the air and all the dangers that lurked within it. There would be no record except in the mother's heart.

Rebecca pressed the little weight to her chest. How vulnerable they were, these little ones. A tenderness rose in her she hadn't expected, as she rubbed the warm tiny back.

"How's my little sweetheart today?" she murmured. "Did you solve all the problems of the world in your dreams? You're going to have a fine day. I'll try to come back later."

Turning to Nesha, she said, "I've got to go. How about it?"

"I don't want to break her."

"She's stronger than that." Rebecca stood up, holding the baby to her. "Things haven't changed that much since you had yours."

"That was twenty years ago."

When he sat down warily, she deposited Miriam on his chest. At first he sat stiff and nervous, unmoving.

"Relax," she said. "I'll tell Alicia to come get her in five minutes." She bent and kissed him on the lips. "You look very handsome holding a baby."

"Don't get any ideas," he said with a crooked smile.

On her way off the unit, when she turned around searching for him, he was peering down at the baby with curiosity. It was a start.


Rebecca was filling out workmen's compensation forms behind the counter when Iris came back from lunch. While removing her coat, Iris stepped to the window overlooking Beverley Street.

"There's a guy out there in a car in front of the building. In the No Parking zone."

"So?"

"I bent my head when I was going by, to see if someone was sitting in the car. He gave me a dirty look."

"You haven't gotten dirty looks from men before?"

She made a wry face at Rebecca. "I'm nervous after what happened to Mrs. Sentry. And you."

"They caught the guy."

"Maybe he has friends."

Rebecca put down her pen and walked to the window. A dark blue Ford sat on their side of Beverley, facing south.

"He's not in front of the building."

Iris peered out the window. "He moved a little. I probably made him nervous."

"Did you see what he looked like?"

"Thin guy. Balding. Dark jacket."

"He's probably waiting for someone."

"As long as it's not you."

Partway through the afternoon, when Rebecca was bringing back a patient file, Iris said, "He's gone. The guy in the car."

Rebecca smiled. "Sometimes a guy in a car is just a guy in a car."

At six-thirty, Iris finished up and left the office. Rebecca sat at the desk, checking the test results that had just come in. Her eyes began to blur and she sat back. What about her own family? She pulled out Jeff Herman's number from her skirt pocket. She dialed and listened to it ring. After six rings, she hung up. She would try later.

After filling in more forms and requisitions, she was finally ready to go.

She stood at the window putting on her coat. The car was gone from the front of the building. But on the other side of Beverley the dark Ford sat facing north. Someone was sitting in the driver's seat. She froze.

Should she call Fitzroy? What if the guy was just waiting for somebody? She'd look like she was afraid of her own shadow. And yet.

She dialed her own number. Nesha answered.

"This is going to sound silly, but there's a man sitting in a car out front that's been there most of the day. I'm nervous about going out."

"Don't move. I'll be there in fifteen minutes."

She sat near the window, watching for Nesha's car. The man in the Ford barely moved. Maybe he was asleep. She began to feel foolish.

Nesha pulled into the No Parking zone in front of the building. As soon as he stepped out of his car, she ran downstairs.

Opening the front door, she watched him stand near his car and stare at the Ford parked on the other side of the street. He looked fearless in his leather jacket. *Sometimes you just need a man*, she thought smugly.

"Nice night," he said out loud.

She could see a man sitting in the Ford, in profile, ignoring the unwanted attention.

"Hey!" Nesha called out. "I'm from the States and I think I'm lost. You know where Queen Street is?"

The man turned his face toward Nesha, assessing him. He pulled down his window, motioning backwards with his thumb. "That way," he said. No accent. "About four blocks."

Nesha swaggered across the street toward him, stopping close to the car. "I thank you, sir. Maybe you can tell me something else. Why've you been sitting here all day? You looking for someone?"

"It's none of your business. I don't want any trouble, so step away from the car."

"Well, we have a problem here. Because you're making my girlfriend very jumpy, sitting here all day."

"Step away from the car!"

When Nesha didn't move, the man opened the door and got out, thin, but half a head taller and at least ten years younger.

Rebecca used the only defence she knew. "I'm going to call the police!" she cried out from the front door.

The man looked toward her. "Don't bother, ma'am. I *am* the police." He flashed a card with his photo at Nesha.

A weight lifted off her. "Well, why didn't you say so? I'm Dr. Temple. Why are you here? Did Fitzroy send you?"

"No, ma'am. I'm special squad. Intelligence."

Nesha smirked. "Better find a new name. Or get tinted windows."

Rebecca threw him a dirty look. "I thought they got the man who ran down my patient. If there's still someone dangerous on the loose, I want to know."

"Your patient? She live in that house?" He pointed to the Sentry place.

"Yes."

He looked at the door she had just come from. "Could we talk somewhere besides the middle of the street?"

She led him into the empty hallway of the medical building. The doctor who practised downstairs had already left for the day. Smart woman.

"You'll probably find out soon enough." The man towered over them in a black coat. He was in his thirties, going bald.

"Find out what?" she said.

"The man they had in custody for the hit and run. Got himself killed."

She was speechless. And curiously not relieved that the man was dead. "How'd it happen?"

"Stabbed with a filed-down pen. Got into a fight with another prisoner."

She tried to picture the disdainful man in the lineup. "He must've had a temper. But I don't understand. Why is Intelligence looking into it?"

He observed her a moment, thinking. "I already told you more than I should."

"He tried to run me down on Saturday. Am I still in danger? I have a right to know."

The cop pursed his lips, pondering.

"How do we know you're really in Intelligence?" she said. "You could be a hired cop."

He tilted his head, amused. "You've been watching too many detective movies. Okay. You'll find out anyway. He had a foreign passport. United Arab Emirates. That's why we were called in. Once it's an international question, it falls to us."

"United Arab Emirates?" she said.

"The passport could be phony."

"Was it just your common-variety prison brawl," asked Nesha, "or was he targeted?"

The cop scrutinized him. "We're keeping an open mind."

"You think he might've been a terrorist?" Nesha asked.

"That's how rumours spread." The cop stood there, hands clasped in front of him.

"So you were watching the Sentry house?" Rebecca asked, trying to keep him talking.

"I can't say any more."

"Am I in danger?"

"That's not my department, doctor."

"Well, what *is* your department?"

"Sorry. Can't say."

When the special agent went back outside to his car, Rebecca returned to her office, Nesha trailing after her up the stairs. Standing behind the counter, she dialed the Fifty-Second Precinct.

"Detective Fitzroy is off tonight, ma'am. Would you like to speak to another detective?"

She left a message for him to call her in the morning.

To Nesha she said, "You think he could've been a terrorist? Here? Why would he go after me or Mrs. Sentry?"

Nesha leaned over the counter, his elbows splayed out. "Sentry. Doesn't sound like an Arabic name. Though they could've changed it."

"They're Jewish."

His eyebrows arched together in surprise. "Not a Jewish name either. There seem to be some pieces missing here. But I don't know if your Detective Fitzroy will tell you any more than this guy. If terrorists are involved, the police won't be broadcasting it."

"If they're watching the house, they must think Sentry's involved in something. Do the United Arab Emirates have a terrorist group?"

"The main organization on the Arabian peninsula is the Muslim Brotherhood, which started in Egypt and branched out like an octopus."

"Sentry has a very odd relationship with an Egyptian doctor. They've known each other for years, apparently, but they're barely polite to each other in public."

"An Egyptian doctor?"

"Remember the medical conference I told you about last week? He was the guest speaker. Runs a drug company."

"Ah yes. Investment opportunities in Egypt after the peace accord. How does Sentry know him?"

"Can't figure that out. I heard them speaking German once. I thought maybe the doctor trained in Germany."

"Is Sentry a doctor?"

"No."

"Well, there were a lot of Nazi sympathizers in Egypt. They had so much in common. They both hated Jews. And they both hated Britain, which ruled Egypt for decades. What's this doctor like?"

She shook her head. "Hard to say. His company's connected to the Egyptian government. He's a little long in the tooth to be a terrorist."

She glanced at her watch. Nearly seven. "I want to go to the hospital and speak to Sentry. He's probably visiting his wife." She came around the counter, ready to leave.

"Do you always have this much energy?" he said, straightening up.

"I'm tired, but this can't wait."

"Well, could we go somewhere for a quick meal first? You could relax a bit."

When she hesitated, he took her coat lapels in both hands and pulled her gently toward him. "You know what a man's like when he's hungry. He gets less discriminating about what he eats." He opened his mouth and played at biting her cheek.

"All right, all right." She wiped her cheek with her palm, smiling. "There's a burger joint on College where the service is fast."

# *chapter thirty-one*

Nesha managed to find a parking meter a block away from the restaurant. It felt odd having a man drive her around. Disorienting. Like Nesha himself. Comforting and disorienting at the same time. What was happening to her? Why couldn't she just be grateful for his company while all hell was breaking loose in her life?

They sat at a booth with high backs for privacy. The waitresses scurried back and forth from the kitchen at the rear, carrying huge trays piled with plates of food. They looked like college students working their way through school, thin cheery girls with muscular arms.

While they waited for their burgers, Rebecca said, "You really think there are terrorists in Canada?"

"It's an easy country to get into. An easy country to hide in. Canadians are decent, so they don't expect people to come here and try to kill them."

"But *why* would they come here? Surely not that promise about moving the Canadian Embassy in Israel to Jerusalem."

"I'd forgotten about that. Your prime minister was reckless to bring up Jerusalem at all. Now he has the Arabs up in arms — any implication that Jerusalem belongs to the Jews is going to boil their blood. This is why the Muslim Brotherhood is so popular — they tell people what they want to hear. That they'll spread Islam throughout the world, and they'll wipe Israel off the map."

She stared at him while the waitress set down their plates. Rebecca picked up a French fry and chewed thoughtfully.

"You don't believe me. You've grown up in a country where Jews are like everyone else. In Arab countries Jews are less than human. The Arabs couldn't believe it when Israel was created. The underlings with their own country? Maybe if it was there earlier, the Holocaust wouldn't have happened. In their rage the Arabs threw all the Jews out of their lands. People who'd lived in Arab countries for generations — they left behind everything they owned. They went to the only country that would take them. Israel."

"Okay, hold on. What about the peace accord?"

"That's between governments. Between two presidents. The radicals on the ground have their own agenda."

He had stopped eating while he talked. Half his hamburger still lay on the dish.

"I thought you were starving," she said, finishing her fries.

He picked up his burger and took a large bite, chewing with a smile. "I get worked up about this."

"I hadn't noticed. What do you want to do while I go find Sentry at the hospital?"

"I'll drive you and wait for you in the car. I hate hospitals. I can snooze and listen to music. And think about your body."

He let her off at the Elizabeth Street entrance of Toronto General, where there was less traffic.

"I'll try to be back in fifteen minutes."

When she found the room, Mrs. Sentry lay sleeping while her husband and son exchanged heated words in low voices in a corner of the private room. Not a good place for an argument, she thought. Though the patient seemed unperturbed, her head covered in white bandage, an IV solution dripping into her arm. Beneath the covers, wires ran to a heart monitor. Otherwise there was little visible evidence of the injuries she had sustained.

When Erich saw Rebecca, the anger in his face slid beneath the surface. He stepped away from his father toward her.

"How is she?" Rebecca asked.

He looked back at his mother. "Sleeping quietly. They gave her something for the pain."

His father nodded toward her without expression, though an energy sparked from him that seemed to issue from his unruly hair. He was wearing dark sweatpants and a jacket.

"It's nice of you to come," Erich said.

Now she was embarrassed. She hadn't come to visit. "Have you spoken to Fitzroy today?"

"No. Why?"

"Something's happened. The man they had in custody. He was killed by another inmate."

Erich blinked. "Right in prison?"

"I'd like to talk to you about something. Your father too, if he doesn't mind."

Erich hesitated, then approached his father, murmuring a few words.

"Killed?" said Sentry. He followed his son to the other side of the bed, near the door.

"I'm sorry," Rebecca said to Will Sentry, who waited with his head tilted, "but something unusual seems to be going on. The man who ran down your wife was an Arab national. He might've been a terrorist. Someone might've had him killed in prison so he wouldn't be able to talk."

"Terrorists? *Here?* I don't understand," Sentry said. "What does it have to do with us?"

"You don't have any Middle Eastern connections?"

"I don't concern myself with politics."

"What do you know about Dr. Salim?"

"Why?"

"He's Egyptian. The man had an Arab passport."

He rolled his eyes. "Doctor, doctor! Salim's company is in the government's pocket. He's part of the ruling class. Can't you tell by his clothes? If there are terrorists anywhere, then they're *against* the government. You're barking up the wrong tree."

"Your wife said your house was broken into —"

"So *you're* the one who told the police."

Her face went hot. "I thought it might be connected to this."

"Very civic-minded, I'm sure," he said, smiling, turning on the charm. "But I told the police. It was one of my students. We had a disagreement about his grade. He's a hothead and wanted to get back at me. So he broke in and made a mess. Nothing to do with anything."

Erich's eyes had shifted away abruptly, his jaw set. Was this what they had been arguing about?

"Wolfie." Mrs. Sentry was mumbling in her sleep. "Wolfie."

"I'm here, darling," her husband said, stepping back to her bed. He took her hand and stood watching her face. "I'm right here."

"She called your father Wolfie," Rebecca whispered to Erich, still beside her.

"His real name is Wolfgang."

She supposed it was too German for Canada. "Is your real name Erich Sentry?" She was only half joking.

"It is now. But it used to be Erich Eisenbaum."

Birdie's name. "My German's rusty. Is it a translation?"

"Partly. *Eisen* means 'iron' and *baum* means 'tree' in German. They took away the 'Ei' from 'Eisen' and were left with 'Sen.' So it became Sentry. He used to tell me that story when I was a kid. He was so proud he could come up with an English-sounding name. When I was old enough to translate for myself, I asked him why he didn't use Irontree. He said it was a ridiculous name because a tree couldn't be made of iron. Nothing could live in an iron tree, including us."

Sentry looked up from his wife to his son. He seemed to be following their conversation. When his wife dozed off again, he stepped toward them.

"You forgot that 'sentry' means standing on guard," he said to Erich. "We always have to be vigilant to protect ourselves."

"Against what?" she asked.

"The world is filled with danger."

"I've noticed," she said.

"I understand someone tried to kill you a few days ago."

She glanced at Erich, the probable source of the information.

"I can't help feeling it's because I met your cousin. If you'd tell me more about her, maybe I could figure this thing out." She didn't mean it to sound like a challenge, but her impatience was probably surfacing in her voice.

"There's nothing to tell." He fixed her with brown eyes that professed sincerity and reason. Then spoiled it by adding, "Leave her out of it."

Rebecca wasn't good at taking orders. "Her name was also Eisenbaum. She never married?"

"Doctor, please! Let her rest in peace!"

Rebecca was startled. As if her question was offensive. And *peace* was not a word she would have used for the murdered woman. If there was such a thing, she doubted the woman was resting in it, but she wouldn't burden him by saying so.

"I wanted to tell you — I'm having doubts about the homeless man. What if he didn't kill her? What if the same man who ran down your wife killed your cousin?"

He suddenly lifted his hands over his ears. "Cousin! Cousin! Stop calling her that."

Rebecca looked at Erich, who stared at his feet. "I don't understand —"

"She was my *sister!*" Sentry leaned back against the wall, ashen. "She was my sister. My beautiful, brilliant sister. Don't ever call her Birdie! Her name was Frieda. She was always the smart one in the family. You believe it?" He appraised Rebecca, his eyes bitter. "You want to know the worst part? She was a doctor once. Can you imagine? Just like you. A doctor. At a time when it was next to impossible for a woman. The insane creature you saw in the backyard was just like you once."

She couldn't move. A cold nausea rose in her. Funny the way your body reacted to words. Only words, but the body took in their import as if they were bullets aimed at the chest. She pictured the dirty heart-shaped face beneath the cap, the unfocused eyes. The horrors of the camp had destroyed her.

"I can't imagine what she went through …"

"You don't want to. You wouldn't have survived what she went through. Did you ever have to kill a baby?"

"Dad ..."

"In the first camp she was sent to. She told me she delivered babies of women who were foolish enough to get pregnant. If the Nazis saw the babies, mother and child would be gassed. So she saved the mother by killing the baby. How can someone stay sane after that?"

She was the doctor his wife had spoken of! The one who had lost her soul. She had not only smothered other women's babies. She had saved her sister-in-law's life by smothering her own niece. Sentry would never know.

Rebecca's heart twisted with pain. In a flash she saw herself delivering Miriam, hearing the plaintive cry for the first time. What would she have done in the other's place? Unthinkable.

"After that," he continued, "she was sent to a camp where she worked in the office. Not practising, of course. Keeping records, that sort of thing. It was better there, but it was too late. The damage was done. You know where 'Birdie' came from? Her Jewish name was Faygele. Little bird. She said that was why she was going crazy. Because a bird couldn't live in an iron tree. She called herself Birdie after that. Even half-crazy she still understood irony."

Rebecca wavered where she stood. Was she still in the room? The hospital? The old woman's face appeared in the air, confused, distressed.

Erich took a deep breath beside her. "Dad. Maybe you should sit down."

His father retreated to the further chair. The old woman dissolved into the wall.

"I'm sorry," Erich said. "You didn't need to hear all that."

In her peripheral vision, a figure appeared in the doorway of the room. Nesha. Bad timing.

"I was wondering what happened to you," Nesha said, observing Erich.

She had to snap out of it. "Sorry. I lost track of time. This is Erich and his father, Will. This is Nesha. He's visiting from California."

"Your friend from the States." Erich nodded at him, but gave her a sidelong glance that implied subterfuge on her part.

She hadn't lied, only omitted crucial information. The gender of her friend. She gave Erich a half-hearted smile and said goodbye.

"You're very quiet," Nesha said on the way to the elevator.

"I'm not feeling well."

"You were okay when I dropped you off. You mad because I came up?"

"Of course not."

The middle-aged woman in the elevator stepped backward to let them in.

"Nice-looking young man. He wasn't supposed to see me?"

She cringed at the woman listening behind them.

"Don't be ridiculous. We just met last week."

"Sometimes things happen fast. I saw the look between you."

"You don't understand." She turned to find the woman staring up at the lighted floor numbers changing as they descended.

The elevator stopped at the first floor. The woman stepped around them and hurried off. They headed toward the Elizabeth Street exit.

"It's a tragic family. I'm learning more about them than I want to know and it's upsetting me." She looked at him sideways. His eyes searched hers, waiting.

"The woman who lived in their backyard. The dead woman. She wasn't Sentry's cousin. He says she was his sister. His *sister*. He was probably too embarrassed to admit it. He says she was a *doctor*. That she was ... he says she was just like me."

Nesha stopped and took her hand. "Impossible. No one's like you. He's distraught and he's lashing out."

"But she was a *doctor*. How could she become what she was?"

"You didn't have to die in the war to be destroyed by it," he said.

Nesha had been one of those casualties. But Rebecca couldn't explain her distress to him, the kinship she felt with the older woman. She could hardly explain it to herself. She was a successful young physician, her future stretching out before her. Yet the small, sad face hung like a moon on that horizon. What if one day she found it looking back at her in the mirror?

"You need some rest. Come on, I'll take you home."

Rebecca was changing for bed when the phone rang. She glanced at the clock on her night table. It was after eleven.

"Hi, Rebecca. It's Susan."

"Susan! Are you all right?"

"I'm feeling a bit better."

Was she whispering? Rebecca sat down on the edge of the bed, relieved. "I can hardly hear you."

"How's Miriam?"

This was a change. "She's holding her own." Don't push. Don't say it.

"Rebecca, I'm so sorry about everything. I know I've made things difficult for everybody. I just ..." She sniffled.

Rebecca's heart contracted at the sound of Susan weeping. "Don't cry, sweetie. It's not your fault. These things happen." She hesitated. "If you're feeling up to it you could drop into the hospital for a visit." There, she'd said it.

"Got to go!" Susan murmured. "Jeff's coming."

# chapter thirty-two

---

I ris was on the phone when Rebecca arrived at the office Wednesday morning. She stood in front of her assistant with her coat on until Iris looked up and put her hand over the mouthpiece.

"Did Fitzroy call?"

Iris shook her head.

Rebecca headed for her inner office. Throwing off her coat, she picked up her private line and dialed the precinct number by heart. For a change Fitzroy was in.

"What can I do for you, doctor?"

"I met the cop from Intelligence last night. He was watching the Sentry house."

"They're watching the house?"

"When were you going to tell me that the guy in jail was a terrorist? Or that he was killed to keep him from talking?"

"We're not sure of any of that."

"Well, someone's sure enough to bring in Intelligence. Didn't you think I should know? Since my life might be in danger?"

Silence. Thinking.

"Is it?"

"I don't know. We don't have a lot to go on. Everything's happening real fast. We had a guy in who could translate the Arabic but so far there's nothing personal in the pamphlets. It's vicious hate stuff. 'Drive the Zionist entity into the sea.' That kind of thing. That's one of the mild ones. But your names don't come up anywhere. Not yours or the Sentrys'."

"Where'd you find the pamphlets?"

"In the house with the guy you ID'd. Place probably belongs to their group, whatever it is. Out in Scarborough. At least two other men living there. Ran out the back and disappeared. Not enough of our guys to chase them down. When we realized what we had, we brought in the troops and combed the neighbourhood. Went door to door. They'll turn up. Anyway, nothing much in the house except boxes of these pamphlets. We're checking the mosques in the area to see if they were handing out this crap."

"So there are at least two men out there who may or may not be part of the Muslim Brotherhood and who may or may not be interested in killing me?"

"I wouldn't put it that way."

"Well how would you put it?"

"They're people of interest. We don't know their connection yet. Just be careful. Be aware of who's around you. Don't take any unnecessary chances."

"That's not reassuring."

"Well, the cop from Intelligence is right in front watching the Sentry house. If you see something suspicious, call him."

"Yeah, thanks. About Sentry, did you buy that story — that his house was broken into by a student?"

"You think he's holding something back?"

"Fencing is a genteel sport. I have trouble imagining one of his students trashing the teacher's house. Did he give you a name?"

"He said he didn't want to get the guy into trouble. If he isn't pressing charges, nothing I can do."

"Or it wasn't a student."

"Or it wasn't a student," he said.

"Mrs. Sentry said they didn't take anything. What would they've been looking for in the house?"

"Something Sentry has that the terrorists or the Muslim Brotherhood — or whoever it is — wants. What's his connection to them?"

"That's just it. I could understand them going after Salim because of his association with the Egyptian government. But why go after Sentry?"

"Maybe there's a connection between Sentry and Salim we're not getting," he said. "We have to start at the beginning. With the old woman."

"Do you still think Stanley killed her? What about Nigel?"

"We found Stanley's fingerprints on a few things in the yard. But the rock with the blood on it — no fingerprints there. We think the killer hit her with it. If all these other things weren't happening, I'd like Stanley for it. Maybe even Nigel if he was flying high. But this Muslim Brotherhood business has got me scratching my head."

She pictured the large head with the scant hair combed forward. "Did you come up with anything on the doll?"

"Turns out it's just a broken old doll. I had forensics take it apart after what you told me she said. What was it again?"

"'Where is it? Where is it? You can't have it.' As if someone had come looking for something and she was repeating both sides of the conversation. At first I thought it might be the doll she was talking about. But you know, after speaking to the Sentrys, I think the doll was a personal thing with her. Part of her war memory. It wouldn't mean anything to anyone else." She wasn't going to tell Fitzroy about the Sentrys' lost baby. He would have to trust her on this one.

"See, it's hard to connect her to the Brotherhood," he said.

"Maybe they came looking to get into the house and she surprised them in the yard. They wouldn't have expected her there, and just killed her on the spur of the moment. She may not have a connection."

"A lot of maybes."

"Have you questioned Dr. Salim?"

"He's a hard man to get hold of. Left a message for him at the hotel."

"The Royal York?"

"He's a VIP. He's got a schedule of talks as long as my arm. We put a man on him for protection, but he kept giving him the slip. Doesn't like guards, he says. We'll catch up to him." Fitzroy cleared his throat. "Anyway, he's kind of peripheral to the investigation. Sentry never mentioned him."

"I'd take what Sentry says with a grain of salt. He keeps secrets on principle." Even if he did divulge something intensely personal about his family to her. He'd managed to insult and offend her while doing it. She was still disturbed by his words. He didn't care if he hurt her; seemed to make a point of it, targeting her with those eyes filled with world-weariness. Yet something else was going on. She sensed it in the combative posture, the evasive words. It was like he was trying to distract her from the real issue. He was playing his cards close to his chest.

"The thing I can't figure out is what *I* have to do with it. How am I supposed to protect myself?"

"Mace."

"Mace?"

"Come down to the station and I'll give you a sampler. If someone gets too close, you spray the bastard in the eyes. That'll stop him. Don't tell anyone, though. Not supposed to be giving these out to civilians."

"I'll send my assistant over. You're around the corner from her favourite Chinese restaurant."

After Iris had left for lunch, Rebecca dialed the number for the Royal York.

"I'd like to speak to one of your guests. Dr. Salim."

"He's not in. Can I take a message?"

Since when did switchboard operators keep track of the comings and goings of hotel patrons? When VIPs gave instructions not to be disturbed.

The grey sky threatened rain as the Dundas streetcar trundled west to the subway. The hotel wasn't far from the office. Her paperwork would wait.

In less than fifteen minutes Rebecca was striding along the plushy champagne-coloured broadloom of the Royal York foyer toward the sweeping reception desk.

An imperious young woman with sleek black hair looked up. "May I help you?"

"I've come to see one of your guests. Could you tell Dr. Salim that Rebecca Temple is here? Dr. Rebecca Temple."

The woman searched through a large-leafed book, then looked up again, her eyes half lidded. "Dr. Salim is unavailable. Would you like to leave a message?"

"Dr. Salim's a friend of mine. I have something important to tell him. I've found an investor for his new drug. He'll want that information right away."

"If you give me the name of the investor, I'll pass it on."

"I'm afraid it's strictly confidential."

The sloe-eyed receptionist assessed her. "I'll try to reach him. Wait here." She retreated to an office.

In a few minutes, she returned to the desk, her face softer. "Dr. Salim says he'll be right down."

Rebecca sat down on one of the silk-covered sofas in the foyer, facing the corridor that led to the elevators. As she undid the buttons of her black wool coat, three men in business suits strolled by, giving her the eye. She uncrossed her legs, tucking them demurely beneath her. While she pulled her tweed skirt over her knees, Salim exited the elevator corridor and walked toward her.

Though he had to be over sixty, he cut a fine figure, his shoulders broad and solid beneath the brown wool sports jacket and ivory-toned shirt.

"What a lovely surprise!" he said with an effusiveness his eyes did not share. "Would you like to go to the bar? It's just down here."

He led her to a room panelled floor to ceiling with oak, books lining the walls. Green damask-covered sofas ranged around dark wood tables. More like a Victorian parlour than a bar.

"They make an excellent martini," he said, motioning her to a sofa, then seating himself at a polite distance.

"I'll just have coffee, thanks. I have to go back to work."

A waiter appeared and took their order.

"Did I hear the lady at the desk right? You've found an investor for our drug?"

She had an uneasy moment about the lie but stared in radiant confusion. "I think she misunderstood. What I said was I had some suggestions on finding investors. I thought of a few organizations you might not have tried. The Canadian Cancer Society. The Canadian Arthritis Society. The Multiple Sclerosis Society. Any place that deals with people in pain. They may have funds they're willing to invest in new research."

He observed her. "Yes. Thank you. What a good idea."

"Did you know that the police were trying to get in touch with you?"

The waiter brought their drinks. Salim sipped his martini.

He shrugged. "They're worried about my safety. As long as I stay here, I think I'm out of harm's way."

"Someone mentioned terrorists," she said. "Would they really try to harm you?"

"Who knows? My brother-in-law has high connections in government. Which clamps down on the Muslim Brotherhood every so often when they overstep their bounds and kill someone important. Right now tension is running high because of the overture for peace with Israel. Since I run my brother-in-law's company, I'm a target." His face brightened with a bemused smile. "Your police don't want anything to happen to me. It might cause an international incident."

"Did they have any suggestions?"

"They offered me protection. But that's impossible. If an Egyptian national has to be guarded in a Western country, then the Brotherhood has won. I can take care of myself. Living in Egypt all these years, I've grown very careful."

"They offered you protection, they put a man outside the house, but I never even got a phone call."

"Outside the Sentry house? I suppose that's wise." He finished the martini. Raised his finger for the waiter and motioned for a second.

She blushed, imagining the cop's reaction to her loose lips.

"Maybe you should take them up on their offer. No one needs to know."

"I'm not afraid of death. I've lived so long near the pyramids and the souls of dead kings. Death doesn't frighten me. It's a stepping stone to the afterlife."

He lifted the second martini glass in the air in a mock toast. "I don't get a chance to savour alcohol in Egypt. So I take the opportunity when I travel. Here's to new places and new friends."

She smiled and finished her coffee while he sipped at his drink.

"Why do you think a Muslim terrorist would be interested in Sentry?"

"Maybe he owes them money. He's an inveterate gambler."

She had always assumed that Muslims didn't drink or gamble. People were always so much broader than their definitions.

"How do you know him?" she asked.

Salim lifted his head back while emptying his glass.

"It's a long story," he said, his speech slower.

One he wasn't about to tell.

"Well *I* don't owe them money. Why would they try to run me down?"

"Dear lady doctor," he said, closing his eyes, opening them, "they are a troublesome, violent bunch whose motives are rarely reasonable. I would stay off the streets and lock your doors." He raised his finger to get the waiter's attention.

After her last patient left that evening, Rebecca tried Jeff Herman's number. While she listened to the phone ring, someone climbed the stairs to her office. Before she could jump to lock the door, Jeff Herman stepped in, stoop-shouldered in an expensive sheepskin jacket. His blonde hair lay in professional waves, but his eyes shifted restlessly above dark half-moons.

"Is Susan here?"

"She's not with you?"

He reached into his pocket and pulled out a note, handing it to her.

> Dear Jeff,
>
> Thanks for all your support, but I have to work things out for myself now.
>
> Love, Susan

"She left sometime before I got home. She's gone."

"I'm sorry," Rebecca said, an automatic response to his distress. She would have been sorrier if Susan had stayed with him.

"Look. Rebecca. I know what you think of me."

She opened her mouth to make a feeble protest. He raised his hand, excusing her.

"But I'm really in love with her. I'd do anything for her. We talked about her getting a divorce so she could marry me."

"Her idea or yours?"

He stopped to think. "Mine." He chewed on the inside of his cheek. "You know where she is?"

"No."

"I tried your parents' place — she wasn't there. I tried Diane's." He rubbed his eyes with one hand. "You know, I still remember her in high school. We were sixteen. She had that stunning blonde hair that covered half her face. She was so sexy. All the guys were after her. And for a while *I* had her. I was cock of the walk. She still makes me feel that way."

"Jeff," Rebecca said, trying to find the right words, "I think she needs some space. If you care for her, you'll do what she asks."

"What she asks?"

"Read the note."

He stared at her glumly. "She's wasting her life. Tell her I can still help her get into law school here. I have connections."

After he left, Rebecca walked back to her inner office to grab her coat. Where was Susan? If she were at their parents' house, they would have called Rebecca by now. Was she lying low at Diane's? A hotel? Rebecca would start at Diane's.

She stepped to the front window, putting on her coat. The Sentry house was usually dark at this hour, but to her surprise, a light shone through the window. Maybe Will Sentry was picking something up to take to the hospital for his wife.

On her way down the stairs, she groped in her purse for the key to the deadbolt, her fingers blindly bumping into the small can of Mace that Iris had picked up for her from Fitzroy.

Outside the back door, she locked the deadbolt, breathing in the chilly air. Walking to her Jag in the little parking area, she looked up to see the dark Ford almost in front of her, sitting on D'Arcy, the driver's side next to the sidewalk. Parked in that direction, the cop from Intelligence would have to watch the Sentry house in his rearview mirror. She supposed he moved the car a few times during the day, trying to avoid notice.

Maybe she should ask him if there had been any developments. He had given her information before. In the light of the street lamp, she saw him leaning over the steering wheel as if looking for something on the floor.

Something was wrong. He still hadn't moved when she reached the car, his face turned to the other side.

She knocked on the window. He didn't move. She tried the door handle. It was unlocked. She pulled open the door.

"Hello!" she said. "Can you hear me?"

No movement. She pushed him back by his shoulders. God! Blood covered his neck and stained the front of his coat. Too much blood to see where he had been wounded.

Adrenaline kicked in. Feel his neck for a pulse. Two fingers pressed against the carotid artery. Nothing. How long had he been sitting here? Check for breath. She put her cheek next to his mouth. Nothing. He had lost too much blood.

She closed the car door gingerly and was about to rush back to her office when she saw a dark-clad figure approaching from that side. The man wasn't running, but he walked with purpose. Were they coming after her now? No more hit and miss with the car. More chance of success up close with a weapon. She jumped away from the car and sprinted across Beverley toward the light in the Sentry house.

# chapter thirty-three

She vaulted up the front stairs. Banged on the door. "Mr. Sentry! It's Rebecca Temple! Please let me in!"

No answer. Damn him! She turned around, searching for the man in the street. Was he hiding? She tried the door knob. It opened.

She leaped inside and closed the door behind her, locking it. Her heart beat wildly, her breath shallow. Had it just been someone walking home quickly for dinner? She wasn't taking any chances. She tried to calm down and remember where the phone was. The kitchen?

"Mr. Sentry?"

She peered into the living room from where she stood. In the lamplight she could see books and photos all over the floor. Hadn't the Sentrys picked things up after the break-in?

She crept down the hall toward the lit kitchen. Where was he? The phone was on the wall, like she remembered. She picked up the receiver and dialed for the operator. No sound. She pushed down the lever to get a dial tone. Silence. Not an empty silence. A bleak silence filled with inevitability. The phone was dead. She felt her armpits go clammy beneath the coat. Pulling on the wire to see where it attached to the wall, she looked down: the cut end hung loose in her hand.

She had to get out! Now! There was a back door off the kitchen — she remembered Mrs. Sentry stepping out of it the night Birdie died. Rebecca was creeping toward it when she heard the groan. *Oh God.* Someone was hurt — was it Sentry? Where did duty to others end? Should she risk her life to give medical attention? What if it was a trap?

She stopped. She couldn't just walk away.

"Mr. Sentry?" she whispered. "Is it you?"

She tiptoed to the living room. This time she stepped inside. Then she saw him. He was sitting on the floor, leaning against a bookcase, legs stretched out in front between two upholstered chairs. Blood stained his shirt around one shoulder. His eyes were closed, his face the colour of putty.

"Mr. Sentry? Can you hear me? I'm going to go out and call an ambulance."

He shook his head. "Run!" he whispered hoarsely.

"Good advice," said a familiar voice behind her. "But I'm afraid it's too late for that."

She whirled around. "Dr. Salim! What're you doing here?"

He held a sword in his hand pointed toward her, his grey cashmere coat open.

"Take note, doctor, that this is not one of those foils with a rubber tip. My old friend was thoughtful enough to collect a real sword and hang it on his wall. The police will see it as an opportunistic weapon for an intruder. The end is very sharp, I assure you. As you can see by the wound it delivered. One needn't take fencing classes to inflict grievous injury. Lucky for me."

"*You're* behind this?"

Salim's eyelids lowered partway. "You should've stayed home, doctor. Eisenbaum convinced me that you didn't know anything and I was prepared to leave you alone. Of course that's impossible, now that you're here. I'm surprised that someone so smart can be so stupid. I knew someone else like that once. In fact, you remind me a lot of her."

"Brenner! *Halt den Mund!*"

"Brenner?" she echoed.

"The way she used to be, anyway. When she was young and exquisite. She had … the deepest brown eyes."

"Don't you dare speak about her, you filthy murderer! You killed my sister."

The reverie in Salim's face went blank. The sword lowered a few inches. "She wasn't your sister anymore. Your sister was a shining beauty, a woman of intelligence. The creature in that yard was a shell. Unrecognizable."

He paused and pressed his lips together. "I came to check out the house — it wasn't so easy to find where you lived. And there was this old *woman* in the yard. When she began to speak, I recognized her voice. You should've *told* me, Eisenbaum. It was such a shock when I realized who she was. What she had become."

He shook his head slowly. Rebecca wondered how many more martinis he had consumed after she had left. Who was he? He had killed Birdie. Why?

"Ultimately I blame *you*, Eisenbaum, for abandoning her in your backyard. People treat dogs better."

"Shut your filthy mouth!" Sentry roared. "You killed her in cold blood — you bludgeoned her to death, and you have the gall …"

"You don't understand at all. I idolized your sister. I loved her from the first time I saw her in the hospital in Berlin. Look!"

He pulled a photo from his coat pocket and held it up for Rebecca to see. The young Sentrys stood behind a sad, beautiful woman holding a child on her lap. The photo from the mantel. He'd removed it from the frame.

"*This* was the woman I remembered. When I found out she was at Ravensbrück — I risked my position to bring her to the sub-camp. How long do you think she would've survived if I hadn't taken her to work in my lab?"

"You were in Ravensbrück?" Rebecca said.

"She didn't *work* with you! She kept the records!" Sentry cried. Then he groaned with pain, his voice dropping. "She was blameless. So big deal, you're human! You wanted her, so you saved her."

"No!" He stared down at the photo. "I *loved* her! When love between us was forbidden. *She* appreciated the danger of my position." He levelled half-lidded eyes at Sentry. "And then to see her dirty and unintelligible ... It tore me apart. She wouldn't want to live like that, the woman I knew. I couldn't bear to see her like that. I set her free."

"Ha! She couldn't tell you where the record book was, so you eliminated a witness."

"Are you purposely obtuse? A witness! She made no sense. What kind of testimony could she give? I left in a quandary, very distraught. When I came back, she began to shout. I tried to speak to her, make her listen — but she was completely mad. I was afraid the neighbours would come out. I knew what I had to do. I picked up the rock ..." He stared at the floor. "And I prayed to Allah."

"*Allah!* You hypocrite! You expect me to believe you have a heart? You thought she might have the book, but you couldn't find it because I took it away from her. If you kill me, you'll never find it. You want it, you know my terms."

"You're *blackmailing* him?" Rebecca said, her voice rising.

"None of your business," Sentry replied, his head back against the bookcase.

"All of this because of money? What the hell's in the book worth killing for?"

Salim tilted his head. "On the other hand, maybe it doesn't exist. You've always been good at bluffing. Did you think I'd just take your word and pay you?"

"I have a photocopy. For insurance."

Salim sucked in his cheeks. "Where?"

Sentry leaned his head back tiredly against the bookcase. "Dr. Temple. If you come on the other side, you'll see my gear case. Reach down inside. You'll feel a plastic bag."

She stepped over his legs. Salim raised the sword again, pointing it at her. She wondered how much force it would take for him to penetrate her coat. Her purse still hung on her shoulder, the can of Mace inside. It was useless unless she could get close enough to spray it into his eyes.

She knelt down and unzipped the long leather gear bag. When she put her hand inside, the first thing she felt was Sentry's foil. Her mind whirled. A weapon! She looked up at him. Their eyes locked. She tried to read his expression, but mostly she wanted to know: how could she combat a real sword with a foil that ended in a rubber tip?

"Well?" said Salim.

She felt around beneath the steel foil. Her fingers pulled out a plastic shopping bag containing a wad of paper. She peered inside the bag — vertical lines divided a page into columns like a ledger, writing in between.

"Hand it over!" Salim demanded.

She'd have to rummage in her purse with her left hand to find the Mace. It would be obvious and he'd have more than enough time to run her through. She'd have to wait.

She stood up and reached out to give him the bag.

"Get back there. Sit down beside him. On the other side."

She stepped back and sat down on the floor. Salim must have known there was a foil in the gear bag. He also knew the rubber tip rendered it useless, otherwise he'd have pushed it away.

He held the plastic bag under his sword arm and pulled a few pages out with his other hand. "Hmm. March 12, 1943. Prisoner numbers. Amounts injected. Procedures. And so forth. All in Dr. Eisenbaum's perfect handwriting. We destroyed everything before the Russians came," Salim muttered, studying the pages. "I'm impressed your sister managed to hide this."

"She was a resourceful woman."

"I can't imagine why she kept this rubbish all these years. Was it a memento, Eisenbaum? To remind her of what was done to you?"

Rebecca glanced sideways. What had Sentry been through?

"You mean what *you* did to me, Brenner."

"You were a Nazi doctor?" Rebecca asked, incredulous.

Salim tilted his head, his face shiny with perspiration. "That was another life. It wasn't me. I mean the me *now*. I've climbed to the highest echelon in my adopted country. Did you think I'd let you jeopardize all that, Eisenbaum? You always were greedy."

Sentry rallied to the challenge. "We could finish the whole affair if you got your brother-in-law to wire you the money. Just tell him the lab here asked you for it. It's all really his fault anyway. He was the one who shipped the venom to the camp. He found the drying process, otherwise it would spoil, all that distance. Frieda told me all about it. Do you ever think of that at family get-togethers in Egypt? That your brother-in-law's shipments helped you torture people? Even he would think of the money as the price of doing business."

"Mohammed thinks of himself as a humanitarian. He only sent the venom because I asked for it. The Nazi doctor supervising the sub-camp — he didn't understand anything. He got his diploma from the Party. They were only interested in their obsessive theories of race. They wouldn't let me do my own research. I was forced to compromise my integrity and use the venom in their experiments."

"The same venom that's in your new drug?" she asked.

"Absolutely no connection. We're developing a drug for pain."

"It's the same venom," Sentry said. "Your brother-in-law a humanitarian! Don't make me laugh. He knew what they used it for." He glanced at Rebecca. "The obsessive theories of race the esteemed doctor mentioned. They included sterilizing undesirables. The lower orders. In other words, anyone but them. Mostly with radiation and surgery, no anaesthesia, of course. But the Herr Doktor added another element to the torture. He injected venom into the testicles."

"That's a lie! I went against Nazi policies and used it to alleviate the pain of the surgery. I couldn't *say* that. But Frieda knew. She kept it to herself to protect me."

"You're dreaming this up. The guilt is making you hallucinate."

"If I wanted to work, I had to go along with them. I had no choice. *You* survived, didn't you?"

"One of the few."

"How do you think that happened?"

"Frieda wouldn't sleep with you unless you let me live?"

Salim blinked, speechless. Rebecca felt her heart shrinking.

Sentry addressed her. "The others were all killed. How do you say? Sacrificed, after the experiments."

The hair on her neck stood up.

"It was a different world," Salim said, finding his tongue. "We needed results. The only way was to get postmortem data. You see, you can't operate like that today. That's why it takes so long to develop the research."

"If I go public with the book, you're finished. The new wonder drug — first used to sterilize concentration camp prisoners! Your investors will dump you like a hot potato." Sentry grimaced. "All the pain and suffering that went into getting that data. Kiss your drug goodbye."

Salim shook, trying to control his anger, his fist hard around the handle of the sword. "There'd *be* no drug if I hadn't used it on prisoners first!"

Rebecca looked at Sentry beside her. Had *he* been one of the subjects?

Salim read her mind. "Yes, Herr Eisenbaum was there. You're wondering, if he was sterilized, how does he have a son?"

"Shut up, Brenner. Shut up."

"Frieda saved your life when she persuaded me to transfer you from the main camp. I can't tell you how many guards I had to bribe. She didn't know what would happen to you. Only that you had a better chance with us."

Sentry lowered his eyes.

"So you see, you owe me. Where's the real book?"

Sentry's eyes were closed. "Why should I tell you? Then you can kill me."

"You think my hands are tied? I don't need to kill you. I can kill the doctor."

Did she hear him right?

"This beautiful young woman's death will be on your head if you don't tell me where the record book is."

Sentry opened his eyes and searched her face as if seeing her for the first time. A chill went through her.

"You don't believe me," Salim said. He took a step toward her, pointing the sword at her chest.

Images of her lifeless body swirled in her head.

"You haven't changed, if you're still capable of such a thing," Sentry said.

"We're *all* capable. Didn't you see in the war? Everyone can kill. It's only human. It just depends on what's at stake. You understand, if the record book becomes public, my life is over. So I have nothing to lose."

He raised the tip of the sword to Rebecca's neck. "Where is it?"

"Mr. Sentry!" she gasped. "*Tell* him!"

Sentry opened his mouth, but nothing came out.

"*Where is it*?" Salim cried. Eyes blazing, he lifted the sword in the air and whipped it down on her arm, the edge of the steel cutting through her coat sleeve and stinging her skin. He lifted the sword again, threatening another blow.

"Stop!" Sentry yelled. "It's in the mantel!"

Salim kept the sword raised and turned his head to look at the fireplace. "Where?"

"The wood lifts off. The book's underneath."

"The doctor will go fetch it," Salim said. He motioned with the sword for her to get up.

She stood up, holding her hand over the painful left arm. Salim moved to one side, letting her step into the middle of the living room and toward the fireplace.

She began to remove the photos from the mahogany mantel, placing them on the stone hearth. She had to keep him distracted. Once he had the book, he'd kill them both.

"Someone else is looking for it," she said. "They've already gone through the house."

"Just the incompetent moron I sent."

"*You* sent? The same one who came after me?"

"You said Frieda told you things you didn't understand. I was afraid you'd figure it out."

"The same man who ran down Mrs. Sentry?"

Sentry's eyes popped open. "You bastard! You tried to kill my wife!"

"No, no. Just trying to scare you off. He was only supposed to graze her. It really is hard to find decent help nowadays. You see, if you hadn't come after me for the money, your sister would be alive and your wife would be cooking dinner in the kitchen."

"You hired a man from the Muslim Brotherhood?" Rebecca asked.

"It's a good thing these fanatics are incompetent. Otherwise they'd rule the world."

"I don't understand. Isn't the Brotherhood your enemy?"

"Egyptian politics are very complex. My brother-in-law supports them because they feed the poor before handing them guns. But it's not politic to back them, in some circles. And since you never know whose side someone is on, it's pragmatic to make everyone think you're on *their* side."

"You're good at that, playing both sides," said Sentry.

She grasped the wood with both hands. "How does it come off?"

"Just lift it straight up."

She pushed on the square edges from below, though her arm hurt. The mantel moved. She lifted the slab of mahogany off and leaned it against the wall. On the unfinished wooden base beneath lay a notebook with a faded green cardboard cover.

"Move away from it!" Salim said. "Sit back down. Where you were."

She knew they had little time left. She didn't like the picture that presented itself in her head: she and Sentry lying dead on the living room carpet, lights blazing. Instead of stepping over Sentry to follow Salim's instructions, she stopped on the side where the long gear bag lay. Salim's attention was fixed on the record book. He didn't notice when she bent down beside Sentry, pretending to minister to his wound. Keeping her body stiff, she inserted her right hand into the bag.

"The neck!" Sentry mouthed, bringing his good hand to his throat.

What damage could she do with a foil that ended in a rubber tip? She had an idea that would require speed and surprise.

Glancing sideways, still in a crouch, she saw Salim flipping pages with the thumb of the hand that held the sword. She quietly drew the foil out of the bag. Adrenaline pumped through her. She had to act while he was distracted.

Holding the foil, she moved between the two chairs, lifted her weapon high over her head with both hands. Salim raised his head in surprise, affording her a clearer shot at her target. He had no time to react before she whipped her foil sideways with all her strength, the rigid edge of the steel catching his neck. She felt sick to her stomach.

The book tumbled to the carpet. She thought he would fall, but he stayed upright, cradling his bleeding neck with his hand. Moaning in pain, he stumbled forward onto the sofa, still holding the sword. His eyes were closed in a grimace as she stepped toward him.

With one quick movement, she pulled the sword from his hand.

As she stood, her chest heaving from the effort, someone opened the front door.

"Dad?"

Erich appeared at the entrance of the living room in his navy jacket, blinking in bewilderment.

"Go next door and call an ambulance!" Rebecca shouted. "Get the police!"

"What's going on?" He looked at the sword in her hand and Salim bleeding on the sofa. "Did you do that?"

"It's a long story," she said.

"Where's my father?"

Salim took a deep noisy breath and opened his eyes. "Look who's here! Where *is* your father? An excellent question."

The blow had just stunned him. But she had his weapon.

"Erich!" Sentry shouted.

"Dad?"

"He's hurt but he's all right," Rebecca said.

Erich rushed behind the chairs to where his father lay on the floor. "Did you do this?" he cried at Rebecca.

"Don't be stupid!" said Sentry.

"*He* stabbed you?" Erich said.

"It's astonishing that he looks like you, Eisenbaum. Since that's impossible." Salim removed his hand from his neck. The bleeding had stopped. "I've been thinking about that and I've come to a remarkable conclusion. It's a *family* resemblance. He looks like Frieda. Am I right? When's your birthday, Dr. Sentry?"

Erich hesitated. "What?"

"Your birthday, please."

"November 30, 1945."

"My God! Let me look at you."

"What the hell are you talking about?" Erich stood up to stare at him.

Salim gaped, running his eyes over the younger man's face. "That means you were conceived in winter. Yes. A very cold February. I remember the wind blowing outside through the pines." He blinked away the memory. "You have to believe me — I never knew. When the Russians were close, I ran for my life. She understood. Your mother was the bravest woman I ever knew."

"My mother?" Erich's eyes narrowed with puzzlement. "You know my mother?"

Salim said to Sentry. "You never told him?"

"Told me what?"

Sentry's eyes were closed, his eyebrows arched together, as he sat against the bookcase.

"Told me *what?*"

Even as he stood, the information was probably filtering into Erich's brain like a trickle of dirty water. Slow but inevitable, it would find a path into meaning.

"Who are you?" he asked Salim.

"That's not so easy to answer. I was someone else when I knew your mother."

"How did you know my mother?"

"We worked in the same hospital."

"When did she work in a hospital? She was an athlete."

Salim peered at Erich with irritation. "It appears we're not speaking about the same woman. You must face the truth, son."

Erich shrunk away, crouching down over Sentry again. "What's he talking about, Dad?"

Sentry leaned his head back against the bookcase, weary. "You can't remember her the way she was. She was so beautiful. And brilliant. She was too sensitive to survive the war intact. Not meant for this evil world.

She sacrificed herself for so many. This is what you should remember."

"Aunt Frieda? My mother?" Erich's face went pale. He stared fixedly at the wall. "I used to have these dreams. Or maybe they were memories. She was rocking me to sleep in her arms. She called me Erich-mouse. She was the only one who ever called me that. I'd forgotten."

"That was our grandmother's pet name for us," said Sentry. "Frieda-mouse. Wolfie-mouse. Luise-mouse. So many gone. Another life."

The fondness for mice, thought Rebecca, recalling the children's books. Not rodents, but a connection home.

"I wish I'd known while she was alive."

"*I'm* alive," said Salim.

Erich rose to his feet and turned to face Salim. "You were in the camp? What were you to my mother?"

Salim glanced at Rebecca and Sentry, neither of whom rushed to speak. "I loved her. She loved me. That's the important part."

Rebecca realized their silence was meant to protect Erich. "The phone's not working," she said. "Please go next door and call the police."

"I'm still confused."

"I'll explain later."

After Erich left, Salim clasped his neck with his hand again and fell back into the sofa, eyes closed. Sentry moaned behind the chairs. Holding onto the sword, she found a clean tea towel in an open drawer of the buffet and stepped toward Sentry. She kneeled near his injured shoulder, cleaning the wound with the towel.

"You okay?"

"I feel like a fool."

"You *are* a fool!" Salim said from the sofa. "You had everything you needed. You should've left well enough alone."

"Look who's talking! A German Egyptian! You changed your whole identity."

"I had no choice. I was running for my life. When the Russians were close, I threw away my uniform and put on a prisoner's jacket. Berlin was destroyed. The buildings, the people I knew. I had no family. I made my way to Hamburg and got on a ship. Mohammed had often invited me to his home. This time I went. They are a remarkably generous people, the Egyptians. Friendly to a fault. I felt at home there. More than in my original home. Mohammed took me under his wing. I fell in love with the culture. And his sister. My friend became my brother-in-law. I converted to Islam. I've been fortunate to have two lives.

"Maryam was past marriageable age in Arab society. They were very grateful to me for taking her off their hands. I just had to convert. It's really very comforting, having religion. The Arabs say only Allah is perfect. They accept that man is weak."

"You expect me to believe you're different? A leopard can't change its spots."

"I'm not who you remember. When you learn a new language and culture, you become a different person, even in your gestures. You give yourself up, your old self, and create a new image, one you could never have imagined. Even your body moves differently. It's like a rebirth. Then when a time comes that you're forced to speak the old language, it's like someone else's mouth moving. That man is a stranger to me now. So you see, I can't go back."

These last words came from right behind her. While she was tending to Sentry's wound, Salim had kept talking and crept toward them.

"Look out!" Sentry screamed.

She turned sideways to see the glint of metal in Salim's hand as he lunged at her. She rolled away, the knife grazing her thigh as he thudded to the ground. She'd been stupid. She'd forgotten he had killed the cop outside. Of course he had a knife.

While he struggled to get to his feet, she grabbed for her purse. On her knees now, she rummaged inside the bag until she felt the cool metal can. He was lifting himself up, his hand holding the knife in a tight fist, about to strike again. In a second, she flicked off the top of the can, pointed it at his face, and pushed down hard on the nozzle. A triangle of spray hit his eyes.

"Ahgghh!" He dropped the knife and brought both hands to his eyes. "Ahgghh! Help! Help!" He groped blindly toward the kitchen. "Water!"

She collapsed on the ground beside Sentry. Her heart was racing. She saw blood trickling down her leg from the cut. It must have hurt, but she was too numb to feel it.

# *chapter thirty-four*

---

S he floated into the forest on icy wings, riding the
wind through the pines. She tried to speak, but
instead a song erupted from her throat. A mournful trill
that made the animals on the forest floor pause and lift
their eyes in acknowledgement.

The wind swept her to the shore of a gunmetal lake,
a mirror of the gunmetal sky. One a grey eye contained by
the boundaries of earth, the other an infinite line, vast with
possibilities. She had flown at the horizon with her heart
full, even forgiving the village by the lake for their indif-
ference. Then the searchlights found her in the sky. In an
instant, the horizon shrank into a vault and closed over
her with the finality of iron. High in that iron sky, stars
twinkled dispassionately, hard as diamonds. No one saw
her tumble to the ground. No one saw her gather every
ounce of energy and fly to the nearest tree for shelter. But
her membraned feet couldn't balance on the iron branch.
She trembled and fell for the last time.

Lifting herself on a broken wing, she gazed into the lake: a tiny heart-shaped face looked back at her from the water. Where had she seen it before? A vague memory of grief squeezed her chest. The face smiled sadly and melted into the water; eyes, nose, mouth stretched upon the lake and dissolved into other eyes, another nose, another mouth, until Rebecca was looking at herself.

She opened her eyes with a start. Where was she? Warm. Protected. She lay in Nesha's arms in her own bed. She wasn't a bird. She wasn't in a camp. She was one of the lucky ones. But what if her mother's family hadn't moved from Poland to Canada when Flo was a girl? Her mother would have been a teenager when the Nazis put her into a camp and killed her, along with her family. Rebecca would never have been born. Where were the millions of unborn progeny of those who had perished? She felt Nesha's breath on her cheek. It was the American Thanksgiving, she remembered. *Thank you, Whoever Is Responsible, for my life.*

A grey November light filtered through her bedroom window. She had taken the day off and told Iris to reschedule her patients. After last night, Rebecca needed some recovery time. It wasn't just the stitches the resident had put into her thigh to close the wound from Salim's knife — four stitches after waiting in Emerg for two hours. It was the stress of having her life threatened, of seeing someone else's blood issue from a wound she'd inflicted.

Fitzroy, all in a lather, had found her in Emerg last night.

"You should've called me! Not try to do things yourself! You could've been killed!"

"I couldn't call you," she said softly. "He cut the phone line."

His large face flushed with anger, then concern. "Yes, of course he did. I'm sorry." He took a deep breath, his barrel chest rising and falling beneath his coat. "I shouldn't have relied on the surveillance cop. It was my fault."

She was sitting up on a gurney in one of the cubicles, holding a wad of gauze against her leg as she waited for the resident.

"I'll go hurry them up," he announced, turning to go.

"Detective," she said. "You saved my life."

"Look, I feel bad enough —"

"If I didn't have that can of Mace, he would've killed me."

Fitzroy's face lit up, his mouth lifting from ear to ear. "Right!" he said. He looked behind himself, snickering. "He's just across the way at the sink. They're washing the stuff out of his eyes. I hope it stings. I hope it stings like hell. The bastard killed a cop."

Nesha had rushed in then, his face pale with worry.

"I'm all right," she said, as he hovered over her in his worn leather jacket.

Fitzroy gave her a grin before disappearing.

Nesha kissed her forehead and took her free hand. "I'm not letting you out of my sight again."

She smiled, taking in the brown, melancholy eyes. She wished he could stay in the country long enough to make that threat count.

Erich stuck his head into the cubicle. "You all right?"

He exchanged a perfunctory nod with Nesha, who gripped her hand tighter.

"I'll be fine. How about your father?"

As soon as she said it, she realized the ambiguity. If Erich had any reservations, he hid them admirably.

"You saved his life. He'll be okay. No fencing for a while."

She hadn't asked him about the man in custody, his biological father, or the matter of his startling origins.

The scenes of last night played over and over as she lay in bed, her head too heavy to lift. Nesha adjusted his arms around her.

The next time she woke up, it was past two. The aroma of coffee and eggs wafted up from the kitchen. Nesha was cooking. Her leg pulsed with pain, but she couldn't lie there any longer. She threw on her bathrobe and went downstairs.

"I was just going to bring this up on a tray," Nesha said.

He was distributing fried eggs and toast on two plates. She poured the coffee.

"I think I dreamt about a concentration camp. The one Frieda was in."

On the way home from the hospital the night before, Rebecca had told him about Sentry and Salim. Eisenbaum and Brenner. And Frieda.

"You know, Ravensbrück was one of the bad ones," he said. "She was lucky she survived. Probably because a Nazi loved her. Very rare in a camp."

"I wonder if she loved him back," Rebecca said. "Or if she knew she'd never see him again. He may as well've fallen off the face of the earth when he went to Egypt. I guess that's what he meant to do."

"They would've welcomed him there with open arms."

"Why?"

"Ever heard of Arab Nazis? The Grand Mufti of Jerusalem?"

"No."

"He was the Muslim Brotherhood delegate in Palestine. Hajj Amin al-Husseini. Organized the murder of Jews in the twenties and thirties. For this, the English appointed him Grand Mufti. Meanwhile, remember in Cairo the founder of the Brotherhood was writing letters to Hitler, telling him what a stellar fellow he was? Well, Hitler saw an opportunity and the Brothers became a secret arm of Nazi intelligence. When Hitler actually got into power, he sent the Mufti arms. In 1936 they fomented the Arab Revolt when they rose up and murdered Jews and Arabs who disagreed with them. After that the Mufti escaped to Berlin, where he spent the war."

"Where did you learn all this?"

"Some people golf. I like to sift through old records at the Wiesenthal Institute in L.A."

"So the Mufti went to Berlin. Then what?"

"He worked for the war effort, recruiting Bosnian Muslim volunteers. He organized them into their own battalions."

"I don't understand. They fought for the Germans?"

"They were put into the Waffen SS and fought partisans in the Balkans. They also hunted down Serbs, Jews, and Gypsies. I've seen pictures of them marching in formation wearing their fezzes. Twenty thousand of them. The Mufti flew from Berlin to Sarajevo to inspect his Muslim army."

"What happened to him after the war?"

"He was declared a Nazi war criminal. But the English let him escape to Cairo."

"Why would they do that?"

"For the same reason the Americans hired ex-Nazis to work for them after the war. To fight the Communists. You're too young to remember the beginning of the Cold War. The Communists were the new bogeyman. So Arab fundamentalists became allies against Arab Communist sympathizers. The ex-Mufti ran Arab Palestine till he died in 1974. Then his relative took over."

"But I thought Yasser Arafat …"

He was chewing on a piece of toast with a smug look. "Arafat is related to the Mufti?"

"His real name is too complicated to remember. But it ends in 'al-Hussaeini.' They belong to the same clan. Arafat shortened his name to hide his kinship because the ex-Mufti was discredited. Even if you supported the Nazis, these days you don't call yourself a Nazi. Especially if you're courting the Western media."

"You must spend a lot of time reading up on this stuff."

"If we don't remember the past, we can't understand the present."

"Sometimes we have to get beyond the past to be able to live in the present."

"You think I'm obsessed. I think I'm a realist. What do you think happened to people who kept their heads in the sand when Hitler was consolidating his power? They didn't survive. The man who tried to run you down? He's a direct link to the Grand Mufti. The Nazis may be gone, but their legacy lives on. Every time an Arab terrorist kills an Israeli, Hitler laughs in hell." He stared into his coffee. "The funny thing is, Brenner seems to be one of the human ones."

The phone rang. Rebecca reached over and lifted the receiver off the wall.

"Hi, sweetheart. Are you feeling better today?"

Rebecca knew her mother had held off calling earlier not to disturb her. "Much better."

"How's your leg?" There was something else in her voice.

"It'll heal. Don't worry."

"Did Jeff Herman call you? Susan's left him. Is she with you?"

When Rebecca got off the phone, she hurried up the stairs.

"Where you going?" Nesha asked.

"Getting dressed."

"Why?"

"I'm going to find Susan."

Nesha insisted on driving. "Where are we going?"

"Mount Sinai."

"You're an optimist."

"It's the only thing that keeps me going."

He dropped her at the hospital, then drove off to find a parking spot.

Rebecca rode the elevator upstairs impatiently, rushing off in the direction of the preemie unit.

Inside, her father stood, enthralled, against one of the walls. She followed his eyes. Wearing a hospital gown, Susan sat in a rocking chair beside the incubator holding Miriam against her chest. Both mother and daughter had their eyes closed as if no one else existed. Alicia, the nurse, stood off to one side, beaming.

Rebecca felt her heart expand in her chest. Her eyes burned with tears.

Alicia waved at her to approach. The nurse opened her mouth in a laugh, barely able to contain herself.

"She been here since yesterday!" the woman said in a hoarse whisper. "Slept in the waiting room. Wanted to know *everything*. About the IV, the baby's heart, her oxygen level. Gave her a bit of a bottle. You know the way it is, drop by drop. Wouldn't leave to go eat. I had to pry her away."

Rebecca took a deep, cleansing breath, feeling her chest clear of this weight finally. She stepped back beside her father, who looped his arm through hers.

"Thank God!" he said. "I can finally stop telling Miriam I'm her mother."

Later that evening, Susan returned to Rebecca's house. Without being prodded, she phoned Ben in Montreal. Rebecca and Nesha left her in the kitchen for privacy, but she could hear her sister's side of the conversation from the den.

"It's me," said Susan on the phone. "How are you?"

Rebecca imagined Ben's surprise. And, hopefully, his relief.

"I'm better," Susan went on. "At Rebecca's. Yes, Miriam's doing fine."

Rebecca knew Ben had been calling the hospital daily to check on his daughter's progress.

"I thought you might come to Toronto this weekend to see her. I miss the boys."

She hadn't apologized. Hadn't grovelled. Things would be different in that household, Rebecca thought. Ben would have to make some hard choices if she knew her sister.

Susan stuck her head in the kitchen, her face drawn with exhaustion. "I'm going to sleep. Can you tuck me in?"

Rebecca gave her a minute to get into the nightgown she had lent her.

"Thanks for being so understanding," said Susan as they sat together on the bed in the guest room. Dark blonde roots peeked through her ash blonde hair.

"I'm your sister. That's my job."

"You knew it wouldn't work out with Jeff, didn't you?"

"I wasn't sure. You were going through a crisis, and people in crisis do things they wouldn't ordinarily do."

"It was so *depressing* being with him. He thought I could fix his life. He had all these plans. About new furniture. Where we'd go for vacation. How great it would be walking into his favourite restaurant with me on his arm. He only talked about *things*. I was just a trophy to add to his collection of stuff. Like his car or his job."

"I think he really loves you."

She sighed guiltily. "In his limited way. I don't want to sound mean, but he's an empty man. He tries to fill that emptiness with stuff. I was going to be the solution to his life! When I'm so messed up."

Inwardly Rebecca rejoiced at her sister's assessment, but she arranged her face in a sympathetic expression.

"He doesn't even like what he's doing. Corporate law bores him, but it pays well. At least when I start law school I'll know what I *don't* want to do. I'm going to look into family law."

She trained eyes on Rebecca that hinted of the mischief from younger days. "I missed the boys so much. Ben's taken good care of them, I can tell. I appreciate him more. But I'll be damned if I'm going to tell him."

She would make a fine lawyer, Rebecca thought.


Rebecca decided to work on Friday, tending to the more urgent patients who'd had their appointments cancelled the day before.

She worked steadily for a few hours, then Iris called her to the phone. It was Fitzroy.

"I won't keep you, doctor, I know you're busy. I'm calling you as a courtesy because you were so helpful. You're going to be contacted by the RCMP about our friend Salim. He's trying to cut a deal with information he says is, quote, 'of international significance.' They're going to ask you if you know anything."

"Is this about the sterilization experiments during the war?"

"What war? No. We're talking about current political affairs here. He claims to have information about a plot to assassinate the Egyptian president, Sadat. Willing to give up big names."

She paused, taking this in. "That surprises me. His brother-in-law is one of Sadat's advisors. Wouldn't Salim have warned them already?"

"His brother-in-law?"

"Mohammed Hassan. Hassan Pharmaceuticals."

"You know more about this than I do. Just tell the RCMP."

"I wonder if his brother-in-law is involved. It seemed strange that Salim knew people in the Muslim Brotherhood."

"The whole thing could just be a story to bargain with. He's looking at a long prison stretch — remember, he killed a cop."

"You don't believe him?"

"We don't want to take any chances. Which is why the RCMP will be calling you."

"He never talked about an assassination plot with me. Have you spoken to Will Sentry?"

"He says it's news to him, too. I don't trust this Salim as far as I can throw him."

"Well, Sadat's very unpopular in Egypt right now because of the peace initiative with Israel. I'm sure there *are* plots against him. The question is, does Salim have an inside track on one?"

"You're very well informed," said Fitzroy.

She smiled into the phone. "My friend from California has been educating me. The thing about Salim is he's very well-connected because of his brother-in-law. And he's a survivor. I can see him betraying his friends if it means things will go easier for him. I wouldn't discount his story. But how can you check it out?"

"*We* won't be checking anything out. Way out of our territory. The thing'll get passed on to the FBI, and you know how *they* share information. We'll probably never know."

"Let's hope they pass it on to the Egyptians."

Mid-afternoon, she opened the door to an examining room for her next patient.

"Mr. Sentry!"

He sat there, like any other patient, his arm in a sling. "Call me Wolfie."

He must have been very persuasive to get past Iris today.

"How's your arm?"

He watched her pensively. "With Aspirin it's not so bad." His hair looked more unruly than usual. She imagined grooming was hard without the use of one's right hand.

"I never got a chance to thank you properly," he said. "You saved my life."

She nodded, embarrassed. She never could take compliments graciously.

"I also wanted to set something straight. I know you misunderstood when I talked about my sister — when I said you were like her. I know you took it the wrong way. Forgive me. Sometimes my temper ..." He lifted his free hand in the air, the equivalent of a shrug. "But I wanted you to understand — I couldn't give you a bigger compliment. In our family I loved her the most. I wish you could've known her when she was your age. She was a noble soul. She sacrificed herself to save so many. Something in your eyes reminds me of her. A sadness. Like you've lost something. She looked like that, a terrible sadness in the eyes, from everything she lost." Tears welled in his eyes. "I like to think that you're what she could've become, if not for the war. If not for many things. She would've been just like you."

Rebecca's breath caught in her throat. Her chest ached, pain mingling with pleasure in a bittersweet pride. "I don't know what to say."

His lips curled up, his eyes contemplating her with affection. "You don't have to say anything."

Rebecca got home late in the afternoon, just before Ben and the children arrived. The three boys burst through the door, but only two ran to embrace their mother. The eldest held back, sullen. Ben, thinner than Rebecca remembered, stood awkwardly in the hall, watching. When Rebecca introduced Nesha, Ben stepped forward to shake his hand.

The two youngest boys clung to Susan's legs. "Where were you?" they asked in a chorus. "We missed you. Are you coming home?"

Susan looked sheepishly at the eldest from under her eyebrows. "Adam, come here."

He stared at the ground, then glanced up at Ben. Ben nodded, gesturing with his head. Susan held out her hand to the boy. Adam crept toward her, anger mingled with confusion on his nine-year-old face. Once he was close enough, Susan pulled him into a tight embrace.

Nesha observed mother and children quietly. "You're a very lucky man," he said to Ben. "Three handsome sons."

"Thank you," Ben murmured.

"And a beautiful daughter," said Susan. She gazed at Ben with steady eyes, waiting for him to respond.

He watched her, perplexed but hopeful. "And a beautiful daughter," he said.

Susan flushed, rewarding him with a remorseful smile.

Nesha put his arm around Rebecca's waist and kissed her forehead. "We should be so lucky," he murmured in her ear.

She let his words buoy her up but was careful not to let them carry her away. If the boys behaved well this weekend, if they didn't have temper tantrums, if their sweet innocence touched him …

"Let me introduce you," she said. "Nesha, this is Adam, the oldest."

Adam lifted his head from his mother's shoulder and blinked.

"This big boy with the curly hair is Sammy."

"Samuel!" he cheeped, his ear still pressed against his mother's stomach.

Susan grinned. "His Grade One teacher doesn't like nicknames."

"And Jonathan, a big boy of four."

"Auntie Rebecca! I'm still little!"

Nesha smiled at them. "You boys like hummus?"

"What's that?" said Samuel.

Adam nodded but said nothing.

"It's a Middle Eastern dip. They eat it in Israel." He glanced at Ben's skullcap. "You tear pita bread into little pieces and scoop up the hummus. It can get messy, but it's delicious. Want to help me make some? You just throw all the stuff into the food processor and it makes a lot of noise. Then you eat it."

The two youngest quickly left their mother's side. Nesha beckoned to Adam with a wave as he headed for the kitchen.

Susan and Ben wavered in their spots until Rebecca turned to follow the boys. Then she heard hesitant mumbling behind her, the rustling of clothes as they crept into the den. Things would be awkward at first, but Rebecca trusted in her sister's charm.

Lights blazed in the kitchen, while the living room lay dusky, now that the sun was setting. She stopped in the shadows, looking toward the brightly lit doorway, enjoying the cheerful din. How lucky she was! Here, in this house, in this country. She was *alive,* unlike so many others. The tiny heart-shaped face that visited her dreams. She was like Frieda, and not like Frieda. Her mettle would never be tested in the same arena, and for that she was profoundly grateful.

But she knew the desolation of a bird trying to land on an iron tree. There were only two possibilities that she could see: hover forever and never land, or look outward to find a more hospitable home. The bird might have to fly in the dark for a while. She would have to trust her instincts and hope she was travelling in the right direction. Maybe take some chances, let go of herself a little, and watch for a welcoming light.

Rebecca heard the ringing of children's laughter. The weekend would be easy. It was after everyone left that she would be flying alone again. The food processor whirred on the counter in the distance. A little boy yelped with delight. Savour the moment. Life was made up of moments. She lifted her feet from the ground and headed for the light.

## *author's note*

Anwar Sadat became the first Arab leader to officially visit Israel when he met with Israeli Prime Minister Menachem Begin. Their initiative resulted in the 1979 Camp David Peace Accord between Egypt and Israel, extremely unpopular in the Arab and Muslim World. The Arab League suspended Egypt's membership, moving its headquarters from Cairo to Tunis.

On October 6, 1981, a month after his widespread crackdown on Muslim organizations, Sadat was assassinated during a parade in Cairo. The assassins were army officers who were part of the Egyptian Islamic Jihad, an offshoot of the Muslim Brotherhood that was opposed to his negotiations with Israel. A fatwa approving the assassination had been obtained from Omar Abdel-Rahman, a cleric later convicted in the U.S. for his role in the 1993 World Trade Center bombing.

As air force jets flew overhead distracting the crowd, a troop truck halted before the presidential reviewing stand, and a lieutenant strode forward. Sadat stood to receive his salute, whereupon the killers rose from the truck, throwing grenades and firing assault rifle rounds. One assassin, Khalid Islambouli, shouted, "Death to the Pharaoh!" as he ran toward the stand and fired into Sadat's lifeless body.

# *acknowledgements*

I am indebted, as always, to my husband, Jerry, for his moral support and medical knowledge; to my friend Dr. Herb Batt, whose outside-the-box ideas and suggestions for the manuscript were generous and invaluable; to my two writing groups, one the appropriately named Midwives, namely Lynne Murphy, Rosemary McCracken, Madeleine Harris Callway, and Joan O'Callaghan, and the other consisting of Priscilla Galloway, Vancy Kaspar, Heather Kirk, Barbara Kerslake, Lorraine Williams, and Ayanna Black; also to Cecilia Kennedy for help early on. I am grateful to Helga Stummer for taking the time to talk to me about her memories of Nazi Berlin, to Dr. Bruno Belfey for his help on the subject of medical schools in Nazi Germany, and to Dr. Martin Kosoy for his recollections of the Mount Sinai Hospital of 1979. I am thankful to two friends: Sylvia Kissin, for recounting her memories of Cairo, her home in the 1970s, and Dr. Ray Steinman for answering medical questions patiently. I am also grateful to my nephew, Constable Rory Hopkins, of the Toronto Police Services, for letting me pick his brain about his employer. My gratitude to members of the University of Toronto Fencing Team, namely Nick Rudzik, who gave generously of his time at the Benson Building, taking me through the paces of a fencing practice, and Thomas Nguyen and Dr. David Kreindler, who graciously made themselves available and answered my questions about the complicated rules of fencing. My gratitude also to Lanna Crucefix of the University of Toronto Athletic Centre for digging up historic information on the centre. Thanks to my mother, Gustava Maultash, for her continual, unfailing support, and my children, Nathaniel and Jessica, for their help along the way. I am especially grateful to my agent, John Pearce, for all his encouragement and support. My deep thanks to Kirk Howard and the dedicated staff at Dundurn: my editor, Barry Jowett; copy-editor, Andrea Waters; designer, Jennifer Scott, who outdid herself with the cover; head of marketing, Beth Bruder, and marketing assistant, Christianne Commons; and publicist Ali Pennels, assisted by Dan Wagstaff.